"A totally original sci-fi thriller that will have you hooked from page one with both riveting action and a sly wit. This is a story of human history, the hidden powers that have shaped it, and one man's transformation from complete nobody to a key fighter in the war for humanity's future."

Ramez Naam, author of Nexus

"Filled with non-stop action and brilliant asides on the history of our species, the book is sure to thrill and amuse."

Ken Liu, Nebula Award winning author of The Paper Menagerie

"Recommended."

Steven Gould, author of the Jumpers *series*

"Tipping his hat to both science fiction novels and comic books, Chu delivers a narrative that is at times pulse-pounding, laugh-out-loud funny and thoughtful. Part James Bond, part Superman, part *Orphanage*. There's something here for everyone."

Myke Cole, author of Control Point *and* Fortress Frontier

"In Wesley Chu's debut novel you meet an unlikely hero in the form of Roen, an out-of-shape, self-loathing, under-achieving computer geek. He is soon transformed into a confident, lean, mean fighting machine under the guidance and influence of the ancient alien Tao, who has inhabited his body and is now working hard to get Roen in shape for an important mission – nothing less than to take on the Genjix and save the planet from an evil plot of destruction. This book is high-octane spy vs spy action with a sly sense of humor. Pure pleasure from beginning to end. Highly recommended!"

Ann Vandermeer, Hugo winning editor of Weird Tales *and British Fantasy Award winning publisher of Buzzcity Press*

ANGRY ROBOT
A member of the Osprey Group

Lace Market House,	Angry Robot/Osprey Publishing,
54-56 High Pavement,	PO Box 3985,
Nottingham	New York,
NG1 1HW	NY 10185-3985,
UK	USA

www.angryrobotbooks.com
Through the ages

An Angry Robot paperback original 2013

Cover art by Bruce Hogarth/Argh! Oxford
Set in Meridien by EpubServices

Distributed in the United States by Random House, Inc., New York

ISBN: 978 0 85766 332 0
Ebook ISBN: 978 0 85766 333 7

Printed in the United States of America

9 8 7 6 5 4 3 2 1

WESLEY CHU

The Deaths of Tao

ANGRY
ROBOT

To my loving wife and most favorite person in the world, Paula Kim.

CHAPTER ONE
REPRISAL

The path of a vessel is strewn with the dead. The journey of a Quasing even more so, for it is that constant cycle of life and death that will take us home.

Huchel, Genjix Council – Eastern Hemisphere,
the Quasing of King Solomon

The lone black car slunk through the dark, unlit streets, a ghostly shadow creeping past the decrepit warehouses and abandoned storefronts along the South Capitol at the outskirts of Washington DC. Sitting in the car, Jill Tan glanced out the tinted windows at the darkened snow-dusted shapes of the washed-out world. Tonight's meeting with Andrews was another bust. There had been far too many of these dead-end nights of late. And each time a deal didn't pan out it put the Prophus one foot deeper into the grave.

Having to sit down with the first-term senator from Idaho, the leader of the slightly-crazed and lowly regarded Trinity Caucus, was a stark reminder of how precarious the Prophus' position was in the United States. Their influence in American politics was slipping, forcing them to reach out and deal with the fringes of government. When a schmuck like Andrews could dictate terms to her, Jill knew they were in trouble.

You should have pushed harder on the Poseidon Bill.

"No one's vote on a bill is worth a committee chair, Baji. I'm not going to hold Wilks or the Prophus hostage to that half-term hack."

Our orders are to make sure the appropriation passes by any means. We desperately need those resources rerouted to us. What is a two-year chair to us?

"I'm not going to sell the farm. It's bad precedent."

We are still three votes down in the Senate.

"I'll dig them up somewhere," Jill murmured absently as she studied the whip count. She wasn't nearly as confident as she sounded, though she wasn't sure why she bothered feigning confidence with Baji. Her Quasing knew everything she did and then some. Still, maintaining the facade was second nature to her. You didn't survive working as an aide in Congress long showing weakness.

She looked out the window again. Leave it to Andrews to plan a meeting in a place like this. He didn't want to be seen with her, he said. She would taint his reputation. Just who did he think he was? The meeting had lasted three hours. In the end, he had given her the runaround and made outrageous demands that he must have known she could not accept. Dealing with him wasted precious time and effort, neither of which Jill could afford to lose.

She checked her watch: 9.14pm. A mountain of work waited for her back at the office. She'd be lucky to make it to her bed by three. Well, it wasn't like she had much of a private life anyway.

Maybe you should reconsider that date with Doctor Sun. He is an MD, not to mention one of Wilks' big donors.

"Baji, I'm fully aware of what the 'Doctor' title in front of a guy's name means. That man is boring, self-centered, and probably a sociopath. And he has yeti paws. What do you use to pick men besides an MD anyway?"

That is about it. That and they are not hosts.

"Worst criteria I've ever heard."

Hardly. Look at Roen. A host and not a doctor; where did that get you?

Jill harrumphed and went back to work. Her personal millions-years-old alien was wise and knowledgeable, but her matchmaking philosophy was straight out of the eleventh century. Still, Jill's romance batting average had been pretty dismal of late. The very thought of dating, even with someone not repugnant, felt wrong.

"Damn that Roen," she said.

A blinding light suddenly appeared from behind and rammed into the rear of the car. Then another came from the side and punched the front, spinning it around.

Ambush!

"Are you alright?" asked Shunn, her driver and one of the men on her security detail, though he was the one with blood trickling down his forehead. Chevoen, the other bodyguard, had already gotten out of the car. Jill could hear the sound of gunfire rattling the side panels.

"Stop checking on me and get out," she snapped, pulling out her Ruger. "Get word to Command. Defensive perimeter. Follow my lead for a retreat." She got out and took cover behind the door. Gunfire filled the air as several shadows appeared out of the darkness. She leaned over the trunk and engaged the dark figures. Two bullet holes appeared in the panel centimeters away from her face.

One flanking you on the roof.

She put her back to the car and scanned the roof just in time to see a dark figure duck behind cover.

"Prophus!" a voice called. "We wish to parlay."

We are surrounded. Two Genjix on the opposite rooftop as well.

"They just jumped us, Baji. Why would they want to talk?"

Only one way to find out. See if you can buy some time. Chevoen must have sent out a distress signal.

"What do you want to talk about?" she yelled.

One of the Genjix appeared and held up a phone. Jill kept him in her sights as he approached. When he was within five meters, he tossed the phone to her. She caught it and brought it up to her ear.

"Hello, Jill," a smug voice said across the line.

She scowled. "Simon."

I hated Biall even before I became Prophus.

"You've repeatedly ignored my calls to your office, so I took more drastic measures. How was your meeting with Andrews? Fruitless? Of course it was. We got to him two months ago. You Prophus are a little behind the curve these days."

Jill bit her lip. "Well, good for you. We both know Andrews is a one-term senator. I hope you didn't pay too much for him. Is there anything else, or are you just here to gloat?"

Two more to the right. Total of eight in range of vision. Take out the one on the rear roof first.

"What's our escape path, Baji?"

Side street to your rear.

Simon continued rambling, as if he wasn't aware that she was in the middle of a standoff with a dozen guns pointed at her. "Gloating is human. The Holy Ones demand better of their vessels. In fact, we want to work with you. A little bipartisanship if you will."

Jill didn't buy it. The last time Simon offered bipartisanship in Congress, the Genjix reneged and caused the financial meltdown of the real estate market. Of course, their people had bet on the collapse and made billions from the betrayal. Scratch that. The Prophus weren't betrayed; they were outmaneuvered.

"Actually, Hogan would like to deal with your boss," Simon said. "Can the misguided senator from the land of Lincoln spare two hours for the noble senator from West Virginia?"

Jill exhaled in exasperation. "All this because you want a meeting?"

"Next time, take my calls. I'm not to be trifled with."

"Let me guess. The South Korea Destroyer contract? The East Seas Minerals Sanction? Or the Japanese IEC Standards Tariff? Which one?"

"Among others. Call it a grand package."

"What are you offering?"

"I'll send your assistant my terms tonight. You will present it to Wilks in the best possible light, and then we will both be praised for working across the aisle. Is that clear?"

"Why would I want to help you?" Jill said.

"Because if you say no, my men will kill all of you."

"Then I guess I don't have much of a choice. I'll need time to look your offer over, though."

"You're not in much of a position to talk terms, but take some time to think it over," he said. "I want your confirmation by next week. By the way, Baji, Biall still owes you one for the Revolutionary War. Here's a partial payment." Then he hung up.

"What happened during the war?"

Biall's vessel at the time was the nephew of Lord Sandwich, First Admiral of the British fleet. He was promoted to captain and sent to the States. My host, John Paul Jones, captured his frigate. Then they gave him a sloop. I sank that. Then they put him on a desk job at the port of Yorktown. When I raided the port, I kidnapped him. Lord Sandwich had to pay ransom three times for the lout. He has held a grudge ever since.

"I would hold a grudge too if I were him."

Jill tossed the phone back to the Genjix agent. "You got your meeting. Now back to your masters, dog."

The Genjix agent looked at her and smirked. "We have orders to let you live unless you cause trouble. The others don't. Kill them!" he barked.

"No!"

The exchange the next minute was deafening as all sides opened fire. Her two Prophus guards, however, were outgunned and out of position. The Genjix made short work of them and before long, she was the only one left alive. Jill huddled behind the car door and reloaded, too angry to mourn the men who just died protecting her.

"Your people are dead, betrayer," the Genjix agent shouted. "Drop your gun and come out. You are free to go. Otherwise, your life is forfeit."

Drop your gun. There is no other way to survive this.

"Baji, shut up. They killed Shunn and Chevoen because they could. Show me their positions. Now!"

Images flashed in her mind of the Genjix kneeling on top of the roof behind her, the two to her right leaning against the van that had rammed them, and then the commander of the ambush who was speaking with her. Jill stood up and unloaded her clip at the three groupings, successfully taking out two more thugs. She didn't stick around to count her kills, though, booking it toward the side street.

"Take her down!" someone yelled.

Bullets kicked up dust all around her as she sprinted down the narrow sidewalk and turned into an alley. Something about running here reminded her of Roen, that bastard. A lot of things reminded her of him these days.

A moving shadow on the roofline of one of the buildings caught her attention. She flattened against the wall and scanned for movement. Then she heard the tramp of footsteps to her right; ten or so Genjix by the sound of them. Jill crouched, taking cover behind a dumpster, and peered over the top. Nearly a dozen men and a white unmarked van bore down the alley toward her.

Looks like a Penetra van.

"Well, there goes hiding as an option."

The advent of the mobile Penetra scanners had changed the course of the war in the past three years. When the Genjix had first completed the Phase I Penetra Program and invented a scanner that could detect Quasing within a host, it had little effect on the war, because the machines were the size of houses. However, over the past few years, the Genjix had successfully miniaturized the scanners. Now Penetra vans were everywhere and the Prophus were finding it harder and harder to avoid detection.

There are too many.

"I've had worse."

It was just brave talk though. They both knew that. As much as Jill had trained over the years, she was never going to be Sonya. Baji's previous host had trained Roen to be an agent, and had been one of the Baji's favorites. She was captured by the Genjix while trying to rescue Jill and

Roen during the Decennial and had died at the Capulet's Ski Lodge in Italy. Baji had never forgiven Roen for Sonya's death and, in a way, had not forgiven Jill either.

Jill leaned over the side of the dumpster and took three shots. One of them found its mark while the other two bounced harmlessly off the van. She ducked just as a hail of bullets banged the dumpster like a drum.

Two on the near side are creeping forward against the wall.

A quick image flashed in her head of two men crouching, edging closer toward her, using the dumpster to stay out of her field of vision. Jill exhaled again and aimed at the position in her mind, taking a Genjix agent square in the face. Another barrage of gunfire exploded around her, and she distinctly heard someone call out for a suppression rotation.

"I wish I had a grenade."

Might as well wish for a rocket launcher while we are at it.

Jill bit her lip, her mind racing to find a way out of this trap. Maybe she had something almost as good as a grenade. The Genjix agents were getting close. She dug in her purse and pulled out a small can of pepper spray. She hefted it in her hand and leaned toward the side.

You are not that good a shot.

"Positive thoughts, please."

Baji was right though; Jill was at best an average marksman. They were going to overrun her position at any moment. And it wasn't like she could hide with that Penetra van close by. She leaned over the side and rolled the can toward them. Then she took aim and pulled the trigger in rapid succession. She missed her first three shots. Flashing lights from the barrel of pistols exploded around her.

Pull back!

Jill ignored Baji and continued to focus on the can. She expended another burst, her fifth shot finally finding its mark. The can of pepper spray exploded and a cloud of capsicum burst into the air. Immediately, the Genjix in that area began to cough. She pulled back, but not before a bullet grazed her cheek. Jill clenched her teeth and stifled a cry. That was too close.

The Genjix were distracted right now. Jill had to move before the cloud dissipated. She sprinted out from cover down toward the end of the alley, firing blindly behind her. She suddenly felt a searing pain as one of their bullets grazed her thigh. The impact knocked her off balance and she fell to the ground. Her pistol skidded across the ground.

Jill cursed and reached for it, clawing and dragging her way across the alley. All she could think about were Cameron and Baji. She had failed them both. One of the Genjix agents appeared and kicked the pistol away. Then she felt the air whoosh out of her lungs as another stomped down on her chest.

"Give it up, Prophus," a voice said. The van lights closed in; she was surrounded. At this point, she had only one choice: get them to kill her to save Baji. She lashed out with her good leg and swept one of the agents. She grabbed for the foot of another. A blow to her head left her woozy. She closed her eyes and waited for the next, which would either end her life or knock her unconscious.

Soft pattering sounds began to rain down around her and all the Genjix agents suddenly fell over. The van screeched and then veered into the wall. The driver got out, falling to the ground as he clutched his shoulder. More pattering sounds came and he stopped moving.

Jill sat up and looked at the dozen still bodies; it looked like a war zone. With a grimace, she stood up and tested her injured leg. The bullet hadn't hit bone. She took a handkerchief out of her purse and tied off the wound. She then limped to the end of the alley toward the main street. Her phone rang.

Jill dug it out of the purse and answered. "Hello?"

A gruff voice came across the line. "You tell Command to send better security next time or I will jam chopsticks through their eyes!" Then he hung up.

"Asshole," she muttered, scanning the rooftops.

An asshole that saved your life.

"Least he could do was offer me a ride."

Jill left the area as quickly as her limp would allow. The Genjix would send a cleaning team soon. It would be wise to be as far away from here as possible. Fifteen minutes later, she made it to a major intersection and saw a local bar on the corner. She was about to continue on when she stopped, a small smile appearing on her face.

"Oh hell, I deserve it," she muttered and walked inside.

You are bleeding. Now is not the time for a drink.

"Now is the best time for a drink."

She walked up to the counter and ordered a margarita.

You are not being wise.

"This *is* me being wise. I almost ordered a shot of tequila instead."

Baji knew better than to press the issue. The bartenders gave the dried blood on her cheek a curious glance but otherwise left her alone. What little wisdom she had must have fled after the second margarita. She moved on up to tequila shots, downing two in rapid succession. That helped dull the pain. All she could think about was the close call;

how she almost lost Baji and almost never saw Cameron again. And then she thought of Roen. She clenched her fist, downed the last shot of tequila, and slammed the glass down on the table. With newfound purpose, she hurried out of the bar and hailed a cab.

The sooner we get back to safety the better.

"I'm not going to a safe house."

Where are you going then?

"I'm going to go find my husband."

CHAPTER TWO
BUCK'S

The crash. A calamity. With over six million Quasing on board, the ship had accidentally passed through an asteroid field and was crippled. It fought to stay intact longer than we thought possible. Courageously, the ship limped through space, dying and desperate to find a place to land. That was when we entered your galaxy.

The Grand Council identified a planet in this solar system that contained atmospheres the Quasing could survive in, though the planet offered them in billions of tiny moving pockets. It was then we realized these pockets of atmosphere were the indigenous life forms on the planet. We had little choice and set a course for the planet we now call Earth.

Tao

The biggest mistake of the twentieth century. Go.

"I'm going to have to say that art school rejecting Hitler's application, leading him toward the career choice of becoming a mass murderer. That or New Coke. You?"

The Japanese sneak attack on Pearl Harbor in 1941 or the 1948 presidential election when the Democrats failed to elect Henry Wallace as Vice President.

"Never got over it, huh? Over half a century later and you're still bitter."

Wallace was Roosevelt's spiritual successor. The world could have been so much different.

"You're just mad because he was the closest you ever got to being president."

I spent two decades maneuvering him for the presidency!

Roen Tan pulled into the gravel lot in his Chevy Impala and studied the cars parked there: Jimmy's; Amy's; Chipmunk Voice Weird Guy's; the owner, Dan's; and the Raisin's. He checked the mirror for any blood on his face. Some of the fighting on the roof had gotten very up close and personal.

He noted his sunken cheeks and the four-day fuzz on his chin. His black hair, cropped in a crooked faux hawk, was tangled and uneven. Satisfied, he parked the car, reached into the back seat for his cowboy hat, and stuffed his pistol into his jeans.

He got out and circled around to the front. One thing about rural roadside bars off the highway in the middle of the Appalachians, the patrons were usually the same folks coming in and out, and there wasn't a bouncer patting you down. That last part was especially important. Roen felt his knife sheath slide down his ankle. He'd have to poke a tighter hole soon. His new weight loss regime of eating only once a day must have reached his calves.

He swung the door open and tipped his hat to Amy, the bartender. She was the hottest young thing within a hundred kilometers, which, truth be told, was probably a sample size of about a thousand and most of them men. He also suspected she was pushing forty.

"Charlie," she nodded. "A late night? We're closing in a bit."

"Just a drink or three, ma'am," he replied. "I'll be out of your hair soon enough."

"No worries, cowboy," she smirked.

You know she does not believe you for a second…

"I'm practicing for a time when I have to really pull it off."

When that time comes, let us hope your life is not depending on it.

Roen wasn't that oblivious. He knew she didn't call him cowboy because she actually thought he was one. He tried his best to emulate the southern mountain dialect of the people here, but he sounded silly. Still, it amused the locals, and over the past year, they had grown to tolerate his presence. It was one thing to be a stranger, but it was another entirely to be one who tried to fit in. It's those who didn't try who tended to piss them off. Still, he was a novelty here even after a year and they often took turns playing guessing games trying to figure out what crime he was hiding from. The consensus was he was running from tax fraud.

You really should just drop it.

"When in Rome, Tao, when in Rome."

I lived in Rome for centuries. The last thing the Romans wanted was for the non-Romans to emulate them.

There was an old sound system playing Buck Owens on cassette. Roen knew it was Buck Owens because the bar rotated the same four tapes every night, and he was berated extensively the first time he asked about this giant of American music. He actually thought Buck sounded a little flat but that could just be the tape after a million playbacks.

Door in the back ajar. Garbage can blocking exit. Shotgun behind the bar. Two men at the far booth. Looks like Howie and his inseparable friend again.

Chipmunk Voice was at the far end of the bar, where he usually sat with his eyes glued to the television, a rickety old tube set that still had dials. Roen half expected to find the television broken every time he came in, and marveled at that wonderful piece of American ingenuity. They really didn't build them like that anymore.

Raisin was sitting by himself at the booth closest to the door. He waved at Roen and beckoned him over. Roen averted his eyes and pretended not to notice the ancient man who smelled like he had been buried and recently dug up. Instead, he took a seat in the middle of the bar where he could keep an eye on both the entrance and the exit.

"What'll it be, handsome?" Amy said in her sandpaper voice. She called everyone handsome, but Roen secretly harbored the suspicion that she really meant it with him. "The same?"

He nodded. "Wait," he patted his pockets; it felt light. He had brought one of his fake identifications with him tonight and had forgotten to transfer his money. "Cutty," he said dejectedly. "Neat. No, better make this one on the rocks."

Cutty gives you headaches.

"So does not eating."

No, that just makes you grumpy.

Amy brought over two glasses of brown liquid and slid one toward him. "Got your usual Glen. I'll just put it on your tab, and this one too." She winked. She thought she was doing him a kindness, but frankly, Roen would rather just get the Cutty than buy her a drink.

He suppressed his sigh and raised the glass. "To the finest lady this side of the mountain." They clinked and emptied their glasses.

She brought the bottle out from the shelf and poured them both another drink. This was about to get expensive on his dime. "So what kept you so late from visiting me tonight, Charlie?" she asked, twirling the bottle in her hand.

"Shooting a dozen guys trying to kill Jill" seemed like the wrong thing to say.

Roen lifted the glass to her eye level and tipped his hat. "Had to check chemical levels at the plant." The local industry in this region was chemical processing and it was common to carry odd hours. Usually, no one batted an eye at his alibis.

Amy leaned in close, her finger running along the rim of the glass. "So what else you got planned tonight, muscles? This ol' bottle and I are all by our lonesome."

Roen hesitated. On the one hand, she revolted him with her ashen face, yellow-stained teeth, and inane prattle. On the other hand, she did come with a free bottle...

The door opened with a loud creak. "He's already got plans," a strong, clear voice butted in, the sound traveling all the way through the entire bar. Roen didn't need to turn to know who it was. Instead, he took the bottle out of Amy's hand, poured himself a double, and threw it down.

Amy looked over lazily at the new voice and turned her back to it, pretending to be wiping the counter. "Sorry, honey, we're closed."

"I'm not here for a drink," Jill said as she took a seat next to him.

"Get her one anyway. Tequila for the raging tempest," Roen said.

"I'm here to talk to this son of a bitch." She swung a closed fist with a thumb extended out toward him.

"Want me to get rid of her, handsome?" Amy asked. "Who is she anyway?"

"She's just some–" Roen said.

"–wife," Jill growled.

And all the good will Roen had worked so hard to build here went up in a puff of smoke. Amy shot him a look that could kill a buffalo. "No good bastard swamp snake," she hissed and poured Jill the shot of tequila. "Here you go, honey, this one's on his tab."

Jill smiled sweetly at Amy, and the two shared a drink on Roen's dime. The next hour went by awkwardly, the ladies lambasting him as if he weren't there. When he shook his glass for another drink, Amy just shrugged and answered, "Pay your tab first, deadbeat," and proceeded to pour Jill another shot.

My advice is to run. I see no path to victory here.

"Thanks, Genghis. At this rate, I might have to start washing dishes if I'm going to cover this tab."

Amy even walked Jill out of the bar when she closed shop, going as far as hugging her and telling her to "take care of yourself, sweetheart, and watch out for the snakes that slither back into your life, you pretty little thing."

And then Jill and Roen were standing alone on the deserted gravel lot of Buck's Bar. They walked toward her car in silence. "She's sweet," Jill smirked. "Now I understand why you left me."

"I left you?" Roen's voice shot up two octaves.

Steady. Do the countdown.

If Jill had been anyone else in the world, his fist of fury would be dropping bombs right now. Instead, he closed his eyes and counted down from fourteen, enunciating each syllable one by one. He used to count down from ten, but as the years went on and the situation worsened, a higher number became necessary. When he had calmed down, he opened his eyes slowly and studied her face. There were dark rings around her eyes and her usually straight brown hair was mussed up. Roen reached toward her and touched the cut on her cheek. "We need to get something on that, or it'll scar. How are you?"

She knocked his hand away. "I think what you meant to ask was how is our son?"

"I'm not asking in the order of importance," he ground his teeth. "How are you?"

"Alive," she shrugged, "for now."

"How is Cameron? Does he miss his father?"

"He doesn't know his father!" Jill snapped.

"I'm not the one who forbade visits," he snapped back. "Might I–"

Stop.

"Tao, butt out."

Stop. Now. You dummies are quarreling in a parking lot at two in the morning off the side of a highway. You can go ahead and be stupid with each other, but at least have your shared idiocy some place safe where I am not endangered.

Roen sighed. "Come on, Jill, it's late. We've both been drinking. Let's talk at my place."

She narrowed her eyes and her mouth curved upward. For a second, the old mischievous Jill he remembered was back. "Inviting me over? That's a bold move. Daddy's been asking where in Africa you Fedexed yourself to. Now I get to save him from needing vaccination shots."

"How are Louis and Lee Ann?" Roen asked. No doubt both her parents wanted to string him up and use him as a piñata. It was really too bad. Roen had spent an inordinate amount of effort to get on Louis' good side. At first, Louis didn't think he was good enough for Jill, but he softened when he saw the engagement ring. Then he hardened up two minutes later when he found out it was going to be a shotgun wedding. He didn't soften again until Cameron was born.

"Busy taking care of your son," Jill replied, deflating. "I just couldn't do it. Couldn't take care of my own son with all that's going on. I'm a terrible mother."

Roen saw a tear sneak out of the corner of her eye and roll down her face. He reached over to embrace her. She socked him in the shoulder. Roen bit his lip and held his hands up in surrender. At least she still hadn't learned how to throw a punch yet, else this conversation might become painful.

He was a bit uneasy about Jill's parents taking care of Cameron, though. He knew that regardless of what happened between them, Jill would never badmouth him, but who knew what poison her parents, Louis especially, were whispering into his son's ears. "How did you know I'd be at Buck's anyway?" he asked

"Because you're always here after one of your watch-over-Jill escapades," she shrugged. "Don't think the Prophus haven't kept an eye on you. You're not as off the grid as you think you are."

She has a point. You have been maddeningly predictable lately.

"On the subject of which, by the way," she added, "who's your mole in Command?"

Roen shrugged, feigning innocence.

"Who's our leak?" she repeated, emphasizing each word. "Come on, your having access to mission tactics and playing shadow on some of my assignments means some jackass with misplaced loyalties is feeding you intel. Who's the dunce?"

"Not some of your assignments," he grumbled. "All of them. I've watched your back on all twelve of those crap missions Command has sent you on over the past year."

"Fourteen," she corrected.

Roen shook his head. "Costa Rica doesn't count. You didn't even bring your gun. And I arranged for you to be watched in Paris. And a mole won't be much of one if you knew, would it?"

"I don't need your help."

"Sure you don't," he said gruffly. "You had tonight completely under control. Come on, my place isn't far. Follow in your car. We can finish this conversation at a secure location."

Jill looked like she was about to protest but then thought better of it. Baji must have seen the wisdom of his proposal. It must have killed her to agree with him. A small victory. Baji barely ever conceded anything to him, and she was like this before Sonya died. It must be ten times worse now.

They got into their cars and drove another six kilometers west deeper into the Appalachians, two lonely sets of headlights weaving through the darkened hills. Eventually, he pulled off the highway and traveled down a sloping gravel road to a dried up ravine. He parked under a small ledge that hid the car from the sky and got out. Moments later, Jill pulled up next to him.

"Either you live in a tent, or you lured me here to murder me," she mused, looking around.

"After you, my lady," Roen smirked as he gestured magnanimously at a crooked myrtle tree growing out of the slope.

Jill rolled her eyes and peered underneath the tree. She whistled when she discovered a concrete tunnel burrowed into the ravine covered by a rusty gate. "When you said you were going underground, you really meant it," she said, impressed. "Gone to live with your kind?"

"Are you calling our son half-rat?" he teased.

"My looks, my brains, thank God," she answered.

They passed through the gate and walked down the dark tunnel. Roen flicked a switch, and a series of dull yellow makeshift lights buzzed on one by one, illuminating a tunnel that continued on for a good fifty meters. They walked in silence for a ways, their footsteps making a series of dull thunks that echoed all around them.

"How did you find this place?" she finally asked.

Roen kicked a rock and watched it bounce around the circular tunnel. "When I left the Prophus, I needed a new supplier. A lead pointed me to Old Alex, a recluse selling illegal munitions. He was a doomsday prepper who bought this old nuclear missile silo back in the Eighties and turned it into one of those underground castles. What we're passing through right now is the exhaust of Launch Pad 2.

"The old man hated the government and thought the world was involved in one big conspiracy. Went on for hours about them coming to take his guns and his Bibles and his moonshine. Finally got busted trying to buy a Soviet tank. Died of lung cancer in prison. Guy never believed in hospitals. Thought they'd harvest his organs or something. Who'd want his dirty kidneys I'll never know. He had no family and all his friends had four legs. When I found out he died, I moved in. Now I have a lifetime supply of munitions to play around with."

They reached the end of the tunnel where a large rust-stained door and a high-tech electronic keypad not unlike the ones on their safe houses barred their way. Roen muttered a phrase in front of a microphone and put his eye in front of the scanner. The door beeped and hissed open, and they entered what could only be described as his living room.

It was a massive silo that spanned upward so far a person couldn't see the ceiling. The room was filled with mismatched furniture; some looked like Roen had found it at a garage sale while others looked like pristine antiques. There was a couch that Jill swore was an authentic French colonial antique, and then a tacky coffee table made from carriage wheels. Three shelves of books lined one side of the circular room. There was also an air hockey table and a lifting bench on the far end. On the near side was a set of six LCD televisions stacked on top of each other.

"Living out your Bruce Wayne dreams, I see," she remarked. "It's actually quite impressive. I spent the past two years imagining you were living it up on some beach in Panama surfing all day and hitting on the locals at night."

"That was the first six months," he grinned. He gestured at the barren kitchen. "Mi casa es su casa."

"Anything respectable to drink or did you go native with the moonshine?" she asked.

He took out a half bottle of bourbon and two glasses "Little low on ice," he apologized as he poured her a glass and mixed it with water. "You're staying for the night?"

Jill shook her head. "I need to be back on the Hill in..." she checked her watch, "seven hours."

Roen took the glass away from her. "It's a three-hour drive. Stay or you get water. Tao would probably like to have a few words with Baji."

"I'm not sure Baji feels the same way. Give me the drink. I'm a big girl."

Roen hesitated before handing the glass back to her. They had more pressing issues to fight about than her drinking habits. He sat down on the couch opposite her and leaned forward. "So how is our Cameron?"

"Sprouting like a weed. Throwing kicks and punches better at three than his daddy at thirty." Jill offered the first sincere smile he'd seen all night. For a few minutes, they forgot about their past and fell into the world of their son. Roen was briefly overcome by guilt and pain as she detailed Cameron's first time on a bike with training wheels. For a few moments, their problems over the past two years were put on hold and they were a family again, sharing proud pictures of their son.

An hour later, she was still regaling him with the latest adventures of three year-old Cameron. It had gotten late and both of them were exhausted, barely able to keep their eyes open. They huddled close together. Roen could smell the faint aroma of smoke, blood, and alcohol over her. It made him even more protective as he held her gently.

"You did this on purpose," she murmured sleepily. "I need to get back to Washington."

Roen mumbled something incomprehensible as he wrapped his arm over her shoulder and closed his eyes. And for that brief moment, they were a couple again.

CHAPTER THREE
BAJI AND TAO

The ship burned up entering Earth's atmosphere, breaking into several pieces that rained death across the face of the planet. It had been bred to harden its membrane when exposed to the high heat of atmospheric entry. It was the only thing that saved us from complete annihilation.

The bulk of our people were vaporized with the main portion of the ship when it crashed into the ocean. Several hundred thousand of us survived in the fragments that were scattered across the Earth. I was in a section of the ship that crashed into the depths of what is now known as Africa.

Tao

"Hello, Baji."

Jill's eyes fluttered open and focused on Roen looking down at her. She pulled away from him and moved to the other end of the couch, a twisted look of anger on her face. "What do you want, Tao?"

Tao, through Roen, leaned forward. "Right now, I want to talk to my old friend. How are you?"

Baji shook her head in disbelief. "You have some nerve

to ask that. Things are terrible. In fact, in the history of our six hundred year war, including that fifty years I spent in the Tower of London, this is the worst it has ever been. Maybe if you had not run out on us, you would know."

"Come now, the Tower of London was nice as prisons go," Tao said mildly. "Besides, you know me better than that. When have I ever run from this war?"

"Then where were you when Capulet's Ski Lodge fell? Where were you when Dubai and Ankara were invaded? Were you with us defending Central Command when they came to Denver? Right when the Genjix brought the hammer down, you disappeared."

"Our bases in those cities were casualties the moment the Genjix infiltrated the old network. My presence there would not have made a difference."

Baji stabbed a finger into Tao's chest, pushing him back. "Six Prophus and a squad of thirty held off four hundred Genjix in Boulder for five days. Reinforcements were three hours too late. Do not dare tell me the great Tao could not have made a difference."

She leaned back and buried her face into her hands. Tao could tell Baji was exhausted.

"We have lost two hundred to the Eternal Sea this year alone. Newly acquired intel uncovered a prison in Tibet holding approximately two thousand agents and hosts. What could be so important for you to run out on us?"

"The Genjix are playing a different game now, and it has nothing to do with controlling humanity." Tao grimaced. "We were not doing a good job of winning the old way regardless." He stood up and walked away, then rounded on her, suddenly furious. "I warned them after the fall of

Toronto. I told those fools to initiate the guerrilla protocol and go underground!"

Baji stood up and glared. "And when the Keeper did not listen and ordered you to focus on other objectives, you left in a huff. And with you, Jill's husband and Cameron's father." She threw her hands in the air. "Did you imbeciles stop to think about the consequences? They were a family. Did you two selfish bastards ever consider what you put her through?"

"Do not put this on Roen. She threw him out of the house!"

"That is because he disappeared for months at a time on off-book missions. On your orders, I might add!" she snapped. "He was not there when she was struggling to raise his newborn."

Tao lowered his eyes and whispered. "Roen struggles with this more than you can imagine, but it was important. He understood."

"You felt it was important! And make no mistake, it was your plan. That imbecile obeys you like a trained dog, so it could not have conceivably been his idea."

"It had to be done," he said more emphatically. "The information I received out of South Korea was too important to ignore. The Keeper chose not to put resources into it. I did what had to be done. Command has been dropping the ball more and more these days."

"By hiding in an abandoned missile silo in the middle of the mountains?" She raised her voice. "By stalking our communication channels and popping up whenever it suits you?" Baji shook her head and turned away. "I have known you since the Inquisitions. You have never been predictable. In a way, that made you the most human of us all. And Sonya paid the price."

"It always goes back to Sonya, does it not?" Tao snapped. "People die in war. Edward died. Do you think I did not mourn him?"

She stalked back toward him. "Yes, it always goes back to Sonya. Edward died on a mission in the line of duty. He accepted the risks. You had twenty years with him. Sonya was just coming into her own. She was going to be one of my greatest hosts, and Roen robbed me of her potential. She left Metropol to save him. He was the reason she was captured. She died for your idiot host because he had a brain freeze and went after his stupid girlfriend."

Tao frowned. "The stupid girlfriend that is your current host? With the way you treat humans, maybe you should fight for the Genjix."

Baji's left hook just missed Roen's nose. Fortunately, with the sluggish control the Quasing had with their hosts, Tao blocked it, if barely.

Baji moved her face very close to his, rage flashing in her eyes. "How dare you!"

Tao had sharp words at the tip of his tongue but he stopped himself from going further. "I apologize, Baji. Sonya meant a lot to Roen as well. His guilt still consumes him."

"As it should." Baji walked away and sat back down on the couch. She looked up at the tall rounded walls that used to house a nuclear missile and then at the picture frames that lined the wall. There was one of Jill, four of Jill and Roen, and nearly a dozen of Cameron and Jill. At the far end, opposite the entrance, hung a map of Earth. Several dozen push pins of assorted colors dotted the landscape. There was another smaller map of the eastern seaboard. It too had several pins stuck into it.

Baji hesitated and grimaced. "I like what you have done with the place," she said finally. "At least he is not as much of a slob anymore."

Roen shrugged. "He even washes the dishes every night."

"That is because she is not around to clean up."

Baji finished appraising the room and took a seat on the couch. "So did you find what you were looking for? Is this information worth not being in the fight?"

Tao put his hands together, mimicking how Roen posed when he was deep in thought. In truth, Tao could have Roen stand on his head and still think just as clearly, but he enjoyed acting human when he was in control. "Remember the theory I had two years ago? The one everyone mocked?

Baji smirked. "Which one? Past couple of years, you've become a grocery stand tabloid."

"The one with–"

Jill's phone beeped and then nearly a dozen messages appeared. She frowned and looked up at the metal walls. "How is reception here?"

Tao shrugged. "There is a signal repeater set up for his phone's frequency. Everything else is a crap shoot."

She went over the texts and gasped. "I need to get back!" She stood up and shook her head violently. Jill's eyes glazed over for a moment before they refocused; she looked confused. Her expression slowly changed to one of concern.

"Oh, my God," she gasped, scrambling for her jacket.

Tao grabbed her elbow. "What is going on?"

She bent down and put on her heels. "The Genjix just crippled the *Atlantis* off the coast of southeast China. There are a hundred Prophus on board and two hundred support personnel. It's our last flagship."

"What was it doing there?" he demanded. "The South China Sea has been under Genjix control for the past five years."

Jill shook her head. "I'm not sure. Only thing I know was they had to rendezvous with a team embedded on the mainland." She hurried toward the exit, stopped, walked back to Roen and gave him a quick kiss on the mouth. "That's for saving my life." She broke off and ran out the door.

Tao ran to the exit and called after her as she was leaving. "What is Command going to do?"

She turned back. "They're mounting a rescue mission." She paused. "Roen, Dylan was on board the *Atlantis*."

Tao clenched his fists and hollered after her. "Wait. I'm coming with you."

He closed his eyes and punched himself in the face.

CHAPTER FOUR
TRANSITION

There is much debate among the Quasing about which Earth creature was the worthiest vessel. Many consider it humans for their advanced cognitive thought. I believe that a weakness as free will is a redundant ability in vessels.

Truth is, the Tyrannosaurus rex and their theropod cousins were the greatest land reptiles to ever walk the earth, and they were also the greatest vessel for one sole reason: there was no other creature on this planet blessed with such a harmonious combination of ferocity and feeblemindedness.

Our true Golden Age on Earth was during those millions of years when we ruled through the giant lizards that walked the planet. They did not aid in getting us home, but for that period of time, we were all kings.

Zoras

Devin Watson was having a bad day. An hour ago he was meeting with Prime Minister Wen and Admiral Wu in Beijing for a private lunch, discussing the placement of the South Sea Fleet and the recent military action off the coast of Taiwan. Then he suffered a heart attack and was now

lying in a very uncomfortable bed surrounded by a team of
doctors at the 301 Military Hospital. The prognosis was not
good; he was dying.

"We can circumvent the transplant list and get you a
heart immediately," one of the doctors was saying. "One can
be delivered within two hours. We will need to prepare you
for surgery right away. You will not last the night without
the procedure."

Devin grabbed the doctor by the sleeve and pulled him
close. "How long before I can get out of this bloody room?" he
said in between labored breaths. "My work is too important
to leave unattended. What are my odds of a full recovery?"

The delay is unacceptable.

The doctor hesitated. "Sir, this is your third heart attack
in five years. At your age, it will be several months before
you can leave the hospital. You may never fully recover."

"I am sorry for my state, Zoras."

*You have been a devout vessel, Devin. However, your frail body
betrays us. Your time is at an end. Call the Adonis Vessel.*

"We are nearing a critical stage. A transition would surely
put the plan at risk."

I have spoken. Initiate the transfer protocol.

"As you wish, my Guardian."

That could only mean one thing. Devin looked down at
his broken body and grimaced. He had hoped to hold up a
few more years. The ProGenesis project was his conception
after all. It would have been glorious to see it through.

Devin waved the doctors aside and beckoned his aide
Amanda. "Get me a glass of Pappy's bourbon, neat, and a
Habanos Cuban cigar." The team of physicians protested,
telling him it wasn't advisable in his current state. One even
had the audacity to remind him that this was a hospital and

that smoking wasn't allowed. Devin zeroed in on the fool
and spoke in clear Mandarin. "If I had a gun right now, I'd
shoot you. Now, all of you, get out!"

The two guards standing in the room drew their pistols.
The doctors fled, stumbling over each other in their haste
to get out of the room. When he was finally alone with
Amanda and the guards, he began to issue orders in rapid
succession. "Have all departments prepare a full status
report. Call Palos and have his team prepared for vessel
transfer. Recall Enzo from the Hatchery and send him to
Qingdao. We leave after I finish my drink."

Amanda bowed and left the room. A few minutes later,
she returned carrying a silver plate with a cigar, a glass
of golden brown liquid, a pill, and a Shilin knife. Palos,
head of Devin's security detail, was with her. Devin stared
thoughtfully at the silver plate as she placed it on his lap.
These were his last rites and he was wearing a gown. It
wasn't how he thought his life would end. But then, Devin
never thought he'd die a natural death. Well, as natural as
someone in his position was ever going to have.

He motioned them all to be quiet as he caressed the cigar,
first sniffing it, then cutting the ends, and lighting it. He took
a generous puff and exhaled with pleasure. It had been two
years since he had last smoked one. The bourbon burned his
mouth, and he relished the sweet flavor of honey and spice.
After twenty minutes of bliss, when the glass was empty and
the cigar nothing more than a stub, he nodded to Amanda.

"Let's begin," he said.

She bowed. "May I have the honor, Father?" she asked.

He shook his head. "Enzo will need you." He turned to
Palos. "I need a volunteer. Not you, old friend. You will be
needed as well." Palos nodded and left the room.

Moments later, Saldhana, the oldest man on his guard detail, walked in. He prostrated next to Devin's bed, his forehead almost touching the ground. "Father, I have the honor."

Devin put a hand on Saldhana's shoulder. "You are worthy, my son." Devin closed his eyes and took a deep breath, saying a prayer to the Holy Ones. When he was ready, he gave final instructions to deliver his body to his wife and ordered those around him to provide Enzo the support he needed to deliver the Genjix's will. Then he picked up the Shilin knife.

The transfer ceremony will not be necessary. Make it quick and painless.

Devin hesitated. "As you wish, Zoras."

Then he looked around the room. "Praise to the Holy Ones," were the last words out of his mouth. Then he picked up the cyanide pill and swallowed it. Moments later, Devin Watson, senator of the state of Alabama, father of four, grandfather of nine, High Father of North America, and a member of the Genjix Council, was dead.

"Praise to the Holy Ones," the voices in the room echoed.

Immediately, Zoras moved out of Devin's body and floated into the air. The agents in the room prostrated themselves and waited. He moved in circles, flitting back and forth before settling into the transfer vessel. Saldhana uttered a shocked cry of pain and he spasmed on the ground for several minutes. He finally recovered and nodded to Palos. The security team formed around Saldhana and they all left the room in unison.

Amanda broke off from the group to instruct the hospital staff on returning Devin's body to his family. Minutes later, they were in a caravan of limousines heading toward the airport. Within an hour, they were up in the air heading toward Qingdao.

Enzo sat at the edge of the infinity pool at the edge of the high cliff overlooking the lush canopy of Santa Rosa National Park. He was a near-perfect specimen for a human. His build was taut and muscular but not bulky, and he walked with the grace of a dancer. Chosen for his genes and natural physical attributes since birth, he was a handsome man: tall, with high cheekbones, chiseled features, and a completely symmetrical face. Symmetry, of course, was the scientific formula of beauty. And in Enzo's case, it was common knowledge at the Hatchery that he was even more beautiful than most. Not only that, he could run a marathon in three hours, shoot an eight centimeter target with a handgun at fifty meters, and run any of the countries in South America better than their current leaders. Like all his brothers raised at the Hatchery, he lived and trained to serve one purpose.

The financial figures of the Eurozone's trading day sped by on a small ticker at the bottom of a tablet resting on his lap. Above the ticker, a chart of Genjix owned assets on the New York Stock Exchange, Tokyo Stock Exchange, and the European Stock Exchange fluctuated in real time. The Genjix were up for the day. The rest of the world, not so much. The state of the Euro was a small cause for concern, though their analysts had correctly predicted this outcome and their liability shield was keeping them safe from the brunt of failing world economies. Enzo picked up his glass of Macallan 24, careful to keep only two fingers touching the glass, and took a sip. On both sides of him, half a dozen of his brothers and sisters, all in similar states of relaxation, sat on recliners analyzing the aggregate data from today's world events broken down into a series of numbers and charts. A report from their South American operations flashed across his screen. He gave it a quick glance before shelving it into one of his archives. South America was of little concern to him.

"Brother," Danette, who sat next to him, said, "The Minister of Finance in Sweden just resigned. Wasn't he one of ours?"

"The position is about to become one of ours," he corrected.

"Supplies of natural gas are down in Spain as well. The Pegasus operation is based there. Why is the Euro Council suppressing it further?"

Enzo turned to another sister. "Jeanine, answer that."

She nodded. "Operations in that region consist of less than one percent of our global presence. Prophus dealings are estimated to be at three."

He turned back to Danette. "Hurts them more than it hurts us."

The group fell back into silence as they continued deciphering figures and reports. Enzo pulled up a three-month history of Genjix figures compared to what they believe the Prophus owned. It painted a flattering picture with the two sides moving in opposite directions.

Enzo finished his scotch, stood up, and stretched. He walked to the edge of the balcony and looked out at the breathtaking view below. The jungle grew in all directions as far as his eyes could see. A single bead of sweat dripped from his brow, down his cheek, careening off his jaw. The gentle churning of the water in the infinity pool was soothing to the ear, though the peace was occasionally broken by the sound of combat approximately thirty meters away. To his left, a young woman butchered the Portuguese language.

Enzo, one of the oldest on the training floor, tore his eyes away from the jungle canopy and looked at the hive of activity in the main training room of the Hatchery. Azumi was talented in many things; languages were definitely not one of them. Her recital of *The Art of War* in Portuguese from memory was an embarrassment. Austin should be nearing half his hundred-lap swim by now. Matthew and Akelatis' sparring session had just finished the second round.

As usual, Elder Mother sat on her throne, overseeing the day's studies. Nearing eighty, Enzo wondered what she was like before she was posted here. Once a very high-profile operative, she was one of the principal architects of the Hatchery program and ruled over them with an iron fist. Being the only blessed vessel, she was at the same time a parent and god to them. This was the Holy One's third and most successful attempt at building such a program. The first two, originating during World War II with the study of eugenics, had mixed results. This third program, however, had been decidedly more successful. Already in the past ten years, eighty-four Adonis Vessels had made the transition. Enzo was currently one of nineteen assigned to Holy Ones. The rest of the one hundred and forty-seven incubates were in different states of training and readiness.

Elder Mother saw him studying her. "Enzo. I see you have completed your appraisal. Come forth and tell me what you've learned."

Enzo tilted his head at Elder Mother and made his way past the infinity pool to the sparring mat. Austin was still swimming at a steady pace. By Enzo's calculations, Austin should be on his seventy-ninth lap in the twenty-five meter length pool, assuming he had maintained the pace he had set when he began. Knowing Austin's fitness and the state of his health, he expected a degradation of roughly fifteen percent.

Enzo winked at Azumi as he passed and was rewarded with a slight stutter in her recitation. He stopped at the foot of the bamboo mat as Matthew and Akelatis completed their round. Enzo settled down and waited, watching with professional interest as two of his younger brothers beat each other senseless. Ten seconds into watching the fight, he knew Akelatis would win. Matthew was constantly half a step slow in his counters, especially on his right. There was a blossoming bruise just below his eye on that side; it must obscure his vision. His arm also displayed an ugly welt just above the elbow. Akelatis was not strong, but had a quick release with his lead leg.

Enzo began to recite his analysis, starting with the technology market in the States and the recent five-day decline of the Dow. Then he proceeded to tie the Dow with the recent fall of the euro in the currency markets and how it was affected by austerity measures on fringe economies of the European Union. Then he moved on to the rise in prices of concrete and industrial cranes, which had had a significant jump of fourteen percent in the past month.

Seven minutes into his analysis, Austin walked out of the pool and approached the mat, standing at attention on the eastern side of the mat. Doing some quick math, Enzo made a mental note on Austin's conditioning; he was twenty percent off his initial pace. The fight in the center of the mat ended with Akelatis chasing a retreating Matthew off the floor.

Elder Mother had long since stopped listening to Enzo. Her focus was on the melee. She beckoned them back to the center. Enzo continued his monologue about the

recent drop in heroin prices on the black market as Elder
Mother gave his two brothers her breakdown on their fight.
Akelatis would make a fine field commander for a mid-
level Holy One. Matthew was fated for an administrator's
life. Neither was Council material though. Then again, few
were. Currently, there was only one Adonis Vessel worthy
of the Council residing at the Hatchery.

"Austin, join us," Elder Mother said. The lad bowed and
took position next to Matthew and Akelatis on the right
edge of the mat. Then Elder Mother finally gestured for
Enzo to approach. He bowed and took position at the end
of the line. Elder Mother put her hands together between
Enzo and the other three and then opened them. She was
setting up a one versus three fight. The men split up into the
two groups and faced each other.

"Would you take these odds?" she asked.

Unconsciously, Enzo flexed his shoulders and felt his back
crack as they loosened up. All three were younger. Austin
might be stronger but he was the most green and his boxing
style was rudimentary. Akelatis was the quickest, preferring
taekwondo as his style. He had also injured his left hamstring
a week ago. Matthew had the most experience, preferring
to fight with judo. He had pillow punches but was the most
tactically sound. Judging by his posture, he was also gassed.
This fight would come down to how much energy Austin
had expended during his swim. Several more factors ran
through Enzo's head as he considered his options.

"Well," Elder Mother said.

"In this scenario, Mother, do I have the option to
withdraw?"

"The combat is optional, though once you engage, you
are committed."

"And the prize for victory?"

"Significant."

"Very well then. I accept." He bowed and walked to the middle of the mat. The three men exchanged glances and spread out to both sides of him.

"You believe this an equal fight?" Elder Mother asked.

"If I believed it an equal fight, Mother, I would not have accepted."

Elder Mother smiled. "Your assessment of this situation is correct. Azumi, please join your brothers and see if you can balance the scales."

Behind him, Enzo heard the sloppy recitation of Sun Tzu's masterpiece end and Azumi's light footsteps approach. The situation had just turned dire. Azumi's standing in combat was just beneath his. In fact, she had the ability to win one in ten against him. Add in the others and he stood no chance of victory.

"Tilting the scales heavily in their favor hardly seems balanced, Mother," Enzo murmured, retreating slowly to one corner of the mat. He could not afford to be surrounded.

"Imposing your will and strength over another is a sign of your superiority. Enzo, you believe you stand above your siblings, that you are their better. Prove it." Elder Mother turned to the other four standing opposite of him. "Children, you are to beat Brother Enzo until he loses consciousness. Begin."

The fight attracted several new viewers. A small crowd of his brothers and sisters gathered around the mat to watch. Many of the servants stopped as well to watch the spectacle. Enzo had to be careful. Even in training, he could lower his standing among them, and that standing would be important for all these future leaders of the Genjix.

Enzo's mind raced. This was not a situation he could win on his own, yet Elder Mother would not put him in a situation that did not have a solution. They spread out, cutting off his escape routes as they closed in on him. He anticipated he had about twenty seconds to solve this encounter. It came down to his opponents. Matthew and Austin would not change the outcome of the fight regardless of which side they fought on. Akelatis was injured but the most malleable. Azumi would give him the decided edge but would require the highest price.

"Sister," he called out, not looking her way. "Why do you fight me?"

"Mother has ordered it so," she answered. "And I obey, praise be the Holy Ones."

"Mother," Enzo kept his voice calm. He had to work hard to appear in control. "What if Azumi chooses to not engage in this encounter?"

"She must," Patron Master said. "Or she will stand guard at the west wing for the next two nights."

"Sister," Enzo said quickly, "I offer to take your place at guard if you come to my side."

"Your offer gains me nothing," She cracked her knuckles and stretched her shoulders and settled into her Muay Thai stance. The other three were already closing in. If they were smart, they would attack immediately to prevent him from negotiating with Azumi. However, none was willing to lead the charge against him.

"Then what do you wish?"

"Such an open ended question, Brother. I wish for world peace and a Holy One."

"Something I can offer you."

"It seems there is not much you can offer me at this time."

Before he could respond, Matthew lunged. Though he was the least threat, he recognized that any successful negotiation with Azumi would turn the tide to Enzo's favor. His decision to attack was tactically sound, if not a bit suicidal. Just as he charged forward, Azumi turned and threw a forearm to his neck, leaving him writhing on the ground gasping for air. A murmur of surprise swept through the audience. This turn of events surprised everyone, including Enzo. However, he quickly reappraised the situation and pressed his attack on Akelatis while Azumi destroyed Austin. The melee was short and ugly. Akelatis and Austin were no match for them. The fight ended with Akelatis unconscious on the ground and Austin suffering a dislocated shoulder. Enzo glanced at Azumi and nodded. She gave him a quick two finger salute and walked off. Elder Mother smiled.

"At this time" is what should have given her away. Enzo had thought today's test was for him. It was then that he realized that he was just a part of the test. Azumi was Elder Mother's real focus. Now Enzo, an already blessed vessel of the Council, was beholden to her. That future favor was far more valuable than anything he could offer right now. Furthermore, her standing in the Hatchery had just skyrocketed. She had proven to be a cunning vessel. Enzo bowed and was about to leave the floor when one of the servants came in and whispered in Elder Mother's ear. She listened attentively, her eyes locked on Enzo.

"Enzo," she called out. "You have been summoned. The plane leaves within the hour."

CHAPTER FIVE
REUNION

Our crash sparked a chain reaction of destruction and climate change that wiped out the majority of life on the planet. Less than a third of the survivors lived through Earth's transition as the planet underwent massive seismic shifts.

For millions of years, we struggled to stay alive, flitting from one dying creature to another. Eventually, we were scattered, all semblance of organization lost. And then we lost our way as sentient beings, eventually becoming nothing more than living mist, parasites that occupied hosts by instinct.

Tao

Jill's car screeched as it turned down a ramp into the parking garage of an abandoned warehouse. They had made the three-hour drive in two, speeding down Highway 82 to the 66 at breakneck speeds. The entire time, Roen held the door rail with a white-fisted death grip. It wasn't because he was afraid of driving fast, it was because Jill was the one driving. Her car making noises like a dying cow when accelerating didn't help matters much either.

She admonished him several times for passenger-side

driving, scolding him whenever he reacted as if they were about to die in a fiery blaze of automobile glory. It took a while, but he finally settled down into a quiet whimper as they sped through the night. Luckily, she had government plates, or they'd surely have been pulled over by now. He certainly didn't remember her driving like this when they were together. By dawn, they reached the outskirts of the city proper and headed south toward a run-down industrial district.

The sun was just past the ridgeline in the east. Their lack of sleep coupled with the alcohol they had both drunk was taking its toll on them. Surprisingly, the dilapidated parking garage attached to the warehouse was filled with cars. She pulled into an open space and hopped out, gesturing for him to hurry. Roen opened his door and promptly nicked the side panel of an expensive-looking Mercedes.

Come on. Really?

Roen looked at the small scratch sheepishly. "I hardly got any sleep."

And you smell like a cask of whiskey.

Jill gave him an exasperated look. "Still oblivious. You know whose car that is, don't you?"

Roen shook his head. "Do I want to?"

"You tell the Keeper you scratched her car when you see her."

"The Keeper?" he gasped. "You mean, this dump is Prophus Command? I thought it was just a safe house."

The Keeper has a few character flaws and living in comfort is one of them. I blame that on her living in pharaohs for a thousand years. Things must be much worse than we thought.

Jill nodded and walked to a door at the end of the lot. "The Genjix has made it difficult to maintain a permanent base within the United States. Most of them now are in third world countries. We still need a heavy presence in the nation's capital though, so this is it."

Roen scanned the garage. This place would definitely not pass the sniff test. The mixture of cars was too strange. The Keeper's car must be over a hundred grand while the car next to hers looked like a Jeep that might have rolled off the assembly line during World War II.

He hurried after Jill. By the time he caught up with her, she was walking through a dark tunnel that looked like it hadn't been used in years, much less belonged to the Prophus command center. There were thick layers of dust on everything. Roen pinched his nose to stop from sneezing. If he didn't know better, he'd think she had a hit out on him. That sort of uneasy feeling was common among operatives.

"Are you sure this is the right place?" Immediately, he regretted asking that. Of course she was sure. Sometimes, he just couldn't help asking. She awarded his dumb question with a hostile glare before walking into a large storage room. She tapped on a hidden panel on the far wall and a retinal scanner appeared. After authorizing herself, the wall swung open.

"Get in," she said. "The dust sprays kick on in thirty seconds."

"Cute," he grumbled as he went in after her. The wall swung closed behind them and they continued down a cleaner, better-lit tunnel. "What about all the cars out there? Looks a bit obvious, no?"

"Most in that lot are registered as DEA impounds," she explained. "This is technically a lot for cars preparing for auction."

They walked through another set of doors and turned right, going down a long flight of stairs. Two guards met them before they reached the end, where a rusty coiling door was rolled halfway open.

"Ma'am," one of them said, "you're clear. This one we have to take in."

Early twenties. Seventy-five kilograms. Chest armor only.

"Not military by the way he's holding the gun. Trigger finger off. Not expecting to use it."

Second target. Even younger. Overweight. Same armor. Rifle at his waist.

"What the hell? Seems anyone can join the club these days."

Sixty degrees right, cut off line of sight on second, disarm first, use as body shield, shoot second?

"These two cubs? No need to get fancy. I might as well just Hulk-smash them."

How droll. How about control right barrel with hand, spin kick to chest on second. I would say face, but you are not quite that limber anymore. A groin pull would be unfortunate.

"It's the jeans; they're too tight. I can body check one, obstruct two's line of sight..."

Jill snapped her fingers in front of Roen's face. "Stop mentally masturbating. I know what you two idiots are thinking."

Roen managed to look a little crestfallen, though if anything, it was an act to get the rookies to lower their guards. This exercise was one Tao used to hone Roen's tactics during fights. Now, it was a game between them to see who could be more creative.

She put on a stern face and glared at the two young guards. "Do you know who I am?"

"Of course ma'am," the one in the rear said.

"Good. The jerk's with me. Let us through."

They exchanged hesitant glances before the one in front stepped aside. Jill thanked them and continued through the entrance. Roen followed dutifully, but as he passed them, he couldn't help himself. He gestured to the skinny cub and flicked the boy's trigger hand with his finger.

"Look, if you're going to point a rifle at someone less than a meter away, keep your damn finger on the trigger." Then he rounded on the fat one in the back. "And you, who do you think you are, holding yours at your waist? Are you in a Columbian cartel? Listen Che, up here." Roen snatched the rifle and stuck it at shoulder level. He turned away and muttered. "You two schlubs have no idea how close you were to getting killed just now."

That will endear you to the troops.

"I'm assuming we're here on a temporary basis, right? We're contracting this gig."

Nothing like contracting for free.

They passed by the coiling door and entered a large open space teeming with activity. The current Prophus command center looked like someone started unpacking and then left for lunch. Roen's eyes followed the cable lines that snaked across the floors to the corners and down the room to another that most likely housed the data center. There were half-unpacked crates everywhere and the entire room felt very makeshift.

Dust on the walls and shelves. Weapons all live on racks.

"How long have you been here?" he asked.

"Four months," Jill replied. "All bases are mobile now. We can't afford to stay in one place for too long these days."

"Why isn't that man under guard?" A voice belted over the constant buzzing of the room. A red-faced Stephen approached with his right hand on his holstered sidearm.

WESLEY CHU 53

"Thirty degree angle left, right arm clothesline?"

It is only Stephen. He has twigs for legs. Go low.

Stephen got close and poked a finger into his face. "We don't take to deserters kindly around here."

Roen held his ground and gave Stephen an even look, half prepared to defend himself. The two stood still for several moments. In the back of his head, he heard that old Wild West music playing and imagined a tumbleweed rolling past them. Then finally, the end of Stephen's mouth twitched upward; he grinned. "It's good to see you again, Roen. I see you haven't let yourself go."

"Not all the way," Roen grinned back. "And I see you still can't hold a poker face." Stephen was one of the few people in the organization who Roen would take a bullet for. He thought of the Field Marshal of the Prophus forces as a father figure and, along with Jill and Dylan, he was the only person Roen felt guilty for abandoning.

Stephen turned and motioned for Roen to follow. "So how's that fact-finding mission of yours coming along?" He was also one of the few to take Roen's conspiracies seriously.

Roen was more than happy to share the information. "The Genjix are planning something big. We know they are heavily invested in ProGenesis, trying to procreate our kind, but I believe that is only a means to an end. Their research divisions have been sourcing raw materials that have nothing to do with the reproduction process. They recently completed a heavy water refinery in Siberia, and they've snapped up every ounce of certain rare metals they can get their hands on in South Africa. It's a large puzzle. One that I haven't put together yet. I believe a large part of their refining is done in the States and routed to China."

Unlike most of Command, Stephen actually seemed interested in Roen's findings. "We found scattered reports that correlate with what you just said, though our intelligence gathering is only a shadow of what it was a few years ago. You have any theories on what they're up to?"

Roen shook his head. "Something Sean told me at the Decennial stuck in my mind. It was about not caring if the Quasing return home or not. Then we discovered those mutated algae in that Newfoundland research facility two years ago. I traced the empty chemical barrels to a testing lab in Mongolia. The CO_2 emissions in the fields there were off the charts. It got me thinking..."

They reached a set of double doors. Stephen stopped and turned to him. "You might want to stick around. We have intel you might find interesting. Besides, we can use your gun. Lord knows we're short on quality men these days. What do you say?"

"Sorry, sir," Roen shrugged. "I operate better without that bitch Keeper always yelling at me. By the way, where are you finding these new recruits? The two kids up front, their voices are still cracking."

"Not much more inexperienced than when Tao found you. Give them time."

Our need to recruit younger and more inexperienced reminds me of the final year of the Third Reich. They were drafting children off the streets.

"And why is Dylan in China?" Roen asked. "No Prophus should go anywhere close to that continent these days."

"That's where the good action is these days," Stephen shrugged. "The Genjix have free rein there. They consider the States too restrictive. The *Atlantis* was providing support for him when it was crippled." He grimaced. "Eighty-three hosts, a hundred and ninety-four crew, not to mention a three billion dollar sub."

"We didn't actually pay for it," Roen said. "We stole it from them."

"Still a three billion dollar asset lost."

"What's the situation now with the *Atlantis*?" Jill asked.

"Still being towed," Stephen said. "The South Sea Fleet forced the sub to the surface but was unable to cut in. They won't be able to, short of blowing it up. They're towing it to the Fuzhou Naval Base. From what I hear, all the maneuvering thrusters on the *Atlantis* are working against the tow. It'll take them a few days."

"Why didn't they just sink her and be done with it?" Roen asked.

Stephen shook his head. "The Genjix, at a very high cost, have been capturing Quasing rather then send them to the Eternal Sea. The ProGenesis experiments demand a lot of host test subjects. Dylan discovered that the Genjix have been stashing all their prisoners in an internment camp in Tibet. It's the logical place for the prisoners on *Atlantis* to go. We're going to try to break them out there instead of in China."

"Is that why Dylan was in China? He was searching for the internment camp?" Roen asked.

Stephen shook his head. "Discovery of the camp was just gravy." He leaned in close. "You want to know why? He was following up on your intel." Stephen's face broke into a wide grin when he saw the shocked look on Roen's face. "You didn't actually think that mole you were using to check up on Jill actually worked for you, did you?"

Roen was speechless. "You... were spying on me!"

Stephen laughed. "Let's say we used you as an unpaid intelligence consultant."

"Tao, oh my god! I was contracting for free!"

I have always considered Stephen's Quasing, Camr, my equal. It seemed I have underestimated him.

Stephen winked. "Do you want to know what he found?"

Roen nodded.

Stephen opened the double doors. "Follow me."

The three of them entered a small room with nine people huddled around a large round table. Roen didn't recognize all of them, but the three he did told him that he was in rare company.

The Keeper looked up from the map they were fussing over and scowled. "Who let that traitor in here? Put him in cuffs right now."

Two guards as young-looking as the ones Roen had met at the entrance appeared. Immediately, an escape plan involving a pretty rough firefight popped into his head. Unfortunately, the plan entailed taking Stephen hostage and shooting the Keeper. Roen put a hand on his sidearm and the two guards raised their rifles. At least they were holding them right this time.

This is certainly going to be interesting if you draw. And no, you are not allowed to shoot the Keeper. Try being civil.

"Technically," Roen shrugged as casually as a person could with two rifles trained on him, "I'm a deserter, not a traitor, and I'd like to see these kindergartners try."

Your interpretation of civil needs a bit of work.

The Keeper had aged quite a bit since he had last seen her, and she wasn't that young to begin with. Her host, Meredith Frances, was a distant Astor through marriage. She and the Keeper had been the head of the Prophus longer than anyone could remember.

The Keeper was the only Quasing from the original Grand Council to side with the Prophus, and she had held the honored post of the Historian of the Ship since they first journeyed from Quasar. She was the closest thing the Prophus had to a head of government. Unfortunately for Roen, she hadn't thought much of him even before he left. Now she thought even less of him. It didn't bother Roen that much though. He hated the Keeper's guts.

You did get her heir killed.

"On a mission. She tried to have me arrested for disobeying orders."

You did disobey orders.

"I was a hundred meters away from the entire Genjix Council. It was worth the risk."

That I agree with.

"So why are you arguing with me?"

I am not. Just reminding you that you disobeyed a direct order and Hubert died for it. He was her favorite nephew after all.

Roen took a deep breath, closed his eyes, and counted down from fourteen. He opened them and looked straight at the Keeper. He could tell from his peripheral vision that the guards were a little trigger-happy. "Look, I'm here to help. I owe Dylan more times than I can count. If you want me on board, my gun is yours. If not, you can try to arrest me."

Jill just rolled her eyes while Stephen tried to defuse the situation. "Put the guns down," he snapped at the guards. He turned to the Keeper and Roen. "Meredith, now is not the time. Roen, grow up. We have bigger issues at stake here. Hundreds of our people's lives are forfeit unless we act. If you're with us, obey orders like everyone else. If not, you know where the door is. Understood?"

Roen nodded.

"Good." Stephen looked down at the map. "The parts are already moving. The bulk of our forces will enter Tibet via commercial transport over the course of a week. Our infrastructure in Nepal fortunately remains intact and will supply us from across the border. That entire region hasn't seen much action from either side in over forty years or the Genjix probably wouldn't have built the internment camp there.

"What's our troop count?" Roen asked.

"Stripping available personnel without crippling world operations, a shade under two thousand," Stephen answered. "This will be largest direct operation we've had since World War II. Advance scouts already on the ground estimate nearly fourteen to twenty-two hundred prisoners. With the *Atlantis* added to those numbers, that's far too many Prophus to leave in Genjix hands.

"I'll need to clear time off with Wilks," Jill said.

"You're not going," the Keeper said. "Through attrition, you're moving up the food chain here at the capital. Adam's dropped the ball around here. In the past six months, we've lost nineteen political operatives. You have an important job on the Hill and I want you to focus on our initiatives there. No more off-the-program work for you. I'm assigning an agent to your protective detail as well. This city's gotten too dangerous, and we can't afford to lose any more, especially a key legislative operative such as yourself."

"You're taking me off the line?" she gasped.

"More like we're narrowing your focus. As much as I hate to say it," the Keeper sniffed toward Roen's direction, "he might have been on to something. The Genjix have been applying pressure in Congress to loosen trade resolutions with China. There are a few bills in particular that seem to be part of a larger initiative. Until we find out exactly what they're after, we need you to shut them down."

Stephen looked at Roen. "That's where you come in. Dylan was following leads from your intel in China and it pointed him to the island of Taiwan. The *Atlantis* was taking him there when it was attacked. Last communication we got from Abrams was that he got away in an escape pod. We don't know if he made it or not. I want you to pick up where he left off, find what he's looking for and, if possible, bring him safely back as well."

"Who's going to protect Jill then?" Roen asked.

"Aw, I didn't know you still cared, Roen," Jill said. "Now, if you only cared enough to not leave me and our child..."

"Can we not do this in front of our friends and alien colleagues?" he said.

Stephen wagged his finger at both Jill and Roen. "And that's why it's a standing policy to not let agents in a relationship, or whatever you two are right now, work together. People get emotional. People get killed. The Keeper has it covered."

"Covered like last night?" Roen spat. "Forget it. She'd be on her way to that camp right now if it weren't for me."

"I know about last night's fiasco. As far as I'm concerned, the only operation Adams is managing from now on is the annual Christmas party," the Keeper said dryly. "I'm taking him off operations in Washington and transferring him to the Midwest." She pointed at the map. "Trust me when I say Jill is an important asset. We are slowly losing the United States. We're bringing someone with a proven track record to stem the tide of Genjix influence in the States, and we're going to need Jill. We need someone she can depend on to protect her."

"I'm sure the Keeper has an able agent assigned," Stephen added just as Roen opened his mouth to tell the Keeper where she could shove that not-so-subtle jab at him.

"I don't trust any of these kids you assign to her," Roen snapped.

"The only one I see acting like a kid here is you," someone piped up from the door.

All eyes turned to the new voice. Paula smirked and walked in. "I see all the best and brightest are here. Well, the brightest at least. Now that I'm here, the best as well." She turned to Roen. "Why does it seem like I'm hearing babies prattle on when you're around, Roen?"

He grinned and shook hands with her. "It's good to see you again. You too, Yol."

Stephen nodded when she gave him a casual salute. "Thanks for making the trip on short notice. You're being reassigned to do here in the capital what you did in London." He looked up at the rest of the room. "Paula will be directing all DC operations from here on out."

Paula bowed magnanimously. "Queen, country, and the Redskins."

"If Paula's handling operations, who's taking Jill's protective detail then?" Roen demanded.

"I'm putting Marco on the job," the Keeper said with a satisfied smile on her face.

"Marco!" Roen's voice rose up three octaves. "I hate Marco!"
I hate Ahngr!

"Ooh, Marco. We really are bringing the big guns," Paula quipped, her smirk getting wider. She turned to Jill. "You're in for a real treat. Marco's so dashing with that nose and jawline and debonair ways. And he's got these..."
There are quite a few Genjix that I like more than Ahngr.

Roen's face turned red and he felt his entire body tighten. "If you think I'm letting my wife hang out with that egotistical self-centered leech and his..."

"...dreamy eyes. A total charmer, but watch out, he's such a cad sometimes," Paula winked at her. "And such a legend at European Command. He makes James Bond look like a pimply virgin. Makes a girl swoon." She pretended to fan herself.

"I'm in love already," Jill winked back. "Guess I'm in good hands."

"Like hell you are!" Roen roared. "I won't have it!"

"That's enough!" Stephen snapped at Roen. "This is a military operation, not high school drama club. The decision's been made. You're either on board or the door is over there."

The room was silence as Roen weighed his options. He felt torn between wanting to protect Jill and the promise he just made to Stephen. Jill had a bodyguard now, and even Roen had to admit that Marco was good. Probably better than Roen, but did it have to be Marco? Of all the jerks in the Prophus ranks, and there were a fair amount of them, Marco took the damn cake.

Did I tell you that Ahngr twice sacrificed my host so his could get away? Once in Sumeria and once during World War I.

"I know! How can I trust that asshole with my wife?"

Roen racked his brain for a few more seconds, warring between his protectiveness for Jill and his respect for Stephen. Finally, after he ran out of alternatives, he grudgingly nodded. "Fine. I owe it to Dylan. If it wasn't for him, I'd be dead ten times over."

Stephen nodded. "Alive preferably. In good health if possible but I'll settle for breathing. I'd love to hunt for Dylan myself but two thousand lives have priority."

Roen nodded. "I'll find our Aussie for you. Alive, in one piece and ugly as ever."

"Good," Stephen nodded. "Find that fat bastard, finish the job in Taiwan, and join up with us in Tibet afterward."

"How many men am I getting on my team for this mission? There are a few guys I'd like to ask for." Roen asked.

"You don't get anyone. I'm attaching you to Wuehler's black ops team. Follow his orders." He paused again, the appraising look returning. "Will that be a problem?" Roen gritted his teeth and swore under his breath. This was just getting worse and worse.

"What the hell, Tao? Wuehler and Marco of all people. I think the Keeper is messing with me."

I know she is. This will be interesting. I wonder how many nights in a row he will make you stand guard.

Roen nodded reluctantly.

"Good then. Alright people," Stephen scanned the group. "You have your orders. Let's see it done."

CHAPTER SIX
MEETING WITH WILKS

I became Prophus in the worst way. At the time, I, alongside many others who did not heed the command of the old order, hid from their decree that all Quasing must come into the fold or face the Inquisition. The simpleton who was my host at the time could not stop talking about the voices he heard in his head, and was eventually taken for questioning. That was how I was found out.

My host was imprisoned by the Inquisitors by command of the Genjix, and framed as the murderer of a Spanish Cardinal, one Francisco Ciserno. For two years, he languished in a damp prison in Valencia. He was near death when a hooded figure appeared and opened his doors. Half a dozen guards lay dead in the hallway.

Terrified, my host asked what the stranger wanted.

The man's answer was, "Your freedom. You have paid for my crimes long enough."

Baji

When the meeting ended, Paula signaled to Jill to fall in with her. Paula, a former MI6 agent, was considered the rising star at European Command. She had twice refused promotion in order to stay in the field and was eventually forced into a command role. Since then, she had been instrumental in keeping the Genjix from infiltrating Her Majesty's Secret Service. If the Prophus ever needed to turtle up, Iceland and England would be their centers of operation. It was unfortunate that Ireland had been compromised the previous year or the Prophus could realistically have kept some semblance of a stronghold in that region. Her Quasing, Yol, was one of the foremost computer experts within the Prophus and Tao's close friend. Jill had a sneaking suspicion that Paula was Roen's leak.

"I don't have a lot of pieces to play with, Jill," she said as they walked through the busy hive of the command room, "so I need all of them working. Marco is en route. You listen to him and don't give him a hard time. He's quite lovely if you're on his good side and a real troll if you're not. Just ask your husband."

"Why does Roen hate him?" Jill asked. "I've never seen him react this strongly to any Prophus before. Not even the Keeper, and he uses her picture as a dartboard."

Paula chuckled. "Imagine Tao, all snarky and self-righteous, add an overdose of self-confidence and a title, and you have Marco. And to double down on that, Ahngr is even more insufferable. Roen and Marco ran a series of missions together in Egypt three years ago. You remember that?"

Jill nodded. "He came home pissy for a month."

"Those two were joint leads on the operation. They were at each other's throats and had to be physically separated four times. According to eye witnesses, Roen lost every fight."

Witnesses say it was not even close.

"That would explain it."

"It gets worse. Tao hates Ahngr even more than Roen does Marco. Yol says they had a pretty bad row during the Thirty Years' War, and it lasted for the entire thirty years. Some Prophus believe their bickering changed the outcome of the war."

You do not know the half of it.

Jill frowned. "So if they have such a long and bad history together, why did the Keeper send for him? She must know it'd just infuriate Roen."

Paula glanced to the side to make sure no one was listening. She leaned in. "Don't tell Roen, but I asked for Marco."

Jill stifled a chuckle. "Why? You're his friend."

Paula shrugged. "Because Marco's one of the best. Taking care of you is the perfect assignment for him. Trust me, Roen will thank me for this. Just don't ever let him know." She paused. "What's going on with you two anyway? Are you..." Paula's voice trailed off.

"Still separated? You don't forgive a father who abandons his son on some alien's say-so."

Paula nodded. "I'm sorry to hear that. He's a good bloke though, and Tao can be very persuasive."

"No need to enumerate Roen's good qualities to me." The words tumbled out of Jill's mouth a bit harsher than she intended. She tried to rein her emotions in. "I know you just flew in, so let's schedule a meeting after you get settled. Dinner and drinks? We'll catch up and acclimate you to the political arena here. It's a lot less civilized than what you're probably used to."

Paula sniffed. "You obviously haven't seen our House of Lords. Would strain anyone's patience." She checked the time. "I'll need seventy-two hours to take control of operations and lay out a new strategy. Then you can brief me on the latest intelligence reports." She gave Jill a nod and left.

Jill watched Paula walk away. She had worked with the British agent before, and they got along well. Paula was a cheerful woman, a rarity in this line of work. She credited Yol for her sunny disposition. But regardless, she was always thoughtful and competent. If the Prophus were ever to change the momentum of the war, they would need more people like her.

There was a lot to do over the next few days. She had a meeting with Wilks on the Hill at 10am. No doubt Simon had already sent his demands to her office. Threat or no threat, she had to do due diligence before making a recommendation to the senator. It was a lot more complicated than determining if a political deal was worth Wilks' support. How would it affect the Prophus? What advantages were the Genjix seeking? There was layer upon layer of intrigue that would need to be vetted first. Working for the interests of both the Prophus and the senator was tricky business. She stopped for a moment and took a deep breath.

One thing at a time. You have me.

That much was true. Jill learned early on that Baji was infinitely sharper than she could ever be. And while Baji's expertise was in covert operations, Jill found that her Quasing was equally proficient in political chess. That was how Jill had risen so fast on the Hill and within the Prophus ranks in the government.

First things first, she needed a shower. She still had grime from the previous night as well as a dozen or so bruises to cover up. That and a gunshot wound to address. Her leg had stiffened up and the cut on her cheek stung; it would probably scar. Jill went to seek out her estranged husband, found him talking with Stephen and pulled him aside.

"Hey," she began, and then the words got stuck in her throat. A range of emotions from anger to concern threatened to pour out of her all at once.

Roen didn't bother hiding his feelings. "Listen, those idiots are sending me halfway around the world. Promise me, if it gets too hot in the capital, you leave. You go into hiding. Alright?"

"You know I won't do that," she said. "I'm not going to cut on the team." She closed her eyes. Even when she was being sincere, she couldn't help but antagonize him. "That wasn't meant to be a dig on you."

He bit his lip and forced a less-than-convincing smile. "You know that was a dig, and I know you didn't mean it that way. It's just the truth." He pulled her in close with a sudden urgency. "I'm not going to be there to watch your back." His voice quavered.

She had to remind herself that he had a lot to make up for. The puppy dog worry in his eyes was touching, though. She stiffened, trying hard to keep her own emotions from bubbling to the surface. "I'm a big girl."

He became serious and his grip on her elbows tightened. "If things get hairy, I want you to hide out at the missile silo. No one knows about it, not even the Prophus. It's stocked with food and ammo for years and depending on how bad your shot is, you can hold off the Canadian army for at least six months. Got it?"

"All forty Mounties?" she laughed, trying to brush off the awkwardness of the moment.

"Front entrance and the mainframe are all authenticated single sign-on via retina. You can override with the master

phrase 'Baby Bear versus the Big City'. The arms locker is
Cam's birthday in reverse. There's a hidden exit in the back
connected to the third silo. The key to that is behind the
ant farm."

"You have an ant farm in your underground bunker?"
she chuckled. "How poetic."

"Can't keep anything else alive down there," he grinned.
"Feed them if you can." He gave her a peck on the lips and
held her tightly. "Be safe," he murmured before running off.

Baby Bear versus the Big City? How childish.

Jill stood there for a few moments, running that last
moment over in her head. "I like it."

It is asinine. I wonder what it means.

"Cubs versus the Yankees. Our first date."

That is strangely romantic in a juvenile way, I guess.

Jill allowed a small smile to break on her face. It was as
much of a compliment as Baji was willing to offer Roen.
She watched as he disappeared with a group of agents,
presumably off to Taiwan, and prayed that she'd see him
again.

She left Command and walked down the newly redusted
corridor toward her car, bottling her emotions back up. It
had been over a year since she last saw him. And just like
that, he was gone again. As she got into the car and pulled
out of the garage, her thoughts raced in circles about the
man she had once loved. Did she still love him even after
the decisions he'd made?

You forgive too easily.

"Who says I forgave him? Trust me, Baji, I just want to
kill him myself."

What Roen did, choosing Tao over her and Cameron was
unforgivable. She still remembered those nights begging

him to stay home instead of running off on his little crusade, but Tao had already convinced him it had to be done. He had no choice, he said. It was during those moments that she realized that he would never truly be hers as long as Tao was with him. And Tao would always be with him. His wife would always be a distant second to his Quasing and to the ghost of Sonya Lyte. And that broke her heart more than anything else.

For Roen and Baji, it all went back to Sonya. Jill looked at herself in the rearview mirror and wondered if there was any part of Baji's previous host in her. She had only met Sonya briefly when they were captured by the Genjix at Monaco. They were in adjacent cells and it was Sonya's steady voice that had kept her sane through the ordeal. She hadn't known about the Quasing then. She didn't even know what Sonya looked like until they were brought to the helipad at the Capulet's Ski Lodge. Sonya Lyte was breathtakingly beautiful. It was just another thing Jill could never live up to.

She heard later on that Roen was forced to kill Sonya in order to save Jill from becoming a Genjix host. He had never forgiven himself. To make matters worse, Roen and Tao fed off each other's vengeance. Tao had hundreds of years' worth of revenge to draw upon, while Roen tried to absolve his guilt for Sonya's death by killing the enemy. In the end, they only hurt themselves and the ones they loved. Even her own damn Quasing couldn't get past how poor a substitute she was for Sonya.

It is not that way, Jill. I do not hold you responsible for Sonya. You are two different souls with different strengths. I never intended to compare you two.

"You never intended to, but you do. You can't help it. Hell, everyone does."

Jill got out of the car and took the elevator to the condo that she and Roen had once shared. Coming into her quiet home was a harsh reminder of all that she'd lost over the past few years. There used to be a husband and squealing baby in here once. Being a single parent now, she couldn't take care of Cameron while working the hours she did for both the Prophus and the senator. Sending him to her parents was even harder than locking Roen out of the house. He had returned home after being gone for a month, and she had changed the locks. He had pleaded outside the door for her to let him in. Huddled in a ball on the other side of the door, she waited him out with tears streaming down her face. It took him six hours to leave. Those were some of the longest hours of her life. She had half feared he would break his way in, but that wasn't his way with her.

Jill kicked off her heels furiously and watched them bounce off the walls. She wandered to the living room, stripped off her dress, and threw it into the trash. It was pretty much ruined anyway. Jill made one trip around the entire apartment, turning on every light. It was a ritual she did every time she came home; she wasn't sure why. Maybe it made her feel less alone. Maybe she hoped to find her husband and child waiting for her. With a sigh, Jill went to the shower to wash off the previous night's madness.

On the plus side, Roen did seem like he was suffering almost as much as she was. In a rather sick way, it made her feel better. She was still furious with him and he would have to work hard to get back into her good graces, but it comforted her to know that at least he was just as miserable without her. Maybe, if she ever saw him again, she'd make him sweat it out for a year or three before forgiving him. It would serve him right. Jill let the warm water from the shower rain down on her face as she pulled her hair back. Then she froze for several moments. The thought of not seeing him again seized her with a sudden terror.

It made her feel better that Wuehler was in charge of the mission. He was a competent commander who wouldn't take chances like Roen would. She had met the man a few times. He was stuffy and by-the-books, having risen through the ranks of Prophus military and earned an equally stuffy and by-the-books Quasing named Ramez. They were an odd couple to match with Roen and Tao. Jill hoped that the more level-headed man could keep Roen alive long enough for her to torture him for a few more years.

Jill got out of the shower and looked at the time: 8.43am. She had to get moving. The Hart Senate building was on the other side of DuPont Circle and traffic was murder at this hour. She threw on a suit, applied ample makeup to cover the nasty cut on her cheek, and headed to work.

At precisely 10am, Jill knocked on Senator Wilks' door and walked in. James Wilks was a four-term senator and the chairman of the powerful Senate Committee on Appropriations. The Prophus had long considered him a kindred ally and much of the committee's pork barrel spending that the senator allocated was steered toward Prophus projects. Jill was assigned to his office by Command soon after she became Baji's host.

"God, Jill, what happened to your face?" Wilks looked concerned. "It wasn't that low-down husband of yours, was it? Because I'll make a call to the Hoover Building and have him put on the Most Wanted list faster than that worthless son of a bitch can take a piss."

James Wilks was an elderly statesman who looked every bit a career politician. He just never sounded like one. Tall and distinguished-looking, with a full head of graying hair and a jawline to make all the ladies swoon, he looked like one of those older models on hair dye boxes. When he spoke, though, people either immediately identified with him or couldn't stand him. Rough around the edges, he might seem out of place in Illinois politics, but his constituents loved him just fine.

"Senator, it wasn't Roen. I haven't seen him in months," she replied, reflexively touching the cut on her face. "It's just a little mishap with heels."

He gave her a doubtful look. "You're either lying to me or you should be banned from wearing heels ever again. It seems to happen a lot with you."

After the small talk revolving around her pitiful alibi was over, she laid out Simon's proposal in the most lukewarm fashion she could muster, glossing over the offer and stressing prudence. On the surface, Simon's deal was very attractive. He had effectively offered her boss everything he ever wanted in exchange for the support of an issue he really didn't care about: the South Seas Trade Sanction. In any other circumstance Wilks would consider this a major coup.

It was Jill's job as Wilks' policy director to encourage the deal, but it was also her job as a Prophus political operative to oppose it as well. She needed more time to figure out what angle the Genjix were really after. Wilks wasn't stupid though. He knew a good deal when he saw one.

"You're reaching there, counselor." He wrinkled his brow. "You don't usually come to me with such half-assed arguments. What's going on? Why do you care so much about these sanctions?"

"I can give you a full account shortly," she said defensively. "I just need some time. I'm just asking you to postpone agreeing to the deal until then."

Wilks shook his head. "I don't know, Jill. It's a more than fair offer from the other side of the aisle. I see no downside to the deal."

"Just give me some time to analyze this and come back with recommendations. Maybe I can leverage this offer for something even better," Jill stressed.

"Fair enough," Wilks said. "Hogan offered me a sweet deal. You give me a legitimate reason to turn him down and we'll talk."

Jill nodded. "Thank you, Senator." She left his office and signaled to Tammy, her assistant. "Find me everything you can on the South Seas Trade Sanctions. I need to know who's for it, who's against it, and how it affects our trade barriers." Then she left for the next round of her morning meetings on the Hill. Now the real battle began.

CHAPTER SEVEN
ELEVATION

For eons, the Quasing functioned as one mind, following the will of the Grand Council, until the Prophus betrayers splintered from the collective. They claim our way was ill-suited for these humans, that we walked a moral precipice.

After millions of years as gods blessing the worthy species of this planet, I find their sudden moral apprehension feeble and hypocritical. After all, we determined the fate of the species of this planet when we first came. Who else but gods can claim such a role?

Zoras

Saldhana, flanked by the contingent of guards, entered Devin's penthouse office at the Genjix research facility in Qingdao, China. Zoras had to admit, he was uneasy. Transitioning to a new vessel carried risks. He had chosen well, though. His handpicked Adonis Vessel was one of the highest-rated humans ever at the Hatchery. In fact, Zoras had to contend with three others on the Council for this vessel.

Stand at the door. On my order, leave the room.

"As you command, Holy One."

Enzo stood at the window, looking out at the Genjix Research campus. Half of the honor guard stayed outside Devin's office while the other half spread out around the room, guns trained on the vessel. Tension filled the air as the ceremony began. Palos and Amanda came in last and took position on opposite corners of the room. On their signal, the guards would shoot Enzo unless Zoras provided the release command.

This was Zoras' safeguard. Early in the program, several Adonis Vessels, raised to believe themselves gods, were mentally unstable and ignored their Quasing's orders. Now, in the third iteration of the program, the Hatchery had optimized the perfect blend of education and physical training for these high-valued vessels.

Enzo looked relaxed, albeit a bit curious. "I have been summoned by Father Devin. Where is he?"

Zoras studied his new vessel; Enzo had control of the room without even saying a word. His face was calm, his chest palpitations normal, and he seemed at ease. Adonis Vessels were never informed of the transition, but the Hatchery did not raise fools.

Enzo's eyes trailed from Palos to Amanda, then he nodded. "I see. Praise to the Holy Ones." Those in the room echoed the sentiments. "And to Father," he added softly. He closed his eyes and murmured a blessing to Devin. So far, Enzo was saying all the right things. The room remained dead quiet as they waited on him. Yes, the boy had gravitas.

"I am ready," he nodded.

Saldhana knelt down in the center of the room and recited a prayer to every Genjix he had ever met, which to his credit, was quite a few. Zoras was satisfied with him receiving the honor of being the transfer vessel. He had been with Palos' detail for over a decade and had worked under Devin for fifteen more years before that. It was a fitting end to a loyal Genjix agent.

With feverish devotion, he kissed Enzo's hand. "I bring you the god to infuse your body. May you serve the Holy Ones well."

Then Saldhana took out a serrated knife and disemboweled himself. His body shook as he dragged the knife across his abdomen with painstaking slowness. Zoras appreciated this final gesture.

The transfer ceremony, created by the Genjix in Japan over eight hundred years ago, was a time-honored tradition. The longer and slower the death, the gentler the transition for the Quasing. Sudden ejections from vessels were painful. The lingering bleed of life pushed them out of the body in much more comfort.

Saldhana's body shook with pain as his mind screamed with agony. Zoras flashed several images of the first time he took a bullet for Devin during the assassination attempt in Cairo, and of the time he was elevated to his personal detail. Then he flashed several more imageries, a montage of his years of service. Then finally, Zoras flashed Saldhana the rise of the Genjix, overwhelming his brain with the entire history of the Genjix through Zoras' eyes in a matter of seconds. Such overload often disoriented and dulled the pain.

Your standing is high. Begin your elevation.

It took Saldhana forty minutes to die. The last image he saw was Quasar, the closest thing to heaven the vessels believed in. Finally, he spasmed one last time and his body slumped over the large pool of blood in the center of the room. At the same time, Zoras felt a soft pull, as if a gentle ocean wave, move him away from the body.

Everything went black and then Zoras awoke hovering over Saldhana's body. His sparkling form, a gaseous stratus cloud, expanded and contracted as he floated in the air. It was the second time in so many days he had been exposed to the planet's atmosphere. Zoras made one loop around the room and then blanketed Enzo, who had waited patiently all this time with hands raised toward the ceiling. Tiny bursts of white light spread all over Enzo's body, permeating his skin until Zoras once again felt the warm cocoon of a vessel.

Enzo gasped and fell to his knees. His stomach churned and he threw up his last meal. His vision blurred as his eyes watered, and he had to take deep breaths to stop himself from passing out. Quasing integrations had always been painful to the beings on this planet. Over the course of several minutes, Zoras waited until Enzo's shocked nervous system relaxed and his heart rate slowed.

Rise.

Enzo lifted his head in exaltation, basking in the voice of a god. "Your command, Holy One," he called out.

Speak with your thoughts, vessel. Heed my words. But first, relay to Amanda that death is the solution to all problems.

Enzo repeated the phrase verbatim.

Amanda nodded and looked at Palos. "Release command accepted."

There is much to do. Devin's place among the United States government is not something you can replace. Your immediate concern is to manage his proxies and oversee the ProGenesis project. The Quasiform program can wait. Everything else is of secondary priority. Amanda will address the succession of his senate seat. For now, you must secure your holdings within the Council.

There wasn't much time for the two to get acquainted, and frankly it wasn't necessary. Enzo's sole purpose in life was to serve Zoras. The Quasing relayed dozens of instructions and was pleasantly surprised at how well his new vessel assumed the mantle of control. Enzo began to dictate to the aides around him as if he were an experienced Councilman. He told Amanda to return to Washington immediately to oversee Devin's burial. He called for a meeting with the head researchers of the programs under his responsibility. He summoned the French Ambassador to China, a Genjix operative, to continue discussions with the Chinese prime minister, and he ordered an audit of Devin's holdings within the organization. They were over budget, after all.

A Council meeting needs to be held as soon as possible to solidify your standing. While Genjix seniority is measured by the Quasing, you will still need to put the Council at ease. Devin's accumulated holdings were vast and the others will move on any perceived weakness.

"I have no weaknesses, Holy One. I do not fail."

We shall see. Assign the rest of the daily operations to Amanda. Lean on her while you grow into your role. Call a meeting of your senior ministers and commanders in two hours. There is something more pressing that requires your attention. The rest can wait. Test lab six is waiting for you to proceed with the test. I wish to personally witness the results.

Enzo nodded and left his office, flanked by twenty aides coming and going as he dictated orders. He left the building and proceeded toward the ProGenesis lab.

By now, word of his ascension had spread and the curious lined his path to pay tribute. Several of the devoted reached out to touch him, a new god walking amongst them. Zoras watched with curiosity at how Enzo dealt with the attention.

The results were mixed. On the one hand, Enzo recognized that he was a blessed being more valuable than a thousand humans and carried himself as such. That was an important trait for an Adonis Vessel to possess. Their sense of self-worth enforced their Quasing's ability to rule. On the other hand, Zoras watched with disdain as Enzo played the crowd like a politician walking the rope line. Keeping his face stoic, he touched the outstretched hands and made eye contact with the worshiping masses. It was a far cry from how Devin, who played the role of an isolated Egyptian Pharaoh, treated his people.

You are a god. Remember that.

"A god who leads, Guardian."

To lead is a human trait. A god demands obedience.

It took Enzo over half an hour to make the five-minute walk across the Genjix campus to the research building. He was met by Chow, the head researcher, at the entrance to the ProGenesis lab.

"Father," the rotund man dressed in blue research robes bowed.

Jikl's vessel.

Enzo noted Chow's figure with disdain. It was a vessel's responsibility to keep his body healthy for his Quasing, something Chow had heretically neglected.

Not all Genjix serve your purpose. Jikl's vessel fills his role well.

"The sacrilege is unacceptable, Holy One."

"We await your order," Chow said.

Enzo nodded and signaled for the test to begin. A large crane hummed to life and lifted a cage into the air. Inside, a prisoner shook at the bars.

"You can't do this," the man screamed at the dozen people below watching him with scientific interest. "I'm not a lab experiment. This is murder!"

"Penetra scanner readings," Chow called out. A few scientists below on the ground level confirmed it.

"Signatures," he directed to another group. A large screen appeared, showing the human and Quasing's life signs.

Then on his order, Chow ordered the experiment to continue. The crane moved the cage over a massive cylindrical glass vat filled with a slow swirling, sludge-like red liquid. A metal cover, split down the middle, opened outward.

The prisoner screamed, hammering the bars with his fists. "We're all humans! Think about what you're doing!" He began to slam his body into the bars in a crazed fashion until blood poured down his forehead.

With a signal from Chow, the crane dropped the cage into the vat and the cover closed over it, vacuum-sealing the container. Immediately, the cage sunk to the bottom and within seconds, the human was dead, a frozen look of terror on his face. Enzo paid attention to the steady beep of his life signs flatlining. The Quasing's life signs, though, jumped as it moved out of the corpse. Several scientists took to typing into their tablets. A sparkling light swam around the body of the cylinder, zigzagging back and forth, trying to escape. After a minute, it settled near the base of the vat.

"Elevated signs, but stable," Chow reported. "Clocking at ninety seconds."

"How long do these subjects survive in there?" Enzo asked.

"The most recent test, using chemical batch 5-8S, lasted nine minutes, Father," Chow said.

Longer than a human could stay alive underwater. Better than one could in many parts of the world.

The life signs of the Quasing remained stable, but slowly eroding. He was dying a lingering death. Enzo waited patiently, watching one of the gods perish. He wondered where gods went after they died. The humans on this planet believed their gods to be immortal. Some believed in only one omnipotent god who had lived since before the creation of this planet. It seemed they were only half right. Gods could live forever but could also be killed like any other. Enzo was now a witness to this truth. After nearly fifteen minutes, the life signs of the Prophus leveled out, turning from a soft blip to a steady tone.

To the Eternal Sea.

Enzo repeated the words under his breath.

"Sixteen minutes, forty three seconds at time of death," a scientist below called out.

Several of the blue robes congratulated Chow. They were on the right path, a step closer to the formula for the Quasing primordial soup. It was only a matter of time.

"Find the cause of death," Chow ordered. "I want an autopsy report of the human and the Quasing within the hour." He turned to Enzo with a large smile. "An advancement, Father."

Enzo nodded. Sixteen minutes was encouraging. "When will you be ready to test again?"

"Immediately after the autopsy and analysis from the Penetra scanner," Chow said. "We'll need to make adjustments to the chemical mixture and synthesize the formula. Possibly a few days?"

"How many Prophus prisoners are on hand?"

"Three, Father. A shipment is being delivered from Tibet as we speak, and I am told the recent captured enemy vessel has plenty more. It should be enough to keep our tests running for the rest of the year.

"Continue on then," he said briskly, turning to leave. A small army of aides trailed close behind.

Enzo looked at them, irritated. "Holy One, must they follow me every step like lap dogs?"

These aides are simply a means to do my bidding. Do you pay attention to your hands when you perform a task?

"I long for a little routine at the gym. My body requires its nourishment to stay strong for your use."

Your dedication is noted. Who was that betrayer sacrificed for the greater good?

Enzo stopped just before he reached the exit and turned around. The group behind him immediately parted ways. "What was the name of that Prophus?" he asked.

Chow looked down at his notes before speaking. "I believe he was named Krys, Father. He was captured when the Prophus Command fell three years back."

Satisfied, Enzo nodded and made his way toward the gym.

CHAPTER EIGHT
CROSS COUNTRY

Consciousness is a human concept. My thoughts were present when our ship crashed. I lost them during those millions of years I struggled to stay Quasing, and eventually became nothing more than a ghost. I regained myself during one momentous encounter.

At the time, my vessel was the alpha in a large troop of ancient primates deep in Asia. The memory of times before I became present were vague. After living for eons in instinctive creatures, my consciousness had dulled.

One day, a gigantic cousin of my species wandered into our territory. He was twice again larger than any of my troop, and carried a dangerous scent of cunning. I could not describe that scent any longer, for all now possess it. Some of the troop tried to drive him off, but he swatted them with ease. Then, it became my duty as alpha to handle this new menace.

Tao

Roen's plane trip across the United States was very uncomfortable and terribly awkward. Sitting in coach sandwiched between the window and Wuehler was a far cry from the good ol' days when he jet set all over the world in G4s and military transports. To squeeze two full grown men into seats the size of bread boxes was inhumane. The budget crunch and the recent losses affected every part of Prophus operations.

"I wish I had showered last night."

I am sure Wuehler wishes you had as well.

"How can we go on missions like this? Do they FedEx our gear?"

You will have to source the weapons locally from the criminal underground. It could be worse.

"What, ship us by cargo plane?"

Consider yourself lucky. It has been done before.

Sadly, that was the good part of the flight. The bad was dealing with Wuehler for seven hours straight. A couple of lifetimes had passed since they had first met. Roen had joined Wuehler's team on his first mission raiding a Genjix warehouse. Back then, the older commander paid Roen the respect due to a host. Since then, because of Roen's growing list of dirty laundry, Wuehler barely tolerated him. Wuehler had the lead for this operation, though as hosts, they were technically equal in rank.

They spent the first hour without exchanging a word. When the older commander had learned Roen was being attached to his team, he threw a tantrum that only a stiff like him could. He told Stephen he objected strenuously. And when Stephen shot him down, Wuehler went to the Keeper and told her he objected very strenuously. When that didn't work, he came and told Roen to be ready at 0900 hours. Roen was in for some very dull few weeks.

At least you have me.

"Yes monkey, dance for me. Tell me a fun story."

Remember the first time you met Lin?

"That's not a fun story. Why does every fun story you tell have to do with me getting my ass kicked?"

Because you have a higher frequency of getting asskicked than most of my hosts.

"Come on, you're telling me Genghis didn't get the sharp end of the spear once in a while?"

Temujin killed his brother when he was ten. Do you really think he lost that many fights? Even Brother Renoir, a devout Catholic priest and pacifist, poisoned forty Nazis and mowed down twelve SS with a machine gun before he died.

"Your definition of pacifism is a little different from most others."

I tend to beat that quality out of them early on in our relationship.

"Roen," Wuehler handed him a notebook. "Here are the men's bios. I'm placing you third after Faust."

Roen's outstretched hands stopped just short of taking the notebook. "Third?" he said incredulously. "I'm a host and the intelligence officer on this mission. It's my work that got this data."

"You're an unreliable rogue," Wuehler snapped. "Faust has been my second for years. I can depend on him. I'm not risking the boys to an unstable, short-fused cowboy."

Unstable? No one has called you that in weeks.

"Man, how many insults do I have to put up with this morning? It's not even lunchtime yet."

"Look, this is against protocol," Roen snapped out loud. "If you go down, a host needs to be in charge. What does Ramez think of this?"

"He's the one that gave me the green light to bust you back," Wuehler at least had the decency to look smug. He pushed the notebook forward again.

Let it go. Faust is solid. You can assume command from him if the situation arises.

Roen reluctantly snatched the notebook and put it on the tray. He signaled to the stewardess for a scotch and scanned the bios. It was a pretty standard shock-team roster. Wuehler's team of ten was a far cry from the thirty he had led when they first met. He had moved from commanding a large general assault group to a smaller, heavier-armed shock unit. Once an agent became a host, his skillset became specialized.

Since then, Wuehler had racked up an impressive list of engagements. His primary theater of operation was the Midwest, mainly in Omaha, Chicago, Madison, and the Dakotas, occasionally venturing out to Kentucky and Pennsylvania where the Genjix had a heavy coal industry presence.

"This sounds like a weird job for Wuehler. His team is as heavy and as non-covert as they come. Wouldn't an urban reconnaissance squad be more appropriate?"

Maybe he's branching out, trying new things. Or maybe his team was the only resource available.

"I doubt it. You don't change stripes this far in your career. Shock troops are beasts of a different breed, and are as subtle as daisy cutters. Usually, you hear them coming miles away, and they leave messes that would make a cleaner cry."

Roen put the notebook down two paragraphs into each person's bio and sipped his scotch. He had read enough. At the end of the day, it didn't matter what these guys specialized in. The fact that Wuehler's team was so ill-equipped for this mission was not too unusual. It wasn't the first time the Prophus had to work with less than optimal resources.

Urban reconnaissance would be key to finding the Genjix supply line. Even though Taiwan was a subtropical island, it boasted a dense population and was heavily industrialized. It would require extensive surveillance and inquiries into the local underground to achieve their goals. This must be the real reason why Stephen had asked him to come. They would rely heavily on Roen to put the pieces of the Genjix operation together. That team needed his expertise, even though he wasn't a perfect fit for this assignment, either. Being silent and deadly was his bread and butter, but this mission required more finesse than his usual handiwork.

Roen hoped Dylan was still alive. The fact that there had been no contact with him since the sinking was worrisome. The Aussie must be laying low while doing his own investigation. It would make locating him much more difficult. Still, he must have made contact with some of the local inhabitants. How hard could it be to find a giant Australian with a half-burnt face on a small island in Asia anyway?

"Hey, Wheels," Roen smiled. "Let's call a truce. I mean, we've crossed paths a dozen times and haven't gotten along, but let's try and make nice this go around. Pretend it's our first date again, alright?"

Wuehler, with his eyes closed, shrugged. "Just follow orders, Roen. Don't get anyone killed."

"See, that wasn't so bad, was it?" Roen grinned.

"I'll shoot you myself if you disobey."

Roen sighed. "And I thought we were about to share a beautiful moment. Why did you have to ruin it?" A few seconds passed. "So do we have the details of what happened prior to the *Atlantis'* capture?"

Without opening his eyes, Wuehler bent down and picked up the notebook that Roen had laid aside. He flipped to the next page and placed it in front of Roen. Then he turned his back to him.

"I didn't realize there was a page two."

Your physical competency seems to directly correlate with idiocy.

Roen skimmed through the rest of the mission summary. The *Atlantis* had picked Dylan and his team up in Shanghai just after he rendezvoused with one of their double agents. He had received intel that led him to Taiwan. The *Atlantis* tried to sneak through the Strait of Taiwan when the South Sea Fleet boxed them in. During the ensuing battle, the *Atlantis* was crippled, but only after she took out two Chinese subs, a destroyer, and six ASW combat choppers.

"Old girl didn't do too badly for herself," Roen murmured, not without a bit of pride.

Wuehler opened one eye and nodded. "Damn straight. Abrams is pretty ace. I hope to see that old dog still alive."

Before she lost propulsion, Admiral Abrams had pushed Dylan and his small team into individual escape pods. The last communication from the *Atlantis* was the pods' trajectory toward the northwestern coast of Taiwan. All five of the ejected pods were confirmed destroyed shortly after launch. Taiwanese authorities had recovered the wreckage of all the pods and four bodies. Dylan's was the only one missing. The *Atlantis* now was in Genjix hands and the status of her crew was unknown.

"That tough bastard. I won't believe he's dead unless I see a body. Not even a torpedo and the ocean could kill him."

Yen likes his hosts like that.

Roen looked at his watch. They were landing in Los Angeles in six hours and then it was off to Taiwan. His mind raced back to Jill and the past twenty-four hours of his life. He hadn't realized how much he missed her until they were huddling together looking at pictures of their son. Tao had him so focused on this Quasiform discovery that it had completely overshadowed the pain of missing his wife and child. Now it was rushing back like water through a broken dam.

As far as Jill was concerned, he'd been holed up in that missile silo for the past year. If she only knew the truth – he had actually spent barely any time there. The two main reasons he had chosen the silo were the munitions stash and its proximity to her base of operations. One thing Roen was adamant about, much to Tao's irritation, was to always be there for Jill when she was on assignment. That he never wavered on. She was the last thing on his mind when he finally dozed off.

When they reached LAX, the team walked to their layover together. The rest of the guys gave Roen the same cold shoulder that Wuehler did. All except for Faust. Faust had always treated him fairly, and Roen was grateful for that. The others only knew him by reputation, which, while not entirely unjustified, gave them the impression that he was as dangerous as the Genjix. They walked by a corridor full of windows, and Roen stopped to admire the sun-soaked landscape. After living in a cave and operating only at night, like a vampire, seeing the sun felt like a surprise visit from an old friend.

"Always seventy plus or minus two in Los Angeles," he murmured, admiring the cloudless sky.

We should build our headquarters here.

"Nah, traffic's a killer on the 405. Besides, too many paparazzi."

Who would want to take a picture of your ugly mug?

"Hear, hear," Roen chuckled. "I wonder what Jill and Cameron are doing right now."

The thought of Cameron brought another stab of pain to his chest. He hadn't seen his boy in so long, and now with him staying with his grandparents in... His thoughts trailed off. Roen stood there in the middle of the pedway, completely blocking traffic. His eyes wandered outside again, and then back at the signs floating above his head. Restroom to the right. Ticketing upstairs. Luggage Claim down the stairs. No entrance after this point. Car Rental to the left. Roen made up his mind and took off running after Wuehler. He grabbed the man by the shoulder and spun him around.

"I need to take a later flight," he said urgently. "I have the safe house coordinates in Taipei. I'll only be a day behind." He turned to leave and stopped. "Sorry," he said finally, really meaning it.

Wuehler seemed stunned and looked like he was about to blow a gasket, but then he noticed the desperate look in Roen's eyes. "One day I can give. Two and I'll shoot you when you walk through the door."

Roen nodded. He appreciated this gesture and reminded himself that whatever happened, he owed Wuehler one. Then he took off sprinting down the left corridor as fast as he could.

CHAPTER NINE
PLANS AND PIZZA

That was my first encounter with Tao. It was not unusual for Quasing not to have crossed paths, but I had heard of him. He had a distinguished history among us, and was reputed to be a firebrand. His work as an empire builder could not be overlooked.

And though the Genjix had captured and imprisoned my host, I was not ready to join the newly founded Prophus faction. It was one thing to passively object to the old order, it was another to outright rebel. Tao made sure I had little choice in the matter.

Baji

Jill rubbed her eyes and looked at the time: 7.15pm. For the past two days, she had pored over all the documentation Tammy had pulled for the South Seas Sanction. It was a behemoth seven-hundred-page stack of trade papers that was as interesting to read as a Latin dictionary.

She looked at the lopsided battle on the white board of her office wall: sixteen Genjix senators against just three Prophus senators for its passage. Its success would come down to a list in the middle column of four senators who were sitting on the fence.

"Tammy," she called as her assistant was sneaking home for the night. "Schedule a meeting with Gastigone, Garritano, Young, and Karn before you go. Make it before next Thursday. Then I need you to pull every initiative these senators are backing. I need it tonight."

The look of disappointment on Tammy's face could kill. Jill wouldn't have ordered this if the fate of the world wasn't on the line. She made a mental note to buy Tammy lunch tomorrow. She watched as her assistant huffed back to her desk and then focused again on the forty-page list of imports/exports in the sanction.

The Genjix were trying to slip something past the Prophus, something that they wanted badly enough to offer significant political capital for it. She notated several possibilities, from military grade electronics to rare minerals to energy sources. Then she compiled a list of elements from heavy water to experimental metals to biological specimens. By 9pm, she had gotten through less than ten percent of the banned list. She was about to order delivery for dinner when a reminder popped up on her computer. Jill grimaced.

"You think Paula would mind if we skip it? I'm not in the right mind for cocktails right now. All I want to do is finish this and get home."

Have her meet you at your place. It is more secure anyhow.

That was a great idea. Jill might get some actual sleep for once. That and she could use a nice hot bath. She called Paula on her way home and changed their plans to 11pm. The first thing she did when she walked inside was kick off her heels and run the water in the tub. Ten minutes later, she was drinking a glass of pinot and soaking her exhausted body in a steamy bath.

She closed her eyes and tried her damnedest to unwind. Jill couldn't remember the last time she wasn't stressed. A few minutes later, she slipped into an exhausted slumber. She woke to a light tapping on her shoulder. It took a second to get her bearings. She noticed the cold silver barrel of a pistol close to her face. With a start, she lashed out.

"Easy there," Paula cooed. "Just me." She holstered her pistol. "Had me worried. Thought there was foul play when you didn't answer your phone. Can't do my job knowing the love of Roen's life isn't safe. I'll feel better when Marco arrives."

"Stop being on his side," Jill yawned and stood up, shivering. She must have been out for a while. The water was nippy and her fingers and were wrinkled like dried plums. "Did I miss our meeting?"

"Not if we have it now," Paula grinned and handed her a towel.

"How did you get in here?" Jill asked, wrapping the towel around her body.

Paula shrugged. "Snuck in through the pool deck of the high-rise. You'll need to get a new lock for your front door. I'll wait outside."

A few minutes later, a bathrobed Jill walked out to the living room. Paula was lounging on the couch watching the cricket score recaps on ESPN. She gestured at a large thin crust pizza on the coffee table. Jill's stomach reminded her of how famished she was.

She grabbed a slice and sat down next to Paula. "So what's the scoop? Is the capital of the free world going to hell in a hand basket?"

Paula handed her a large manila packet. "Here are the latest intel reports. DC is already crispy. All I can do at this point is keep you lot out of the fire, or at least not too badly burned. What's happening on the political front?"

Jill told her about the offer Simon made to Wilks, cutting through the fat and focusing on the sanctions that the Genjix seemed desperate to lift. She then laid out her alternatives to prevent Wilks from agreeing to the Genjix's proposal.

"Start with the list of materials the sanction blocks," Paula said, mouth half full. Jill handed the stack of paper to her. Paula glanced at it and frowned. Then she skimmed through the pages. "That's a long list."

Jill nodded. "We need better specifics. A lot of the banned tech on the list is predator drone technology. Could that be it? Are the Genjix trying to build a fleet of unmanned drones?"

"None of our intel suggests Skynet coming online."

Doubtful. Control through a host is difficult enough. It is doubly so to control a proxy through another proxy. Besides, we harbor prejudice toward artificial intelligence.

Paula finished her slice of pizza and helped herself to another. She stared at it lovingly. "You know what I love about America? Your food. Now I know why you're all so fat. You have the best food. It's just too bad your tea is so awful."

Jill went to the table and began to pull notes from the reports. She was going to need more time to go through everything. That meant she had to delay Wilks' meeting with Hogan – by weeks if possible. "I need a better excuse to keep this meeting from happening," she muttered. She turned to Paula. "I'm going to be busy for a while. You heading back out?"

"In a bit. If you don't mind, I'd like to finish catching up on today's breathtaking cricket replays," Paula replied.

"Be my guest." Jill began laying out a new plan to entice Wilks from Hogan's deal. It would have to be a large package with several things from his wish list. The first thing she did was write down all of Wilks' goals, from his pet projects to his major initiatives. Then she made several lists of other senators' goals that Wilks could support. Then she connected the dots and packaged several potential deals.

Two hours later, she finished her plan and reviewed it. It was a solid start, though she was dubious about pulling it off. She stood up and stretched, bending her torso side to side. She looked at the clock: 3.42am. She'd better head off to bed. It was another early day tomorrow.

"You alright there, Paula?" she asked, turning to see what the other woman was doing.

Paula was sprawled on the couch with a half-eaten slice of pizza on a plate resting on her belly, sleeping in what seemed like a very uncomfortable position. Jill smiled and went to get the extra blankets. She moved the plate of pizza aside, layered the blankets over the sleeping agent, and tucked a pillow under her head. Then she dimmed the lights and went to her room.

Paula knocked on Jill's bedroom door. Without waiting for a response, she walked in and sat down at the foot of the bed.

Jill's eyes fluttered open. "Hello, Yol," she said.

"Baji," Yol answered through Paula. "It has been too long since we last spoke."

"October 1944, just before the death of the Desert Fox," Baji said solemnly.

Yol nodded. "Rommel was a good man, even if he was on the wrong side of history."

"I did what I could for him, though the SS had long decided his fate."

"You saved his family," Yol replied. "That was more than enough considering the circumstances. Your host's hands were tied at High Command." Yol looked off into space and shook her head. "I had high hopes for him as a boy. In any other time, he could have become a great person. He was my Sonya. It was too bad we could not prevent the rise of the Third Reich."

"Nor the Japanese imperial expansion," Baji added. "Our entire network in China dissolved in under a year. We should have rebuilt it immediately after the war. But we focused on America and the reconstruction of Europe, allowing the Genjix to gain a foothold there. Now it is the base of their power and nearly impossible to crack."

"Many mistakes were made. The twentieth century was a catastrophe for us and for humanity. The blame for a dozen wars lies at our feet," Yol shook her head in disgust. "Sometimes, I wonder if Tao is right."

"Tao is a hypocrite," Baji snapped. "He rants that our influence over the humans is just as bad as the Genjix. That we are the cause of as much misery as they, yet he wages a personal war that cuts a path of destruction as wide as Sherman ever did. Now, with Roen a willing accomplice, he is a loose cannon no one can control. At least Tao's previous host, Edward, had a good head on his shoulders."

"But you heard Stephen," Yol mused. "He found truth in Tao's claims. That means Camr does too. Stephen is cautious and Camr even more so. We cannot ignore the facts. Global temperatures have increased three percent since the turn of the twentieth century. Carbon levels by nine. The Genjix are pushing for the industrialization of humanity in the most inefficient way possible. That cannot be coincidence."

"It is the path of least resistance."

"That's the curious thing. It is not; everyone knows that. The Genjix are playing a cruel joke on this planet. Humanity could advance far quicker utilizing more efficient means of industrializing, yet the Genjix take the most toxic path possible."

"You give them too much credit. The Genjix do not care about being cruel to humanity. That would imply that they cared enough to be cruel. Their only concern is the Return. The evil they do is simply a byproduct of their means."

A thought occurred to Baji. She turned to Yol. "What is the longest you have ever survived in this atmosphere?"

"Thirteen minutes during Waterloo. I had to jump among nine French military officers, including three captains and a general. It was a messy day."

"Back during the second Ice Age, we lost hundreds of thousands of Quasing to the atmosphere. Survival outside of a host depended on seconds. Now, it is minutes. With the current ultraviolet levels and carbon levels, the rate the planet is increasing in temperature..."

Yol shook her head. "It will still be five hundred years before we can survive an hour. Not even the Genjix could be so ambitious."

"Ambition is something the Genjix have ample supply of." Baji stood up. Jill's leg ached from the wound she had sustained last week, and she had forgotten to take her antibiotics. More often than not these days, Jill was forgetting to take care of herself. She went to the counter, took two pills from a small bottle, and popped them in her mouth. Then she paused. Tao had ranted for a year leading up to his disappearance. Now, Yol was here with the same conspiracy theories.

She squinted at Yol. "Are you Tao's mole?"

Yol laughed. "That is the second time this week you have accused me of that. I will tell you again that I am not. And if I were, I would not admit it. From what I can tell, the only thing Tao has done with the information is look after Jill."

Baji waved her off. "I would love to plug that leak. I do not care if Camr is using the mole to spy on Roen as well. Tao is just so smug about always appearing at Jill's missions."

"He saved her life more than a few times," Yol countered. "We ask a lot of our hosts. They make sacrifices most others would not dream of. Do not be so hard on Roen, or Jill, for that matter."

Baji walked to the window and looked at the night sky. The stars were rarely visible from the city. Tonight was no exception. On the horizon, a thick layer of clouds sped east. They would be directly overhead shortly, and with them, rain. The swamp in the nation's capital would be rising tonight.

"Part of the reason I have not embraced Jill to the same extent as my previous hosts is because I do not think she will survive long with things the way they are. Her area of expertise is political, and they are always the first to the headsman during regime changes." Baji bowed her head. "I should have kept her in the Midwest."

Yol chuckled. "Maybe you should worry more about getting a mole into the Genjix Council than finding one working for Tao in Prophus Command."

"It is not just that." Baji turned to her. "When I had Sonya, Tao chastised me about not giving her a life outside the Prophus. With Jill, I tried to not lay a heavy hand upon her. Jill marries Tao's host, and then he abandons her!"

"At least it was not for another woman," Yol shrugged. "From what I understand, she kicked him out, yet he still hovers in the shadows protecting her. It was not like he ran off with his secretary."

"Whose side are you on?" Baji snapped.

"Everyone's, obviously." Yol shook her head. "I have known you for a very long time. You were not like this a hundred years ago. Take a step back and look at what has been happening. You need to forgive yourself for Sonya and open up to Jill."

Yol stood up and followed Baji to the window. The two of them stood side by side, looking up at the darkened sky. "I am tightening the sloppy DC operations for our operatives. Adams was versed at policy but useless in matters of security; it is a dangerous combination. Any success in the political arena just pushes the Genjix toward solving the problem with a knife instead. I need Jill to help push policy while I address our defensive position. Expect a visit from Marco in the next few days."

"Ahngr was never my friend, but I do not question his host's competency."

"I will see you soon then," Yol gave her a reassuring pat on the shoulder and walked out the door.

"At least I hope so," Baji said before turning off the lights and going back to bed.

CHAPTER TEN
PRISONERS

The Prophus argue that we cannot treat humans as we do the other beasts on this planet. They say that humans are complex and not driven by instinct, that their evolutionary level required a new set of standards of judgment.

I find that assertion preposterous. All animals are motivated by pain, pleasure, and self-preservation. Humans are no different. When the rift occurred among our ranks, the Council decided to be merciful and only commanded all the Prophus vessels imprisoned or killed in order to keep the betrayers out of the way. After all, we were all still Quasing.

Zoras

Enzo watched from the upper platform as the tugs dragged the *Atlantis* into drydock, his knuckles white as he gripped the hand rails. It was a massive sub, the only prototype of its kind. Originally christened the *Scimitar* and commissioned through the Soviet Navy, the Prophus had pulled a coup and stolen it the night before her maiden voyage. Now she was returning home. While she might be showing her age – some of the newer submarines were faster or heavier armed – none had the sheer scale and imperial might of the *Atlantis*. Yes, she was back to her rightful owners.

"Close the gate. Get the Red Army out," he ordered. Standing next to him, Yuki, Admiral of the Genjix Orient Fleet, ordered the gates closed. Two massive gates that made up one wall of the drydock rolled shut with a jarring squeal.

Yuki paused at the next order. "The situation is volatile, Father. We may need the extra manpower if the Prophus resist."

"Your concern is noted," Enzo remarked. "This is Genjix business. Get the humans out. Assemble a defensive perimeter around the *Scimitar*. Non-lethal force only. We need the vessels."

He watched as his minions scurried like ants on the ground level. The Chinese commander raised a ruckus about being ordered out, but eventually, he and his men were ushered out at gunpoint. He might claim jurisdiction, but he knew who wielded the real power here. The Prime Minster wasn't a vessel yet, but it would only be a matter of time before a Genjix assumed that mantle of leadership. Regardless, there were already enough of theirs in the upper echelon of the party for them to operate unhindered.

When all the Chinese soldiers were gone, the Admiral called for "all phasers on stun". Technically, the guns weren't phasers and didn't stun anything. The small gas pellets they fired released a neurotoxin that could knock out a rhino. And in case the targets wore masks, the pellets were hard enough to pierce flesh, directly injecting the toxin into one's bloodstream. "Phasers on stun" was a tribute to Yuki's Holy One, Galen, whose previous vessel created some silly television show an odd half century ago.

Respect your predecessors. Each vessel's role in the Genjix is different. Devin never fired a gun in his life. Not all excel militarily.

"Apologies, Zoras. I meant no disrespect."

An engineering crew approached the primary armory bay, originally designed for a nuclear payload. Enzo doubted *Atlantis* had those in her hull. The weak-willed Prophus would never have the gall to use a weapon of such power, so why bother lugging them around? It was the largest opening in the sub and gave his men the widest bottleneck to work with. A laser cut straight around the hinges should take less than an hour. He leaned forward eagerly and watched the sparks fly.

Hand the responsibility of the prisoners to Yuki. You must prepare for the meeting with the Council tonight. Your place among them rests on their acceptance.

"I am an Adonis Vessel, Zoras, raised only for this purpose. Why would the Council not accept me? I am the epitome of the human and Quasing merger."

Since the Hatchery's inception, only a handful of Adonis have been blessed. Its record since the Second World War has been inconsistent. The first two programs produced catastrophic failures. There are those in the hierarchy who still question its product. You must not make a bad impression upon them.

Enzo dismissed that dated theory. "The program was perfected years ago. The early Adonis recruits were poor samples. Training back then was imperfect. I am living proof of its success." He unclenched his fist on the railing and then clenched even tighter, his excitement replaced with growing irritation. It was insulting to question the Hatchery's effectiveness.

We shall see.

"Father," Yuki said, bowing. "Myyk is asking to meet with Zoras."

"Abrams wishes to speak terms?" Enzo chuckled. "What terms could they possibly offer?"

All information is useful. It is wise to know your enemy.

"As you wish, Zoras."

He took the phone from Yuki. "Admiral Abrams," he said respectfully.

"A young man by the sound of it," Abrams's calm, aged voice spoke on the other line. "This is Zoras' new vessel then? Last time I spoke with Devin, he was hacking up a lung."

"A pleasure, sir," Enzo turned on the charm. "I am the new vessel of the Holy One."

"How unfortunate." There was a pause on the other line. "Devin was formidable. Though on opposing sides, we shared a mutual respect. I am saddened by his passing."

"Thank you for your kind words. Father Devin is greatly missed." Abrams's voice reminded him of a doddering old man, nothing like what an admiral's would be. "I offer you the opportunity to convey your condolences in person at your surrender."

"We haven't discussed terms yet, son."

Being called son only reinforced his image of the old feeble fool. Enzo blocked it out of his mind and pressed on. "Apologies, Admiral, but there is little you can offer. If you value the lives of your crew..."

"You do not want to have to board the *Atlantis*."

Enzo masked his growing annoyance. "Abrams, the *Scimitar* is in a military naval yard surrounded by a thousand Genjix and twenty thousand Chinese soldiers. Your defeat is not in question."

Offer him terms of surrender.

"Why bother, Zoras? He is trapped in the tin can. Unconditional surrender is his only recourse."

Whichever entryway we cut through will be heavily defended. Our casualties will be high. You also want to take them alive, so that rules out incendiaries. There is also the question of nuclear armaments on board.

"Casualties are acceptable. They are only humans."

Abrams continued speaking as if he were talking about watering his garden. "I never said victory was an option. However, taking *Atlantis* will prove difficult. The *Atlantis* will bleed you before you take her."

"My men will do what is necessary to take the *Scimitar*," Enzo accentuated the true name of the submarine. "You still have nothing to offer."

"I offer the lives of the men you will lose if you take *Atlantis* by force."

"Forgive me if that incentive holds little value to me. I am a vessel of the gods. The lives you offer are there to be expended, so here are my terms. Come out unarmed and surrender unconditionally. You have until we cut through your doors to decide if you want to save your crew's lives." He handed the phone back to Yuki and continued to stare intently at the work below.

That was inelegant. You should have listened. You have much to learn.

Enzo grunted and continued to watch the dancing sparks of the laser as it bounced off the submarine walls. Six minutes into cutting, the bay doors made a clicking noise and began to lift. The engineers stopped and took a few steps back.

"See, Zoras? The Prophus are weak and have already given up."

The door stopped a quarter of a meter off the ground, making a booming sound that bounced off the drydock walls and echoed through the room. Half a dozen metal objects rolled out from the opening, followed by the sound of automatic fire. The engineering crew was cut down immediately while the guards surrounding the submarine scattered. Two of Enzo's bodyguards pulled him down to the ground. The resulting explosions rocked the drydock.

He heard the screams of men and the creak of metal as another explosion shook the building. Red lights flashed, and in the distance, a siren wailed. Enzo threw his men off and scanned the carnage over the railing. Smoke was everywhere and several dozens of his men lay dead.

Yuki walked up to him cautiously and held up the phone. "It's for you, Father. The Prophus wishes to discuss terms."

Enzo snarled and snatched the phone.

"Let's try this again, shall we?" Abrams said. "I want guarantees for my crew."

Offer imprisonment and guarantee the safety for the crew.

Enzo reluctantly relayed the offer.

"Now that we've established a baseline," Abrams said, "I want the entire crew and half of the Prophus agents released. We choose which half."

Enzo gritted his teeth. "You forget who has the upper hand."

That is his opening salvo. Do not react to every offer. Guarantee the safety of the crew. All Prophus agents will be held by us. The crew will be transferred to a Chinese Military prison instead.

"How is that a better offer than the first?" was Abrams's response to that.

"Why don't we meet like gentlemen over a glass of wine. I can have my men bring a table next to the *Scimitar*."

Abrams laughed. "Possibly if it was still Devin. However, I am perfectly comfortable in my quarters."

And thus the negotiations continued for the rest of the day and well into the night. They haggled over prisoner counts and prison locations. They bargained over the submarine database and the activation codes. They even argued over protocol for surrender. The Prophus were adamant about keeping their people together and not separated into a Chinese prison. The Genjix were equally adamant about none of the Prophus agents being freed.

Enzo had initially tried to stall for time in order to call in another engineering team to finish the job. Abrams would have none of it. When the second team was killed off, Enzo had to take the negotiation more seriously. Even in better faith, it proved difficult. Three times, twice because of Enzo and once because of Abrams, negotiations broke down and the cutting began again, resulting in more deaths on the Genjix side.

Finally, twelve hours later, they had come to an agreement. The non-Quasing crew would be imprisoned for a period of six months, kept in good health, and then released. Sixty percent of the Prophus vessels, chosen by the Genjix, would be given the same accommodations. The other forty percent were prisoners of the Genjix to be treated as they pleased. In return, the Prophus surrendered peacefully, kept the integrity of the now-renamed-again *Scimitar*, and released all access codes.

Enzo was furious at these concessions, but maintained a calm demeanor in front of his people. He was even more angry that negotiations had taken so long. The Prophus were trapped in a maximum-security naval base. To concede so much was a slap in the face. Not only that, he had to beg the Council to postpone the meeting, citing the negotiations as an excuse. To show weakness right before his ascension shamed him.

The fault was yours that we conceded so much. Abrams could tell you were hurried and dragged the terms. You must learn patience. We are Genjix. Time is irrelevant.

Being berated by Zoras did not help Enzo's mood. While he worshiped the Holy Ones, he was an Adonis Vessel, a chosen messenger in his own right. All his life, he had known he was special. His rise to a vessel of a Holy One had been impressed upon him since he was a child, and he was unaccustomed to not having his way. The lack of deferential treatment he received from Abrams was unsettling. The enemy had showed respect to Zoras' previous vessel after all. Why not to him? Devin was not even an Adonis Vessel. Enzo watched the bay doors opened as the Prophus finally surrendered, their heads held high as if they were on a victory march.

"Stay alert," he told his guards as he made his way down to the ground level.

"Zoras, tell me what you know of Abrams."

You walk a thin line, vessel. Myyk is a high value Prophus. We share extensive history. I have known him since before mankind harnessed fire. He was part of the very first group of Quasing scouts sent to find others of our kind. I do not care for most of the Prophus but Myyk has value.

"And the old man?"

Abrams has been with the Prophus for forty years, rising through the ranks via their military arm. Watch your words around him. He is clever and spent twenty of those years on the front line. Do not engage him in singular combat. Even at his age, he is dangerous.

"Sounds like a challenge. My will is superior."

You are no longer at the Hatchery. This is not a game.

"I never treated the Hatchery like a game."

You will soon discover that the reality you knew is not what you will experience.

His men came to attention when he reached the ground level. The tension in the air was thick. Though the Prophus were unarmed, as agreed, the Genjix agents were trigger happy. He noticed Abrams and the rest of the Prophus eying him. One wrong move and a battle could erupt. Something must be done to cement the peace before his plans were destroyed. Enzo put his hand on the shoulder of the nearest Genjix agent.

"Stand down," he said in a loud, assuring voice. "Blood won't be spilled today." The soldier lowered his rifle without question. The rest of his men followed suit. Out of the corner of his eye, he saw the Prophus relax as well. Abrams did not. Enzo gave his man a reassuring pat on the back before strolling toward Abrams as if on a Sunday walk after church. He got within two meters of the Admiral and bowed.

"By the power bestowed on me as Admiral of the Prophus fleet," Abrams said formally, "and by the terms of our surrender, I give you the codes and the guarantee of my subordinates to offer no resistance." He stood at attention, awaiting Enzo's response.

Enzo studied his enemy for a second. At first, Abrams looked exactly like any other elderly man. Upon closer inspection, he noticed Abrams's distinguished facial lines, his skin pale undoubtedly from years living in a submarine, his lean, tall figure, and his resilient penetrating eyes. This was not a man to be trifled with. He was also standing with both his feet pointing slightly inward, a sign of a trained martial artist.

Enzo stuck out his hand. "Admiral Abrams, it's a pleasure. I wish we could become acquainted on better terms."

Abrams hesitated before taking his hand. "Myyk feels the same way. He and Zoras have a history of mutual respect."

"Zoras still remembers what you did for his vessels during the Stone Age, how you brought him from the darkness and into the Quasing fold."

Abrams relaxed. "It was a difficult time for us. I still believe our goals remain the same, and that one day, we can all work together for the greater good of all." He handed the notebook to Enzo and saluted. "The *Atlantis* is yours."

Enzo took the notebook and then handed it off to Yuki. She scanned the codes and then nodded. Enzo turned and scanned the rank and file crew. According to the terms of the surrender, over three quarters of the enemy would be free in six months. And while it was a low price to pay for an intact nuclear submarine, it still reflected badly upon him.

"You are a shrewd diplomat, Admiral," he mused. "I missed my induction into the Council because of our negotiations."

"Convey my apologies to your Council." Abrams sounded anything but apologetic.

Enzo smiled. "Of course. Please." He gestured for Abrams to follow. "I will arrange some accommodations worthy of your rank."

Abrams nodded and followed in step next to Enzo. "Thank you. Now if possible, Myyk would like to speak with Zoras tonight..."

He never finished his sentence. As they were walking, Enzo took a step back and cut the back of Abrams's knees with a kick, sweeping his legs out from under him.

Enzo, no!

Credit was due to the old man: as Abrams fell to the floor, he rolled away and got back to his feet. Immediately, Enzo was on top of him, lashing out with his fists. He connected with Abrams's face, shattering an orbital bone. But the old man was a tough old nut. He stayed on his feet and retreated to the protection of his people. In his peripheral vision, Enzo saw the Prophus agents closing in to protect their Admiral.

He heard the footsteps of his own guards approach from behind. A pitched battle was about to commence.

What do you think you are doing? An arrangement has been agreed upon!

"I have this under control, Zoras."

"Come out, Admiral, if you value your crew," Enzo yelled. "Your sacrifice will save their lives."

To his credit, the old man held his arms out and ordered his men back. Enzo waited while he gave final instructions to those around him, and then came forward. Enzo waved his guards back as well, and the two met in the center of the circular opening.

Abrams shook his head. "Is this the honor of the Genjix now?"

"This is the honor of the victor," Enzo smirked. "We will dictate what history says."

"It is a pity," Abrams remarked. "Devin was honorable. He would be ashamed of Zoras' new host."

"Shame is reserved only for the defeated," Enzo growled and attacked.

This time though, Abrams was ready. As Enzo charged in, he nimbly sidestepped and danced away. He ducked Enzo's leaping swing and kept his distance, feinting and bobbing his way out of reach.

"Clumsy, lad," Abrams said. "I expected more from a Hatchery-raised Adonis. I could have countered you twice there."

Enzo pressed the attack, covering ground quickly and sweeping low with his foot. He relished this real combat. Trained by the very best in jujitsu and boxing, he had always been considered too valuable to deploy to the field. Now, he enjoyed the adrenaline of a real life-and-death fight. He grazed Abrams's foot as the older man skipped back again.

"Predictable," Abrams chuckled. "A low counter or a step down would have shattered your kneecap there. It is a pity I still honor our agreement, or I would have taught you a lesson, pup."

Enzo grunted and doubled his aggression. He was not going to let this ancient weakling make him look a fool in front of his men. He swung a hard right, folding it into an elbow that grazed Abrams's nose. Still, Abrams shifted out of the way and kept his hands up, emulating a strike. "Another two blows to your exposed left side. Your guard needs work. If I had..."

"Then do it!" Enzo snapped. "Defend yourself if you can."

Enzo, no! You do not know who you are dealing with.

A wicked grin appeared on Abrams's face. "As you wish."

Abrams's attack came so fast that Enzo barely even noticed it. He felt the air pop near his left ear and then a hard pull that lifted him off his feet as Abrams grabbed his collar and threw him across the room.

You are being foolish. Myyk was Dong Haichuan, and Abrams was once a deadly assassin in his own right.

Enzo recognized the name of the creator of Bagua Zhang as he landed unceremoniously on his rump. He rolled away just as a foot came stomping down. The challenge of this fight piqued his interest even more. A real opponent. Enzo picked himself up off the ground and brought his guard up. His face turned crimson red when he heard the cheers of the Prophus and the mutters of his own men.

"I will not lose to this feeble man. I will impose my will and strength on him!"

Your standing among the Genjix will fall if you do. This is a terrible risk you take to gain nothing.

Abrams pressed the attack. Enzo blocked three quick strikes and countered. Abrams dodged an uppercut but ate a side kick. Enzo followed up with a flurry that missed its mark. Enzo was stronger and quicker, but Abrams was by far the craftier fighter.

Abrams continued to throw him off balance, tugging his sleeves and tripping him. However, the old man eventually tired and Enzo's attacks got closer to their mark. Finally, two jabs followed a leg sweep and he was on top of Abrams. Once he had locked down the slippery old man, the fight was a forgone conclusion. Enzo rained punches on Abrams, striking him repeatedly in the face. The Prophus gasped and a wave of them surged forward to protect their leader.

"One more step and my men will open fire," Enzo screamed. Immediately, a hundred Genjix rifles trained on the prisoners. The Prophus officers barked orders to stand down.

Victory is yours. End this display.

But Enzo was not done yet. As the old man lay unconscious on the ground, Enzo began to kick him in the ribs, breaking more bones.

Stop this at once. You are acting mad!

"I am in perfect control, Zoras. Watch."

Enzo continued beating on Abrams, playing the part of a madman intent on pummeling this helpless old man to death. And while he had a look of fury on his face, his mind was calm. He was no more angry beating on Abrams than a butcher hacking a side of beef. He pulled Abrams up by the shirt and clocked him in the jaw. Abrams groaned and lay sprawled on the ground, not moving. Enzo stomped down hard on Abrams's knees, relishing in seeing exposed bone. The old man would never walk again. Enzo then pulled his knife from his belt and knelt down to cut the Quasing out of this undeserving human. There was a flash in the corner of his eyes.

"You animal" was all he heard before one of the Prophus collided with him. Then Palos and his guards appeared, pulling the idiot man off. Enzo smirked. This was exactly the effect he was looking for. The rest of his bodyguards pulled Enzo back to safety.

The powder keg had been lit and the room exploded into a full blown melee; chaos ensued. The unarmed Prophus prisoners attacked en masse, a futile display of courage that was rewarded with barrages of gunfire. Enzo had to admit, even in the chaos, the enemy was organized. Their line reached as far as the Admiral's body. He was dragged back into their ranks and then they tried to retreat into the submarine. It was too late, however.

The Prophus were surrounded and outgunned. It became a bloodbath as the Genjix soldiers mowed them down. Fortunately for them, his men were still using non-lethal munitions. Before long, three hundred Prophus agents lay in heaps of bodies lining fifty meters long.

Enzo watched a few familiar sparkles of Quasing float into the air. Some of the Prophus must have died after all. Non-lethal munitions could kill just as easily as lethal ones if they struck a vital area. No matter. A few casualties were acceptable.

What were you thinking? You risk your standing. Terms were agreed upon! You will never be able to negotiate with the Prophus ever again.

Enzo wiped the blood from his face as his engineers brought out Penetra scanners. "I do not intend to ever negotiate again, Holy One. The terms of the surrender were that forty percent of the vessels were ours to handle as we saw fit. I was treating Abrams as I saw fit and was attacked. I have honored our terms. They have not. We are no longer held by the terms of surrender. They are all my prisoners now."

CHAPTER ELEVEN
CAMERON

When I confronted the strange beast, my host realized that he could not be beaten, that this monstrosity was a new form of my kind. I later learned that this strange cousin was the next step in my host's evolution known as Gigantopithecus.

When I attacked and wrapped my teeth around his shoulder, something awoke in me, and for the first time in millions of years, I remembered. I was sentient and present once more. To my great shock, I recognized a presence; it was Myyk, and he had come searching for us.

Tao

Roen pulled up to the front driveway of Louis and Lee Ann Tesser's house in his rental car and turned the engine off. He stilled his rapidly beating heart and tried to collect his thoughts. He was actually going to see his boy! It was a three-hour drive from Los Angeles to San Diego, and his mind had raced the entire way.

This is not a good idea.

"He's my son. How is it ever a bad idea to visit him?"

I was referring to his grandparents. You are probably in mortal danger.

"That's the truth," he muttered as he got out of the car and scanned the premises. A winding brick path led to the front door. There was a three-car garage at the west side, and if he needed cover, a grove of trees to the east within sprinting distance.

Originally from New York, Louis and Lee Ann were living out their golden years on seven acres of hills and woods on the outskirts of the city. It was the perfect place for Cameron to grow up, except for the fact that he wasn't with his parents.

Filled with apprehension, Roen made a trip around the house to scout the grounds. He stopped in his tracks when he saw Louis working in the backyard. He decided to face Louis and get the hostilities over with. There was more room to maneuver outside. If he accidentally broke one of Lee Ann's figurines while dodging Louis, then he would definitely have to suffer both their wraths.

Roen walked toward Louis, more nervous making than he would be crossing a mine field. He wondered what he'd say to the grandfather of his son. Maybe Louis, having time to have calmed down, would embrace him. They were family after all. That had to count for something, didn't it?

Doubt it.

"Pessimist."

I wish you had left the engine running.

Louis was whistling and shoveling dirt with his back to him, gathering mulch or raking or whatever one does with landscape. Eva, their Airedale Terrier, padded around the lawn, sniffing and rolling on the grass, generally being the worst guard dog in history. It looked like Louis was scooping a mound of black soil from a wheelbarrow and building another mound on the ground next to a bed of white flowers. He was also sprinkling the black dirt around a small area enclosed with white rocks. It seemed like a lot of work moving all that earth back and forth.

Roen was not one of those suburban types who ever understood the purpose of a lawn. The lure of having a patch of grass that needed mowing every week escaped him. Yeah, there was a lot of open space, but that just meant more work to do. But then, Louis grew up in the country on a farm or the swamp or the jungle or something like that before he moved to New York, so this had to be what farm country jungle people did for fun.

As usual, the world's worst guard dog did not even notice him until he was practically on top of them. And staying true to form, instead of barking a warning, Eva cocked her head to one side and began to thump her tail. Louis finally noticed him when Eva's butt began to join in on the wagging. He looked up and stared, mouth agape.

"Hey, Louis," Roen began. "How's it going?"

Louis swung the shovel over his shoulder. "Hey, Lee," he yelled.

"Yes, dear?" Her voice came from somewhere in the house.

"You know where my varmint gun is?" he said, eyes still intent on Roen.

Well, this is panning out exactly as I expected.

"It's locked up in the cabinet where you keep all your guns," she replied.

"Look, I know you're upset," Roen began. "And I get it. I messed up a bit."

"Could you bring it out?" Louis continued. "And some shells too."

"Where did you put the box of ammo?" she asked.

"On the top cabinet of the kitchen counter. In the far back behind the sugar," he answered.

I wish you had worn your Kevlar.

"Louis isn't going to shoot me. Besides, a varmint rifle's like a .22. It'll barely break the skin."

If you say so. I do not relish living the next ten years in Louis or Eva.

"I'd go with the dog."

Roen raised his hands in surrender. "I don't have a lot of time and don't want any trouble. I just came to see Cameron."

"Hurry please, Lee. The varmint might get away."

"I'm not having a lot of luck getting through to him."

You should consider a tactical retreat.

Roen heard a door creak open and then the shuffling of footsteps on the wooden deck. "I don't know why you keep trying to shoot these rabbits, Louis. You never hit one. Your eyes just aren't what they used to be. Besides, even if you do, what do you think you're going to do with... oh. Hi, Roen."

"Hey, Lee Ann," Roen said, not taking his eyes off of Louis.

Lee Ann handed the rifle to Louis and shook her finger at them. "Now boys, don't do anything you're going to regret. I'm not bailing anyone out of jail today." She gave Louis a peck on the cheek. "I'll set another plate for lunch. You good for omelets, Roen?"

"That sounds wonderful."

Lee Ann gave them a boys-will-be-boys look and walked back into the house. Louis upended the box into his palm and picked out a few bullets.

"He won't shoot."

There is cover at your three. Louis is left handed and has a bad hip, so if you go in at forty degrees...

"I am not taking out my wife's father."

Just giving you options.

"No. Just no."

Louis loaded a round into the rifle and pointed it at Roen. "You saved me the effort of getting immunization shots. Now, you have ten seconds before I pop a couple holes in you. You better start running, boy."

Remember, cover at your three.

"He's not going to shoot."

"One," Louis began.

"I don't want any problems. I just want to see my son." Roen pleaded, feeling a little nervous.

"Two."

"I'm still married to Jill," he said more emphatically.

That was the wrong thing to say.

"Three."

"Come on, let's be serious for a second. You're not going to shoot me. Let's talk this over."

I see your negotiation skills are as sharp as ever.

"Seven."

"Wait, what happened to four?"

"Eight."

"Fine. I dare you. Give it your best shot."

"Nine." Louis uncocked the safety and lifted the rifle to his shoulders.

Roen threw up his hands. "Wait, wait. OK, you're going to shoot. Hang on!"

"Ten."

Roen prepared to dive to the right. He could have dived to his left onto the bed of flowers, but crushing Louis' hydrangeas or whatever they were wouldn't help the situation.

"Daddiieeee!" a high pitched squeal rang through the air. Standing outside with Lee Ann's arms around his shoulders, Cameron waddled toward Roen as fast as his three-year-old legs could carry him. Barking enthusiastically, Eva bounded up to Cameron and bowled him over, licking his face as he writhed around on the ground like an overturned roly poly. Cameron didn't cry though; not his boy. After failing to defend himself against her vicious barrage of dog kisses, Cameron went on the offensive and smacked her lightly on the muzzle. Then it became a game of tag. First Cameron would waddle after her while she barked and pretended to pounce, and then he would book in the other direction while she ran circles around him. Obviously, in all the excitement of playing with a brown and black dog that he saw every day, his father had already become an afterthought.

To Roen, it was the most beautiful scene in the world. He swelled with pride up as his boy ran with reckless abandon, playing with the furry beast twice his size. He caught a lump in his throat in the tender moments when Cameron gently hugged Eva, and saw his son stand up for himself when she tried to maul him. And he looked so joyful, so wonderfully happy. A tear escaped Roen's eye and trickled down his cheeks. He forgot about the gun still pointed at his head. Frankly, he didn't care. If Louis shot him dead right now, it would be alright. He would die looking at his son giggling and laughing. What more could a father ask for?

How about a little recognition that he has not seen you in a year. He prioritized the dog over you. Are you just going to stand there or go give him a hug?

"I don't know. I didn't think past this. Right now, I just want to watch."

Probably for the best. Louis still has you in his sights. He might shoot if you make any sudden moves.

Hesitantly, Roen walked toward the two. They were rolling around on the ground; Eva still trying to drown him with licks, and Cameron using her face as a punching bag. Out of the corner of his eye, Roen saw Louis grudgingly lower the rifle. He wasn't sure how serious Louis really was about shooting him. Knowing the old man and having played poker with him dozens of times, he knew Louis rarely bluffed. Lee Ann gave him a neutral look. She was always a hard one to read. Being a former trial attorney, she kept her emotions close to her vest and rarely rushed to judgment.

Eva, on the other hand, was thrilled for another playmate. She disengaged from Cameron and promptly pounced on Roen, knocking him over and licking his face. This in turn made Cameron jealous, so he joined in on the festivities and leapt on top of Roen as well. For the first time in almost two years, Roen held his son in his arms.

"Last time I saw him, he had to use the wall to stand. Now he's running around all by himself," Roen said, his voice cracking.

"We can't get him to stop running all over the place," Lee Ann remarked. "Nowadays, we just tie him up to the dog and let them run each other ragged." She went to Louis and took the rifle away. "Go wash up. It's time to eat." She patted him on the cheek. "Be on your best behavior, dear." She turned to Roen as she walked back into the kitchen. "Clean the slobber off Cam's face before you put him at the table. Make sure he washes his hands."

Roen wouldn't have it any other way. Cam hated having his face washed and fought the towel just as hard as Roen remembered. And when they sat down at the table, he made just as big of a mess as he always did. Roen loved every minute of it. Lunch was much less uncomfortable than he thought it'd be. It was mostly because the three of them focused their attention only on Cameron.

Lee Ann was pleasant as always, and Louis was minimally civil. And though feeding a toddler was time-consuming, it felt like the shortest two hours in his life. He was sad when Lee Ann took the plates away. He looked at his watch: 2pm.

We have to leave soon if you want to catch that flight.

"I don't want to go."

There are many reasons why we do not want to fight. Your son is a reason why you do.

"You're right. If what we think is happening is true, then Cam won't have one."

Exactly.

"Roen," Louis said, standing up. "Walk with me."

Without looking, he turned and headed out of the house and back to the mound of dirt from this morning. He picked up a shovel and began building new piles of dirt. Roen checked the time again. Should he tell Louis he had to leave now? He thought better of it and picked up the extra shovel. Then he joined in with the digging.

Every once in a while, Louis signaled that the new pile of dirt they were building was large enough, and then he'd point to another spot to build another. Roen would then load the wheelbarrow with dirt, move it to the new spot, and unload. Then Louis would sprinkle the new earth evenly over the ground.

"I wonder if they have to replace the top soil every year. Sounds like a drag. If this was my lawn, I'd pour cement over it and make a tennis court."

You have seen the reports. The weather patterns are changing. Global temperatures are increasing. Do not think this was natural. The Genjix have been intentionally pushing the temperatures and carbon concentrations up for decades now. If we do not stop them, in a few years, losing top soil will be the least of your concerns.

They landscaped for the better part of three hours. Roen thought about bringing up his flight a few more times, but it was never the right moment. By the time 5pm rolled around, it was too late. He had broken his promise to Wuehler but he really didn't care. For now, moving this dirt with Louis was all that mattered.

"I looked you up," Louis said finally around sundown. They were building the last pile of dirt.

"You did what?"

Louis wiped his brow and looked him straight in the eye. "After Jill told me about you being gone for months on end, I got suspicious and looked you up. Thought maybe you were with the mob or running from bad debt. Hired an ex-IRS agent and a federal investigator."

"I didn't know you cared enough to hire a snoop," Roen said.

"I do when it's my baby girl involved."

"What did they find?"

Louis scratched the crown of his head. "That's the thing. They didn't find anything. All the records about you were a bunch of crap."

Remember the time I said Louis was a genius? I rest my case.

"How do you know it's a bunch of crap?"

Louis chuckled as he finished spreading the dirt around. "I was a corporate raider for thirty years. You think we just looked at financial statements and forked over a hundred million? I knew if a CEO liked heroin with his eggs, or if the trustees preferred domestic or imported hookers. We sicced guys on the entire board of companies for months. And that's what I saw in your records."

"I don't like imported hookers," Roen stammered.

You are obtuse to the point of stupidity.

"It's too clean," Louis drawled. "Like someone typed it all out and made sure every piece fits just like it's supposed to. Done well, I might add, but not passing this sniff test." Louis tapped his long schnoz for emphasis.

"I don't know what you're talking about," Roen shrugged.

A little too late for that.

"Tao, our cleaning teams suck."

All they care about is preventing the Genjix from tracing you, not inquisitive father-in-laws.

"So what are you? FBI? ATF? You don't seem smart enough to be CIA."

"I didn't know you had to be a genius to be in the CIA," Roen muttered.

Louis shook his head. "Don't matter. You won't tell me anyway. Is this why you had to leave Jill alone for so long? You doing something for our country?"

"Yes." There was no hesitation in Roen's voice. It was close enough to the truth, though in his eyes, he was doing this for the entire world. In any case, if it got Louis off his back, a little half lie was acceptable.

Louis paused. "Does Jill know?"

Roen nodded.

"I see, and you flew all the way here to see your son for a few hours. You're heading somewhere, aren't you? Somewhere you might not come back from."

Brilliant man. If I had only found him forty years ago.

Roen nodded again. It was close enough to the truth. He didn't actually think this mission was any more dangerous than any other, but today made him reevaluate his life. He needed to be around for his son.

Louis finally softened. "Alright. Sun's setting. Cameron goes to bed at eight. You have until we tuck him in."

Roen thanked him and took off into the house. He spent the rest of the night with Cameron, reading a story, playing building blocks, racing toy cars. He tried to memorize every detail about of his boy, from how he smiled to what his new favorite toy was. And for a few hours, he was just a guy playing with his son.

When 9.30 rolled around, Lee Ann stopped by Cameron's room and knocked on the door. "It's past his bedtime," she said softly.

Roen nodded and helped put Cameron to bed. "You be good to your grandpa and grandma, alright, buddy?" he murmured.

"Will you keep watch so Eva doesn't eat Poopsie?" Cameron said, his large round eyes imploring Roen.

Roen's heart broke for the tenth time in so many hours. "Sure buddy," he choked.

Cameron sniffled and reached out to him. Roen sat on the bed and held onto his son for another half hour until he finally fell asleep. When he was sure Cameron was out, Roen pulled the blanket over him and just stood there trying to memorize the picture.

I have it for you whenever you need, my friend.

Would he ever see his son again? This could be the last time. Roen fought the tears that began to roll down his face. Lee Ann came into the room and put her arm around his shoulder, and together, they just watched Cameron sleep.

There is a red eye flight at two. If you do not make this flight, you will have to wait until tomorrow afternoon. We have to leave right now.

Roen looked at her. "Thanks for the few extra hours."

"Just make sure you're in his life, regardless of what happens between you and Jill," Lee Ann said.

He nodded, giving her one last hug. On the drive back up north to Los Angeles, Roen kept the mental video of Cameron playing with Eva running over and over in his head. He was determined to watch his son grow up to be a man. This wouldn't be the last time he saw his boy.

Are you ready? Is your mind clear?

"Damn straight. It's exactly what I needed. Now, let's get this job done. I have my son's future to fight for and a wife to win back."

CHAPTER TWELVE
MARCO

*Our escape from the prison in Valencia was typical of Tao's hosts,
even today. He cut a swathe of death through the prison guards'
ranks, utilizing a style never seen on this side of the planet. It
wasn't until later that I learned that it was Tao's own invention,
the Grand Supreme Fist. The carnage was spectacular, and he
captured two Genjix Quasing, forcing them into two rats. Then he
caged the rats and took them with him.*

*By then, the Genjix had spread their Inquisition, and the
situation had deteriorated into a civil war. For the next few years
I assisted the Prophus in capturing dozens of Genjix and trapping
them in small animals. Thus, the Chest of the Menagerie was born.*

Baji

It was a small victory that Wilks grudgingly pushed his
meeting with Hogan back, but only after Jill had promised
him the moon, stars, and six solar systems' worth of
concessions. It was a tall order, but she made the promises,
so now she had to deliver.

Jill had just returned from a meeting with Senator Young
of California. She had assumed he would be the easiest

of the on-the-fence senators to sway since he didn't care either way about the sanctions. However, he was a sneaky one and resisted all her offers. It wasn't until she reminded him of the explosion at the Port of Los Angeles – courtesy of a firefight between the Prophus and Genjix over nine tons of biological weapon agents – that he saw the profit in supporting her. Even then, he extracted concessions, including a tax break for solar panels in the richest homes in Hollywood, and an endowment for the Young Museum of Lithuanian Arts. Boy, did that guy love to talk. They had wrapped up the solids of their deal an hour in, but he kept going for another thirty minutes just because he enjoyed the sound of his own voice.

Afterward, she met with nine aides of six senators whose votes she already had. It was important to make sure no one jumped ship. She knew that Simon was working his ranks as well, and it would only be a matter of time before he realized that she was playing him. By the time she got out of that meeting, it was already well into the afternoon.

"Lunch at 2 in the afternoon. Must be a light day."

You need to take better care of yourself.

"No one said running the country offered a healthy lifestyle. Not to mention the pay is comparable to my first job scooping ice cream."

You are pulling a double paycheck from the Prophus.

"Oh yeah, that pitiful thing. It's even less than this one. Between my two checks and what Roen sends me, that's almost half of what I made at my old job before hitting the jackpot with my own Quasing."

Tammy practically ran up to her as she returned to her office. "There's someone in the office for you. Where did you find him?"

"What?" she said, puzzled.

"He's really good looking and charming. And he brought you a present. It must be serious. How did you hide him from us?"

I see Marco is here.

"I don't know what you're talking about," Jill replied. Instinctively, she checked her suit for wrinkles and calmly walked in. Between Paula's description and Tammy's gushing, she was definitely curious about this Marco.

Standing next to her desk was a tall man in a charcoal pin-striped suit. He turned toward her as she walked in and smiled. Tammy was right. Jill wasn't sure what to gape at first: his Ken-doll peppered hair, the high cheekbones, or those kissable dimples. The guy also had a smile that had popped out of a dental brochure. He held a small gift-wrapped box in his left hand and extended his right.

"Jill," he said, his voice a low pleasant rumble that tickled the bottom of her chest. "Marco. It's a pleasure. I believe you're expecting me."

"I was expecting someone," she said, suddenly very self-conscious. If Paula had exaggerated, it wasn't by much.

Marco was tall and lean, yet she could tell he was in very good shape, built proportionally like an athlete without looking like a bodybuilder. His face was tan and weathered, but the age lines only made him look distinguished. And Paula wasn't kidding. Those deep hazel eyes were whispering sweet nothings just by looking at her.

"Well," he smiled. "I hope I exceed the expectation of just someone."

Someone inhaled behind her. She turned to see Tammy jittering like a nervous fool, the pad and pen in her hand a pitiful excuse to eavesdrop.

"I'm good here," she said, giving her assistant a get-out-of-here look.

Tammy had the audacity to look disappointed. "I'll be at my desk, if you need anything. Just... call." She turned to Marco. "It was nice meeting you."

He tilted his head toward her in a way that with any other man would seem condescending. "Pleasure is all mine." After Tammy left, he asked Jill. "There's much to cover. Can your employer survive without you for the rest of the day?"

Jill shook her head. "Congress is in the middle of session. My hours are pretty much..."

"Nonsense," Wilks said, walking into the room. "Marco here says he wants to kidnap you for the rest of the day. I say kidnap away."

"Do you two know each other?" Jill looked perplexed.

Marco smiled. "The senator was good enough to entertain me while I was waiting for you. We seem to have a shared interest in golf and the European commodities market."

"Marco here tells me he once swung a sixty-eight at Augusta. I told him if that's the case, he's in the wrong line of work. You still up for a game next weekend?"

"Why, but of course. Tee time at six?"

Jill's mouth dropped open. "Senator, you're going golfing with a man you met five minutes ago?"

Wilks laughed jovially. "I can tell Marco here is one of the good ones." He leaned in close. "Make sure you do a background check before next weekend. Can't be seen golfing with a serial killer or a gossip columnist, right?" He nudged her playfully.

Marco is not only a ladykiller but a man's man as well.

"Great, that's all I need. Bromance between my boss and my bodyguard."

Marco handed her the small box. "Excellent. It's settled then. I'll see you later today, dear Jill. Something to remember me by until then. Adieu."

He tried to kiss her hand; Jill would have none of that and kept her arms glued to the sides of her body. She tried very hard to not let her eyes roll. She and Wilks just stood there and watched as Marco left the room. She wasn't sure what had just happened.

He leaves quite an impression, right? A host but not a doctor. In his case, I will make an exception.

"What a pompous ass!"

But you are still attracted to him?

Jill caught herself nodding unintentionally. There wasn't much she could hide from Baji.

Wilks chuckled almost gleefully as he pat her on the back. "What a charming fella. I say, you do recover well with your men. That Marco guy is really something. You should keep this one. Anyway, break's over. Do you have Beckman's whip count? We need to get moving while the momentum is on our side."

Jill gave the door one last look before getting back to running the country.

Jill walked out of the Hart Building after work and found Marco waiting. He was leaning on what she could only presume was his car, a sporty and impeccably shiny Tesla Roadster. She made a mental note to give her little Ford a bath the next chance she got.

"Rental?" she asked.

He shrugged. "Well, the cars the Prophus had available just wouldn't do. Dreadful choices really, and I didn't have time to arrange to have my Aston shipped over, so I did the next best thing. Fun little bugger."

Jill couldn't help but smile as she shook her head. "You're an awful spy; you know that?"

"Why do you say that?" he asked.

"Because you look the international superspy with your flashy car and demeanor. You stick out like a sore thumb. Supermodels are supposed to be kept in New York City or cages."

His smile brightened when he saw his gift wrapped around her wrist. She had to consciously tell herself to not touch it. It was a beautiful silver bangle bracelet with a single diamond in the center and several intricate grooves running along its edges. It was overwhelming, and she felt more than a bit uncomfortable wearing it.

"Do you like it?" Marco asked, opening the passenger side door, which made her feel warm and fuzzy inside. She appreciated a man with manners.

Roen has not opened the door for you since your first month together.

"I'm not going to play that game, Baji."

You should, then maybe you will know what you are missing.

"It's lovely," she replied, "but why did you get it?" She got into the car and inhaled that fresh new car scent.

Marco got into the driver's side and pulled away from the lot. "The bracelet has a microphone and monitoring device. If your life signs fluctuate past a certain point, the audio channel opens up and a tracker kicks in. So if you have been knocked unconscious, I can come to your rescue as fast as possible." He turned to her. "I'm your security now and I take that role seriously. We'll go over the ground rules over dinner and a nice glass of wine."

They went to dinner at the iconic 1789 restaurant, housed in an old federal building in the affluent Georgetown part of the capital where, over dinner and several drinks, they went over the protocols of her protection. He would pose as her boyfriend for all public functions and would never be further than a klick away any other time. Marco was exact on every minute detail, from her positioning when they walked together to what their emergency rendezvous points were. By the time they were on dessert, he had combed through every part of her daily routine.

"So here's the deal," he said as he drank his bourbon. She noted that it was his third glass of a particularly expensive bottle of Glen Garioch and wondered how someone on Prophus salary could afford it.

Old money. Lots of it. Marco's family once reigned over the Duchy of Brittany. Ahngr has been with his family for almost a thousand years.

"A rich kid who fights for fun?"

You would be surprised how many bored wealthy young men choose this path.

"Boarding school must really be dreary."

"Sometime this week," Marco continued, "I'm taking you through your paces. You will need to understand not only my role as a bodyguard, but yours as my ward. If I'm taking a bullet for you, it had better be for the right reasons. I also need to know how well you take care of yourself. Your file says you only took basic training. As a civilian host, that's usually all that is required."

"I'm a political operative," she said stiffly. "Fighting and all that jazz I leave for you roughnecks. Tomorrow's going to be a little tough to fit in my schedule. I kind of help run a country, you know."

"We'll see about that," he grinned. "We'll call it a first date. Paula did tell you to follow my instructions. I believe

I have rank in this matter. Your file says you used to be a gymnast?"

"In high school," she grimaced. "Twenty years ago."

"And you haven't maintained yourself since?"

"I'm not that out of shape," she felt insulted. "I did the Wisconsin Ironman a few years back."

"As spectacular an accomplishment as that is, unless you plan to jog away from the next Genjix you come across at a meandering pace, you will require more training," he replied.

Jill had a bad taste in her mouth as they left the restaurant. She sat in his little Roadster and brooded. She already had three people's worth of work on her plate. The last thing she needed was a personal trainer filling up her busy schedule. Well, he could try his best to bust in on her time, but she had her priorities. Still, she admitted it might do her good. A little brushing up couldn't hurt, could it?

Reserve judgment on how little that brushing up is not going to hurt you until you have experienced it. I knew Marco's father. If the man is half as crazed about calisthenics as his father was, we are in trouble.

And she was.

CHAPTER THIRTEEN
TAIWAN

The next ten million years were called the Time of the Gathering. Those of us who were found were sent out again to search for others who were still lost. Slowly, the hierarchy of the ship reorganized. The Grand Council built a kingdom of primates in what is now known as Africa, and sent out searchers through migratory animals to seek more Quasing.

I was one of those searchers. The odds of finding another were low. To find one of our kind within a thousand years was considered a great success. I personally found twenty-four. I was not a good searcher.

Tao

Roen landed at Taiwan Taoyuan International shortly after ten, three days late on his promise to Wuehler. It had been a long, draining flight. He was delayed in Los Angeles, missed his connecting flight in Tokyo, and forced to go on standby for six hours. Wuehler must be frothing at the mouth.

It is not all bad. You got to miss having to unpack and set up the safe house, though you probably got the worst bed.

"Probably have me sleeping in the bathtub."

Taoyuan was a busy hub and the lines were long even at this time of the night. It took almost an hour to get through customs and pick up his luggage. By the time he was finally ready to leave the airport, it was midnight and he was in a decidedly crappy mood.

Taiwan, like many subtropical islands this time of year, was very wet. The instant he stepped out of the air-conditioned airport, the humidity smacked him in the face and beat on him until his body dripped like a leaky faucet. After five minutes standing on the curb, his shirt was saturated with sweat. Roen's time with the Prophus had taken him from the ice peaks of the Himalayas to the deserts of northern Africa, but nothing ever bothered him as much as the tropics. He didn't have, as Tao often said, the pores for this sort of climate.

"These austerity measures suck. I'm on a world-saving mission. I shouldn't have to fly like a common pleb."

Our apologies, Mighty World Savior. Would you rather travel like a peasant or run out of bullets and armor?

"There has to be something else we can save on other than transportation."

Taco Wednesdays at the office were already cut.

"I miss tacos."

Hailing a cab and figuring out how to get to the Shilin district in Taipei proved to be challenging. Unlike many Prophus agents who were fluent in several languages, Roen was completely ignorant of the Taiwanese language, and though most locals spoke Mandarin, his knowledge of Mandarin consisted mainly of important phrases like "where's the bathroom?" and "hello, you are beautiful, and I am single". Luckily, being a former Chinese emperor, Tao was able to help him through some of the trickier questions, though truth be told, Tao's Chinese was dated by some eight hundred years. Roen ended up sounding like a bozo speaking in an archaic Ming Dynasty dialect. By the time he stepped out of the cab at the Shilin Night Market, he was starving and irritated at the entire world.

Taipei was famous for night markets that ran, as their name suggested, all through the night. Roen passed by throngs of people browsing the many booths and stores that lined the narrow streets. Here, street vendors sold anything from all kinds of foods to plastic toys to bootleg DVDs.

His senses were overwhelmed by the sheer size and magnitude of the market. The most interesting thing he saw by far, though, was the food. Between racks of raw chicken claws, glazed sugary cherry candy on a stick, and flavored shaved ice desserts, it seemed he could find everything here. From fried cuttlefish to small ghastly looking black eggs, much of the food here looked like it came from another planet. And almost everything smelled great. There were more than a few times when he had to stop and stare, mouth wide open, at some of the strange contents on the carts.

It might seem strange to have a safe house in such a high-traffic place, but these areas usually made the best safe houses. There were so many people milling about that it was easy to lose oneself in the crowd. He sniffed the air as he passed by a particularly repugnant-smelling stall.

"What is that?"

I believe the locals call it stinky tofu.

"Name certainly fits. Smells like road kill."

It is supposed to be delicious. They say the stinkier it is, the better it tastes.

"Then that tofu must taste like filet mignon drizzled with cocaine. I guess that's the first thing up to bat. I still haven't met a delicacy I couldn't stomach."

Except durian.

"Ugh. That foul fruit is the devil!"

Roen passed several other unusual smells. Some made his mouth water while others kicked up his gag reflex. His stomach was making a ruckus though. Airplane food didn't satiate a guy who regularly consumed upward of four thousand calories a day. Still, he decided to forgo a meal until after he reported in to Wuehler. He didn't want to antagonize the guy any more by getting caught scarfing down food when he was already three days late.

It took another twenty minutes of wandering through the maze of stalls before he found the entrance to the sub-level market. He went down the steps two at a time and entered another market similar to the one above, but even more cramped. The stalls were minuscule here and the corridors so narrow they reminded him of a submarine.

His pace slowed to a crawl as he elbowed and pushed his way through the throngs of people in narrow sewer-like passages. Eventually he got turned around and lost. Roen finally found where he was going when one of the men on the squad found him wandering aimlessly in circles. In a pissy mood, he nearly kicked the hinges off the safe house door and trudged in. He dropped his bag on the ground and looked around. Things went even more downhill from there.

The cherry on top of the entire night's fiasco was that the safe house was a total dump. Now, a safe house disguised as being run-down was expected. Safe house exteriors were supposed to look like places no one stayed in. Gone were the days when they were ski resorts nestled on top of the Alps or penthouse suites located in five star hotels.

The interior, however, was another matter. Roen expected these havens to have weapons, medical supplies, two exits, a communication system, and a stocked fridge. That was the minimum. However, he also expected a clean room, a warm bed, a hot shower, and enough space to house all the personnel. This was where this dump was woefully inadequate.

The agent in front must have notified Wuehler because the grumpy old guy was sitting in a chair in front of the door like an angry parent waiting for his kid who had snuck out in the middle of the night. Roen walked into a room the size of a small truckers lodge and was taken aback by five pairs of eyes staring him down.

We might want to consider an escape plan.

"Hi?" he said with forced cheerfulness.

That probably was the wrong expression to come in here with. Wuehler's teeth grinded so loudly the entire room could hear them. Faust, standing behind Wuehler, kept his face neutral, but he was suppressing a grin. At least someone thought it was funny.

"I expected you to be a day or two later than promised. Somehow, you exceeded even my lowest expectations. I didn't think that was even possible. Yet I can't say I'm surprised." Wuehler began. "Just because you've been stuffed down my throat doesn't mean I have to put up with your insubordination."

Be civil. Remember, you owe him one.

Roen swallowed a snarky remark and took the rest of Wuehler's berating with as much dignity a full-grown man could muster. It was his bad after all; he had missed his self-imposed deadline. Besides, butting heads with your commanding officer usually led to unpleasant jobs, like all-night guard or latrine duty. Wuehler wouldn't make a host clean the toilet, would he?

Just to be safe, he appeared properly chastised when Wuehler was done. "You're right. Circumstances had changed on the ground and I was delayed. I would have contacted you except for the radio silence. Please accept my apology and, on my honor, I will follow your orders to the letter for the duration of this mission."

Not too shabby. I almost bought that.

"See, all that money I lost in poker went to a good cause."

Still a far cry from an Emmy.

Wuehler seemed taken aback by Roen's sudden capitulation to his authority, his prepared words stuck in his mouth. He gave a stiff nod and motioned to the back. "Stow your gear. You got second watch tonight."

"Good ol' second watch. And thus my punishment begins."

At least you can get some dinner first. We are pretty hungry after all.

Roen perked up. That was a bright spot. Now in a little bit of a hurry, he plopped his stuff down and raced out of the safe house before Wuehler could say anything else. He had about three hours before first watch ended. A good soldier kept his stomach full. His porker days were behind him, and Tao had long since stopped regulating his diet. It was something he now did on his own. Still, it was hard to maintain his diet while on missions, so he didn't bother. Besides, exotic cuisine was one of the few joys of traveling.

Faust caught up with him as he left the claustrophobic underground market. "Getting a bite?"

Roen grinned. "Going native and trying that stinky tofu."

Faust made a face. "Passed on it the first day. Haven't built up the courage to try yet."

A few minutes later, the two sat on rickety plastic stools at a counter and snacked on the hideously smelling tofu over a plate of veggie pickles. It was delicious. By then, the crowds were thinning just a bit, and the two caught up on old times. When he had first met Faust, things were quite different. Roen had just learned how to shoot a gun, and Faust kept him from panicking during his first firefight. In return, Roen saved Faust's life by chucking a rifle at a Genjix sniper because he momentarily forgot how to reload a clip. The two had kept in touch ever since.

That felt like a lifetime ago. Roen was now a deadly host with a reputation within the organization as a maverick, often disobeying orders and going off on his own. Faust had faithfully followed Wuehler and was on the short list for peaceful or voluntary transition. Those were pretty rare these days though.

They exchanged photos of their family and talked freely about the dire situation with the Prophus losing on every front. Faust told him about the action he saw at Boulder and how his entire squad had perished while defending the sewage entry point. That was the battle where Wuehler had earned Ramez. A portion of a ceiling had collapsed on top of Jacques, the general in charge of the defense of the base, during the siege. Wuehler had dug him out just in time for Ramez to make the transition.

Roen talked about his suspicions about Genjix plans and regaled Faust with his exploits of the past two years. Prophus command had initially declared that some of his projections were so outlandish that he was a conspiracy theorist. Now, each small piece was falling into place just as he feared. The only question was whether things were too far along for the Prophus to stop.

"Quasiform," Faust mused, tapping his fingers on the counter. "Like a bad sci-fi flick. Is it even possible?"

Roen, who was busy with a second helping of stinky tofu, shrugged. "They think it is. All the live data backs it up."

"Does the data back up the conspiracy or does your conspiracy back up the data?" Faust wondered.

"That's what the Keeper accused me of when I first showed her the data," Roen replied. "It comes down to this. We know that the Genjix had two large-scale programs in the past ten years: the Penetra Scanner and this ProGenesis. The Penetra Scanner allowed for detection of Quasing inside hosts. The ProGenesis allowed their species to reproduce. Two dramatic leaps that changed the rules of the game. What does that mean?"

"That they're dying out one by one and want to make sure their species continues?" Faust suggested.

"Or they aren't trying to go home anymore," Roen said.

"That's a bit of a stretch," Faust, munching on a meat lollipop called pig's blood cake, grunted. "You're telling me the Quasing, who have been trying to go home for millions of years all of a sudden decide they like this dump and want to stay?"

"Well, if you put it that way," Roen grumbled. "I'm sure they had deeper discussions than the planet's hygiene and our four seasons."

It has been speculated for some time that we would be extinct before technology advanced enough for deep space travel.

By the time they finished dinner, the two were quiet. The grim news had sunk their spirits. None of the agents these days talked much about the future, especially when none of them were confident they had one. There was hardly a worse feeling than knowing that the game was lost and that the only thing the players could do was run out the clock. It was even more terrible that both men knew how the consequences of the loss would affect their children.

"Have you made any headway locating Dylan?" Roen asked.

Faust shook his head. "Still too early. We got three guys out around the clock digging up what's left of our network: local police, crime syndicates, Buddhist temples, a couple of corporations. From their reports, it's pretty barren. The Genjix were pretty thorough wiping out our footprint on the island."

"And remnants of the escape pods?"

"Ashish and I were at the docks the first night. Local authorities confiscated the wrecks and they all somehow conveniently disappeared."

The vendor came by and took the plates away. Faust left a few bills on the counter and the two made their way back to the safe house. The two walked in silence through the now-sparsely peopled market down to the lower levels. There, Roen replaced Ashish, the soldier dozing off on watch. Faust gave Ashish the evil eye as Roen settled in.

"Listen," he said, "I reviewed the parameters of the mission with Wuehler. My team is great at busting things but all this espionage stuff is French to us. My boys would rather level a building and just dig through the rubble for info. You're the closest thing we've got to a subject matter expert, so I'd like them to follow your lead."

Roen nodded. "I'll see what I can do."

Do what? You do not know the first thing about espionage.

"Either me or that crash of rhinos. Who would you rather do the sensitive work?"

That is a toss-up.

"Anyway," Faust continued, "You must be jetlagged. You going to be alright taking watch? If Wuehler catches you napping, he's going to raise all sorts of holy hell."

Roen grinned. "I'm an old pro. See you in the morning, brother."

Faust gave him a casual salute with a flick of his finger. "Hutch's got you at 0800. If he is a minute late, you tell me. I'll bust his balls. That guy tries to get away with sleeping in way too much."

Roen nodded. "Someone once told me that was a sign of a good soldier."

He watched as Faust disappeared into the safe house. Then he entered the guard nest feet first and pushed himself through until he was hidden in the shadows of a cubbyhole near the ceiling across from the safe house entrance. It provided him a decent view down the entire corridor. He checked the safety and the clip in the rifle Hutch had left.

"Tao, does it bother you that we aren't being utilized to the best of our abilities?"

Are you referring to the shock unit playing clandestine ops? I would not worry too much about it. Times are lean. Command must make do with what they have.

"Forget about that. I'm talking about being a super host and you an all-wise alien, and we're on guard duty."

I have heard that my presence qualifies you as a bona fide super hero.

"I heard that too, but my powers don't seem to be working. I must have a broken Quasing."

Broken? Please. More like my brilliant mind is bottlenecked by this weak and aging body. Oh, how I miss Edward.

This was always a source of contention. The Quasing often judged a host by comparing him to their prior host. Jill often complained about being compared to Sonya, and Tao did the same with Roen and Edward. Roen lived in the shadow of always trying to be Edward-good. The difference between Roen and Jill though, was that he embraced striving to be Edward.

"Come on, you told me I was as good as Edward ever was."

You told me to lie to you. So I did.

"You suck."

You are too old to be this insecure.

"Too old for a lot of things."

Roen shifted in his prone position. It was going to be a long couple of hours. He wished he had something he could lean against. His neck was going to cramp up at this rate. Now he wished he had eaten that banana the vendor was selling earlier. It took him the better part of twenty minutes to finally get comfortable. For the next few hours, he performed his duty until Hutch, twenty minutes late, finally relieved him. He let it slide, earning a little good will from the guy. By then, jetlag had taken over and Roen nearly didn't make it into the safe house room before he crashed onto a mattress in the back. He was asleep before his head touched the pillow.

CHAPTER FOURTEEN
GENJIX COUNCIL

Our mercy was scorned when we discovered the existence of the Chest of the Menagerie. To force Quasings into these small animals and trap them in these chests was inexcusable, a throwback to the dark times when we were nothing more than living mists surviving without thought. The betrayers again forced us to relive that nightmare.

I was the only Quasing on the Council to endure such torture. When Chiyva discovered the chest and freed me, we had no choice but to show the betrayers true Quasing justice.

Zoras

Enzo tapped his fingers in succession on the marble table in the solarium attached to his office as the weekly status meeting continued at a crawl. His eyes wandered outside and then back to the time: 11.04am. He should have finished his second jog by now. The meeting was running long and had cut into his daily workout. He bit his lip, reminding himself to tell Amanda to move this meeting to not affect important personal matters. Already, the responsibilities of this new position felt overbearing. The Hatchery had never trained him to handle such tedium.

Pay attention. These matters are important. You missed the last four results for P2.

"The fat scientist won't say anything new. There is little value in his drawn out ramblings."

Indeed, Chow's latest tepid update was identical to his last. All he probably had to do was change the date on the top of the report. The most recent test subject lasted an additional fourteen minutes, breaking the hour barrier. They were getting closer to creating an environment that could sustain Quasing life. Chow was optimistic about finding the right formula sometime in the second quarter. If he was successful, Enzo would almost be willing to overlook the blustering fool's many flaws. Then he could switch his focus toward the P3 catalyst.

And the sacrifice?

"What was the betrayer's name?" Enzo asked, after Chow finished with his update.

"Duc," was the reply.

Duc's influence with Earth was very understated. His host once piloted a plane known as the Enola Gay. *It was a momentous achievement for Prophus and Genjix alike, though they would argue otherwise. It was a large step forward for humanity's evolution. Your species matured that day.*

It was a routine now. Zoras made it a point to eulogize every Quasing that was sacrificed in those vats, making sure each Quasing's history was recorded. To Enzo, the deaths of the enemy were hardly sacrifices. And more importantly, history was told by the victor, so the only reality that mattered was who did the telling.

Do not let your arrogance temper your potential. Learn from the past to not repeat the same mistakes.

"Apologies, Zoras." The problem with a Holy One in your head was that they always knew when you were

disingenuous. Change and humility did not come easily for
Enzo. At the Hatchery, an Adonis wielded confidence as a
weapon, used to beat down the lesser Adonis. It took an
iron will and strong resolve to survive the Hatchery.

He had been raised his entire life to believe himself better
than human. And he was. Faster, stronger, more intelligent,
and more beautiful, Enzo was the highest rated Adonis
the Hatchery had ever produced. And now with Zoras and
unlimited resources at his command, nothing could stop
him. He was not overconfident. He just knew his abilities.

*Maintain pressure on Chow and make sure he is well supplied.
Shift your focus to the final phase. You will need to escalate the
process now that its end cycle is in sight.*

"Your will, Zoras."

Enzo interrupted Chow's rambling. "These progress
reports of their survival times are irrelevant. Report to me
only once a subject has survived twenty-four hours. How is
your supply of subjects?"

Chow nodded. "The new supply has been fortuitous,
Father. These updates further exemplify our progress–"

"Get me results, not updates," Enzo snapped. "You have
my authority to expend as many of the prisoners as you see
fit. Double the size of the shipments from Tibet if you need.
We have more than enough to spare."

"Your generosity is great, Father. On that subject, there
is a report regarding a missing shipment of prisoners from
Tibet. Our people–"

Enzo waved dismissively. "Security during transport
of the prisoners is Newgard's responsibility. I cannot be
bothered by this."

*All that touches you should be under your influence. Do not
separate authority from responsibility.*

"Your will, Zoras."

It is an important lesson you must learn if you are to grow your influence on the Council.

Enzo conceded the point. "Send for Newgard's report on the situation in Tibet and let him know I will not tolerate delays," he said. He scanned the others in the room. "Our focus now will shift priorities to Phase III. What are the current projections?"

The P3 focus was misleading. The truth was that the Genjix had been implementing P3 for almost a hundred years now. Bit by bit, ever so subtly, the Genjix had manipulated the planet to match their core requirements. The colder parts of the planet were being warmed, the polar ice caps melted, and the ocean ice layers thinned. The planet, blessed with an abundance of water, was slowly increasing in temperature. At nearly two degrees Celsius in a hundred years and exponentially climbing, Genjix scientists predicted they could increase the rate of its rising to within catalyst range in less than twenty. All the planet needed was another fifteen-degree erosion of the ozone layer before it could be matched with the specifications of Quasar. All the pieces were falling into place.

"How is the design of the catalyst coming along?" he asked, reviewing all the figures laid out in front of him.

One of the scientists in the back spoke for the first time. "We are ahead of schedule. Production of the catalyst sparks is contingent upon the ProGenesis formula. We can begin once the mixture is perfected. We estimate at the current tonnage output, forty-two catalyst sparks would be sufficient to kick start the cycle past the breaking point."

Jair, Guardian of Mustafa.

"Forty-two sparks to create paradise," Enzo murmured. He turned to the scientist in the back. "You are the lead scientist for Phase III?"

Mustafa nodded.

"Have you tested the catalyst alpha yet?"

Two have already been tested over Hiroshima and Nagasaki.

"Yes, Father," Mustafa said. "The process has been refined since World War II. We can initiate the same effect without the massive collateral damage the previous generation models afflicted on the environment."

Another scientist sitting in the back piped up. "Tests running in Pakistan and India have progressed well. The working prototype is close. When it is completed, we are confident there will be no explosion necessary for the catalyst sparks effect."

"Why couldn't we just modify the nuclear arsenal this world already possesses?"

"Current working models are inefficient, Father. There is too much collateral devastation and too little catalyst effect."

The planet is of little use to anyone if it is left inhabitable.

"Very well," Enzo said, closing the binder. "Moving on."

"There is an issue that requires your attention, Father," Mustafa added. "Several critical elements can only be sourced from refineries in America. Right now, trade regulations are hindering our progress. We are resorting to trade by proxy through Taiwan. It is hindering operations."

Enzo frowned. "Who is in charge of the supply chain from that region?"

Biall. His vessel Simon is a chief of staff to a senator in the government.

"Why is our blessed one in such a lowly vessel?"

Standing goes to the Quasing, not to the human. It should be the same with you.

That not so gentle reminder gave Enzo pause. He still had much to prove, and Zoras was letting him know that.

He nodded to those in the room. "Continue then. I do not need to stress the importance of your work. The Holy Ones' numbers have been dwindling since man's early days. If we are to usher in paradise, it is imperative we bring about the change they need. Do not fail."

The room of scientists bowed and cleared out. Enzo waited until they were out of his office before he closed his eyes and rubbed his temples. He had been working long hours ever since the incident at the dry docks. Even though he had captured all the Prophus, Zoras was infuriated by his tactics. Enzo was ashamed at having failed his Holy One. What he deemed a brilliant stroke of war, Zoras deemed a costly waste of his mandate. Since then, he had redoubled his efforts to serve the Genjix.

You reminisce on that encounter?

"I still feel shame, Zoras."

What is done is done. You have more important tasks at hand. We need to address the matter of the supply chain in the States.

"Why couldn't we just source the refineries on the mainland?"

Much of the catalyst must undergo a specialized refinement process only available in the States. It is then shipped to our trade hub in Taiwan for delivery to our facilities in China.

"Why not directly to China?"

There are fewer trade barriers between the United States and Taiwan. The States are more reluctant to trade rare militarized compounds with another superpower than with a small island who is a political ally. This workaround is bottlenecking our progress. Biall is working on removing these obstacles.

"Why are we still playing such a soft hand with the Prophus? Why was Operation Eagle Purity not put into play last year? From the reports I read, Father Devin had everything in place and was just waiting for the Council's approval."

Devin was overruled by the Council and ordered to stand down. With our near absolute power in the States, they deemed it an unnecessary risk. While Devin and I did not agree with the Council, we also did not fault their logic.

"Are the pieces of the operation still in place?"

Devin made sure Eagle Purity could be revived at a moment's notice. However, we cannot proceed without the entire Council's approval.

Enzo disagreed with the Council on the operation. Increasingly over the past few decades, they had erred on the side of caution. It felt good to know, though, that Zoras agreed with Enzo's assessment. He ordered Amanda to get ahold of this Simon. In less than a minute, a rat-shaped face appeared on the screen in front of him.

"Praise to the Holy Ones, Father." Enzo could tell Simon was nervous and uncomfortable.

"Simon, my son," Enzo began. He accentuated the word son. "My scientists here tell me they're slow to receive components from the States. That is your jurisdiction. What is the hold up?"

"Forgive me, Father," Simon spoke quickly. "Our legislators are slowly stripping away the trade barriers. Progress is slow and deliberate so as not to tip off the Prophus on the specifics. They have proven more cumbersome to remove than we anticipated. It shouldn't be long now."

Enzo gave Simon a steely look. "Delays are inexcusable, my son. Have it removed quickly, or we will resort to more drastic measures." He closed the channel before Simon could respond. The daily reports from the States, and the news generally, couldn't be much better. The entire country was practically theirs, but until then, there were still a few hoops to jump through.

Enzo thought they should stop playing these silly games and just seize the country. It would be a bold move, and there would be casualties, both political and in lives, but it was a risk well worth taking. Unfortunately, he did not see eye to eye with the Council on that matter.

We Genjix operate in the shadows. To attempt a physical takeover would raise our profile more than the Council is willing to risk. If Simon fails in his task, we can explore those options.

"Of course, Holy One."

Enzo left the solarium and went back to his desk. He had barely sat down when there was a knock on his door, and a young agent walked in. Enzo grimaced. The responsibilities of a leader never ended. No wonder Devin had so many heart attacks. "Speak."

"Agent Jacob Diamont, Father," he bowed again. "I have the latest surveillance report of the South Seas theater. A Prophus team has been dispatched to Taiwan. We detected them upon entry through Taipei but lost them once they were in the city."

"Do they know about the trade hub?"

"Unknown, Father."

An enemy team could wreak havoc on our operations if they are not stopped. Any delay is unacceptable!

"What is our response?" Enzo asked.

"A team is prepped and ready to depart. They can be on the ground within three hours."

"See to it." Enzo looked away from the young man and promptly forgot about him. A few minutes later, he looked up again. The agent was still there. "Is there something else?"

Jacob hesitated, and then stood at attention. "Permission to lead the intercept task force."

An unusual request. Enzo studied the agent and realized that he was an Adonis, albeit an unblessed one. He was a fair human specimen, built very much like Enzo, though younger and not fully grown into his body. His blond hair was cropped short, and he bore the presence of one given the blessing of the Hatchery.

"And why would you wish to lead such a team? It is hardly worthy of us."

The young agent fell to one knee. "The team that landed covered their tracks well. However, another lone Prophus agent was detected coming in a few days later. Surveillance monitors have identified him as Roen Tan. We believe he is rendezvousing with the main team. I wish to deal with him."

Roen Tan. That sounded vaguely familiar. Enzo recalled seeing it pop up a few times on scattered reports but the name was hardly important. A minor player most likely. He was definitely not high on the Target List.

"You are young and unblessed."

"I am seventeen, Father," Jacob replied stiffly, "recently elevated to the active ranks."

"Have you been assigned?"

"No, Father."

Enzo waved him off. "Far too green to lead a team, even for an Adonis. You should be spending your time seeking a patron, not wasting mine."

Jacob's face twisted in anguish as he walked right up to Enzo's desk. For a moment, Enzo thought he might have to beat the boy. "I beseech you, Father," he pleaded. "I have a debt to pay to this Roen Tan."

Enzo studied Jacob closely. There was a fire in his eyes he had not noticed before. "What did you say your name was again?"

"Jacob Diamont, Father."

Diamont? Is he related to Chiyva's prior vessel?

"Who was your Hatchery sponsor?" Enzo asked.

Jacob bowed his head. "Sean Diamont was my grandfather. I was to be blessed with his Holy One."

Roen Tan killed Sean Diamont. Chiyva was lost at Capulet's Ski Resort and has not turned up since. He is presumed to have been sent to the Eternal Sea.

Enzo smiled. "So you wish to hunt this Roen Tan for vengeance?"

"And for justice!" Jacob's eyes shone with desperation. "I beg of you, Father, from one Adonis to another, allow me my retribution for a Holy One lost."

Enzo approved of the fervor. The Holy Ones were best served through fanaticism.

An Adonis Vessel is too valuable to waste. The boy is young.

"We are Adonis. If I were he, I too would beg to retrieve the stolen honor of a promised Holy One. There is no greater sin that can be inflicted on us."

Enzo stood up and walked around the table, putting his hands on young Jacob's shoulders. "You have my blessing to lead the team. Fulfill your vengeance and I will see to it that your standing rises."

Jacob sank to one knee. "Thank you, Father. Blessings of the Holy Ones on you."

Enzo put his hand on the boy's head. "Bring me the head of this Roen Tan. You may still earn your Holy One." He watched as the boy bowed and left the room.

You are too prone to gamble.

"I prefer a man with a personal stake in his mission."

Judgments can be clouded.

"But efforts twice as strong, a trade-off I am willing to make."

What if he is not ready?

"He is an Adonis Vessel, Zoras. All we ever are is ready."

Enzo looked at his schedule and saw the rest of his day booked solid. He had to remember to warn Amanda not to override his workout times. While he had ordered her to keep at least four hours of his day open to the maintenance of his body, she always ended up double-booking and pushing his time for training aside. This was unacceptable, and Enzo would no longer put up with it.

He stood up and adjusted his suit. His next meeting was an important one. He walked around his office and stretched his limbs. The shock of such a dull office life was unsettling and his body, used to the rigors of the Hatchery, protested this new sedentary life.

You were bred to be a warrior and a leader, but a leader first and foremost.

"Of course, Zoras. I only wish to maintain this body for your use."

It is your mind I will wield as a weapon, not your body. Are you ready for this meeting?

Enzo nodded, straightening his jacket one last time, and went back into the solarium. He sat down in the center of the room and pressed a button on the table. The wall on the opposite end of the room shifted, revealing over a dozen large darkened screens. Then, as if on cue, each of them flickered on one by one, revealing the members of the Genjix Council. Enzo studied each Councilman as they appeared on the screens.

They were the most powerful Genjix vessels on this planet, yet they couldn't be more different. Chu on the left end was one of the youngest, barely a few years older than Enzo, yet he was being groomed to be a future Prime Minister of China. Vinnick, the Russian billionaire, had just celebrated his ninety-second birthday, and in between was an entire spectrum of humanity from diverse backgrounds. Reilly the American celebrity, Puko the African warlord, Chevaz the Mexican crime lord, Brennen the supermodel with a bestselling pop album in Europe. Enzo couldn't help but be a little jealous of Brennen. Her form of power seemed much more appealing.

Brennen is only a rainmaker and a peddler of influence. You control the destiny of all Quasing. Consider yourself blessed.

The much-delayed coronation of his rise to the Council was about to begin. Enzo held his stoic exterior, but inside, he was a jumble of nerves. This should only be a formality. After all, Zoras was the highest ranking among all of them. However, Enzo was the youngest vessel, so the results could be unpredictable. Still, it was the Holy One who held the seat, not the vessel. A few of Zoras' rivals might try to take advantage of this perceived moment of weakness and seize some of his power.

"Greetings, brothers and sisters," Enzo began.

"The child just called me a brother," Vinnick chortled. "I must commend my plastic surgeon."

Enzo bit back a sharp retort. They were testing him. "We are brothers in the only way that is important, Brother Vinnick," he began diplomatically.

"We shall see," Sugano, an electronics magnate proclaimed. "First, we have heard some disturbing reports regarding the reclaimed *Scimitar*..."

The meeting went downhill rapidly from there.

CHAPTER FIFTEEN
FIRST DATE

*The strategy of deploying the Chest of the Menagerie was a mistake.
We had thought our intentions of the menagerie humane. After all,
unlike the Genjix, the Prophus did not have control of castles and
prisons. The Chest of the Menagerie's discovery, however, enraged
the Genjix and escalated the war. After the Thirty Years' War
ended, the Prophus had been decimated and scattered to the winds.*

*Tao fled to the new world while I ventured south from the ruins
of the Prussian lands to Italy. It was there that I met Yol, who at the
time was hiding in a young philosopher known as Galileo Galilei.*

Baji

The putting-Jill-through-her-paces first date didn't happen
the next day. In fact, their first date didn't happen for an entire
week, though not for a lack of effort on Marco's part. Every
time she left her apartment or office, he was outside waiting
for her. And while he was gently insistent on this stupid first
date, he was so polite about it that she could weasel her way
out of it. She knew it was only a matter of time before she'd
have to give in. And it wasn't like she purposely avoided him.
She really meant it when she said she was busy.

You cannot avoid him forever.

"Look, I'm busy. Shit needs to get done."

You will hurt his feelings.

"Hah. Like that's even possible."

Paula finally called and gave her an ultimatum. Either she did what he asked or Paula would come and toss her in the car trunk. Jill grudgingly had to agree on the date. That Sunday, he called her at dawn and told her he was waiting downstairs.

Grumbling, she changed into her workout clothes and brushed her teeth. She looked at her makeup kit and thought about putting on her face. She wasn't one of those women at the gym who did that, but something about Marco made her feel exposed without at least something. She checked the mirror and noticed the tired lines on her face.

Stop stalling. The day will be long enough as it is without you blathering on about how you look.

Jill sighed. "I used to be so pretty."

You are still prettier than Roen deserves. Get this over with, so we can move on to some real work.

Marco was leaning on his car when she walked out of the building. He beamed with his pearly white teeth as he held the door open for her. "You look fetching this morning."

"You never turn it off, do you?" she said as she got into the car.

"Pardon? I have no idea what you're talking about," he grinned.

They drove thirty minutes southwest down 395 to Mason Neck State Park. During the drive, he entertained her with a steady stream of stories. He had one for everything. When he saw a duck, he had a duck hunting story. When he saw a

single engine plane, he told her about the time he crash-landed
his second Cessna – because it was important for her to know
which of his planes had the mishap – onto a frozen lake in Nova
Scotia. He had to outrun the cracking ice to shore. And when
they passed by a horse ranch, he talked at length about the
difference between an Arabian's gait as opposed to other breeds.
To her surprise, he admitted he had never delivered one.

Marco didn't seem like he was trying to brag. He was
just someone who lived on another plane of existence from
mere mortals. And with every tale he told, he had a moral
point to make, as if he were explaining to her what made
him *him*. She hated to admit it, but he fascinated her. He
was like an alien from another world and that wasn't taking
into account the actual alien in him.

"Who lives like this? I mean, really!"

*Old aristocrats live unlike mere mortals. They might as well be
from another planet.*

"And now he's working my security."

*You are moving on up in the world with such a distinguished
bodyguard.*

They reached the park, and Marco began to put her
through her paces. It started easily enough with basic
stretches. Then he took her jogging to test her cardio.

"Run as fast as you like," he shrugged when she asked
how fast.

There was something condescending about that tone in
his voice, so she did what he asked. She pushed the pace
to blistering six-minute miles. She experienced no small
amount of satisfaction when after the fourth, she wiped
that grin off his face.

"Tell me about Roen," he said, wheezing deep breaths
five miles into their run.

Here we go. This will be fun.

"Not much to tell. We're separated, and I've barely seen him over the past two years."

"Are you... aware of the small bit of unpleasant history we share?"

A molehill out of a mountain.

"Something like that," she said offhandedly.

Baji had already given her the lowdown on Marco and Ahngr. Ahngr was an active Prophus in medieval Europe. While Tao hated Ahngr, Baji and he shared a much more pleasant history. Jill was going to leave it at that but couldn't help herself. "I hear you and Roen went to war a few times in Egypt."

"Pardon my saying so," he sniffed, "but your husband has quite a chip on his shoulder. Hardly a war though, more a tiff. Ahngr and Tao had wars. What Roen and I had was nothing more than a disagreement among pack leaders. I must say, I had my concerns when Paula asked me to run your security detail. What kind of person would marry him, after all? However, I have been pleasantly surprised."

Something in Jill snapped. She had had enough of all this Roen bashing. Between Baji and her parents and now this near stranger, this was more than she could take. Roen might be an insensitive idiot, but he was her insensitive idiot.

She stuck a finger in his face. "Cut it out. No one bad-mouths Roen but me. We might be on the outs, but he's still my husband."

Ahem.

"You too, Baji. Honestly, I'm tired of everyone crapping on him. That's my job. I'll deal with him however I see fit. You'll have to learn to live with him because I say so."

There was a pause in the conversation as they ran up a

steep eight percent incline. They reached the apex and he finally capitulated, signaling for a stop. Jill gave him credit for keeping up this long. He bent over and sucked in large gulps of air. Jill felt lightly winded but was otherwise ready to keep going.

"You gave me quite a go there," he said, still heaving. "If that's your warm up, I would hate to see what your actual run looks like."

They took a break at the top of the hill. It overlooked a large forested area that continued up to the thin dark line that was Belmont Bay. The morning sky above that continued, turning progressively lighter shades of blue.

"I owe you an apology," Marco said. "First concerning Roen; he and I have our differences and naturally, you two being separated, I thought we would agree. I will refrain from referring to him in a negative light. Secondly, you are in much better shape than stated in the reports."

Man enough to apologize when wrong.

"Good trait for a guy."

"Apology accepted," Jill replied. "You don't swim 2.4 miles, bike a hundred twelve, and then run a marathon, and be out of shape."

"Of course," Marco conceded. "Let's move on to self-defense. How about a few rounds of fisticuffs, shall we?" He gestured to a small clearing.

Maybe you spoke too soon.

"God help me."

Jill cursed. This wasn't going to be fun. Her hand-to-hand combat training consisted of all of five weeks during basic and four years of Billy Blanks to techno music.

But God didn't help. The melee was short, brutal, and embarrassing. The first round, Marco treated her with more respect than she deserved. At first, Jill did alright. She had taken the required boxing classes, and her punches were crisp. He complimented her clean form. It was when he went on the offensive that she fell apart. She was too slow to block his attacks, and the round ended with a hip toss that left Jill writhing on the dirt.

Marco rubbed his chin and shook his head. "Unfortunately, you fight as well as I feared."

"What's that supposed to mean?" she demanded.

"You fight like a lady, which, by the way, is a compliment of sorts."

"Sure doesn't sound like it."

"It isn't really," he admitted. "Shall we go again?"

In the second round, things got worse. This time Marco put her through a series of tactical scenarios, gauging her response to attacks from behind, being tackled to the ground, and being put in a choke hold. She failed every single one. Even Marco looked discouraged by the end of the round.

Lastly, he tested her firearms skill. This she performed better at. In all the missions she'd ever run, not once had she ever had to throw a punch. She fired pistols plenty, though. She was also fond of the gun range and practiced regularly.

After two hours, Marco gave a frank and brutal assessment. "The good news is we won't have to work your hand to hand fighting. The bad news is, it's because you're basically helpless unless we put you through a yearlong program. However, your skill with a pistol is better than I expected and your accuracy is... average, which is again better than I expected."

"So I'm hopeless?" Jill's heart sank. She wasn't a fan of fighting anyway, but it annoyed her that he validated her ineptitude.

"I wouldn't say that," he said. "I just have a different plan for you. You don't have the strength or reflexes to match fists with the Genjix. That requires years of training. However, you are naturally quick and agile, and you can run like a gazelle. Have you ever heard of free running?"

I like his plan. It will work with your strengths.

"You mean like not running in a totalitarian country?" she joked. He gave her a blank look. Obviously, the humor was lost on him.

"I mean like this," he said. He turned and ran toward a large boulder that was at least as tall as he was. She gasped when he jumped at the boulder and somehow scampered to the top. Then he flipped off it gracefully, landing softly and somersaulting onto his feet. He continued running toward a tree and grabbed a branch as he ran past, flipping until he perched on top of it. Jill wasn't sure if she was supposed to clap.

"I don't understand," she said with a frown on her face. "You want me to do circus acts when I fight the Genjix?"

"No," he grinned, jumping down. "I'm going to teach you to slip away from danger and become a ninja."

CHAPTER SIXTEEN
THE SEARCH

The Quasing kingdom in Africa was immense. With our influence and the natural intelligence and hands of the primates, we gathered strength until we were many hundreds of thousands again. It was a far cry from the six million on the ship before the crash, but still a remarkable feat to have brought so many together.

The Council had grander ambitions, though. They wanted more, yet these primates were at the end of their evolutionary path. We could not advance further with them. It was then that several of our searchers returned with information about new species of bi-pedals, the Neanderthals and the Cro-Magnons.

Tao

Roen watched with a bemused expression as the barefoot old men in white undershirts played mahjong at the small table in the dimly lit room at the back of the warehouse. These four underworld bosses combined controlled twenty-seven percent of the docks, five percent of parliament, and sixteen percent of the chip market in Taiwan. What was even more amazing was that the bald guy on the left was blood enemies with the fat guy on the right. While both were part of the Bamboo Union, they led separate divisions that often warred over turf.

The fight between the Crane and the Tiger divisions had raged for twenty years now, yet these two still played mahjong together at least once a month. It went to show – either the Taiwanese were really good at keeping business and personal life separate – or good mahjong players shouldn't be killed because they're hard to find.

Contrary to the Genjix, the Prophus had no qualms cooperating with the criminal elements of human society. The Genjix never had any use for the triads, yakuza, Ordo Templi Orientis, or any other secret societies of the sort. They were considered too autonomous and difficult to control. In fact, it was the Genjix who were responsible for the destruction of several of these groups.

These conflicts made the triads a strange but natural ally of the Prophus. Over the years, they had forged a loose alliance with many of the underground groups, sometimes venturing as far as integrating them into the Prophus, as they had with the Hashshashins during the thirteenth century, or simply by keeping them at a wary arm's length, as with the Italian and Russian mobs.

The local connection the Prophus had in Taiwan was with the powerful Bamboo Union syndicate. Though weakened by Genjix expansion, the organization still held sway over the island and was involved in many aspects of Taiwan's society. The mahjong game the four men partook in was part of their monthly sit-down, during which the major players hashed out their differences. They must have had a lot to talk about, because they kept Roen and Hutch waiting over an hour.

Hutch, standing next to Roen, coughed and fidgeted with his jacket. Thirty-six gangsters, dressed to the nines, surrounded the small table, drawn guns half pointing at them and half at each other. Roen poked Hutch and gave him the don't-get-us-shot glare. The gangsters were already on edge. The last thing they needed was to see an anxious foreigner making sudden moves.

Sixteen behind you. Ten on both sides. All armed and probably awful shots. Four bosses in front. Oh, and you have Hutch, the narcoleptic guard. You got a plan to get out of this?

Roen swiveled his head to his left and counted the number of armed thugs wielding bats, machetes, and guns, and then he counted the ones to his right.

He shrugged. "I got nothing."

I find it ironic that you had a plan to fight your way out of Prophus Command, but not out of a triad warehouse. I am starting to doubt your loyalties.

"Or intelligence."

Or will to live.

"Or delusions of invincibility."

Okay. You win this one.

Roen and an increasingly nervous Hutch waited another twenty minutes for the four old underwear-wearing mobsters to finish their game. His faithful compatriot had taken to standing at attention as if he was in the North Korean army. Roen occupied the time by debating hypothetical historical scenarios with Tao. This debate in particular was what would have happened if Fanya Kaplan, a Genjix agent, had been successful in assassinating Vladimir Lenin. Roen believed that without Lenin, the communists wouldn't have unified to defeat the Mensheviks. Tao believed otherwise.

"No way Stalin could have wrangled them all together. He was just a jerk with a mustache back then. What's with all these warlords and mustaches? Maybe I should grow one."

Because looking like a Seventies porn star will make you a better agent.

"I'm just kind of bored of my face."

You should burn half of it off like Dylan. You would be much more interesting. Why are we discussing you again? I thought we were talking about Lenin. And, yes, having met Stalin, I believe he would still have consolidated power, though the succession might have been more bloody.

Their conversation was interrupted when Hutch nudged him. Roen looked up and noticed the four pajama-party men looking his way. The one in the far back beckoned them closer.

They are ready. I am going to tell you what to say in English first and then you repeat it in Mandarin.

"Follow my lead," Roen whispered as he walked to the table and bowed. The four maintained bored expressions as he presented a stack of half million Taiwanese dollars as a gift. Roen bowed again and took a step backward next to Hutch.

One would think they would be happy being presented free money.

"No kidding, right?"

The old man on the right picked his nose and then spoke in a clear voice. "It has been a long time since the Prophus has come to us. Our island has not seen your kind for many years. We thought with the Genjix's great power on the mainland, that you all were dead. After all, why have you not appeared to fight them?"

"Our enemy is your enemy, big man," Roen struggled with the broken Mandarin, "and we still fight to this day."

"A poor job then," the lazy-eyed man on the left said. "These Genjix have no sense of business. They are unwilling to negotiate, moving like locusts across our operations and listening neither to reason nor overtures. Beasts like them cannot be tamed, only put down."

They do not understand the way of the people.

Roen repeated the message.

"And it seems neither do the Prophus," the one with his back to them said. Roen decided to call him Bug Eyes because of his tremendously large glasses that covered half his face. Bug Eyes shook a finger at him. "The Prophus claim to be friends, yet when their enemies come and take our livelihood, they are nowhere to be found. Friends do not abandon friends."

Roen bowed again. "The Prophus beg forgiveness. The fight has gone poorly, but we assure you we still fight to the last."

Catfish Face, the one in the far back, waved the other three off. "Friends know friends are busy. The Prophus have been family for hundreds of years. You come with a request. What do you wish?"

At least one of the four amigos was on his side. Booger Picker and Bug Eyes seemed irritated while Lazy Eyes and Catfish Face were far more receptive. Roen first asked if any of the divisions had seen Dylan, describing his friend physically in less than flattering detail.

The syndicates should be Dylan's first contact for supplies. Guns were illegal on the island and the few safe houses here were not equipped with weapons, another victim of Prophus budget cuts. In the end, he received little actionable information, just like every other lead the team had pursued over the past two weeks. There were scattered rumors of a "burned snowman" that could only refer to Dylan, but there weren't leads behind those rumors. All the

WESLEY CHU   169

Bamboo Union bosses would acknowledge were sightings, be it two weeks or five days ago, at the illegal casino or market or docks, but nothing more. They almost seemed intentionally vague.

Roen knew the bosses were wary of dealing with the Prophus because they did not want to incur the wrath of the Genjix. The triads must have been hit really hard. All they wanted now was to lie low and wait things out. Little did they realize that if things continued this way, there would be nothing to wait out.

"We are seeking information regarding Genjix trade operations. Your noble organizations control much of the labor that works the trade in the airports and ports. Surely there is information you might share with friends," Roen pleaded.

"We have an arrangement with the Genjix," Bug Eyes remarked. "They made it perfectly clear what they want on this island. As long as we are invisible and do not affect their dock operations, we are left alone."

"Abandon markets the Genjix have an interest in and they leave you alone?" Roen muttered in English. "Doesn't sound like much of an arrangement to me. More like a full capitulation."

The four bosses' face darkened. Roen bit his lip and mentally rapped himself on the side of the head. Of course these guys understood English. They were forcing Roen to speak their tongue as a sign of deference.

That or they enjoy listening to you butcher their language. He did just give away information on the Genjix operation. There are a dozen major ports in Taiwan though.

"You speak without knowledge," Booger Picker growled. "What else do you wish to waste our time about? Otherwise, be on your way." He was openly scowling and went as far as to nod toward someone off to the side. He heard the snap of several safeties going off and Hutch's quick intake of breath.

You just do not know when to not improvise, do you?

Roen bowed again hastily. "I just mean that it is wrong of the Genjix to take what is yours without offering fair value. It is an injustice the Prophus will remedy soon."

He spent the next several seconds apologizing profusely, bowing so many times his back ached. Roen snuck a peek up at the group. Booger Picker was still scowling but Catfish Face nodded ever so slightly. At least he was getting through to someone. It was quick, barely an exchange of glances. Of course, they were hiding something. Something they didn't want him to know. The clues were slight and barely noticeable: a quick aversion of the eyes or a little hesitation in their voice. And then just like that, it was gone. Booger Picker abruptly ended the meeting with a dismissive tone, telling him any further questions would be a waste of their time. Bug Eyes even went as far as to admonish him for meddling in syndicate affairs and warned him to stay out of the southern part of the island, which he claimed was his jurisdiction.

Roen was tempted to swipe the half million Taiwanese dollars off the table and make a break for it. At the end of the day, Tao and approximately twenty automatic rifles talked him down from his brazen stupidity.

That is the difference between Edward and you. I admit that once you dedicated yourself, you were a fast learner and now could be Edward good. However, he was never foolhardy. Your old sense of self-preservation was one of your redeeming qualities. Now, I feel like I am always talking you off the ledge. You are not a comic book hero after all.

"If I were, I'd be Batman."

No, you would be Manikin.

"Ooh, obscure yet fitting reference. Bonus points for that. Are you the primeval goo or the ape-man?"

In this relationship, you would be the goo.

Roen and Hutch left the meeting pretty much empty-handed. If they weren't at a dead end now, they would be soon. The Bamboo Union had the widest network out of the gangs, so Roen had hoped they could provide a lead. Earlier this week, Faust and Jim had approached the two other large gangs, the Celestial Way and Four Seas, and had both came back empty-handed as well.

Roen stewed as they were ushered out by the henchmen. These guys basically just took his money and ignored him. He could see this kind of crap from the Russians or the Italians, but not from the triads. It was inappropriate for an Asian syndicate to act this dishonorably.

Calm down. It is what it is. Seventeen thousand will not break the bank.

"Tao, I lived on fifty bucks a week for food for the past eight months. Don't tell me I couldn't find a better use for that dough than give it to a bunch of millionaire gangsters."

As they turned the corner, one of the gangsters sauntered up next to them. Roen guessed by his suit that he was some sort of higher-up. The gangster leaned in and passed him a white envelope.

"Han Da-Ge offers a gift and asks your fathers to simply remember the Dragon division in the future in a preferable light," he nodded before veering off back into the shadows.

In case you are wondering, Da Ge Han was the one in the far back: Catfish Face.

Roen ripped the envelope and took out a crinkled piece of paper hastily folded. Tao translated the words. It was a standing order for all Bamboo Union members to avoid the large Genjix port operation in Kaohsiung harbor.

Southern tip of the island. Largest port city in Taiwan. That is the most solid lead we have received so far.

"At least it wasn't a complete waste of time."

A few minutes later, Roen and Hutch found themselves standing outside the old circuit board warehouse on the northeastern fringe of the industrial district of Hsinchu county. It was a balmy sitting-in-a-steam-bath night that drenched them both within minutes. Roen had never missed air conditioning as much as he did being here in Taiwan. The only other times he felt more suffocated by the heat was when the Prophus had attacked the Genjix thermal plant at the basin of the Erta Ale Volcano in Ethiopia, and the time he went to Disney World in Orlando in July.

Three minutes into their walk down several rows of darkened warehouses, Roen whispered to Hutch. "Tail to our five. Next intersection, continue north and east. If I don't find you within twenty minutes, rendezvous at the secondary site. Do not report back to the safe house. Oh, and walk slower." He waited until they turned left at the next intersection before splitting off.

Now, Roen wasn't worth much in the field of espionage. He couldn't turn the charm on like Edward could or become a chameleon like Sonya did when it suited her. These were just skills he had never developed. Tao often called him a Phillips screwdriver, a single-purpose tool that did one job well. That suited Roen fine because what he was talented at, he was now very good at.

Within steps of leaving Hutch, Roen had disappeared into the shadows and was soon perched on top of the low-hanging roof of one of the warehouses, watching the dark shadow that followed Hutch. He had a few seconds to position himself to set up the tail. Whoever it was would soon realize that he was only following one person now. If the guy was smart, he would back off. And when he did, Roen could follow him to something useful, hopefully.

He waited just outside the shadow's range of vision, skulking along the ledge. Roen saw Hutch strolling down the dark streets and cursed. With the way Hutch overplayed his part, any self-respecting spy would be able to tell something was amiss. However, whoever this tail was was not smart or self-respecting. He continued to follow Hutch.

Roen cursed again. "He didn't even notice he lost a guy. Damn amateur hour."

Well, so much for that. What is plan B?

"We wait. I want to see what he does once Hutch stops moving."

What if he kills Hutch?

"Hutch is not going to die at the hands of a two-bit punk who doesn't know when to abort a tailing mission. Besides, Hutch knows the guy is coming."

Roen continued tracking the shadow, moving from rooftop to rooftop. He didn't worry too much about being noticed. Whatever this guy's day job was better be stable, because he wasn't cut out for covert work. Roen had his doubts that Hutch, who was a smash-first-think-later kind of guy, wouldn't have eventually noticed him himself.

He did take the time to study the shadow though. He was a young man with an upper body disproportionate to his legs and was obviously military. It was evident not just by his build but by the way he carried himself. The casualness was too forced and the man's hands strayed far too often to his ribs, a sign of someone armed and trigger-happy.

Roen wondered if he was dealing with an especially inquisitive syndicate member tracking them or if it was the Genjix.

Hutch was now sitting on a bench at the intersection pretending to wait for the bus. Not exactly the brightest alibi considering the next bus wouldn't stop by in this remote area for eight or so hours, but the man was trying at least.

Remember your first tailing assignments?

"Hey, we all start somewhere, right?"

Some people's somewhere are much different from others'.

And then the espionage version of musical chairs – a game Roen detested – began. For the next fifteen minutes, Roen sat in the sweltering heat waiting for the tail waiting on Hutch to make a move. Hutch ended up waiting nearly thirty minutes for Roen. When Roen never showed, he stood up and walked along the river, the direction opposite of the secondary site.

Roen couldn't believe it; he wanted to tear his hair out. The dumbest thing Hutch could do was to lead a tail directly back to their safe house. The second dumbest thing he could do was be too obvious, and wandering in such a roundabout way, where he would eventually need to double back, fit that category.

For the better part of the next two hours, Roen tailed the tail who tailed Hutch as they made a merry scenic tour of the city, going from the warehouse district to the red light district to the downtown area. Twice, Hutch stopped to get something to eat; the first time at a noodle shop and the second for shaved ice. Roen's stomach grumbled both times as he sweated the night away, waiting for something to happen. Finally, at 2am, Hutch got to the secondary site. In a minute, he would go in, take the back room to the sewers, and hole up at a hostel across town before reporting back to Wuehler.

Roen followed the tail until dawn. By this time, he was so tired he didn't care where this damn guy went, but he stayed with it. What was another hour or two when he'd already done this for six anyway? The chase mercifully ended at a house on the far end of an affluent residential district. Roen was grateful. In his nearly all-black garb, he wasn't exactly dressed to blend in with the morning crowds. Satisfied, he took the information down and made a beeline back to the safe house.

CHAPTER SEVENTEEN
WORTHY SACRIFICE

The Prophus proved their appropriateness of their name by becoming traitors. True Quasing would not choose humans over their own kind. True Quasing would not value a servant over a master, an animal over a god.

After the Thirty Years' War and the incident with the Chest of the Menagerie, we began to treat the Prophus as true enemies. The mercy we extended them was no longer offered. We began to send both the vessel and Prophus to the Eternal Sea.

Zoras

The meeting with the Genjix Council did not go well. He had thought his handling the *Scimitar* and her crew would have cemented his status on the Council. Instead, they berated him on the concessions he made to Abrams. When he pointed out that he actually conceded nothing because he had cleverly manipulated the Prophus into breaking their word, they berated him even more!

They said his tactics stained their honor, that the price they paid was too high, and that the Prophus would never trust them again. Why should they care what the enemy thought of their honor? He retorted that there shouldn't be trust between them anyway.

His first meeting with the Council did not get any better from there. They accused him of brashness and of disregarding his Holy One. They said he was too young to understand the way the real world works and that their relationship with the Prophus was more complicated than technicalities. In the end, he was placed on probationary Council status. In six months, they would re-evaluate his position to see whether Zoras kept his seat.

They are correct. You did not listen as you should have. That is a common issue with vessels from the Hatchery. Many on the Council believe that your experience in such a sheltered incubator ill-prepares you for reality. I see that they are right. No amount of training can replace actual experience in command and combat. I will make a note of this and speak with Elder Mother regarding her wards' training.

"My results exceeded our goals. What more could you ask of me?"

Pyrrhus, vessel to Galen during the height of the Hellenistic age, won every battle he ever fought against Rome, yet lost the war.

"That wasn't the case at the *Scimitar*, though. We suffered fewer than thirty casualties. In return, we captured their entire force."

Your ruse will work only once. The Prophus will never trust you again. You, and more importantly I, will never be allowed to join diplomatic negotiations. That cost is far too high.

He had been hearing it non-stop from every Genjix vessel of note since the Council meeting. From the Council to Zoras to even Amanda, everyone had tried to steer him toward what they considered proper conduct for a Genjix of his standing. Well, he was having none of it.

The phone on his desk rang and Amanda's voice popped up. "Father, Abrams is here, as you requested."

Enzo was grateful for the change of topics. After nearly a week of dealing with the unbearable logistics of inventory, costs, and critical path project plans, dealing with what he had in stored for Abrams would be a welcome diversion.

"Send him in," he said.

He cleared his desk and pretended to be busy going over the delayed schedule for one of the Quasiform plants, code named Catalyst Sigma, as Abrams, pushed in on a wheelchair by a nurse and flanked by half a dozen guards, rolled in. Enzo continued studying the schedule, not bothering to look up at his prisoner.

Abrams had aged since Enzo last saw him. No longer possessing the noble bearing of Admiral of the Prophus fleet, he was now an old cripple who had to be fed intravenously through a tube. His body was a mass of bruises and his head was bandaged in a way that only exposed his eyes, nose, and part of his jaw. He looked tired and broken.

Finally, Enzo leaned back and acknowledged him. "I trust our accommodations have been adequate, Admiral?"

Abrams's head tilted up and down in what Enzo assumed was a nod. When he spoke, the words came out muffled, the bandages and metal wiring holding his jaw together inhibiting his speech. "I've had better. Genjix hospitality isn't what it used to be. Are all these guards necessary? Do you think I'm going to wheel myself to freedom?"

Enzo smiled. At least the old man still had his sense of humor. "For your own protection, of course. I assure you the medical staff is making every effort toward your recovery."

There was a moment of silence. "Why are you treating me? So you can torture information out of me? You're wasting your time."

Enzo laughed. "Please Admiral, we're not savages. I hold you in too high a regard to torture you. Besides, an old soldier like you? You wouldn't talk anyway."

"Then what do you want, boy?"

Enzo stood up and walked around the table. The nurse stepped aside as he grabbed the handles of Abrams's wheelchair and spun him toward the door. Enzo leaned in close to Abrams's ear. "You are healthy enough now to participate in a momentous occasion. You will go down in history as the human who saves the Quasing. Myyk should be proud."

"Myyk *is* proud," Abrams responded. "Though he is ashamed for Zoras."

Enzo kept his smile plastered to his face as he wheeled Abrams out of the building. Behind him, the nurse and guards followed. He leaned in close again. "What makes you think the Holy One isn't? We are about to accomplish something, you and I, that will mark a first among Quasing."

"I know Zoras, boy," Abrams said with disdain, "better than you ever will. He is harsh and totalitarian, but he knows honor. Something you know nothing of."

That stupid word again.

"Honor, like history, is nothing more than a thought, easily changed," Enzo said.

A few minutes later, they entered the ProGenesis lab. The room was a hive of excitement as scientists and techs prepared what was expected to be the crowning achievement of thousands of hours of research. Enzo wheeled Abrams in front of the glass vat and looked at the dark red swirling liquid inside.

"Myyk said it almost looks like home," Abrams remarked solemnly. "How many Quasings did you exterminate to get this far, Zoras?"

No sacrifice is too great.

Enzo repeated the words.

"And therein lies our differences," Abrams said. "I have known you for an eternity, my old friend. You weren't this way on Quasar."

Times have changed. We are no longer on Quasar.

Chow walked up to Enzo and bowed. "Father, we are ready to begin." Then Chow touched Abrams's arm and spoke in a gentle and respectful manner. "Myyk, I am saddened that we are meeting under these circumstances. Jikl has always held you in high regard. You once saved his host when Alaric and his hordes sacked Rome."

"Hardly a horde, Jikl. They were Roman-trained legions. Leave it to the father to lose control of his sons. There is a lesson there for all Quasing," Enzo said. "Besides, Seurot had also warned your host to leave the city."

"Then it is a lesson the Genjix have not learned yet. One day, when the truth of the Quasing comes out, none of us will be safe," Abrams added.

"The real lesson then is to make sure to always keep them in control," Enzo smiled. "Which we have done. Quite well if I may add."

Abrams snorted. "You can't control humanity forever."

Enzo chuckled. "We don't need forever, just a few more years."

Abrams leaned forward and put a hand on the glass. His eyes followed the swirling liquid inside. "So if you are successful, Myyk could survive in there?"

"We are fairly confident," Chow said.

Abrams nodded. "Then, in that case, just this time, I wish the Genjix success." He tore his gaze away. "I'm ready. Do what you wish."

Irritated, Enzo snapped at Chow. "Stop playing with the lobster before you cook him. You might get sympathetic. Proceed."

"Yes, Father." Chow bowed. He gestured to one of his assistants, and the young man wheeled Abrams away to prepare him for the experiment.

Enzo watched them leave; then he sat down in a chair directly in front of the vat and waited. "I do not like our people fraternizing with the enemy."

Our failure on this planet is that our conflict became personal. If it had not come to this, our progress might have been far greater.

"All the more reason to disdain the betrayers."

A few minutes later, Enzo watched as the crane arm lifted Abrams's cell over the vat. He clenched his fists in anticipation as Chow called for the final checks of Abrams and Myyk's life signs. The large Penetra scanner housed at the back of the lab hummed, its vibration rising until the sound was out of the ear's pitch. Then when all was ready, Chow looked to Enzo, who nodded. Chow barked out a few more orders and then the vat doors lifted open.

"Any last requests, Admiral?" Enzo called out.

Abrams looked straight at Enzo, his back arched and his head held high. He saluted with his remaining good hand. "May you all find peace in the Eternal Sea," he said, his muffled mumbling words still carrying across the room. "Please see that my family receives my body, and if the Genjix do prevail, have mercy upon this planet. We provided you a home when the Quasing most needed it."

A low rumbling swept across the room. Enzo scowled as he watched several of his people pay the old man respect. He had thought he was being magnanimous in his gesture. It figured even in his last moment, Abrams knew how to stick it to him.

You were not being magnanimous; you were being prideful. You are still young and prone to error. Learn from my wisdom if you wish to maintain your standing.

Then the squealing pitch of gears turning sounded, and Abrams's cage dropped into the vat.

Enzo got a sense of satisfaction from watching Abrams's calm demeanor betray him as the liquid poured over him. He opened his mouth and struggled, pulling at the bars as he sunk to the bottom. A few seconds later, Abrams let go of the bars and his body floated listlessly in the cage. There was a flatlining beep somewhere behind Enzo and then he heard the time of death called out. Then Myyk leaped out of Abrams's body and swirled around in the vat as if a young stallion stretching his legs. He swam around the vat like a glittering fish, moving much faster than any other Quasing that Enzo had witnessed inside before.

"Life signs?" Chow called out.

"Steady," was the reply.

Enzo stuck his face close to the vat. Myyk, who was near the surface, sunk down and met him on the other side of the glass. Enzo took a few steps left, and Myyk followed. When he stepped right, the Quasing came as well. Then Myyk's gaseous form began to blink in quick succession.

Enzo watched with concern and turned to Chow. "What's going on? Is something wrong?"

"Life signs are normal," Chow responded.

He is speaking to me.

"You understand him?"

Partially. It has been a long time since I have seen these patterns.

There was a strange edge to Zoras as he spoke, a hesitation that Enzo did not think the Quasing had. Every time Zoras had spoken to him, it was with an assured voice.

"What did he say?"

That is not important right now. Check his status.

Chow was already on it though. Myyk's life signs were on half a dozen screens, drawing information from the Penetra scanners. Everything looked steady.

"How long was the last test?" Enzo asked.

"Seventy-four minutes, Father," one of the techs piped.

Enzo walked back up to the platform and leaned forward on the railing. "Very well, then. Now, we wait."

Two hours later, Enzo had not moved from his spot.

CHAPTER EIGHTEEN
GIRLS' NIGHT OUT

Yol was another dissident who hid directly under the gaze of the Genjix. It wasn't until after his host had risen to high prominence that they discovered his true intent. Yol was working for the Prophus spying on the highest seat of Genjix power, the Papacy.

Unfortunately for the Genjix, by that time, Galileo was far too respected for them to kill. They did the next best thing and convicted him of heresy, sentencing him to house arrest for the rest of his natural life, no doubt waiting to kill Yol once Galileo passed away.

Galileo died at the age of seventy-seven. My host at the time was able to spirit Yol away, and we fled to the New World. We both operated in the maritime ranks for many years, until eventually, we both settled back down in Europe at the turn of the nineteenth century.

Baji

Jill met Paula for tapas and sangria at Bodega on M Street for a much needed girls' night out. Though this was technically an intelligence meeting, it was the closest thing she had to a relaxing evening. Between the mountain of deals on the Hill she was juggling and the new training regimen Marco had put her on, just talking about something other than politics and climbing walls like a monkey felt like a vacation.

They started the night sharing a pitcher of white sangria with small cuts of apples, oranges, and peaches floating on the surface. Appetizers were cold potato salads, marinated Spanish olives, and some delicious bacon-wrapped cheese. Jill helped herself to a little of everything. That was what she loved about tapas; she could order half the menu and not feel guilty about it.

"So, how are things with Marco? He's a handsome handful, isn't he?" Paula said as she sipped her sangria.

Jill furrowed her brow. Well, maybe something else besides politics, monkey climbing, and Marco. She was already seeing too much of him every day. Right now, he was drinking at the bar across the street, probably charming some unsuspecting Georgetown law student bedazzled by his perfect hair and King Tut chin. It's not that she minded him, quite the opposite actually. It was just that she had never ever spent this much time with any man other than her husband. And while Roen could cause a ruckus at times, he was a pretty low-key guy. Marco was up-tempo and the life of the party no matter where they went. It was draining.

He is unlike your husband in every way, which is a good thing.

"He's just swell," she replied as she pretended to pick at the fruit in the glass.

That is an understatement.

"That's it? He's swell?" Paula raised an eyebrow. "No other developments?"

"None worth mentioning," Jill shrugged. She changed the topic and slid a stack of papers across the table. "Here's where we're at with processed minerals. Here's the list of over one-ton shipments of processed rares. The United

States has a pretty small list of unrefined exports that can't be had more easily in another part of the world. The commons we can ignore since they can be had anywhere."

Just from this list: diamonds, platinum, and iridium from South Africa. Bauxite, thorium, hafnium from Australia. Palladium, samarium, and rhenium from Russia. Nothing in the States that the Genjix cannot obtain from a neighboring country.

"There's something," Paula talked with her mouth full as the first plate of patatas bravas came. She took out a sheet of paper and slid it to Jill. "Here's a list of Genjix-related industries on the eastern seaboard. Thirty-five are in manufacturing and refinement, fifteen are in electronics. Two are military."

"Can you get eyes on them to investigate?" Jill asked.

Paula shook her head. "Not necessary, nor do we have the manpower even if we wanted to. Ninety percent of them are redundant. China can build or refine everything those places can. The problem with the rest is we don't know what we don't know."

"I'll cross-reference these two lists against each other," Jill said. "Any word from our overseas network?"

Paula pulled out another stack of notes. "We've intercepted communications between Russia and China. They're screaming up their supply chain, escalating their grievances from the research bases to the ports to a neutral trade hub in a country friendly to Western countries. What that tells me is they need something on the restricted list with the United States and are smuggling it through a third party country."

It has to be a country friendly to both the United States and China.

Jill ticked off her fingers. "My guess is a port on the continent. Cut out the extra sea route."

Paula made a face. "That's a lot of countries that are friendly to both superpowers."

Start with the south Asia countries. The recent instability in the region is ideal for the Genjix to set up shop.

The two continued spinning theories as the waiter brought several more hot and cold dishes. They took a break from work and helped themselves to spiced pork bellies, Spanish meatballs, cheese croquettes, and bacalao fritters. That last plate they ended up placing triple orders of. Six more dishes came in rapid succession until they had fully gorged themselves.

Inevitably, they moved from white to red sangria, and the night dissolved into a psychotherapy session on Jill's love life, with Paula playing Oprah.

"That jerk left me while I was pregnant, jet-setting around the world on Tao's fool errand," Jill complained, draining her cup. "What kind of husband does that?"

"He thought he was doing the right thing for the world," Paula said. "He always arranged to have someone watching over you."

"What are you talking about? He was never there!"

Paula drained her glass and slammed it down on the table. "You know that conference you had in Paris last year? Roen pulled me away from Beerfest to watch over you. I was on vacation, and he made my entire team babysit you. I bloody love Beerfest!"

Jill picked at the fruit in her empty cup. "That was an economic summit. Why would I need protection? I had six Prophus with me."

Paula shrugged, pouring them both another drink and signaling to the waiter for another pitcher. "He doesn't trust anyone else to do the job. Roen's very protective of you."

"He has a funny way of showing he cares," Jill groused.

Paula looked exasperated. "You want to know how much he cares? Let me tell you. Stephen's been asking me to take over DC operations for years. I kept turning him down. Had my hands full keeping Europe from falling apart as it is. But three months ago, I took the job. You know why? Because Roen begged me to. Said he couldn't handle protecting you and working his leads at the same time. He begged me; hands and knees begged." Paula's words slurred as she clasped her hands together, shaking them back and forth. "'Please, Paula, come to the States and watch over my fool wife. They've got morons watching her back. There's no one else I trust!'"

That surprised Jill. "And you came? I didn't know you two were so close."

Paula shrugged. "Yol and Tao share a special bond. That makes Roen my brother."

"I'm glad Baji doesn't have that with Tao," Jill said. "That'd be weird."

"Has Marco charmed you into submission yet?" Paula asked.

"I don't know," Jill said. "He's dashing for sure, but he's constantly flirting, so I don't know if he's serious."

"He's so smooth you'll wake up in bed with him and be unsure how you got there," Paula chuckled.

Jill gave her a startled look. "You didn't. Did you?"

"Once, maybe three times," Paula admitted. "Well, I did work with him for five years. Can't keep up my defenses all the time."

"Why did you assign him to me then?" Jill said, exacerbated. "I don't need someone like him right now."

"He's still one of the best," Paula shrugged, "and I owe it to Roen to send you the best. Besides, Marco's not a bad person. He's just a man of loose morals."

And then something clicked for Jill. "You know, for a while, I wondered what it was I loved about Roen. And that's it. He's safe and he's sincere. I worry about a lot of things with him, but never his intentions. He's always been committed to me even when he does boneheaded things like follow Tao to the end of the Earth."

"You have him pegged right about that. He is boneheaded and will follow Tao into hell and back, but he is also committed to you."

"So again, why send me Marco?" Jill asked. "There's got to be other agents who are just as good."

Paula poured herself another glass of sangria and looked Jill squarely in the eyes. "Because I'm not daft enough to be completely on his side. You're your own woman."

That gave Jill a lot to think about, and for the rest of the night, Roen stuck in her head. He would never be as handsome or charming as Marco, and she would always have to share him with Tao, but she would always be his. Well, Cameron's also, but that was a plus. And while she faulted him for abandoning her, she knew that in his mind, no matter how wrong he was, he did it with them in mind. That night, after Paula had dropped her off at home, Jill crawled into bed and called her son.

"Hello?" Lee Ann's voice came across the other line.

"Hey Mom," Jill said in a small voice. "I know it's late. Is Cam still up?"

"Jilly! How are things leading the free world?"

Jill didn't have it in her to tell her mother about the situation. She choked up a little. "Good, good. Just wanted to say hi to my little man."

"We were about to put him down but he can stay up for a bit. Oh, by the way, Roen stopped by a few weeks ago."

Twinges of anger passed through her. It was his fault Cameron was thousands of miles away, and now he was able to see her son before she was? It was unfair. Still, he made the effort, and she would have been more disappointed if he hadn't.

She forced a chuckle out. "How did Dad treat him? I hope he wasn't holding any sharp objects at the time."

Lee Ann laughed. "Oh, he got the rifle out and was about to shoot him. He didn't, of course. You know your father. All bark and bad aim."

"How'd Roen look?"

"Looking a little haggard to be honest. I wonder what he's been up to. I tell ya, he actually looks pretty distraught about being away from you and Cam. What happened between you two? Why won't you tell me?"

Jill sniffled and wiped the tear trickling down her face. "It's complicated, Mom." She paused and regained her composure. "Can I talk to Cam?"

She heard some shuffling and then a squeal. Then a sleepy child's voice piped up. "Mamma?"

The waterworks began to flow down Jill's face. "Hey Cam Cam. Are you being a good boy?"

"Yes," he said. "Grandma gave me ice cream and Eva ate it." Jill laughed through her tears as her son told her the fantastic and exciting adventures of his day as only a three year-old could. It seemed that he and Eva had become best friends and best enemies, and the two waged a never-ending war over his toys. "And then Eva chewed the ear off of Pooples," he said as he finished the story.

"I'll get you a new teddy bear," she promised.

"I don't want another teddy bear," he protested. "I want Pooples."

"I'll have grandma fix it then," she paused. "Did you see your daddy?"

"Yeah," he said slowly. "Daddy looks dirty."

"Oh?"

"Yeah, he has dirt all over his mouth. I tried to wipe it off, and it pricked me."

Jill laughed. "Daddy's a porcupine?"

"Yeah, he's like a..." He struggled with the word. Then the line became quiet. "I miss you and Daddy," a subdued Cameron said. "When are you coming home?"

Jill almost lost it right there. For the next few seconds, it took everything she had to hold it together and to not break down. Finally, after a few deep breaths, she put the phone next to her face. "As soon as possible, Cam Cam. So tell me more about your day?"

For fifteen more wonderful minutes, she listened to him babble on about his life. She ended up promising to ask Lee Ann if Eva could stay with Cameron once he came back home. That would be a tall order to fill. Jill remembered her mother saying that she would rather give up Louis than part with Eva. But still, it was a wonderful way to end the night. She fell asleep dreaming of sleeping next to Roen and holding their son in between them. The war and all the dangers and trappings of it were a distant memory, at least for one night.

The phone rang sometime between when Jill's head hit the pillow and when she was supposed to be at work six hours later. It rang forever, and eventually, the incessant chirping penetrated her subconscious and slapped her awake. Jill was not a happy camper when she fumbled for the source of her disturbance on the nightstand.

"Yes," she mumbled, scowling at the clock and plopping her head back down on her pillow.

"It's me. Did I catch you at a bad time? You sound tired."

"I sound tired because you are calling me in the middle of the night. What do you want, Roen?"

"Just finished lunch. Wanted to check up on you. So... what's up?"

"Did I mention it's the middle of the night?" She rolled her eyes. What was wrong with him?

The concept of Greenwich Mean Time escapes him. And why is he chit-chatting? He hates small talk.

That was true. Hell, Roen hated talking on the phone. He must either be worried or wanted something from her. As much as she hated to admit it, he could be cute when concerned.

"So how are things with Marco?"

Ah, of course.

Jill shot up into a sitting position. "Is this why you called? To check up on me and Marco?"

There was a pause. "No." Another pause. "Of course not."

"It is!" Jill's grip on the phone tightened. "Well, he's fine. In fact, he's more than fine. He's a pretty terrific guy!"

"You don't have to lie just to be mean to me." He sounded sullen.

This made Jill's blood boil even more. "No, I mean it. He's nice to me. He opens the door for me. He calls me pretty. All the time, Roen. All the frigging time!"

"That asshole! I'll kill him!"

"No," Jill hissed. "That's nice. I like it when a guy says I'm pretty. Now, is there something you want or are you here just to ruin my sleep?"

There was another long pause. She could tell that he was struggling to keep his voice steady as he swore at someone away from the phone, presumably Tao. He had that habit when he lost his temper.

Finally, he got back on the line. "Actually, we have a lead. There's a Genjix op in the Kaohsiung province of Taiwan. It's a massive harbor though, and too large for us to reconnoiter. Can you cross-reference the port with known Genjix companies?"

A Genjix trade operation in Taiwan? We assumed all the major ports would be on the main land. We have been looking in the wrong place.

Jill was wide awake now. "That's a bit broad. It'll take some time. Any luck with Dylan?"

"Not a clue. Been poking around the underbelly of the island. For a guy who sticks out like a sore thumb, he pulled off an amazing disappearing act. Can you check for me? I don't want to direct my team down there without getting some intel first."

"Sure," Jill got up and threw on a bathrobe. She was all business now. "I'll dig around and get back to you." She paused. "And take care of yourself. Cam still needs a father."

"Don't worry about me, hon. And you tell that dick Marco that if–"

Jill hung up the phone.

"Baji, how're the trade barriers in Taiwan?"

They are an ally of the United States. Barriers are negligible. This could be a major development. Dylan might have stumbled onto the Genjix's workaround to the sanctions.

Jill went to the living room and rummaged through several of her files. Twenty minutes later, after skimming through a large stack of US Department of Commerce reports, she jotted down several notes regarding the trade policies and programs, as well as companies that traded heavily with Taiwan that had suspected ties to the Genjix.

"There are hardly any trade restrictions with Taiwan. It's an open door."

The Genjix must have infiltrated the island after we pulled out. This could be our trade leak. We have been looking in the wrong places all this time.

She checked the time and called up Tammy, ignoring her assistant's groan of indignation as she ordered several more reports prepared by the time she got into the office. Then she set up an appointment with the Deputy Assistant Secretary of Trade. If the trade list was expanded to Taiwan, Japan, and South Korea, there was suddenly a frightening list of materials that could pose a serious threat to the Prophus after all.

CHAPTER NINETEEN
AMBUSH

I was in the first wave sent to test these new evolved creatures. Several hundred of us migrated our primate hosts into their valleys and joined Cro-Magnon tribes. Another wave was sent to various Neanderthal tribes. It was then that I realized the potential of this new species.

To this day, an argument still rages about whether the Neanderthal or the Cro-Magnon was worthier of being raised. Make no mistake; it was the Quasing who raised your forbearers. We were your evolution. That decision, though, did not come without conflict.

Tao

That is your third bowl. Stop eating.

"You know what, Tao? I have a new rule. As long as I have a six pack, I can eat as much as I want."

You have not had a six pack in four years. And when you did, you kept it for less than a week.

"You know what, Tao? As long as I have a four pack, I can eat as much as I want." Roen reached out with his chopsticks and picked up a piece of blood pork sausage for emphasis. This stuff was damn good. Over the past three weeks, he had learned the secret of cuisine on the island. The people of Taiwan cared little for aesthetically pleasing food. Half the stuff he'd eaten looked downright indigestible – stuff that Jabba the Hutt ate. The other half looked like it would leap off the table and eat him. After the first week, he had overcome his fear of ugly food and now tried every morsel of Taiwanese food he could get his hands on. He was rarely disappointed.

We did not come all this way for you to could dim sum your way to obesity again. When this is all over, you are going back on the regiment.

The consensus was that Ahfu was best hole-in-the-wall restaurant in all of Taipei. Roen knew that to be a fact because there was a sign in front of the restaurant declaring just that. And after discovering this little gem in a side street off the market and eating three meals a day there every single day, Roen wholeheartedly agreed with the assessment.

The restaurant was in a rickety wooden building that defied gravity just by standing up. The walls were a patchwork of metal, wood, and flaking paint that probably violated a dozen health codes. But the dumplings were delicious, the taro puffs were spectacular, and the sesame balls were... Roen had no words to describe how good they tasted. There was this sticky rice wrapped in khaki green bamboo leaves that could cause world peace.

You can start your new job on the Food Network another time. We have work to do.

Roen reluctantly agreed. Faust and Wuehler sat across from him at the wobbly table. Faust had discovered this gem of culinary mastery with Roen, and the two single-handedly kept the place in business. At first, Wuehler objected to planning in a public place. Then he tasted their pork buns. Now, he held all their meetings here. Today, they had the restaurant to themselves except for an elderly woman sitting in the corner drying bamboo leaves on a small line hanging from the wall. Roen suspected she lived in the back, seeing how she was there every time they came.

"Taipei's a dead end," Faust was saying. "Almost a month; not a trace. Not one hit at the other safe houses and nothing from the locals." It was shocking that Dylan had somehow not registered a blip here. Roen was now entertaining the possibility that his friend had died. "You'd think he'd meet up with one of our established contacts," Roen mused.

"Except one's dead, one is senile, and the last one is a double agent," Wuehler remarked. "I wouldn't risk those odds either if I were him."

"Wait, we've got a double agent on the payroll? Why are we putting up with this? Hell, let's go take him out." Roen complained with his mouth full. "After dinner, that is."

"Because the others are dead and senile," Wuehler repeated.

We have too few eyes on here as it is. Better to receive information we don't trust than to receive nothing at all.

Roen shook his head. "I make minimum wage, and we're paying double agents? We need to vote in fresh blood in Command."

Faust raised an eyebrow. "I didn't know we were a democracy. In that case, I'd like to be Secretary of Transportation. My campaign motto will be 'No more flying coach.'"

Roen gave him a thumbs up. "Got my vote there."

Wuehler threw up his hands. "Do we have any leads at all?" His frustrations would have seemed more impactful if he didn't have a pair of chopsticks in one hand and a steamed bun in the other. "What about the escape pod debris? Anything worth sifting through? They did find one intact."

Faust shook his head. "Quarantined by the police. The closest Ashish got to it was two hundred meters when they dragged it to shore to repaint."

"Why would they do that?" Wuehler frowned.

Faust grinned. "I believe that escape pod has been officially drafted into the Taiwanese navy."

"Maybe if we redirect our focus away from Taipei..." Wuehler said.

Roen, blond-haired man in dark sunglasses just passed by three times in the past two minutes. Confirmed visual on you every time.

An image of a young familiar-looking guy wearing a brown leather jacket popped into his head. Flanking him were two others in similar attire. Roen had seen his share of operatives to detect the forced casualness in their demeanor. These were apex predators about to spring in for the kill. He slowly put up a hand and cut off Wuehler mid-sentence.

"Go hot," he mouthed. "Out the rear."

Faust and Wuehler, with their backs to the entrance, followed the order without question. They slipped their hands in their coats and clicked their safeties off.

Wuehler nudged Faust with his elbow. "Get on the comm. I'll go first."

Faust nodded as Wuehler lazily stood up, stretched, and strolled toward the back exit.

"You next," Roen said.

Faust shook his head. "Not leaving a host to cover our rear. Get going."

"I got the visual. You go. That's an order."

Faust hesitated before standing up. Roen heard an "I outrank you" as he walked past. Just as Faust left his line of sight, he heard four sharp pops in the air behind him.

Different barrel signatures. Not a one-sided exchange.

Immediately, Faust sprinted toward the back. Roen overturned the table and ducked behind it. The blond kid and two men suddenly appeared, spraying bullets through the entire restaurant.

Full automatics. You are outgunned.

"You mean my peashooter doesn't do thirty rounds in four seconds?" Roen peeked over the edge of the table and returned fire. He grabbed one of the table legs and pulled it with him as he retreated. Behind him, he heard the two-tone popping exchange again, soon joined by a third. Faust must be getting in on the fun. In front, Blondie's two friends were at the sides of the entrance laying suppression fire while he stood behind them with his arms crossed over his chest. There was something serial killer eerie about the kid.

Stay near the side flank. Civilian on your right.

The old lady screamed and she tried to crawl toward the kitchen on all fours. The Genjix were spraying fire indiscriminately through the entire restaurant. The stupid woman was actually moving toward the crossfire! Roen peeked over the side again and was rewarded with an exploding splinter that nearly took his eye out.

Leave her. You will only draw fire to her.

Roen cursed. Tao was right. He began to drag himself toward the exit when he caught sight of the old woman pleading for help. Roen swore again. There'd be no way the big guy in the sky was going to let this one slide if he left grandma out here like this. He took a deep breath and unloaded his clip at the one of the guys in the entrance.

Once they retreated behind cover, he leaned out, grabbed her by the collar, and yanked her behind the table like a rag doll. A fresh hail of wood splinters exploded around them. A jagged seam appeared down the middle of the table. This thing wasn't going to hold out much longer.

After all these years, you still listen like crap.

Roen motioned for her to stay low. The table was quickly being whittled down into firewood. He had to draw their fire. Roen waited for a good time to jump toward the door but the gunfire didn't let up. Then, a voice called out to him.

"Roen Tan, Come out!"

Roen perked up. He peeked over the jagged edge and saw Blondie stride into the restaurant without a care in the world.

"This kid must be mentally challenged."

Or overly confident. Reminds me a bit of you.

"He must be really good then."

Or just stupid. Like I said, reminds me of you.

"Roen Tan," Blondie repeated. "I have waited a long time to finally meet you."

"How did you find me?" Roen shouted. "Let me guess; you love the dumplings here too."

Blondie smirked. "You're not as good as you think you are. My men followed you after the meeting with the Bamboo Union."

The one following Hutch must have been a lure!

Now, Roen took pride in tailing targets. He was very good at sneaking around, staying hidden, and following someone without being noticed. That skill, however, was far different from detecting targets. In that respect, Roen was only passable. So the tail he did find on Hutch must have only been a decoy to draw Roen out. He had fallen for their trap and led them right to his doorstep! Roen cursed his own stupidity.

"You are pinned down and my men have both exits covered," the kid continued. "I am offering you a chance to live."

Roen forced a laugh. "You think I'm going to surrender? Get a grip, junior."

"Oh, I don't expect you to surrender. I expect you to take my offer for a fair fight. No weapons. Hand to hand. To the death. If you win, my men let you go. If you die, well, you were going to die anyway."

I do not like it.

The offer sounded too good to be true. Who did this kid think he was? Miyamoto Musashi? He didn't even look old enough to shave yet. Roen could admit he wasn't the best fighter in the world. In his book, Lin held that title, but he'd like to think he'd take the bronze.

About that overconfidence thing…

Roen slowly stood up, hiding his pistol behind the shattered remnants of the table. "Why are you offering me this?" he asked. "Selling life insurance too?"

The kid's mouth curled into a sneer. "My name is Jacob Diamont."

Roen shrugged. "And that means what?"

He was rewarded with pure rage on young Jacob's face. That alone was worth the price of admission. Looking at the boy more closely, Roen noticed something familiar about him. Sean Diamont's face had haunted Roen for years, that fatal night playing over and over in his nightmares. Most of Jacob didn't resemble Sean, except those eyebrows. Those were definitely Sean's eyebrows. But where Roen saw most of Sean in this Jacob kid was that smirk. And the nose maybe. The nose and those eyebrows and that smirk.

Interesting.

"Think I can take him?"

He is half your age.

"That's what I'm worried about. At least I have a weight advantage."

"So," Roen said. "I put down my gun, and you put down yours, and then we try to kill each other like civilized men?"

Jacob raised the pistol in his hand, and then let it go. Time slowed as Roen's eyes trailed the falling pistol. Another old memory he had long buried crawled back up his consciousness. Sean once offered a similar deal and had dropped his gun. Except when Roen had put down his gun, Sean murdered Abdul and Sonya. The pistol clattered as it bounced off the concrete floor. Roen gave that smirking Jacob one look and wanted nothing more again than to wipe it off his face. He raised his pistol and fired.

Roen had to admit; young Jacob was good. In the split second that Roen pulled the trigger, he closed the distance between them, blocked the trigger pull with his finger, and kneed Roen in the abdomen, followed by a left cross to the chin. In other words, he kicked Roen's ass and did it really fast.

Highly skilled shotokan movements. Fast. Leads with left.

"You mean that punch to my face was his weak hand?"

Afraid so.

"Crap. I am in so much trouble."

That would be the logical conclusion.

The kid was nearly as fast as Lin, though Roen could tell his speed was more a function of youth and talent than technique. Not that it made a difference to the end result. Roen ate two more punches to the face, and a kick to the ribs knocked the wind out of him. He collapsed on the ground.

"You beat grandfather?" Jacob snarled. "I don't believe it."

"He didn't believe it either when I killed him," Roen shot back.

That earned him another whack to the face. However, this time, Roen was ready for it. Like many younger fighters, Jacob was easy to goad and liked to headhunt. Roen caught the punch, wrapped both legs around Jacob's torso, and scissored him. Jacob crashed to the ground, giving Roen the chance to give a little payback with his own elbow to the face.

Now get out!

Probably a smart decision with Jacob's men nearby. Roen scrambled to his feet, grabbed his pistol, and darted out the back. Another eruption of gunfire zinged past his head and he felt the heat of a bullet cut through his hair.

Take your own advice and stay low. Your brain is not much, but I cannot accomplish anything without it.

"I can't believe how fast he was."

Better hope you do not meet again.

"I am never that lucky."

Roen sprinted through the kitchen, past the terrified cooks, and out the exit where Faust and Wuehler were pinned down behind a dumpster in a narrow alleyway.

"What took you so long?" Wuehler yelled.

"We have bogies coming out here shortly," Roen said, reloading his pistol.

Faust nodded and motioned for them to retreat. "You hosts get out of here. I'll cover."

"Like hell," Roen growled, taking his turn on the firing line just as Faust ducked down to reload. A symphony of sirens began ringing in the distance.

Assume local authorities are on their side.

"Why can't we ever assume they're on ours?"

Because they rarely are.

"Where does the back of this alley lead to?"

Splits fifty meters back. Take the left until it curves and then another left.

Roen grabbed Faust by the collar and forcibly pulled him back as they retreated. He signaled to Wuehler to go left at the end of the alley as they sidestepped the clutter, hurdling debris and carts as if they were on an obstacle course. Taking up the rear, Roen toppled refuse and pushed dumpsters to block the path. For a second, he thought they might have escaped and thrown off their pursuers.

"Did you get word to the team?" Wuehler asked.

"Hutch's stowing the gear now. Ray's mobilizing the rest for an intercept."

It is too dangerous. Send them to the second safe house.

"Too hot," Roen yelled. "Eight more guys aren't going to make a dent here. Send them to the second site. We'll meet up with them."

"We have two hosts here!" Faust snapped. "You two are the priority."

"It's a direct order from Tao," Roen replied.

"Ramez concurs," Wuehler added.

Faust gave them a disgusted look before getting back on the comm.

They reached the end of the alley, which opened to a busy street. The sound of the sirens was getting louder. With the docks to the north and their pursuers to the south, they had little choice.

"Push away from the team," Wuehler was saying. "Second site is to the east. We'll circle around; give the guys a chance to sneak out with the gear."

Roen nodded. Wuehler might be a dick, but he always thought of his men. They scampered across the intersection and entered an even tighter alley, forcing them to move single file. Twenty meters in, Roen heard a shout. He turned and opened fire, taking out two uniformed police officers. He hoped they were actually corrupt and not innocent men just doing their jobs.

Unfortunately, with the Genjix having much deeper pockets, more often than not, they had already bought the local government. The Prophus just couldn't afford to buy influence anymore. The United States and Great Britain were the only two countries they still had significant pull in, and even there they were losing ground. Before long, they would become an entirely underground group.

"Up top!" Faust said, pointing to a ladder attached to the side of a three-story building. The ladder was barred by a small gate locked by a rusty padlock. Roen shot the lock and gestured for Faust to get a move on. Faust shook his head. "Hosts first."

"You're a goddamn broken record!" Roen pushed him to the ladder. "Just get up there and cover us!"

Wuehler and Roen stayed at the base of the ladder as Faust reached the top in a matter of seconds just as Genjix agents appeared. He began to lay down suppressing fire.

"Age before beauty," Roen said to Wuehler, pointing up.

"Yeah so what are you waiting for? Get going then!" Wuehler shoved him to the ladder. "That's an order."

"What is up with everyone not wanting to go?" Roen snapped and began to climb. All around him sparks exploded as bullets banged against the metal grate covering of the ladder.

He was about a third way up when Wuehler called out from below. "You're right, Roen."

Roen looked down. "What?"

"Beauty does go last" Wuehler smirked and emptied another clip. At the far end, a Genjix agent went down. He holstered his pistol and climbed after them.

And who says he does not have a sense of humor.

"Strange time to show it."

Roen reached the top and took position opposite of Faust. "I'm down to two clips," he yelled.

"Last one," Faust replied. "There's rocks up here we can throw down."

Wuehler was halfway up the ladder. Roen had eyes on five enemies, though there were bound to be more incoming. It was a good thing the alley was so narrow or they would have been easily overwhelmed. Wuehler was about two thirds up the ladder when he suddenly flinched. He wavered and then plummeting back down to the ground.

"No!" Faust jumped back on the ladder.

"Don't do it." Roen grabbed Faust by the shoulder and neck and pulled him back onto the roof.

Faust struggled in his arms. "We can't leave him!"

"There'll be twenty guys down there in fifteen seconds. This building will be surrounded in two minutes. If we're not out of here now, it's over. Let's move!" Faust's face twisted with frustration before he finally nodded.

Continue west deeper into the slum two roofs over and into the building. It is residential with many empty units. Hide until aerial surveillance is gone.

"I think staying is a mistake. We should continue west and get as far away as possible."

I study for every contingency while you sleep. How do you think you have stayed alive for so long?

"Fine. Thank God one of us does."

Ten minutes later, Roen and Faust watched from a fifth story window of a half abandoned apartment building as dozens of uniformed police officers milled around the streets. He counted twelve Genjix. The young psychopath was obviously the one in charge of the entire operation. He was furious they had escaped, shouting orders at both his men and the police sergeant in charge. One interesting thing he noted was that the boy didn't speak Mandarin or Taiwanese but American English, with a faint New England accent by the sound of it. The kid was a ringer from the States.

They stayed hidden and surveyed the activity. The Genjix had turned the street into their base of operations. Roen recognized two hosts among the Genjix while Faust identified three of their commandos. It was another shock unit, one that he had dealt with in the past.

Roen and Faust tensed when two police officers dragged a hooded figure toward a van. The hooded figure, arms handcuffed behind his back, walked with a bad limp. As he got near the van, half a dozen of the Genjix closed in around him.

Faust immediately got on the comm, recalling men to the area. Roen had only to glance out of the window to know that Faust's plan was a terrible idea. Improvising a rescue operation against these odds was suicidal. They had better odds stealing from a Vegas casino. The local police being involved just made this entire island a death trap. The only thing that would come out of the rescue attempt was ten more body bags.

You have no choice.

For the second time in an hour, Roen was whisked back to that night at the helipad when he had had to shoot

Sonya. He remembered her final words as she told him to kill her. He had tried to bury those memories, but now they came rushing back. Roen felt a chill wash over him as he leaned against the window.

"I can't do it again."

You must. I am sorry.

"We can rescue him! Just like we did with Jill and..."

Roen couldn't finish the thought. Actually no, they didn't rescue Sonya. Her life was taken from this world by his own blood-washed hands. He killed one of his best friends, and she thanked him for it. All this a sacrifice for the Quasing, because their lives were more precious than a human's. He had vowed afterward that he wouldn't do it again.

The painful truth was, this was the right call. The situation was different last time. He had the entire strength of the Prophus at his back when he had tried to rescue Sonya and Jill. And still he had failed. Now, with only a ragtag group of exhausted men, they had no chance. Wuehler was as good as dead. And with him, Ramez. Unless he did something right now.

Roen looked over at Faust. "Abort. Call the dogs off."

Faust paused mid-sentence. He scowled, turned his back to Roen, and continued giving orders. Roen swiped the comm from Faust's hand and turned it off. Faust drew his pistol and aimed it between Roen's eyes.

"I'm the second. I'm in charge," he snarled.

"You know it's a lose-lose situation. You're not sending our guys to their death." Roen paused. "We have one option."

For a second, Faust looked like he was about to pull the trigger, then he slammed his pistol into the drywall. "Damn!" he screamed.

Roen put his hand on Faust's shoulders. "We don't have much time. You were his guy. I think you should do it."

Faust shook his head. "That's a long shot for a pistol. I'm not comfortable at that range."

Roen gritted his teeth and glanced out the window. It was a very long shot. He wasn't sure he could do it either. Wuehler was almost to the van. If they didn't get a shot off in the next few seconds, Ramez was lost. Roen didn't want to be the one to do it, but it seemed they had no choice.

Roen pulled out his flashlight and handed it to Faust. "When I get the shot off, I want you to flash it on and off at the street for five seconds."

"Why?" Faust asked. "Won't it just call attention to us?"

Roen took aim at Wuehler's head. "Yeah, but Ramez will see it too. I hope you can recover fast from a transfer because we're going to have to make a break for it while you puke your guts out."

CHAPTER TWENTY
OUT OF SUBJECTS

Control of mankind is a simple theory, yet complicated in practice. Like most primitive but sentient beings, they seek to understand what is beyond their grasp. That is the void that the Genjix fill. That is why it is fitting that, for over a thousand years, we assumed control of humanity through the Papal States. The rule of Rome is shrouded in irony and truth.

Zoras

"Time of death: 21.17."

Enzo stared at the corpse floating in the vat. They were close. It had been five days since they sacrificed the annoying old man. When Myyk's life signs had hit the six hour mark, Chow had declared the test a success and popped the champagne bottles. Enzo had reported his accomplishment to the Council, telling them that they were moving on to the final phase.

Word had spread like wildfire that Enzo's project had successfully created a functioning habitat. The next logical step was procreation, something that had been impossible on this planet until now. Initially, there was a surge of

Quasing volunteers for the next step. Every Genjix not vested in their vessel wanted to partake in the experiment. It was a historic event after all.

However, during the second test, Myyk's life signs faded, and Chow had the unfortunate job of notifying Enzo during breakfast. The failure leaked, and within hours, the volunteers had disappeared. It made Enzo look foolish. Receiving the smug looks of disappointment on the Council's faces was one of most humiliating experiences he'd ever had to endure. He passed his anger and wrath onto Chow and his team.

Since then, Enzo had not left the research lab. For three days now, he worked Chow's team around the clock, and short of actually carrying a whip, pushed them as hard as he could for results. There were now seven vats being experimented on at all times as the scientists tweaked and synthesized the formula. Seven formulas. Seven vats. Seven Prophus test subjects being sacrificed continually. Each formula was varied only slightly. Just like the mix of air for humans must be perfect, so too must the synthesized environment for the Quasing. They burned through subjects at a faster rate than could be transferred from the internment camp. Enzo didn't care though. He wanted results and his pride would not be satisfied until he got them.

"Life signs in four are fluctuating," one of the techs called out.

Enzo's eyes darted to four, just glimpsing the Quasing inside spasm, his membrane expanding and contracting in a desperate jerky way. This scene was common now. An hour earlier, vat two's subject had had the same reaction. Six hours before that, vat one actually exploded.

"That's it," Chow yelled. "I want that entire strain shut down."

Enzo waited until the beeping sound of the subject's life signs became a steady tone.

That subject's name was Hume. I have never interacted with him, and he was never a Quasing of importance, though in his confession, he said one of his vessels invented the Hittite method of wool dyeing.

"I don't know what that means, and I really don't care."

Nor do I. He was a worthless Quasing. Forty-nine subjects in three days. You have now killed more Quasing than any other human. A dubious distinction.

"Chow," Enzo called. "Drain vat four. Pull the hybrid strain from one."

The head researcher fell to one knee. "Father, that was our last subject."

"I ordered a shipment from the camp days ago," Enzo snapped. "Why aren't they here yet? I can Fedex a yak to Greenland in two days. Why can't I get my prisoners here in my own country?"

Chow lowered his head. "Forgive me, Father. I do not know. The internment camp lost contact with another supply van two hours after they departed. There is an ongoing search now."

"Have you sent for more?"

"No, Father."

Enzo suppressed the urge to reach out and choke the life out of Chow. "Well, what are you waiting for? Go get me more Prophus!"

This is disturbing news.

"Of course it is! How can our head scientist be such an idiot?"

I am referring to a missing convoy filled with what should be thirty Prophus prisoners.

Enzo shrugged. "That's Newgard's concern anyhow."

That is the fourth shipment out of the last six that have gone missing.

"How many?"

Four of six. The Prophus must have engaged us in Tibet.

Enzo sprinted out of the research lab toward his office, quickly outpacing his staff. By the time they caught up, he was already pulling up the reports of the missing shipments and calling the commandant of the internment camp.

"Father," Newgard was saying on the comm. "My scouts report a large contingent of Prophus operating in this area. They have been intercepting prisoners. At dawn this morning, a team of Prophus breached our western walls and another sixty escaped. I am shoring up the defenses and asking for reinforcements to address these incursions."

Sixty Prophus. Escaped. Enzo stared open-mouthed at the screen, and then put his fist through it. That idiot! Enzo looked up at his terrified staff.

"Assemble all research heads," he yelled. "I want the Chinese governor here within the hour and a division ready to mobilize by tonight to Tibet."

Newgard is under Vinnick. He will see it as encroachment onto his authority.

"Then maybe that old fool should handle his resources better. It became my authority when the failure of his internment camp affected my program."

Vinnick was one of the most vocal opponents to his standing in the council. Enzo had originally written the ancient man off but was surprised when nearly half the pushback came from the Russian. At one point, Vinnick had dared propose to take the ProGenesis project away from him, saying it was too important for one of Enzo's experience. Enzo had smiled at the old man's lack of respect for his standing but vowed to avenge that insult.

Now with the siege of the internment camp affecting ProGenesis, this was the perfect opportunity to pay Vinnick back. Enzo could have his forces mobilized and in Tibet far quicker than Vinnick could. And after he defeated the Prophus, control of the internment camp would be his. Then the Council would have no choice but to acknowledge his standing.

You play a dangerous game. Vinnick has greater financial resources than us. His influence with the Russian government is stronger than ours with China.

"As you've often said, Holy One, standing is the only currency. And the only way to obtain standing is to be the most important cog in the machine. He tried to steal the ProGenesis project out from under me. I shall take the internment camp from him."

I approve of your ambition, but tread carefully.

"I will prove myself Vinnick's better."

It took the rest of the day to complete preparations to depart Qingdao. His scientists were ordered to continue their tests and to keep him updated, and he instructed Amanda to file a separate report. He had little faith in Chow and was prepared to yank him off the lead of the project, regardless of whether he was a vessel or not. It was clear to Enzo now that many vessels were unworthy of their blessing.

Within a short amount of time, he had stripped down his available resources to create an army nearly a thousand strong. Two thousand more would be en route within the week. Newgard had claimed that the Prophus had ten thousand men on the ground in Tibet. Newgard was a fool. All projections of Prophus strength had their global capacity at less than ten thousand. For them to muster every single man to Tibet would be an egregious tactical blunder. Besides, hiding ten thousand men wasn't easy, even in a backwater place like Tibet.

Reliable intel from Tibet confirmed a sizable uptick in commercial travel over the past few weeks, estimated at somewhere between two to three thousand above norm. With three thousand men at his disposal on top of the one thousand already in a fortified defensive position, Enzo held the definite tactical advantage.

By nightfall, a small Chinese military fleet would transport their forces to Lhasa Airport in Tibet. From there, it would be another five hundred kilometers on the ground through thick forested areas to the isolated internment camp.

Enzo's blood boiled with excitement as he oversaw the last of the men loaded onto transports. This was what he imagined his life would be like once he became a vessel. Being chained to a desk was such a slow and painful death. This was his true calling, and Enzo was determined to become the greatest vessel the Genjix had ever seen.

CHAPTER TWENTY-ONE
REINFORCEMENTS

In a way, it was the first great Quasing war, though we played both sides. When the Grand Council deemed migration into Cro-Magnons and Neanderthals our next revolutionary step, all Quasing moved toward one of those two camps.

There was much debate regarding which species the Quasing should migrate to. Neanderthals were stronger and more ferocious, and were also easier to control. The ancient humans were more intelligent and better runners, but many of our kind considered their intelligence redundant.

To decide which species would become the Quasing's new home, for tens of thousands of years, we pitted the two sides against each other until one species remained. This was the precursor of the Genjix doctrine that conflict is the key to innovation and evolution on this planet.

Tao

Roen tossed his bag onto the torn-up plaid couch where springs stuck out of a cushion, and plopped down in an exhausted heap. The couch felt as lumpy as it looked. He yawned and surveyed their new digs. This was the only safe house left in all of Taiwan, if it could even be called a safe house. If they lost this one, the team would be out on the streets like all the other homeless people squatting in the city.

He leaned back, put his feet up, and felt the sharp jab of an exposed spring in the small of his back. He was so tired he didn't care if it was a rusty nail. The escape from the market went as smoothly as a disaster movie. Roen's shot with the pistol hit true. Under different circumstances, he would've been impressed. Even Tao complimented his marksmanship. Wuehler died instantly from a bullet through the head. Ramez rose immediately from his body and floated toward Faust's blinking flashlight. Moments later, Faust was on the floor puking his dinner out. Everything went according to plan for those ten seconds.

Then all hell broke loose, a barrage of small arms fire ripping through the exterior wall of the building. Faust was in no shape to do much of anything. Roen actually saw tears streaming down his face as he writhed in pain. For some reason, he thought a tough guy like Faust would have handled it better. Roen ended up carrying Faust on his back as they escaped the old apartment building, down an old fire escape, across an alley, and finally down through a sewage tunnel where they hid for the night until Roen felt it was safe enough to leave.

See to the men.

Tao was right. Wuehler was dead and Faust's life had just been turned upside down. The transition was not easy, especially while on a mission. It was up to him now to lead the team. The men would always follow a host. The rest of the team's retreat from the safe house went just as poorly. Shock units weren't nimble. The guys grabbed every weapon they had on hand and ignored almost everything else, leaving behind clothes, toiletries, food, and even some of the computers.

"Leaving the food and schematics was okay, but God forbid they leave a gun or ammo."

They brought what they thought was necessary. You cannot blame them for following their training.

Right now, three men were missing. Rich and Will fell covering the team's retreat from the lower market. Ashish was missing in action, and the team held onto hope that he'd show up later. The rest of the guys had assorted minor injuries, the most severe being a grazing wound to Stan's leg. They were lucky; it could have been much worse. Local police bands were on high alert, forcing them to skulk through back streets. It took the team six hours to get three klicks across Taipei to this safe house. It was a minor miracle that the group of brawny foreigners wasn't picked up by the authorities.

Everything had happened so fast Roen hadn't had time to process everything yet. How were they discovered so fast? They had just settled in a few weeks ago. No one anticipated such a strong response from the Genjix. Their intel on Taiwan didn't indicate that the enemy even had a military presence on the island. Considering the local police was working hand in glove with the Genjix, their reports were critically mistaken. Thankfully, Tao's steady guidance got them through this crisis.

The irritating needle sticking into Roen's back began to hurt. He lifted his weary head and decided to show a little leadership. He should take charge and help his men move what was left of their supplies. He muffled the sigh crawling up his throat and willed his exhausted body up. Faust was on the rooftop getting acquainted with his new until-death-do-they-part friend. Jim was backtracking their escape while Hutch stood watch on the ground level.

That left Roen with three guys. Every single one of them looked exhausted. They were lucky the Genjix never caught onto their trail. He doubted any of them would get far if discovered. Now would be a good time to be a leader. He wished he had read their bios more closely. He didn't even know all their names.

Grant is the chubby one and the best cook. Stan is the nerdy-looking engineer and the most lethal with the rifle. Ray is the tall one with the crooked receding widow's peak. Smartest of the bunch.

"Too many names." Roen picked himself up and went to go help the one stacking the ammo cases. "Who's crooked hairline guy again?"

I just told you: Ray. Worst memory ever.

He walked up to Ray, who was struggling with an ammo case and helped him carry it to a corner. He checked the contents inside. "How many did we leave behind?"

"Three, sir," Ray replied, eyes glazed over like the walking dead.

He was about to pick up the next crate when Roen put a hand on his shoulder. "Stand down, Ray. I'll take over from here."

Roen dragged over the remaining crates and ordered the rest of the men to get some rest while he stood watch. Within minutes, they were all asleep. Roen leaned against the wall and kept watch out the window. They were in a corner unit of an old apartment complex. In its heyday, it had been a fully-stocked safe house. However, like all other budget casualties, the place had gone into disuse. He had hoped to restock their supplies since they left most of it behind, but the place was bare.

Twenty minutes later, Faust and Hutch returned with takeout American food: pineapple and chicken pizzas. He woke the team up, and they sat around the makeshift cardboard dinner table eating quietly while Roen continued keeping watch.

Just as they finished up, a hooded stranger burst into the room, holding an unconscious Jim. The team immediately reacted, guns trained at the stranger.

"How did I miss that?"

He did not come from the front entrance.

"This building has no rear. The roof then?"

Carrying a body over the rooftops?

Faust, pistol pointing at the stranger, stepped forward. "Let him go now and put your hands up. Slowly." When the figure bent forward to put Jim down, Faust raised his voice again. "No sudden movements. Drop him and step away. Now!"

With a perceptible sigh, the hooded figure let go of Jim, who promptly plopped face first onto the ground.

"I'm closing the door behind me," the hooded man replied, motioning at the entrance.

That voice, sharp and gravelly, sounded familiar. Nostalgia, good and bad, washed over Roen. He couldn't quite place his finger on it. Both hands on his pistol, he crept forward past Faust and stopped a meter away from the mysterious figure. He knelt next to Jim, putting his finger on the unconscious man's neck.

"Pulse faint," he said. Then he stood up and jammed his gun into the stranger's face. "Pull your hood back," he ordered.

I think this is...

Roen could just make out a hairy chin covered with white tufts of hair sticking out of the bottom of the hood when the stranger suddenly disappeared from sight. Well, technically, he didn't disappear. The faucets in Roen's eyes turned on when the mysterious man flicked out his hand and struck Roen smack dab on the bridge of his nose. Before his team could react, the stranger charged forward. Roen saw the back of a hand fly toward his face. Instinctively, he dropped his gun and covered up.

Roen blocked the bitch slap, as he liked to call it, ducked under a follow-up punch, and countered with an elbow of his own that just missed the stranger's face, instead punching a hole in the wall. Immediately, his ribs let his brain know that they had just eaten a crushing blow.

Watch for the trip!

Roen saw a flash of the stranger planting a leg just behind his. He sidestepped and grabbed his assailant by an elbow. Before he knew what was happening, the stranger swung his wrist in a whipping motion and reversed the grip, twisting Roen's arm and flipping him onto his back. He landed with a hard thud, the impact knocking the wind out of him.

"Holy shit," gasped one of his useless men, having just stood there while he got beaten up.

The entire melee lasted less than three seconds. The stranger brought his open palm down and stopped a scant inch from Roen's face. He knew that if it had landed, the blow would have crushed his nose and probably pushed the cartilage up into his brain; a killing blow. The stranger's hand hovered in the air before he offered it to Roen.

"Same clumsy oaf," he growled, pulling back his hood.

"Silk reeling," Roen groaned. "Always fucking silk reeling. I hate silk reeling."

He took Lin's hands. Halfway up from the prone position, Lin let go and dropped him again. Roen landed with an oomph back onto the floor. "I am not your father, and you are not a child. Pick yourself up."

"You mean old bastard," Roen barked. Lin gave him a look. "Master Lin," Roen added hastily.

This time, Lin grabbed Roen by the wrist and pulled him up. Faust and the rest of the men still had their guns trained on Roen's former teacher.

Lin looked at them with disdain. "Put your guns away before you get hurt."

"Lin?" Faust said slowly. "The Cold War assassin?"

Lin tipped his hood. The rest of the team looked awed.

"It's an honor to meet you," Ray whispered as if a little girl to a teen idol. "You're a living legend."

"Wait, he's still alive? The guy who took out nine Genjix Russian ministers?" Stan added.

"The one who singlehandedly handicapped the Soviet space program, so the States won?" Hutch gushed.

As someone who had had his noggin rung literally hundreds of times by Lin, Roen was a little less than impressed. "What, you want an autograph?" he snarled as he massaged his sore neck. He asked Lin in a more respectful tone. "What brings you here, Master?"

"I retired," Lin snapped. "And came home. And what do you do, stupid boy? You bring the war to my front steps."

"Still as cuddly as ever," Roen grinned. "What happened to softening up with old age?"

Lin gave a rude bark. "With the way you are screwing everything up? I'm just getting ready for the end of the world."

"Did Command get in touch with you?"

"What part of retired do you not understand? The Keeper tried to a few times. I didn't return her call."

"How do you not return the Keeper's call? I hate her guts and I still come running when she beckons." Roen paused and looked down at Jim's still inert body, suddenly remembering that he had a man down. "What's wrong with Jim?"

"Your ugly mug was plastered all over the television at the pachinko parlor. Once I got to the site, there was an army of police combing the area as if the ghost of Mao was on the loose. It wasn't hard to follow. Then the world's worst scout here got himself seen, and I had to rescue him." He shook his head in disgust. "No wonder the Prophus are losing. Army of incompetents." He watched as Faust and Ray went to check up on Jim. "He should be alright when he wakes. Ground hit him in the head when he jumped out of a second story window."

Faust looked at him suspiciously. "Jim is a special ops sniper. Before that, he was an Army Ranger. You're telling me he doesn't know how to tuck and roll out of a five meter drop?"

Lin shrugged. "We were in a hurry, so I threw him off. He needs more training."

Roen signaled for the men to stand down. "It's been a long night. Grant, you have next watch. Then Stan."

Lin looked around at the room. "It's too late for me to go home. I will sleep there." He pointed at the couch, and then his face brightened. "You have pizza. I'm starved." Lin went to the dinner table and helped himself.

Faust was patting Jim on the cheek.

"Leave him," Roen said.

"What if he has important intel?"

"We're in no position to mount anything actionable anyway," Roen replied. "Get some shuteye."

Roen watched with a sense of resignation as Lin finished inhaling a slice of pizza and then lay down on the couch, the only place with cushions. Stan magically appeared with a blanket and pillow, offering them to Lin as if they were tribute. Roen later found out it was the only pillow and blanket in the entire place.

"I don't suppose you have a nice place we can stay, Master?" he asked hopefully.

Lin chuckled. "A very nice place. I had a very nice pension with the Prophus. You are crazy if you think I'm going to risk it for you sorry lot."

A total pipe dream.

"Ah, well, it was worth a try. Tao, we get pension?"

That program was canceled years before you joined. On account of us losing the war and all.

"Man, I want pension."

I am still working on that Brazilian lingerie model you asked for five years ago.

Roen waited until the rest of the team settled in and then took an unused corner in the kitchen. Before he turned in, he took the time to clean out his pistol. The soothing ritual helped clear his mind as he went through the process of disassembling the gun and wiping down each part. When he finished, he placed it in its holster, stood up and stretched. His back wasn't happy about being hunched over for so long, another indication of the wear and tear on his body.

He made one final jaunt around the apartment to check up on his men. He nodded to Grant, who was on watch, and then brushed his teeth with his forefinger in the kitchen sink. Toothbrushes were another casualty of the night's escape.

"Excuse me, sir," Grant said as Roen turned to leave. "Those stories about Lin, are they true? Is he as good as everyone says he is?"

"Even better," Roen replied, chest puffing up a little. Lin was his master after all.

Get some sleep. Tomorrow's another long day. The team is fragile and will need your leadership.

"What leadership?"

That is why it will be a long day.

CHAPTER TWENTY-TWO
TRAINING

During the hundred years that we stayed in Europe, I climbed the ranks of French and Prussian nobility while Yol moved in philosopher circles. Eventually, I reached the pinnacle of the empire and my host became the Royal Prince, Archduke Franz Ferdinand, at the time still a young child.

Nobility of birth, however, did not guarantee nobility of stature. Franz was a strange host. He was hard to influence, and prone to reckless and self-involved ways. I admit that he would have made a terrible emperor. However, we will never discover what his rule could have been. The Black Hand who assassinated Franz and his wife Sophie saw to that. Unfortunately, it also paved the way for the Great War.

Baji

Jill stared at the black hole of the gun barrel pointing at her.

Uneven ground, fifteen degree slant. Cover to your right, three shrubs and a cliff edge. A flat clearing to the left. Go now!

She dove just as Marco pulled the trigger. The hammer slammed down on the empty chamber with a loud click. She rolled off her shoulder into a kneeling position, her own pistol pointing at his head.

Well done.

"Good," he remarked. "Again. This time, don't telegraph. Your eyes wandered. Trust Baji's signals."

Jill nodded. They were three weeks into her training and had just started integrating free running into combat. They were working on basic techniques, from coordinating leg and hand movements during a climb to tucking the body during a jump to rolling out of a high drop. It was physically exhausting, and she went home every night a walking mass of welts, but she was starting to get the hang of it. Tonight, the ground was a wet mush of dirt, gravel, and grass, which left her looking like she was wearing a ghillie suit. If anyone from the Hill saw this, it would probably end her career.

They rehearsed the encounter several more times, each time putting her through a different scenario. At a distance, she trained to juke and angle toward cover. Close up, she was taught to dive forward and sweep her assailant's legs. And as a last resort, she now carried a rack of knives strapped to her thigh.

This was the plan that Baji and Marco had devised for her self-defense: dodge, counter, and flee. They called it her Flight and Flight tactic. It took Jill a while to warm up to it, but eventually, she found herself enjoying the game. It was a demanding mental exercise and wasn't yet second nature, but she was getting the hang of it.

Always have a dodge direction ready. Angle at opponent's sixty degrees. Stick and move.

"Alright," Marco said an hour into their session. "Let's free run."

Jill grinned. This was her favorite part. She took off and disappeared into the forest, hurdling over rocks and brushes. A second later, she heard Marco crashing through the trees behind her. The forest was dark but her eyes had already adjusted and as long as she paid attention, she was fairly confident she wouldn't smash into anything.

She scanned ahead and zigzagged around cover, constantly taking angles and changing directions to throw him off her trail. She grabbed a tree trunk to her right, swinging around and changing directions without slowing down. She caught a glimpse of him cutting toward her. She jumped over a fallen log and flattened herself to the ground, her pistol aimed up. A moment later, Marco passed by and she pulled the trigger. He stopped when he heard the click.

"Good," he said. "Continue."

Jill smirked, held up one finger, and then took off running again. They played this game of tag for another five minutes until she found her next ambush point. She scampered up a short cliff, using free running to climb over a three-meter rock. A moment later, Marco passed by and she pulled the trigger again. She held up two fingers once he acknowledged the kill.

The next few attempts weren't as successful. When they reached a clearing with sparse coverage he drew his gun at the same time she did. That was a point for him. It was imperative she always drew first. The last encounter was near the river. Jill crossed the brook, backtracked upstream and doubled back. Several minutes later, she caught sight of Marco and tried to get the jump on him.

But just as she was about to pull the trigger, he heard her rustling among the leaves and faded back into the woods. They played a game of cat and mouse, each looking for an opening. However, Marco won this round and somehow corralled her back to the river.

He advanced on her with a large smile on his face. "Situation change. Holster your sidearm."

You should have retreated and regrouped.

"Duly noted."

Jill grimaced, put her pistol in its holster and crouched, trying to make herself a smaller target. She tried to circle away from the river, but he cut her off. Watching his eyes, she stayed out of his arm's length as he advanced.

Right thirty degrees... now!

She dove toward the river bed and rolled onto her feet as he pulled the trigger.

Sixty left... now!

Again she just got out of Marco's sights.

Two meters range. Attack!

Jill instinctively followed Baji's instructions. She slid in close to Marco and kicked at his legs. She felt the satisfying contact of her heel digging into his ankle as he readjusted his aim. The blow knocked him off balance. Unfortunately, he toppled directly on top of her. She grunted as her body cushioned his fall.

"Well," he said, "if this was your plan all along, I say mission successful. What was your mistake?"

"I should have swept from the side of the ankle instead," she replied.

Exactly.

There was a moment of awkwardness. Jill's heart rate quickened and she felt a sudden urge to lean forward and see what came next. Paula was right. He did have nice eyes, a combination of blue and turquoise that could keep a girl mesmerized for hours.

Instead, Jill tore her gaze away and pretended to act annoyed. "Okay, you can get off me now."

His face was very close to hers. "The view's pretty good from here."

She slapped him playfully on the shoulder. "Get off me. I'm not one of those peasants your lordship can just have your way with."

He grinned, rolled off and pulled her up to her feet. "Next time, coming from the angle you did, kick higher at the knees or sweep the ankles."

"Yes, sir," she replied, brushing the chunks of mud off her pants. She was doing laundry almost every day now.

He looked up at the sky and checked his watch. "Let's call it. We'll move training to the city from now on. You'll have more encounters in the urban jungles than the wilderness anyway." That was music to Jill's ears. She couldn't wait to stop rolling around in the dirt.

"First thing tomorrow night?" she asked as they walked back to the car.

"Double sessions," he said. "One at dawn and at night."

She sighed. Sleep was becoming a rare commodity.

Baji initially wanted to call Roen at four in the morning over there just to give him a taste of his own medicine. It was tempting but Jill decided to be the bigger person. She waited and called at what should be lunch local time. Instead, she was surprised to catch him just waking up.

"Starting the day a little late?" she joked. "Wuehler have you on permanent guard duty?"

She knew she had hit a nerve when he mumbled something too low to make out. At first, he pretended things were fine, but like all good wives, she knew how to dig the truth out. Eventually, he caught her up on the events of the past few days.

Killed by the Genjix? What about Ramez?

"What about Wuehler's Quasing?" Jill asked. This tale was becoming all too familiar these days. It seemed far too often these days, another of Baji's friends was sent to the Eternal Sea.

"I got him out," Roen sighed. "I had to do it. Shoot Wuehler. It was the only way."

Jill felt his grief right there. It was the one tragedy that he could never get over, and now it had happened again. Granted Wuehler didn't own Roen's heart like Sonya had, but it still must have hurt. A little itch of jealousy bubbled up in her as she thought of Sonya, but Jill pushed it out of her mind. This wasn't the time.

You honestly need to get over it.

"I'll get over it when you do."

"Any hits on Dylan?" Jill asked.

"The fat bastard's fallen off the face of the Earth."

"Have you considered heading south to that Genjix operation?"

"I thought about it, but I don't know. It's a large port and we're undermanned. Might be more than we can chew. We lost most of our supplies and are in pretty bad shape. There's a lot of heat on us too."

Jill picked up the piece of paper. "I got a name for you: Punai Corporation. Found some docs through the Department of Commerce. Much of it was redacted but that only shines a bigger spotlight on it. That means someone from up on high in this administration is covering for them. And of course, their primary refinery and export hub is in southern Taiwan. I don't think it's a coincidence. It should help narrow your search."

"I'll give it a shot." Roen sounded so deflated. Jill couldn't remember the last time he had sounded this insecure. Ever since she found out about Tao, Roen had tended to exhibit an overabundance of confidence.

"Listen, Roen, you take care of yourself," she said softly. "You have a son. Remember that."

There was a long pause.

"Jill, when this is all over, I want to talk. About us being us again."

Something got caught in Jill's throat. No words came out, and she suddenly felt the need to turn away and face the window. The last thing Wilks and Tammy needed to see was her crying at her desk. Wilks would fly into a rage and Tammy would gossip. Politics was a rough sport, and there was no place for crying in it.

"I have to go," she said quickly, hanging up. She kept her face turned for several seconds.

Maybe we should talk about this. Marco is confusing you.

Jill wiped the tears falling down her face and breathed in sharply. "No he's not, Baji. There's nothing to talk about. Let's get back to work."

CHAPTER TWENTY-THREE
NEW MANAGEMENT

The war between the Cro-Magnons and the Neanderthals was wider in scale than any humans have seen since. There was little strategy and coordination, save for what the Quasing could coax out. It was genocide by any definition. By the end, only one species remained.

After the Cro-Magnon established their dominance, the next several thousand years became a time of great innovation. We harnessed our new tools and showed them how to bend fire to their bidding. We taught them how to follow the stars when they traveled and showed them how to cultivate the land for sustenance. Then in Mesopotamia, the Keeper, in all her wisdom, offered the humans a new gift: the written word.

Tao

Roen and the team stayed at the safe house for three more days. The men needed to recuperate from their dozens of minor and not-so-minor injuries. Jim complained of dizziness from his concussion, Hutch had cracked a tooth and needed dental work, Stan's bullet wound festered, and Grant somehow came down with an intense itch that required a doctor. It ended up being gonorrhea. Ashish never returned and they were forced to presume him dead.

Roen had hoped to speak with Lin the next morning, but his hopes were dashed when he saw the empty couch. That was too bad; the team could have used his help. Not only was he familiar with Taiwan, he was easily one of the deadliest fighters in the world.

Roen knew better than to beg Lin to join the team, though. First of all, he'd be a terrible teammate. There was no way his master would follow Roen's orders. Even when Lin was active, there was a reason he was a solo operative. Second of all, Lin was a man of his word. He took that whole retirement thing seriously and meant what he said about not being involved with the Prophus anymore. If his master felt his service to the world was done, it was.

The team had to be more careful now with a strong Genjix presence close by. This was the last safe house in Taipei and discovery would be catastrophic. Operations in Asia were inherently risky these days. Gone were the days when Prophus Command could ship support within twenty-four hours. Once a team was isolated, especially in the enemy zone of control, they were on their own.

For Roen, taking charge was a learning experience. In all his years as an operative, he had never owned a team. Sure, he had led tactical operations before, but this was a beast of a different nature. At first, he thought Faust would help run the day-to-day operations, but he was having a tough transition with Ramez. The two did not seem to get along and were waging a war of wills in Faust's head. Roen pitied them both.

You should be glad you got lucky with such an agreeable Quasing.

"Pfft. I bet Ramez doesn't put Faust on a diet right away and torture him with hot ass-kicking women."

Admit it. You liked being beaten up by Sonya.

"You know what I wish? I wish I had trained Jill. Why wasn't I allowed to again?"

Because Jill, as a political operative, cannot be seen as a battered wife. That and you know how she gets when you tell her to do something she does not want to. Not everyone is as malleable as you.

After the first two days, Roen decided he hated being the team lead. He never realized all the little things Wuehler did behind the scenes until he had to do them. Details from feeding the men to whose turn it was to wash the dishes to the guard duty schedule had to be considered. It was as if he had suddenly adopted a household of strong-minded teenagers and had to play stepfather to all of them.

He had to consider each man's individual quirks and personality instead of thinking of them as assets on a mission. For instance, Stan, the straw-thin stick figure, ate three times more food than anyone else. Hutch might be a narcoleptic, considering how often he slept. And Grant with his gonorrhea... Well, now everyone knew where he disappeared to during his off hours.

"This sucks. It reminds me of my old desk job, except without the paperwork. And the pay. And any benefits."

You start missing your old job at least once a year. At least you have the option of pulling yourself out of guard duty.

"That's the worst part. Wuehler regularly took watch himself. I don't get any perks being the boss. I doubt the lads would put up with me taking myself out of the rotation."

The final nail in the coffin was their next plan of action: they had none. Or more specifically, Roen had none. They had exhausted all their leads on the Genjix operation and on Dylan. They were also now being hunted by the local authorities. The only thing they had to work with now was Jill's lead and that unsubstantiated vague note from the unnamed gangster.

So after several days of laying low and recuperating, Roen finally decided on their next plan of attack. They were going to head out to investigate the Genjix operation in the south. It was their only lead after all, so it really wasn't that hard a decision. Plan B did not exist. It did cheer the men up to finally be doing something.

By this time, Faust and Ramez had formed an uneasy truce, seeing how they were stuck with each other until death. Roen had originally thought that he was the only one who had had it rough with Tao. It gave him a little satisfaction to know that not all hosts got along swimmingly with their Quasing.

The next thing to do was move the seven surviving members of the team down to Hsinchu. Again, this was not as easy as it sounded. Seven foreigners moving around in public would be easy to spot. The syndicates could not be relied on for anything more than ammo. Most of the bosses were already too leery of the Genjix to offer much assistance.

And to top it all off, they were running low on money. For some reason, when Ray packed up the gear during the attack, he decided to grab the sniper rifle instead of the suitcase full of cash. That decision, on top of dentistry bills, doctor's bills, and crime syndicate bills, put the entire team in a precariously poor financial position. Roen had to utilize whatever funds they had on hand to restock their supplies.

By the end of the week, the team was almost broke. He was tempted to put them all to work as waiters or dishwashers at restaurants. He'd get a mutiny on his hands in a second though. Roen racked his brain trying to find a workaround for all their woes. Finally, unable to come up with a solution, he decided to use their one get-out-of-jail card and grovel to Lin. His master would assuredly make this experience as painful and soul-sucking as possible, but he had little choice.

Roen had thought his master would maintain a low profile. After all, he had lived in hiding in a suburb of Chicago for over twenty years. Roen knew how much Lin valued privacy and wasn't sure if he could even locate his master. Finding Lin, however, proved surprisingly easy. It seemed real bona fide Tai Chi masters were a big deal here. And that made Lin one of the biggest deals in the neighborhood. After an afternoon of inquiries at local Tai Chi hangouts, mahjong parties, and pachinko parlors, Roen found himself up a steep forested road in a mountainous region on the eastern side of the island.

A white tiled wall with a massive red iron gate surrounded the house. Next to the gate was an intercom, and to neither Roen nor Tao's surprise, it didn't work. There was a hidden camera on the southern corner of the wall that was blinking and following his movements, so someone in there was watching. It would be just like Lin to mess with him for fun.

After pushing the buzzer and waving at the camera for ten minutes, Roen took matters into his own hands. After all, as he often said, breaking and entering was his specialty. He wandered around to the northern perimeter, his fingers brushing along the cracked and moss-covered tiles. The wall on this side pushed up against a steep incline, which made scaling it a tad easier. A hop and a hurdle later, Roen landed softly on the other side and flattened into a crouch. Who knew what kind of crazy was in store for him here?

Roen found himself in the back of the estate, if you could call it that. The house was a large two-story behemoth that was easily twice as large as the others in the surrounding area. Roen didn't begrudge Lin wanting something bigger after living in a tiny warehouse for twenty years.

The place looked typically Lin. There was a large koi pond populated with dozens of the large orange fish. An array of wooden poles rose from the water in a figure eight pattern. He crept along toward the near deck and peered into the window.

"Maybe he's asleep."

If he was, your constant buzzing of the doorbell will have woken him up. I am sure he is in a fine mood then.

"Damn! Tao, now I'm scared."

You should be.

Roen decided against entering through the back door and climbed into the living room through the side window. It was quiet except for the wind whistling this high up in the mountains, and a chorus of cicadas chirping incessantly. Roen did a double-take and grinned at the same pinball machines and arcade consoles that lined the walls. And just like the old warehouse, in place of a coffee table was a circular fighting mat in the center of the room. Some things never changed.

"It's dark. He's either not home or asleep."

So go check. Why did you suddenly become so indecisive?

"Look, I just broke into Master Lin's house and don't relish sneaking up into his bedroom and waking him up."

Sounds like a good way to get yourself killed.

"No kidding. Lin is grumpy after a nap. Sounds like a recipe for suicide."

Your options are either search for him or sit on the couch until he finds you. It is not that hard.

Napping on the couch didn't seem like a bad plan. He could catch up on some sleep. But knowing Lin, he would receive a cruel wakeup. Best to try to get the jump on him. He glanced at the couch longingly; it did look comfortable.

It took Roen five minutes to creep up to the second story. He was sure Lin was waiting around the corner ready to jump out and box his ears. After all, the guy had spent two decades hiding not only from the Genjix, but also the CIA, KGB, and supposedly the still-functioning White Lotus Society. No one survived that many people trying to kill him for that long without being careful.

By the time he got into Lin's bedroom, he was sweating bullets from anxiety. Thank God Lin wasn't in his bed. That meant Roen didn't have to wake him up. The wave of relief that washed over him was so palpable he almost giggled. Roen wasn't afraid of much these days, but there would always be a mixture of awe, respect and fetal position terror when it came to Master Lin.

Search the rest of the house.

A few minutes later, he had searched the rest of the floor and come up empty. He did, however, find Lin's torn-up coat on the rack and the old man's soft slippers put away neatly at the top of the stairs. The old man never left the house without those. Roen began to suspect foul play.

Go get some fresh air. You are sweating like a pig.

Not a bad idea. Roen's shirt was drenched. He stepped out onto the deck and felt the breeze coming down from the mountains. It was still jungle humid outside but much more bearable than in the city. He closed his eyes and inhaled and then slowly exhaled, counting down from fourteen, willing his heart rate to decrease. The urban legends of masters who didn't sweat weren't totally untrue. There were techniques that a person could train for to keep their heart rate low and their body temperatures regulated. A large heavy, hard object struck him right between the eyes.

"Gah!"

Roen fell to his knees, spun onto his back, and drew his pistol. Looking up, he saw Master Lin standing on the roof waving. A rock the size of a child's fist lay next to Roen's head.

You should have checked the roof.

"I could have used that advice five minutes ago!"

Lin turned away and disappeared from the ledge. Swearing, Roen picked himself up and went up onto the rooftop. He found Lin sitting on the ground with his back to him. Roen knew his master wasn't meditating. The old guy thought meditating – like yoga and baseball and white wine – was for pansies. He sat down on the ground across from Lin.

"You move quieter than you used to," Lin remarked as he approached. "Not like a three legged bull in a china shop anymore."

"I think there's a direct correlation between moving quietly and long life. For some reason, when I move too loud, people try to kill me," Roen said.

"Is Master Tao well? Has he been pleased with your progress?"

"You'll have to ask him, Master, but he tells me I'm the greatest thing since the invention of the toilet."

"Like the toilet, you both are full of shit."

You stepped into that one.

Lin became solemn, looking very serene and masterly. "I have one more thing to teach you. The last piece of your training."

"Like the dim mak?"

"Stupid boy. Every move I have is a dim mak. That's why I'm the master." Lin swung at him with his stick. Roen blocked it and grinned. He wiped that smirk off his face when Lin scowled. Subdued, Roen moved closer and allowed Lin to give him a light thump on the back of the head. "Come, let's see how much you've forgotten."

They stood up and moved to the center of the roof. Lin began the Chen 42 form. Roen joined in, running through the movements he'd worked through thousands of times, from Six Sealing to Buddha Pounds Mortar through to White Crane Spreads Wings. It had been years since he practiced, but it came rushing back like an old memory.

Goodness, you are rusty. San Feng is rolling in his grave.

"Why do you always talk like every host before me is continually rotating in the dirt?"

By the time Roen hit the second segment of the form, Lin had stopped and was watching him flow through the movements. Roen could feel his master's judging eyes make note of every little mistake.

"Sloppy," was all he said. "You are a bigger oaf than when we met. How is that even possible? Are your parents alive? If they are, they would be ashamed."

Roen continued working through the form. He knew what game Lin was playing. He moved into cloud hands, feeling the energy course from the base of his feet up to his fingers, and began Parting the White Horse's Mane.

"Could you move any less smoothly? I feel like I'm watching a video on YouTube on a dial-up."

So Lin discovered the Internet finally?

"Appears so."

Roen, being used to Lin's snide comments, kept his face neutral.

"Has Master Tao forgiven Edward yet for leaving him with you? We know the Keeper sure hasn't. What is your son's name? What is five plus seven?"

"Cameron and twelve. And I don't remember Edward ever asking for forgiveness."

"What is your mission here in Taiwan?"

"We are searching for a large Genjix trade operation. We're also hoping to find Dylan as well, Master," Roen responded. "He escaped from *Atlantis* before it was captured."

Fair Maiden Works Shuttles to Lazily Tying Coat back to Six Sealing.

"You haven't been practicing."

"I've been a little busy. You know, getting married, having a kid, fighting a war to prevent alien world domination."

"From what I heard, you've been doing a pretty lousy job at all three."

Roen stumbled out of Sparrow Dashes Earth Dragon and temporarily lost his train of thought. Biting his lip, he emptied his mind and continued.

That one cut a little deep.

"You don't say. One more snarky remark about my family and I'll..."

...do nothing. Remember what happened the last time you two scuffled?

"I wasn't ready last time."

I actually believe Lin has improved, scary as that thought might be.

"He's still a miserable old man."

Better miserable old than miserable young.

"Did your brain just have a fart?" Lin chortled, obviously enjoying himself. He saw the kink in Roen's armor and had zeroed in on it. "Your wife tracked me down once when you were on one of your fool's errands. Asking me if I knew where you were. Said you disappeared."

"I was on a mission for Tao, Master. I had no choice."

"Is that so? I venerate Master Tao as much as any, considering he is the father of Tai Chi, but if anyone told me to abandon my wife and young child, I would tell them to feed themselves to drunk pandas."

"Pandas are vegetarians, Master Lin."

"Shut up!"

Roen felt his hands involuntarily clench, disrupting the flow of his chi. And as much as he tried to stay relaxed, his reservoir of calm had become precariously low. He counted down from fourteen. And then he did it again to no avail.

Hold it together. This is only a test. You know that.

"Maybe I should offer to adopt your son. He deserves a father after all. Though with your genes, I have little hope of him ever accomplishing anything."

Roen's lip bled as his teeth gnashed down on them. It was all he could do to force himself to go through Wave Double Lotus.

"You failed me years ago. So now you will fail Jill, your son, and Tao. Your fatherless boy will probably grow up to be a hateful punk who will be a useless blight on society and probably try to rob me when I'm too old to teach him a lesson."

"Don't talk about my son like that," Roen roared. Skipping the last few moves, he lashed out at Lin's stupid ugly beard. He whiffed as Lin pulled back and counterattacked. Roen ate a smack to the face. A common saying for an old fighter was that power was the last thing to go, and in Lin's case, it was true. The guy still hit like a Mack truck. A few years ago, a blow like that would have buckled Roen's knees and crumpled him to the ground, but now he was made of tougher stuff. With a healthy dose of rage added in, he was practically impervious to pain.

He walked through the blow and smashed a Buddha Pounds Mortar down on Lin's shoulder. Lin spun away and followed up with three quick blows to Roen's solar plexus. Then he grabbed both of Roen's elbows, pulled, and bounced him three meters back. Roen landed with a hard thud and skidded another five from the force.

He actually is better than he was. Impressive.

"Stop commentating and help me!"

When two of my students fight, I stay out of it.

With a growl, Roen charged again, throwing rapid combinations of kicks and punches, possibly landing two hits out of the five. Their exchange was blinding as the two stood close together, throwing bombs with their hands and feet. Combat is like kissing, Lin often said. In this case with two high level practitioners, the melee was more like a game of high-speed chess. They covered the entire rooftop, constantly retreating and feinting to get the upper hand.

Roen had a few new tricks up his sleeve and he unloaded all of them at once. Some of them even worked. A particularly sneaky spinning back elbow popped Lin right on the mouth. Unfortunately for him, Lin spat out the blood and smirked.

"Cute," was all he said before they engaged again. The rest of Roen's tricks were decidedly less successful. His Superman punch left him exposed and rewarded him with a bloody lip. His Fanzi fist combination got him popped in the ear, and his flying scissor takedown attempt actually left Lin standing over him roaring with laughter.

You should break. This is a losing situation.

Tao was right. Their fighting styles were too similar and Lin was smarter, stronger, and faster. He was able to predict what Roen was going to do before he even thought of it. Slowly, Roen was forced to retreat. He was landing one for every ten against Lin. Every time he tried to break away, the old fox was right in his face. Finally, he made the mistake of overreaching on a left hook. Lin trapped both of his arms, gave him one measured grin, and then slapped him hard across the face.

"That's enough," Lin said calmly. Roen's face contorted into a snarl before another slap hit him so hard he ended up facing backwards. "I said that's enough." Then his master locked him in a choke hold and dragged him to the ground. Feeling himself losing consciousness, Roen tapped Lin's leg.

"I don't know what that means," Lin's chuckled. "It's terrible foreplay though."

Just as Roen's vision darkened, Lin released his grip. Roen collapsed onto his back and heaved huge gulps of air. Lin stood over him and waited for him to recover.

"Don't you know that tapping is the universal sign of surrendering during a submission?" Roen gasped in between breaths.

"Maybe in your professional wrestling, but in combat, we wait until our opponent is dead. I just saved your life by not killing you."

And then for the first time, Roen saw something new in Lin's eyes: sadness. He was actually pitying him! Lin was not one to get emotional, but to show pity was the worst thing he could do to Roen.

"I have failed you as a teacher," Lin looked resigned.

Roen sat up, legs still sprawled on the floor. He gingerly touched the right side of his jaw. "I don't know. I thought I was doing pretty well, at least for a while."

Lin snorted. "I'm not talking about your fighting. You've been good at that for years. Never good enough to best a true master, but adequate enough for me to acknowledge you as my student."

"Thanks, I think."

That is the nicest thing he has ever said to you.

"Really? That's it?"

What do you want, a colorful belt?

Lin put a hand on Roen's shoulder. "I have given you the skills to be great, but not the mind. Your focus is weak. Too easily angered and you are fighting for the wrong causes."

"I'm fighting for the Prophus!" Roen protested. "That's what you trained me for."

"I did not train you to be Master Tao's puppet."

I resent that.

"Yeah, so do I!"

"I am no one's..." Roen snapped.

"Come," Lin interrupted him. He turned and walked away, leaving Roen to hurry after him.

"Where are we going?" Roen asked.

"I am hungry. I was waiting for you to have dinner but it took you too long to find me."

They left the house and walked down the mountain to a line of street vendors in a small market. There, Lin ordered two hot bowls of congee and they feasted on the mushy rice filled with strange-looking herbs and spices. It took Roen a while to get used to using chopsticks with the porridge. Lin enjoyed watching him drop half of his meal onto his lap.

"Two left hands and ten thumbs," he smirked.

"Eating congee with chopsticks is unnatural," Roen grumbled.

"Do you have a picture of your son?" Lin asked, mouth full as he slurped the soupy meal.

Roen pulled out his family picture and showed it to Lin, his chest swelling with pride.

"Strong legs," Lin observed. "A good base. Perfect for Hsing Yi."

"I'm not letting him anywhere close to the Quasing," Roen said sharply.

You do not want to pass me down like an heirloom?

"I'll get him a Rolex instead."

I come far cheaper. Will only cost your life.

Lin finished his breakfast and picked his teeth with his fingers in a way only an old person could get away with. "Why not? You do not approve of yourself?"

"What kind of a father wouldn't want their kid to fight an alien war. And not only that, they get zero benefits, crappy health care, and a paycheck a paperboy would laugh at."

"I see," Lin replied thoughtfully. "You fight for your wife and son?"

"Of course."

"Then why did you leave them?"

Roen felt his anger boiling up inside again. "First of all, she left me. And second of all, because I had to. Tao told me–"

"Why is Tao dictating your life? Isn't that what the Genjix do?"

Hey, I resent that even more. Tell Lin he is dead to me.

Roen opened his mouth to tell Lin exactly what Tao thought of his words but his master had already finished his meal and stepped away from the counter. Roen looked down at his three-quarters eaten bowl and then back at Lin already walking back up the hill. Finally, he scooped one last mouthful of congee, paid for both meals, and hurried after Lin.

"That's the final lesson you must learn," Lin said without turning when Roen caught up. "A true master must know when to do the right thing. You are lazy and just listen to Tao."

"Shouldn't you be on his side?" Roen asked.

"I'm on humanity's side," Lin replied. "Always have been. It's just that the Prophus usually fight with us. Now go away. I am tired."

"What about that final lesson?"

Lin grinned. "That was it."

"What does that have anything to do with Tai Chi?"

Lin shrugged. "It doesn't. Your Tai Chi is good enough. The lesson is about being a good person."

They stopped at the intersection and Lin held out a hand. Surprised, Roen shook it. "After this mission, boy, go home. Your family needs you more than the Prophus do. No matter what, they should come first." And with that, Lin turned to go.

"Hey, Master," Roen called out. "You know, we're a little short-handed. Think you're up for helping your old pals out one more time? You know, for old time's sake?"

Lin turned around and for the first time that Roen could recall, his smile was genuine and warm. And then he shook his head. "My fight is over. I do not expect to ever see you again, Roen Tan. Good journey, my son. Honor your ancestors and Master Tao. Now, you have a war to fight and I have a retirement to enjoy."

Before he could leave again, Roen tapped him on the shoulder. "One last request, Master," he said as formal and deferential as possible.

Lin gave him a wary look. "Yes?"

"Can I borrow some money?"

CHAPTER TWENTY-FOUR
TIBET

Huchel, one of our brightest, once inhabited a scientist named Charles Darwin. His vessel claimed to discover evolution, but the truth is, all he discovered was our kind's millions-year-old methodology. Humans are our children, and are only alive by our mercy. We made them the fittest to live, and for that we are owed everything.

Zoras

Enzo looked out the window of the Mi-171 transport as it buzzed over the canopy line of the thick Tibetan forest. Having grown up in the mountains of Costa Rica, he was reminded of his Central American home by this land. Sure, the trees looked different and the sharp biting edge of the Tibetan mountain air was a sharp contrast to the humidity of the jungle, but both were a far cry from the oppressive steel, concrete, and smog of Qingdao.

You miss your sheltered life at the Hatchery?

"Incubation had its pleasures, but Hatchery life was no life at all. I am now truly alive, fulfilling my destiny."

We shall see. Your actions have been bold and successful to an extent. However, you assume too much risk.

"My apologies, Zoras. I shall work harder to earn your favor."

A few minutes later, the dense forest opened into a clearing, and the tops of the internment camp buildings appeared. As the transport hovered in the air, Enzo took the time to study the camp below. The entire place was a mess.

He had assumed the internment camp was run like most Genjix facilities: controlled, uniform, and clean. However, the scene had no semblance of order. The buildings were a sad-looking bunch, made from wood and plaster. Several showed the blackened burns of battle while others seemed decrepit from lack of maintenance.

The center building was in much better shape than the smaller outlying facilities. It was a two-story structure reinforced with steel beams and riot control windows. Enzo watched as groups of men congregated at the western fence. Upon closer inspection, he noticed that some of the buildings on that side still smoldered. Approximately twenty meters of the fence had been torn apart as well.

We seem to have come at the right time.

With the helicopter still five meters from the ground, Enzo jumped out and landed gracefully on his feet. "You," he called to the nearest officer directing a squad of men clearing wreckage. "Report."

Looking irritated, the officer turned and stopped, his mouth dropped open. A man young enough to be his son was barking orders as if a general, and carrying himself as if a god. And in this case, he was right on all accounts. The officer looked him up and down and then noticed the helicopter still hovering in the air.

He did the rational thing and saluted. "Father."

Enzo noted the tiredness around his eyes and the trembling in his hands. His left hand was wrapped hastily and blood seeped through the bandages. This man, a career soldier by his bearing, probably had not slept in over thirty-six hours.

Enzo saluted back. "What happened here?"

"Latest attack fifteen minutes ago, an explosion on the western perimeter. Six confirmed enemy dead, thirty friendlies. Seventy prisoners escaped."

"Seventy!"

Newgard has lost control of the situation. That or it is much worse than we anticipated. You were right to come.

"How many of the escaped were vessels?" Enzo snarled.

The officer averted his eyes only for a split second. "Fifteen. The Prophus knew exactly where to hit us."

Then Enzo frowned and scanned the field. Many of the buildings were damaged, and the ground was scarred from battle, but this couldn't have been all from one attack. The Prophus had to be precise in their assaults to avoid injuring their own.

He assumed a softer tone to the officer. "How many attacks have there been?"

To the officer's credit, he didn't bat an eye when he spoke. "Sixteen in the past forty-eight hours, Father."

Relieve that fool Newgard at once!

Enzo reached out and put a hand on the man's shoulder. "Your performance is commendable. Get that hand seen to and stand down. Relieve the men in similar states. The remainder will be relieved in a few hours when my men reach the base." He patted the officer one more time and watched as a wave of relief passed over him.

"Thank you, Father," the man breathed before jogging to the fence and calling half a dozen men to follow him to the central building.

Your die has been tossed. Now take ownership. There is no backing out now. Expect blowback from Vinnick.

"Palos," Enzo barked sharply. The head of his bodyguards approached and bowed. "Assume command of this rabble and clean this mess up. Send the men who are injured for medical care and have your team take their place. Seal this section by nightfall, and station guards at twenty meters. Pull all able-bodied men to establish a defensive perimeter until the rest of my forces arrive. Reallocate non-military personnel to double duty that the guards would normally have. I want fighting men to do nothing but fight, guard, and sleep. Is that clear?"

"Yes, Father," Palos bowed again and signaled to one of his men.

Enzo stormed into the main building, followed closely by his entourage. The startled guards at the front door stood frozen with terror. The building was just as chaotic inside as outside. Personnel scampered around as if they were still under siege. A quick image flashed in Enzo's head of Chateau Gaillard. Zoras' host at the time was one of twenty knights who had held the castle for eight months before it finally fell.

The right wing of this building was a makeshift infirmary. There must have been fifty men lying on the floor, bloodied and battered. Enzo clicked his tongue in disapproval. This entire triage was a mess. Near the front, officers barked orders to soldiers and engineering crews in a large room serving as a makeshift command post.

An uncomfortable-looking aide approached him and bowed. "Father Enzo, we heard you were coming at the very last minute. Unfortunately, there have been several unforeseen–"

"Newgard," Enzo said in a low, soft voice. "Where is he?"

The aide stepped aside and gestured down the left hallway. "In the war room, Father. Allow me to–"

Enzo strode past him down the hallway and barged into the war room, startling the fool commander of this sad camp. Newgard and the three men with him froze hunched over a map.

Enzo looked each in the eye and spoke one word. "Out."

The herd nearly stampeded out the door. Enzo kept his face neutral, but a small piece of him was enjoying the intimidation and terror he inspired as a vessel of the Council. Only Newgard stood erect before him, simultaneously defiant and cowed.

His eyes met Enzo's and did not flinch, but the nervous quiver in his voice betrayed him. "Father, this is a pleasant surprise. I thank you for your support. However, everything is well in hand."

"Well in hand?" Enzo kept his voice so soft that Newgard had to strain to hear. "How many prisoners have been lost?"

"Six hundred and thirty–"

"I don't care about the humans," Enzo snapped. "How many vessels?"

Newgard averted his eyes. "Eighty-four."

"And yet you believe matters are well in hand? Even after losing three convoys?

"Yes, Father," Newgard stammered. "The Prophus have been raiding us continuously with the aid of the Tibetan Underground. Then a few days ago, they began making incursions into the facility. I have contacted Father Vinnick for additional support, which should be here in a few days."

"At the rate you're going, in a few days, you won't have any prisoners left," Enzo replied. "Newgard, I am relieving you of duty. You will report to Commander Palos."

Newgard's eyes flashed, and for the first time, Enzo saw real defiance in them. "Apologies, Father, but I will not abdicate my command. I report to Father Vinnick of the Genjix Council and am out of your jurisdiction."

Careful how you tread. Push too softly and you will undermine your position in the Council. Push too hard and you risk conflict with the Council. If you take command of the facility and fail, Vinnick will have every right to remove you from your position and assume your holdings.

How dare this man question his order! Enzo took a step forward. "I'm on the Council, Newgard, and you will hand over your command." He turned to Palos. "Send the rest of your men out."

Palos bowed and complied. A moment later, it was only Enzo, Newgard, and Palos in the room. Newgard was still standing at attention next to the table while Palos guarded the door. The tension in the air was thick as each waited for someone to back down.

Perhaps it is best to hedge your bets and allow Newgard to maintain official capacity while you operate in the shadows. That way, a loss will not reflect badly upon you, but neither will a victory. However, a refusal to a member of the Council cannot stand. A lesson must be taught. You must act.

A line must be drawn. If not, Vinnick and the rest of the Council would believe he was a lion without claws. He could have Newgard detained, but what would that prove? He could order Palos to beat him. That would be humiliating to a vessel to have a human take him to task in such a matter, but the other vessels would disapprove.

The Blessed Ones would look down upon that and somewhere down the line, it might give humans ideas. If anyone was to do the deed, it had to be Enzo. But would this lesson be clear enough? Strong enough? Would the rest of the Council respect his standing then? Would they fear him? There was only one thing he could do to prove his might and resolve. Without taking his eyes off of Newgard, Enzo took a step back, drew his sidearm, and shot the man through the head.

No! What are you doing? There are lines that you must not cross!

"He insulted you, Zoras! I will not tolerate it!

Madness! Newgard and Zauw are not without rank, and have proven themselves in the past. There will be a reckoning for this.

"So be it. I will not be handicapped by the Council to do what needs to be done."

You are walking on the edge, vessel. While I agree that the Council plays things too safe, there are other factors to consider.

"Those factors are irrelevant. You even said yourself. Only the final goal is important. The time for half measures is over. Politics should not affect our decisions."

Your single purpose of mind is noble, but with experience, you will understand there is more to victory than just winning.

Enzo holstered his sidearm and watched as Zauw left Newgard's body and floated just in front of his face, as if trying to scold him. Enzo averted his eyes respectfully. "I offer you the vessel of my trusted commander," and gestured to Palos, who stood frozen by this sudden boon. Nearly all Genjix operatives hoped to be a vessel, but this must have come as a shock.

Slowly, Palos knelt. "I serve the Holy Ones," he said, head lowered.

Zauw passed by Enzo and flitted around Palos, as if inspecting the flesh of a new horse about to be purchased. Then finally, he moved on top of Palos' head and sank into his body. Enzo closed his eyes and waited while Palos gagged in pain.

When he finally recovered, he bent a knee to Enzo. "Thank you, Father, for this blessing."

Satisfied, Enzo turned around and nodded. "Good. Let's get to work. Take an account of all human prisoners. They are expendable. Place them standing three meters apart blindfolded, bound, and gagged along the perimeter fence. Let's see if the Prophus are willing to shell their own people."

Newly raised vessel Palos, with adulation now in his eyes, bowed deeper to Enzo than he ever had and hurried away. Enzo watched in satisfaction. He had effectively neutralized Vinnick's hold on this camp and secured Palos' loyalty in one move.

Enzo turned back toward the map of the surrounding area and began to familiarize himself with the landscape as he planned his next move.

What is done is done. Now, the first thing needed is a scouting perimeter three klicks out. And then we will need to send engineering crews to clear away the jungle. Next we need to consider supplies for our increased numbers.

For the next two hours, Zoras and Enzo alone planned their next defensive measures against the encroaching Prophus. If the notes that Newgard had were accurate, this could be the largest Prophus force on the ground in nearly a century. If Enzo could deal a crushing blow here, his standing would certainly be assured. He smiled as he listened to Zoras' plan. This was going to be glorious.

CHAPTER TWENTY-FIVE
TRIP SOUTH

*Empires rose and fell under our hands. It wasn't until just before
the birth of the Babylonian Empire, with Hammurabi at its helm,
that we began to understand humanity's potential. The Council
observed that with every successive rise and fall of an empire, the
primitive man evolved even quicker. Thus, the Conflict Doctrine
became our method of developing humanity.*

*I was a Quasing of low standing during the early years of the
Mesopotamian empires. We were still learning to adapt to the
higher levels of human cognitive thought. We could not treat these
humans as we did the dinosaurs or saber-tooth tigers or primates.*

*I did not rise to prominence until one day, I inhabited the second
son of minor kingdom. His name was Shamshi-Adad.*

Tao

The trip to the county of Kaohsiung in the southern tip
of Taiwan proved much easier once the team secured
financing. Roen didn't realize it, but it seemed one of Lin's
many hidden talents was financial genius. Supposedly,
his master had done so well on the Nikkei that he was a
millionaire. When Roen asked what his secret was, Lin

shrugged and said he picked stocks that rhymed. The old man was either full of it, or the greatest idiot savant stock broker in the history of trading.

Regardless, for old time's sake, and after much begging and pleading, Roen left his meeting with Lin three million Taiwanese dollars richer, which was supposed to bankroll the team for a few weeks. He wasn't sure exactly how much the conversion to US dollars was, but he based his calculations on the fact that an order of stinky tofu at the street market cost forty Taiwanese dollars, so he had roughly seventy-five thousand stinky tofu worth of funds.

They rented vans from the Bamboo Union and stayed off the grid. The Genjix undoubtedly watched for financial transactions. The team never moved in groups of more than two, and made sure to stay away from areas with surveillance. A week later, they had settled into a rental apartment near the port in Kaohsiung. Ray found it in the classifieds from a couple who were studying abroad in South Korea. It didn't have all the perks that a standard safe house had in the States, but compared to their previous digs, the small two-bedroom condo was a mansion. And it only cost twenty-five thousand Taiwanese dollars a month, or six hundred stinky tofu.

Roen tossed his duffel bag to the corner of the living room and did a quick walkthrough of their new home. They still bunched three to a room, and one on the couch and floor, but it wasn't too bad. They had just enough time to settle in and get a reconnaissance team going. Having sat on their collective asses for a week, the team was raring to go. He ordered Stan and Ray to get some supplies at the local grocery store, Jim to get a detailed map of the Linhai Industrial Park, and Grant to make dinner. He put Hutch on guard duty and left Faust to his bonding sessions with Ramez.

Roen wouldn't admit it to the guys, but his concern for Faust was growing. His friend had good and bad days, and was often caught arguing with himself in the corner. Obviously, he hadn't learned to use his inside voice yet when speaking to the Quasing. Or maybe he just didn't care. The conversations never sounded pleasant either. That night, Roen watched from inside the condo as Faust spent all of dinner sitting outside on the balcony ranting at the air.

"Maybe you should have a talk with Ramez. See what's going on."

That would be rude. Quasing do not tell each other how to deal with their hosts.

"Maybe he and I should talk to him."

That inappropriateness extends to you too, Roen. Let them figure it out.

Roen kept an eye on Faust as the rest of the men ate. His friend had not moved from the balcony all night. Finally, as they were clearing the table, he brought dinner to Faust as an excuse to chat. He walked out to the balcony with a bowl of brown rice with tofu in one hand and a six-pack of Taiwan beer in the other. He placed the food and beer on the small table and pushed it over. Faust didn't seem to care about either and continued staring out into the night. Unfazed, Roen sat down next to his friend and put his feet up. They sat in silence for ten minutes. Roen had hoped that Faust would open up first. When he didn't, Roen decided to give it a go.

"Kind of muggy tonight, huh?" he said casually.

Eloquent as always I see. You must score quite often in speed dating.

"Hush. I'm trying to break the ice."

"Is there something I can help you with, Roen?" Faust spoke in a dull, tired voice. "If it's okay with you, I'd just like to be left–"

"You know," Roen quipped. "Did I tell you how I used to be this fat dude who weighed over two hundred pounds? Was wearing size forty-two pants. Huffed and puffed going up and down an elevator. Then one day, this crazy voice started talking in my head. Made me do all sorts of crazy shit like jogging and throwing out pot pies. Hell, he hurt my feelings and called me names. Made me go shopping for clothes." He paused. "Did you know that I never shopped for clothes until I was thirty? My mom used to do that for me." Roen swore he saw the end of Faust's mouth tilt up just a smidgen.

"Look," Faust put his hands behind his head and stared straight up. "I know what you're trying to do and I appreciate it, but I don't need a pep talk. And honestly, just don't even try."

"I'm just saying, as a host, I can sympathize," Roen struggled for the right words.

Faust's eyes narrowed. "Just because you're a host doesn't mean you went through the same things. You're not a mind reader. You don't know what I'm thinking. And by the way, it's none of your goddamn business anyhow." His voice trailed off, and the two ended up sitting in silence again.

Is this unfolding as you planned? I told you this was not a wise idea.

"Did I ever tell you about my pregnancy theory?" Roen quipped again.

Good Lord. Not this.

"I'm pretty sure I know how pregnancy works," Faust said dryly.

"I'm talking about the pain."

"You mean how my wife always lords over me about how much pain it was to give birth to my two kids?"

"Exactly. So you know what I told Jill? We were coming back from a Nationals game. I had drunk too much beer and we were still twenty minutes from home. I told her that it hurt so much holding it in that now I knew what it felt like to give birth."

Faust choked on his beer and gasped at Roen in disbelief. "You didn't!"

Roen shrugged. "As a guy who has been shot a couple of times, I have a pretty good gauge for pain. I think holding the bladder ranks up there. Pregnancy couldn't be that much worse."

And you wonder why Louis thinks you are an idiot.

"Well, Tao, she didn't have to announce my theory to her entire family and force me to explain myself."

Faust held his hands up in front of Roen's face as if holding an imaginary ball. "You realize that a baby comes out of a woman's vagina about the size of a cantaloupe." His hands extended out a little more. "It has to expand to that size."

"Maybe a fat baby," Roen grumbled.

"That's the dumbest thing I've ever heard," Faust said in dismay, giving Roen an incredulous look. "My wife would whack me on the side of the head if I told her that."

"Jill did," Roen admitted.

Faust frowned. "And how exactly does this relate to a Quasing in my head?"

"It doesn't," Roen admitted. "Just wanted to see if you still had a sense of humor. But look, you're going through some stuff right now, much like how I did when I first got Tao. Yeah, both our circumstances were different, but just because I don't know exactly what you're going through doesn't mean I don't recognize the pain and confusion you're dealing with. Not sure if you've noticed, but you just had a sudden change in your life that's akin to a woman getting pregnant, except for them it's nine months. For you, there's no going back. For a woman, it's mostly biological. For you, it's completely psychological. And to be honest, I bet Ramez's an asshole to boot."

That earned a chuckle from Faust. "You got one thing right so far."

"So what is it?" Roen continued. "You feel exposed? No more privacy in your world? Is Ramez harping because you're not subscribing to his every whim?"

"You were a blank slate when Tao found you," Faust said stubbornly. "He was able to mold you. I'm an old dog. You can't just teach me new tricks. You don't know how I feel–"

"You mean about losing control of your life? How you're suddenly not sure if the sounds inside your head are from yourself or this alien presence?" Roen shrugged. "Maybe you're right. Every other Quasing since the dawn of time has gotten along swimmingly with their host except you. The problem must be you." He took a swig of the Taiwan beer and passed it over.

Faust stared at the can for a moment before taking it. "It's a lot to get used to," he conceded. "Nothing like how I thought it'd be."

"Just remember," Roen said. "We're not the Genjix. We don't consider the Quasing some form of holy angel from up on high. You're Ramez's partner and you both have to treat each other with a certain degree of respect and deference.

Set up boundaries. You two are stuck together for a long time."

Faust downed the beer and crushed the can in his hands. Roen picked up two more and handed one to him. They clinked cans and sat in silence again.

"A long, long time," Roen finally said, really elongating those vowels.

"Like being pregnant forever," Faust added, lighting a cigarette.

Roen finished his beer and patted Faust on the shoulder. "Anyway, I'm here if you need someone to talk to. Figure your crap out, because we need Faust back." He turned to leave.

"Hey, Roen," Faust called. "Thanks."

Roen nodded. "Any time, buddy. By the way, since you can't seem to sleep right now, you get first watch. Make happy with Ramez and get your ass back to work."

CHAPTER TWENTY-SIX
DINNER PARTY

The Great War almost saw me to the Eternal Sea. I was unprepared for Franz's death, and survived only by flitting through a Serbian national. All that I had built to obtain a host in the Prussian royalty was lost in an instant. In those four years, I occupied over forty hosts.

It took until near the end of the war before I was able to regain my equilibrium and inhabit another young Prussian nobleman. It took several more years to re-establish my lines of communication with the Prophus network. Then World War II happened.

Baji

Jill's eyes started drooping somewhere in between Senator Gastigone's diatribe about defense, the deficit, the debt, and some other d-something. Her brain wasn't computing on all cores right now. He had this monotone voice that had an inflection range between middle C and C sharp. His monologue became a *Peanuts* episode with the teacher making *wah wah wah* noises.

Wake up!

Jill shook herself and stifled a yawn. She spent the next few minutes willing her eyes to stay as peeled open as possible. She picked up a glass of water and sipped. It was her fifth sip in as many minutes. She wasn't even thirsty, but the pretense of drinking helped keep her awake. Her body swayed as if she was at sea and she desperately sought a way to conclude the meeting. Then she noticed that Gastigone had finished talking and was looking at her expectantly.

"What did he say?"

He asked if Wilks was serious about the tort reform compromise.

"I don't remember. Help me, Baji. I'm dying here."

Repeat after me.

Jill launched a rather eloquent defense of Wilks' tort initiative and how he felt that addressing that issue along with campaign transparency would have a trickle-down effect on all of government. Then she continued with how cap limits of contributions would hurt Gastigone's party much less than hers.

"Baji, Wilks won't touch tort reform with a ten foot pole. We can't sell this to Gastigone."

You mean we are going to lie? Oh, the travesty.

"You're writing checks I can't cash."

We will cross that bridge when we get there.

At the very end of the meeting, she received his lukewarm support, which didn't leave her with any fuzzy feelings about their chances.

"Will you be attending the Exxon Gala tonight?" he said as he stood to leave. "I would like to discuss this further."

Jill cursed. She yearned for an early bedtime. Marco had gleefully informed her about a particularly grueling session tomorrow and she wanted to rest for it.

"Of course, Senator," she smiled. "Wouldn't miss it for the world."

"Do you have a date?" he asked, a bit too coy. "My wife couldn't make it from Kansas."

"I do," she replied hastily. Her heart panicked at the thought of being his date. An entire night sitting next to Gastigone might end up with one of them dead. She just hoped Marco was available.

Of course he is. His job is to protect you. You will have a wonderful time. I know the perfect dress for you to wear.

"Quiet, you. Stop trying to set us up."

Imagine how dashing he would look in a tuxedo. You would have such beautiful, intelligent children.

"I swear if you're calling my son ugly and dumb, I will never speak to you again."

Jill made a polite exit and hurried back to the office. If she had to attend this gala tonight, her day was just cut in half. She crossed Pennsylvania Avenue, her eyes wandering to the White House as she passed. She reminded herself to make sure Marco's background check went through alright. It usually took Secret Service weeks to clear someone. Paula had ordered him cleared expediently. Hopefully there weren't any problems, or she'd end up with Gastigone all night.

Speaking of the devil, Marco miraculously materialized next to her, strolling as if he didn't have a care in the world. He kept looking straight ahead and murmured just loud enough for her to hear. "Your bangle blipped, showing an elevated heart rate. Is everything alright?"

"I got asked out on a date," she growled.

Marco's mask of smug confidence was momentarily shattered. He laughed. "That cad," his voice quivered as he covered his mouth. "Tell me... did he offer to buy you dinner as well?"

Jill scowled. She wasn't in the mood for his patronizing. "Your job is to protect me, not give a running commentary on my life."

"Oh, come now, Jill," he said jovially, "why so peeved? You're a beautiful single woman. You have to know men would come calling."

Jill crossed 14th Street and cut through Freedom Plaza. She might actually get to have lunch today at a decent hour. She stopped near one of the food trucks parked on 13th and ordered bibimbap tacos.

"You want one?" she asked, already stuffing half a taco in her mouth.

"Oh, no, thank you. I have a delicate palate." He grimaced at the heavily fermented kimchee. Jill dropped the other taco into her purse. She'd have to eat on the go. Wilks had a conference call in ten minutes and she had to be there to babysit. "I'm not going to make it," she said, raising her non-taco hand to hail a cab. She turned to Marco. "I'm heading back to the office. Do you have a tux?"

"I am a gentleman," he exclaimed, lifting his chin as if that were all the answer she needed.

"I must live in a country of Neanderthals," she muttered. Neither Roen nor her father owned one. "Wear a tux tonight. We have a dinner function. Six thirty." She got into the cab and stuck a finger out the window. "Don't be late. I want to be in bed by ten, so we can do your stupid monkey jumping thing tomorrow."

"It's called dash vault," he called out as her cab pulled away. "And we're going to do hundreds of them. It'll be fun!"

Jill paced nervously on the corner waiting for Marco, who moments earlier had notified her that he was five minutes away. She was wearing a strapless black dress that showed off a bit more of her figure than she was comfortable with. She had originally bought this dress before she had had Cameron. Some of the fitting here and there was tighter than she liked.

Tonight would be something different. This would be the first time she brought a date other than her boss to one of these gatherings. People would talk. The Hill was a small place and just as bad as any high school in America. Everyone in town knew everyone else. And tonight, Jill was bringing a new player to the party. There would be talk.

Her separation from Roen wasn't a secret, and it was perceived as a weakness in many political circles. If you can't even keep your marriage together, how do you expect to run the country? Something bad and underhanded must have happened to break up a family with children. The real reason aides separated was much less salacious than the gossip. People here at the capital just worked too damn much.

Four minutes after Marco called, she caught eye of his silent little toy car zipping up. He got out and jogged around to open the passenger side door. Jill hid her smile. Having the door opened for her never grew old.

Polite and punctual. There are just some manners that one cannot teach.

"They just don't make them like they used to anymore."

Marco was dressed like a model in one of those catalogs. He wore a custom-tailored gray charcoal tux with a blue tie that suited him perfectly. One could always tell when a tux was made just for the man. He was also clean-shaven, and while she hadn't minded his manly five o'clock shadow, he cleaned up nicely. She had to check herself from staring.

"You look lovely as always," Marco said as he held the door open.

"You look alright, I guess," she sniffed with an exaggerated air of indifference. She got in and they sped off toward the party. On the way, she reminded him that they were in her world now. She showed him a hand signal for him to step away, and more importantly, another to rescue her from an unwelcome conversation. Then he refreshed with her the signs she should use for help, follow, danger, flee, kill, and a dozen others. By the time they got to the party, they had built an entirely new sign language of their own. To be honest though, Jill only remembered help and bathroom, the two she considered most important.

"Why can't we just use the military ones?" she said as they parked four blocks from the party.

"Because then our secret sign language will be known by probably a dozen others in the room," he said. "How am I supposed to profess my undying love with ten complete strangers eavesdropping?"

He held out his elbow, and they strolled to the party leisurely. She cursed her high heels. As was standard practice, he had parked his car several blocks away. If something went down, it would give them space to maneuver. Wearing flats would have been a glaring and gossiped about mistake. Still...

"Could you have parked a little closer?" she grumbled.

"I can carry you if you'd like," he said.

"I just never get to take advantage of valet anymore," she said. "Especially in this town."

Hard to make a quick getaway when you have to wait for the valet to pull your car up.

"You're not the one wearing heels day in and day out."

The price of beauty is never cheap. Ask Helen of Troy.

"That's just mythology."

If you only knew how many silly wars were started over a woman.

Parties at the White House were never small events. Security was tighter than Fort Knox. Background checks had to be done weeks in advance, and getting invited to one was like pulling the golden ticket out of a chocolate bar. It was the highlight of any political operative's existence in the capital. Most aides never got to see the inside of the West Wing. This was Jill's third trip here and it still filled her with awe as she walked past security into the ballroom. She stopped at the doorway and soaked in the atmosphere.

"I can't believe I wanted to skip this," she said as they mingled with the crowd. The truth about the White House was, being two hundred years old, it looked dated and didn't have all the luxury of say, the Four Seasons. It was the White House though, and for Jill, this was hallowed ground.

She turned to Marco. "It's a good thing the British Embassy pushed your clearance through so fast. Otherwise, we'd be missing out."

"Well, I am a lord," he shrugged as if he were saying he liked pancakes.

"Excuse me, your majesty," she said playfully.

"Did the royal family and the forty or so in line ahead of me suddenly keel over?" he grinned. "Your lordship will do."

Jill rolled her eyes. "The day I call you that is the day–"

"Your lordship," Wilks approached them with a glass of whiskey in each hand. He handed one to Marco. "So good to see you again. Hello, Jill."

"Marco will do, Senator," Marco replied, taking the glass and shaking Wilks' hand.

"Senator," she replied. Marco and Wilks began chatting away as if they were two fraternity brothers, leaving Jill feeling invisible.

"How did he leapfrog me on Wilks' totem pole?"

Strong bromance.

"And I even wore heels and a cute dress."

With the two men busy, Jill helped herself to a glass of white from a passing waiter and made her rounds, greeting acquaintances and enemies alike. Inevitably as at all such functions, talk turned to politics. Within a span of ten minutes, she had lost half a dozen votes to two of Wilks' bills and was offered to cosign another. Then she got her second drink.

These events felt more like an extension of work than they did parties. The venues were different, the drinks flowed, and she wore a tight dress, but the discussions were always the same. After thirty minutes, she took a break from deciding the fate of the nation and looked for her date.

Marco was across the room, still chatting with Wilks. However, his entourage had quadrupled in size. There was a football team's worth of men surrounding them, hanging onto his every word. The group suddenly erupted in laughter, and someone patted him on the back. Jill didn't know how he did it, but in less than an hour, he had become the second most popular person in the capital. It was a good thing the president wasn't here, or they'd be two colliding attention-grabbing black holes destroying the galaxy.

He has a way about him.

"I give him that. The few times I dragged Roen to these events, he looked like a cornered mouse in a snake pit."

Marco is a man cut from a different cloth.

"Hello, Jill."

She turned around and tensed. "Simon."

He pointed to one of the side corridors. "Could I speak with you in private for a moment?"

She looked desperately toward Marco, but his back was to her as he held court on the other end of the floor. So much for being her bodyguard.

Play it cool. Simon cannot act here.

She followed him out into the hallway adjoining the main room, and he immediately rounded on her, whispering in a heated tone.

"What the hell are you trying to pull?" he snarled. "Word is out you're building an alternative plan. We had a deal!"

"You had a deal. I'm exploring options," she said, refusing to back down. "You think the Prophus are just going to be your lap dog because you threaten us?"

He grabbed her elbow and squeezed. "The Genjix are allowing you to play in the game because it's easier for all of us. We can do this alone if necessary. You won't like it."

She pulled her elbow back. "You'll still have your meeting with Wilks. You just might have to sweeten the pot."

Simon looked like he was about to lunge at her when suddenly he stiffened up.

Marco materialized behind them, talking with his mouth full. "Have you tried the shrimp cocktail yet? Wonderful, really. I must commend the chef." He leaned in close to Simon's ear and spoke in a whisper only he and Jill could hear. "It's messy eating though. Good thing it comes with toothpicks. I have one right now sticking into the base of your neck, Genjix. A little jab and it goes into your brain stem. You'll be paralyzed and eating apple sauce for the rest of your life. So let me ask you, do you really want to continue this conversation right now?"

Simon froze and slowly raised his hands.

"Are we done here?" she said coolly. "I have better things to do. Now back to your masters, dog. I'm sure we'll speak again."

Simon turned to Marco and studied him. "I don't recognize you, betrayer."

Marco stuck out his hand and they shook.

Simon hissed. "Ah, the famous Ahngr. You're far from home. What brings you to the colonies?" He suddenly winced and his knee buckled.

"Biall," Marco said, iron grip on Simon's hand. "I see your latest host is another weasel, just like all the others you inhabit. I thought you'd have learned your lesson after the beating mine gave yours in Frankfurt. What's with you and tadpoles?" He gave Simon one final bone-crunching squeeze. "Don't ever threaten Ms Tan again. I will end you."

"Just talking shop," Simon said, quickly retracting his hand back. "It's what we do here in Washington."

"Walk along, Genjix. And if I so much as see you look her way tonight, we will have words again, and they might be the last you'll hear."

Jill watched Simon beat a hasty retreat. "You know I had him right where I wanted him," she said.

"Of course," Marco replied, wiping his hands with a handkerchief. "I just didn't want him to have you all to himself." He held out an elbow. "Now that the unpleasantness is over, and I've run dry of stories for your stuffy diplomats, may I have this dance?"

"You're calling them stuffy, kettle?" she laughed, accepting it.

Marco led her to the center of the ballroom, where for the rest of the night, they fox-trotted to a quartet. A few times, Jill had to change partners when several ladies in attendance cut in. She had to admit she felt a twinge of jealousy. He was her date after all. Still, by the end of the night, her feet were sore and she bowed out of the last few songs, leaving him for all the other ladies. She walked out to the balcony for some fresh air and saw Wilks.

"Oh, there you are," he said. "I barely saw you all night, and when I did, you were preoccupied."

She blushed. "My apologies, Senator."

"Nonsense," he exclaimed. "Marco's an awfully fine gentleman. You have my blessing."

"For what?" she exclaimed. "Senator, this is a personal matter."

"You're on my team," he said, lighting a cigarette. "When someone's on my team, all matters are personal to me. I'm just saying his lordship is a good guy." He paused. "You deserve it."

Yes you do.

"I appreciate that, but my personal life is none of your damn business," she replied.

"And it's not your business either, Baji."

Of course it is. I have as much stake in this matter as you do.

Wilks took a puff and looked out across the lawn. "I'm just saying you're not wrong."

"Sorry, Senator?"

"You're not wrong. Marco's a good guy, and you do deserve better than what you've been getting." He took two more puffs and then saw a small group approaching. Jill recognized the lady in the black dress as the Surgeon General.

"Damn it," Wilks growled. "Guy can't even clog up his lungs in peace anymore." He stamped out the cigarette and began to walk inside. "By the way, Hogan's aide, Simmons, Sam, or whatever his name is, says you're sabotaging some deal. Wants me to rein you in and bump our meeting up."

"And what did you say, Senator?"

Wilks gave her a lopsided grin. "I told him to schedule it with you." He wiggled a finger. "You're on my team. I watch out for my own." And then Wilks was gone, leaving Jill alone to her thoughts.

CHAPTER TWENTY-SEVEN
SCOUTING

Shamshi-Adad was my first taste of success with empire building. He started without a kingdom, but ended his reign master of all of Upper Mesopotamia. That was when I first understood the incredible strength humans as a species possessed.

Through him, I had risen from one of low standing to the cusp of joining the Grand Council. However, that was a role I held no interest in. I wanted to explore this vast untapped potential and see what successes his offspring could accomplish. Unfortunately, that was not to be. Unlike Quasing, human qualities are not innately transferred to their offspring. His second son, Yamshah-Adad, was a shadow of his father, and soon, all that I had built was blown away, washed away like tears in the rain.

Tao

Roen stared at the bright plastic yellow flowers that lined the grass as he rode up the escalator of Central Park Station in Kaohsiung. It was the most cheerful sight that he'd ever seen leaving a subway. He had always assumed the large port city, like most others of its kind, would be a cesspool of humanity. However, he found it clean and well-maintained, surprising for an industrial district. Or in his own metrics, New York times three on the cleanliness scale.

"Whoever designed these stations must not be functioning on all cylinders," Faust tapped his head with a finger. "I was at the Formosa Boulevard Station yesterday. They had these glass murals on the ceiling. One of them was some white tree nymph stabbing a black monster. Kind of like *Alice in Wonderland* meets Salvatore Dali on acid."

Roen grinned. "I don't care if he's on crack. This sure beats the New York's ant farm subways."

I prefer the Moscow Metro Stations. There is something poetic about underground cathedral domes.

"Bah, it's the same patterns over and over again."

Patterns are fun.

"Patterns cause seizures."

The team reached the top of the escalator and parted ways as if total strangers. Each man had a job to do. It was Roen and Faust's job to contact the local Bamboo Union, the Dragon division, replenish their ammo stores, and inquire about Dylan. The rest of the guys were on surveillance, mapping the harbor and surrounding factories. Grant was on food and hygiene duty: they were out of toothpaste.

What they did know was that the Punai Corporation was based inland on the mainland and had thirteen buildings – four refineries and nine warehouses – in a prime strip of real estate just south of the second harbor entrance. In the old days, they could just call up satellite imagery or bribe the port officials. Now, it was all leg work.

"I miss being at the top of the food chain. What was it like being the Chinese emperor?"

Being emperor sucks.

"Why do you say that? You get to boss everyone around. It's good to be king."

It is too much work and responsibility. Not to mention there is always someone trying to assassinate you. The best job in the world is the third in succession.

"All the power and respect, none of the work?"

Exactly. When I was in Zhu, life was terrible. Every day, we would get inundated with ridiculous requests. No one could make a decision for themselves.

"Well, Zhu was a frigging tyrant. That's what happens when you consolidate power to just you."

Times were different back then. You give a guy too much power and they raise an army and lay siege to your house.

"Yeah, but as the younger brother to the crown prince, aren't you worried that your older brother will throw you off the parapet or lock you in the Tower of London?

During the reign of Christian V, I hid from the Genjix by living in the second heir to the crown. Tensions were high between the brothers as Frederick, the crown prince, was a bit of an insecure control freak. I made young Charles tell his older brother that he had no desire for the crown whatsoever. Once Frederick believed him, Charles was free to do whatever he wanted for the rest of his life.

"He must have had a lot of free time on his hands. What form of debauchery did you encourage him into?"

He hunted Genjix in Denmark. Had to stop when he was accused of being a serial killer. Frederick had to save Charles from the executioner.

"It's good to be the serial killing brother of the king."

The two found the Dragon's base of operations behind a knick-knack shop that sold thousands of useless trinkets on the edge of the harbor near the National Sun Yat Sen University. The tiny storefront was much larger inside than it seemed out front. They were led to the back and passed through a wall of beaded curtains into a maze of dark corridors and small side rooms. Several groups of thugs lounged around, their wary eyes watching Roen and Faust's every move. A few minutes and two levels down later, Roen was hopelessly turned around.

I know how to get back.

"Haven't seen anyone worth breaking a sweat over. Most of them I can take with one hand tied behind my back."

They will swarm. You did leave your gun at the entrance.

"We're low on bullets anyway."

They were finally led to a small dimly lit room. Six men sat at a round table beneath a floodlight shining down from the ceiling. Wads of crinkled cash, two pistols, and several pieces of jewelry were piled in the center. The men looked up from their card game once and then ignored Roen and Faust for the next ten minutes. At first, Roen assumed these gangsters were playing poker. It took him a few minutes to realize the game was pinochle.

"I thought only grandmothers play pinochle. And what's with these guys and making us wait all the time?"

We did come to them, after all.

One of the gangsters looked up and gestured for them to approach. Again, it was the one facing the door they came in from. "You're the one Da Ge sent?" he asked in passable English.

"We need supplies," Roen took out a sheet of paper and placed it on the table.

The leader, Roen had nicknamed him Sloppy Eater for the half a dozen stains on his cutoff white shirt, glanced it over and then handed the note off. "You a friend of Da Ge Han, I give you good deal. Two hundred thousand."

Roen blanched at the number. Unless he was hunting werewolves and needed silver bullets, there was no way ammo cost five thousand stinky tofu.

Let it go. We are on an island where firearms are illegal.

"Someone must have written 'sucker' on my forehead or something."

"We also need harbor identifications," Roen said. "For Punai Corp."

The room erupted in low mutters as the mobsters exchanged uneasy looks. They definitely hit a nerve bringing up Punai.

"What you want with Punai?" Sloppy Eater said. "Da Ge Han said my boys don't touch them. It will be expensive. Fifty thousand for two to get past security."

"We need eight," Faust replied.

"Five hundred thousand for eight."

Roen made a choking noise like he just swallowed a golf ball. "That doesn't even add up!" he stammered. "How could two cost fifty and eight cost five hundred? If anything, it should be a bulk discount."

Sloppy Eater's face darkened, and Roen hear the distinct click of safeties being switched off.

"Steal one and no one will miss. Steal eight and people get suspicious. Cause more problems," he growled.

That makes sense. Just buy them and be done with it.

Roen reluctantly paid the extortion and silently mourned the dwindling pile of money he had just acquired a few days earlier. At this rate, he'd have to ask Lin for more money in a week. They waited around for an hour and watched Taiwanese soap operas while Sloppy Eater's men got their identification cards together. At the end, nearly a million Taiwanese dollars lighter, they got what they came for:

three crates of ammunition and the fake IDs they needed to get into Punai.

"Do not trace these back to us, or you will have trouble with the Dragons," Sloppy Eater shook his finger.

Roen nodded. "Understood. My boys just want to poke around the refinery and the warehouses."

"These IDs work for the office building and refinery only. Warehouses use different locks. We cannot get those," Sloppy Eater added as they were ushered toward the exit.

"Wait a minute!" Roen said. "We just paid good money. You should have told us this earlier!"

Sloppy Eater glared at him. "Everyone knows warehouse should be kept safer. Else workers will steal everything."

Roen wished he had a clever retort. Instead, he just scowled and stomped away. As they were walking out, Faust looked back and asked. "By the way, we're looking for someone. Face burned, real ugly. Aussie. Kind of big like an ogre. Have you seen him?"

Sloppy Eater gave a surprised start and shook his head emphatically. "No such person."

They know or at least heard something.

"We could really use some help in locating him," Faust added. "We will pay handsomely."

Roen nudged Faust in the ribs. "Stop throwing money at them. You want to go back to instant noodles?"

Be careful! Sloppy Eater just exchanged glances with three others. Four more are approaching from the back, weapons out. Two batons, a tonfa, two bats, and three metal pipes. No guns.

"Why are you looking for this Dylan?" Sloppy Eater asked.

They know where he is!

"I didn't mention his..." Roen frowned.

He noticed two men walk up to either side of him. Things were about to go down in here. Ramez must have just told Faust as well. Suddenly, he tensed in a not-so-subtle fashion. Out of the corner of his eyes, Roen saw a shadow move. He lashed out reflexively, swinging the ammo crate in his hand like a baseball bat and struck a mobster in the face.

The room suddenly got very crowded.

Three to your left. Two right. More pouring in from the back entrance.

The gangsters mobbed them.

Roen was barely able to get his hands up when a machete cut into his forearms. He was lucky the Kevlar was thick. He lashed out, grabbing the kid and throwing him with a hip toss. Faust meanwhile took on several mobsters at a time. He had knocked three of them down already when someone clocked him with a baton. Then more Dragons converged on them.

There are too many! Take the exit behind you, second right, up the stairs.

"What about Faust?"

Nothing we can do for him.

"No way! I'm not leaving him with these punks!"

Roen barreled into the two standing over Faust, shoulder checking one and elbowing the other. He bent down, grabbed Faust by the collar, and dragged him to his feet.

"Come on, man," he shouted in Faust's ear. "These guys couldn't have hit you that hard. Ramez, wake his ass up!"

Three of the toughs converged on him. Two were smart enough to stay out of his reach. The third one, the dummy, got too close. Roen plucked the baseball bat out of his hand and smacked him on the temple. He was about to finish the kid off when Tao intervened.

Do not kill him!

Roen paused in mid-swing. "Why? These odds aren't bad enough yet?"

Think about it. Not a gun drawn. They are trying to take you alive. If you start killing them, they will change their minds. As long as there are not any casualties, they might not draw a gun. If they do, you have zero chance of survival.

Roen scanned the dozen or so guys in the room. Tao was right. There wasn't a gun to be seen. Sure, there were several baseball bats, lead pipes, and knives. Hell, he even saw a cricket bat, but no guns.

One of the two standing in front of him swung a tonfa in his hand. Roen parried with the heavy end of the bat and let the blow glance to the side. Then he lunged forward with the handle and stuck the guy in the throat. He collapsed.

"Let's hope he is still alive. Maybe I can get him a Band-Aid."

No need to get touchy. Take the door behind you.

A trickle of blood ran down Faust's forehead. Roen dragged him backward, swinging the bat at whoever got close. The gangsters gave him more respect after he took down four of theirs in a span of twenty seconds. He reached the back wall and grappled for the doorknob.

They entered a long, thin storage room with shelves stocked with liquor. Roen slammed the door shut and tried to catch this breath. He cursed. They were in a bad spot. It was a dead end. He had hoped for another exit, but it was obviously too much to ask for.

Faust was regaining his senses. Roen put him down next to the metal door. It was sturdy commercial door, but it had no lock. He would have to guard it the entire time until they came up with an escape plan. Hopefully, it would buy them enough time to figure a way out of this mess.

"Why did they attack us? Was this a trap all along?"

I do not believe so. They were not aggressive until Faust mentioned Dylan. Perhaps the Genjix have an arrangement with these triads down south.

Roen's heart sank. If that was true, then those Dragon guys would be sending for the Genjix right now. Then the two Quasing would be screwed as well. The door knob turned slowly and Roen charged just as it opened. He stuck his bat through the opening and smashed someone's face. He slammed the door shut again.

"Next guy that tries that is getting his face rearranged!" he screamed.

Then he looked around the room desperately for another opening. A vent, a sewage hole, anything. Unfortunately, the room really was a dead end. Roen exhaled and leaned against the door. Their only chance was to buy some time in here until Faust regained his senses. Roen would need him if they were going to fight their way out. Or better yet, maybe if they were missing long enough, the rest of the guys would come looking for them. Both plans seemed farfetched, but it wasn't like Tao was providing options.

Negotiate.

"I'm stuck in their liquor closet. What exactly do I have to offer?"

To not go down fighting. They already saw what you could do. I am sure the triad do not relish having more of their men injured.

"Something tells me the bosses here don't care much about the welfare of their men, but I guess it's worth a try."

Roen stood up and shouted at the door. "Hey, let's talk this over. Can I talk to your boss? We can work something out."

Someone on the other side shouted something. Tao translated it as "Fuck you."

So much for that. Roen sat back down against the door and waited. If they were going to be unreasonable, so be it. He could wait them out. Not like he had much choice anyway. Eventually, one of these pricks would have to either talk to him or try to take the room by force. Roen was a patient man; he would be ready.

Twelve hours later, Roen was about ready to throw a fit. He paced the room and muttered obscenities. He thought at the very worst they would wait an hour or so. Now, half a day later with nothing to drink but hard liquor and plum wine, Roen's patience had run out. He was hungry, thirsty, and completely hammered. And to top things off, it seemed the door locked on the other side! Now they really were trapped.

Faust had recovered and was currently keeping watch. He hadn't drunk as much as Roen and was relatively sober. Eventually though, they would have to sleep. Both were exhausted already. And if they were both caught asleep, it would be the end of them.

As the thirteenth hour approached, there was a knock on the door. Both Roen and Faust stood up, weapons in hand. "What do you want?" Roen snarled at the door.

"Don't worry about the world coming to an end today," someone spoke in English.

It cannot be!

It took a second for the statement to register, then a wave of relief swept over Roen and he broke into a grin. "It's already tomorrow in Australia."

The door knob turned and a large figure stepped into the room. It was dark, but he could make out the outline of a disfigured face. Roen moved forward, and the two embraced in the only way straight military men were comfortable doing, with rough pats on the back and what Roen referred to as the clamp of doom. Laughing, Dylan picked him off the ground and shook him like a rag doll. He then gave Roen a playful smack on the shoulder that nearly knocked him off his feet.

"What the blazes are you doing here? Did you actually come crawling back to the Prophus? Run out of lunch money or did you finally come to your senses about your wife? And why do you smell like you've been on a binger?"

"I never lost my senses about my wife," Roen grinned back. Only Dylan could talk to him this way and not get a rise out of him. "We got a problem here. There's an army of triad mobsters trying to kill us. How did you get past them?"

Dylan frowned and beckoned him to follow. Together, they walked through the door to the next room where at least two dozen Dragon members in full battle gear waited. This time, Roen saw guns; lots of them. Sloppy Eater was standing in front with murder on his face. For a split second, Roen thought Dylan had changed sides. An angry rumble erupted from the group. None seemed too happy to see them.

Yen changing sides is laughable. It would never happen.

"How many times have you said that?"

Too often, unfortunately.

Dylan held up his hands trying to calm everyone down. "Da Ge Chang, there seems to be a misunderstanding."

Chang came forward and jabbed a shotgun into Roen's chest. "I offer you our support and you attack us!"

"You were moving in on us," Roen said. "Don't think we didn't notice that."

"We were watching out for Brother Dylan. He warned us the enemy was hunting him," Chang shot back.

Dylan gave Roen a shut-your-mouth glare. "Da Ge Chang, we will gladly make this situation right."

"We generously provide you shelter and weapons, and your idiot attacks us!" He emphasized each syllable of idiot with a jab of the shotgun. "One of the injured is my nephew. He is only seventeen."

"Maybe you should be a better uncle and not steer him toward two-bit thuggery as a career," Roen muttered under his breath.

The look Dylan gave him could have killed a lesser man. He turned back to Chang and tried to explain the misunderstanding. He shot Roen that same look again when he found out that it was him who had thrown the first punch. Then he finally buried his face in his hands when Chang explained that nine of his men were in the hospital.

Nine in two minutes. Color me impressed.

"Half teenagers though. It was like being the only adult in a kid's karate class."

I fear teens more than adults in a fight. If I may remind you of your encounter with Jacob.

"You may not. In fact, we must never speak of it again."

If anything, it might actually be a good time to go over it. I doubt it will be the last time we encounter him. I believe him to be an Adonis Vessel.

Roen harrumphed at the thought. Of course that punk would be an Adonis Vessel. More and more over the past few years, these young, annoying superhumans had been popping up like weeds among the Genjix ranks. And he hated to admit it, but those kids had been eating their Wheaties, or whatever genetically modified formula the Genjix were feeding them. In the past few years, these

Adonis, some barely old enough to drive, had begun to form the backbone of a new generation of Genjix officers. And in every encounter, they had proven to be difficult adversaries.

Finally, it all came down to restitution. Fortunately, Roen hadn't killed or injured any of them too seriously, or the triad might have been honor-bound to kill him. Instead, because of Dylan's longstanding relationship with this particular group, Roen was allowed to pay for the damage and dishonor he caused. In the end, it came out to another cool half million Taiwanese dollars. Roen had somehow spent two-thirds of Lin's money in the first few days. At this rate, they would be broke by lunch. After paying up, the Dragon members ushered the three out and told Roen to never show his face again.

Once they were outside, Dylan cuffed him on the shoulder. "Really? How did you make this big mess in such a short period of time? I've been here for weeks and haven't made a peep. You haven't unpacked yet and already they almost put a hit out on you."

"Sorry?" Roen smiled sheepishly. "How did you find us anyway? What are you doing here?"

"What am I doing here?" Dylan looked surprised. "One of Chang's boys runs to my place saying some guys were looking for me. As far as I know, the only people after me were the Genjix. Then he tells me they locked you in their closet, so I came."

Roen grimaced. "More like we locked ourselves. So you were working with them all this time?"

Dylan nodded. "Chang and I go way back. I used to help them run guns during our pirating days. So what the bloody hell are you doing here? I didn't send for you, nor am I dead."

"Wait, you knew we were here all this time? We've been looking for you!" Roen stammered.

Dylan smacked his forehead with his palm. "Wuehler's team is supposed to stay up north and cause a ruckus."

"I don't get it. Why?" Roen said.

I do. We were never supposed to find Dylan. We were decoys.

CHAPTER TWENTY-EIGHT
NOT AS EASY AS IT SEEMS

We call ourselves your gods, and it is true in every sense. We are the parents who raised humanity, and like any gods, we own your future to use as we feel was necessary. The vessels who follow us do so knowing that those who serve live an eternity through their Quasing.

Elevation is not without cost, though, and our will not without consequences. There is a price to pay for our blessing. The humans who serve will be adapted. All others will perish.

Zoras

Enzo's first priority was to stabilize the situation until reinforcements came. That had proven more difficult than anticipated. The very next day, Vinnick's two thousand reinforcements arrived. Its commander, a stubborn vessel named Nguyen, had refused to hand command over to Enzo. He had to be put down and Vuru, his Holy One, given to another of Enzo's hand-picked men. Genjix forces now numbered three thousand, yet Enzo would not feel at ease until the rest of his men came, for a total of five thousand men at his disposal.

A significant portion of Enzo's training at the Hatchery since he was old enough to walk was war, be it hand-to-hand combat, planning a coastal invasion, or organizing an underground resistance. He had begun studying historical battles as soon as he finished his alphabets. By the age of four, he had read Sun Tzu's *The Art of War*. By six, he had memorized it. By twelve, he had an equivalent to a PhD on the history of war, from Assyrian chariot tactics to Lieutenant Napoleon's first artillery formations to Captain Winter's assault on German fortifications at Brécourt Manor. Enzo knew his calling and dreamed that if given the opportunity, he would shine at his first command. So far, it hadn't worked out the way he had thought it would. For one thing, this Prophus commander wasn't playing fair.

The enemy continually probed the camp's defenses, even with the prisoners lined along the fence, seemingly willing to risk friendly fire. They would hit a part of the perimeter at its weakest, just as shifts ended or if there was a gap in the coverage. Somehow, they had a way of signaling the prisoners. The guard on duty would be taken out, the gate blown, and then a quick raid would nab a dozen men. And it would all happen before any of Enzo's people could react.

In the first two days, there must have been at least twenty attacks. It finally stopped on the third day, when Enzo's men finished burning the forest back a hundred meters. He had cursed that delay. It should have been the first thing he ordered when he got here. However, the constant Prophus attacks forced him into a reactionary role, and he had not had time to assess the situation. He now had a healthy respect for this Prophus commander. Whoever led them was good.

After the no man's land was burned on the fourth day, the enemy did not have a single successful incursion. By the fifth, the attacks had stopped altogether. This gave Enzo the reprieve he needed to strengthen their defenses. On the eve of his sixth day there, Chow sent Enzo a message begging for more subjects, saying they were desperately close to a solution but had no more prisoners. Enzo was tempted to tell him to use Genjix vessels instead.

Out of the question! I do not care how close we are to our goal. Is that understood?

"Of course, Holy One. It was just a thought."

Enzo walked out of the war room and signaled to Palos. "Prep the transport. I want a full security team on board. Get a line to the Chinese military and have two more helicopters delivered. Larger ones this time. We'll never finish this project if we shuttle prisoners ten at a time."

After a slight pause, Palos nodded and left without a word. Enzo watched him disappear around the corner. He was starting to believe he had made an error giving Zauw to Palos. His first was loyal, but would he remain so after being blessed with a Holy One whose loyalty lay elsewhere? Zauw must be incensed with Newgard's death. Who would Palos follow if their orders contradict?

Your decision was not wrong. Palos was best qualified to become a vessel. The vessel follows the Quasing. If Zauw chooses to continue with Vinnick, you must let him go.

Enzo grimaced. He had come to rely on the older commander. To let that valuable resource go to his opposition felt like defeat. But if it was the will of the Holy Ones, he would not question their way.

That night, under cover of darkness, the Mi-171, laden with an equal number of prisoners and guards, took off and headed north toward Lhasa Gonggar Airport. Enzo watched it take off and hover just above the tree line, and then thought no more of it. After all, Genjix controlled the airspace in this region. Fifteen minutes later, however, the base received a distress call.

Enzo was shocked to discover that the Prophus had shot down a transport filled with their own people. He didn't think the Prophus had it in them. They found the wreckage fifty klicks from the camp. All fifteen Genjix operatives were accounted for: nine bodies inside the helicopter and six outside, the furthest nearly a hundred meters away. He was shot through the head.

None of the prisoners' bodies was present, so he could not tell how many had died. This complicated matters. It was clear now that the commander of the enemy would rather kill his own people than let the Genjix experiment on them. Enzo was impressed. He did not think the soft Prophus had the fortitude to make these hard choices. It was what he would have done in their place.

This delay is unacceptable. Send another shipment by morning. Two if necessary.

"Your will, Zoras."

• Enzo spent the rest of the night devising an alternative. This camp was so remote that there were few options available to him. Helicopter transport was easiest, but that idea was off the table now. Land convoys proved too vulnerable. The next option was a plane. However, the airport in Lhasa was five hundred kilometers away, and the Prophus controlled too much of the land between the camp and the city. The alternative was to build a landing strip in the camp. Materials and engineers would have to be flown in, and it would take time.

There is another option. Cross the border and use the Langtang Airport in Nepal. It is a scant fifty kilometers from the camp.

"We have no jurisdiction in Nepal."

The Genjix have jurisdiction everywhere. If we order the Chinese government to speak with their government, we will not be refused.

Enzo's eyes traced the route heading south to the airport from the camp. It was a much shorter journey but would be over mountainous terrain. It was doable, though dangerous. The important thing was to get the convoy out into open space. It was a risk they had to take.

Enzo sent off a quick email to Amanda to arrange the clearance with the Nepalese government. For now, he had to sit tight until reinforcements came. The logistics of sending two thousand men to a remote region of the world was a task the Genjix rarely undertook. The Quasing war did not usually resort to these types of engagements. He was pulling in men from as far away as Europe. That was the only way he could fortify the camp and adequately guard a convoy.

A loud explosion suddenly rocked the camp. Dust and debris rained down from the ceiling. While such things happened regularly, this explosion seemed larger than usual. After the dust had settled, Enzo dusted off his shoulders and studied the map again. Then a series of bigger explosions erupted from every direction, and perimeter alarms began to howl.

"Father," an officer ran in and bowed. "It's a full coordinated attack. All sides."

Get the vessels into the main building. None must escape.

Enzo began giving commands, setting up the defenses for an all-out attack. There was another explosion: west side again. He left the building and waved his personal guards forward as they rushed out into battle. The floodlights on the towers had been taken out, and the northwest corner tower groaned as it lit up the night. It would collapse any minute. The no-man's-land between the camp and the forest was ablaze with bursts of muzzle fire.

"Status," he barked.

"Enemy concentration in the west," Meyers, the commander of the west flank reported. "Under heavy fire."

"We're engaging and pinning them down. The enemy are unable to advance," Tomlinson, commander of the north flank, reported.

"Dead quiet here," Rowe, commander of the eastern flank called in. "Moving men west to support Meyers."

"You stay right there!" Enzo roared. "What's going on with the south?"

"South is confirmed quiet," Palos said. "I still have patrols returning into base via the southern gate. No enemy sightings."

"Cut the lights off the base." Enzo screamed over the din of the battle. "We're painting their targets for them. Focus floodlights three meters above the forest line."

His men quickly complied. The height of the floodlights would temporarily blind the Prophus. It also gave Enzo targets to shoot at. This was his first pitched battle, and two things surprised him. The first was the rush he felt being in the thick of it. His blood boiled, and he had never felt more alive. Every fiber of his being tingled, and he wanted to howl a battle cry as he moved into position, aiming shots at the yellow bursts that lit up the otherwise completely black forest.

The second thing that surprised him was the noise of battle. It was much louder than he could have possibly imagined. So much so that he had trouble communicating orders.

You should be in the war room, not engaged in combat.

"I need to feel the pulse of the battle in order to direct it."

In truth, Enzo reveled in the carnage as he took out several of the Prophus soldiers. He turned to Palos. "Bring your unit. We'll flank the enemy from the south."

That is not wise. You should command.

"I cannot command men hiding in a room. They need to see me lead."

You do not require their respect. You only need to demand they follow.

Another explosion in the center of the camp nearly knocked Enzo off his feet. He continued with Palos and his men as they crept out of the southern entrance and made the sprint to the tree line. There he spread them three meters apart as they cut their way west. It was quieter here in the forest, the sounds of battle far away.

"We must be outnumbered here three to one on this side," Meyers' voice came hurried over the comm.

"Eastern flank is completely dead." Rowe said. "Pulling my men to assist Meyers."

"You stay put!" Enzo whispered angrily. However, he wasn't sure if Commander Rowe heard him. Furious, he tore off his headset. Palos motioned for him to be quiet as they neared the enemy. Something sounded strange up there, as if the sound of the battle was echoing through a pipe.

They found a Prophus soldier firing from an isolated position. He died before he knew what was happening. In the next ten minutes, the team encountered several Prophus fighting in isolated groups. Enzo began to feel uneasy.

"The enemy is scattered here. No nests. How could the attack force be spread so thin?"

They are not. The tree line is three hundred meters long, and the Prophus have been spaced out nearly exactly five meters apiece.

*That means the attacking force could not be more than sixty men.
It is a decoy.*

Then Enzo's team encountered a large speaker sitting on
a tripod piping in the sounds of battle. Enzo took off in a
full sprint following the route he came. The undermanned
Prophus had effectively lured the camp's defenses into
committing to the west.

Enzo rushed back into the camp, trying to call up Rowe
for an update. However, by that time, it was too late. The
enemy was already inside the perimeter, and the base had
erupted into heavy close-quarter fighting. Enzo and his
team mowed their way across the field to the building,
cutting a swathe of death. His ranks grew as more and more
of his men joined in to push the enemy back. By the time
he reached the building, there were over a hundred fighting
alongside him. The enemy thought they had victory in their
grasp. He would show them how wrong they were. He felt
like Achilles killing Trojans.

Dawn broke as the battle raged on within the confines
of the camp. The Prophus had gained a foothold on the
perimeter but were unable to take the main building
housing the vessels. By the time the sun was fully up, they
were forced to pull back. In the end, they had failed to
rescue any vessels. They did, however, release two hundred
humans, no doubt swelling their ranks. That, Enzo could
not care less about.

He watched as the Prophus retreated and disappeared
back into the foliage. Without missing a beat, he summoned
all the officers and had Rowe put in cuffs. The idiot had
disobeyed and deserted his position in an attempt to
improve his standing. His foolishness had allowed the
Prophus to infiltrate the base and almost steal victory. The

298 THE DEATHS OF TAO

Genjix commander begged forgiveness up to the moment Enzo shot him.

"From now on," he declared, "all orders come through me. Follow without fail. Is that understood?"

Enzo then ordered Palos to see to the wounded and begin repairs on the fence. He rushed back to the war room and ordered a convoy of prisoners prepped to leave within minutes. They had just waged a large battle, so both sides were exhausted. Enzo now gambled that the enemy was not prepared to enforce their blockade.

That is clever. You have done the Genjix proud.

He was right. The next day, Chow received a shipment of twenty Prophus prisoners to continue his testing.

CHAPTER TWENTY-NINE
A DEAL WILKS CAN'T REFUSE

In the Quasing's defense, neither the Prophus nor the Genjix were involved in the rise of the Third Reich. In fact, both factions considered the Nazi party an oddball group of madmen. After all, one of Hitler's inner circle was a butcher's apprentice. We thought they were a political party of clowns. Both the Prophus and the Genjix were badly mistaken.

All the Quasing with hosts in Germany during this time were swept into the service of the Reich. We had little choice but to make the best of the situation. My host nobleman, Rolf Hindler, became a young officer of the SS. It was ironic that Yol, never a warrior, was in a decorated general by the name of Erwin Rommel, the Desert Fox.

Baji

"You're not pulling my leg are you, Ms Tan?"

Jill batted her lashes at the sun-baked raisin sitting across the table. Senator Garritano must be the tannest man in his home state of Washington. Having been on numerous trips to Seattle, she didn't think there was enough sun to cook Garritano to that golden crispy hue. He must either spend all his time in Florida or have a tanning booth at home.

Senator Garritano was the number six man in his party and one of the most popular in Congress. He was also so old that he might have been alive when the Roman Senate was in session. And one thing about those who were permanent fixtures on the Hill, they all had their kooky pet projects that everyone else thought were insane.

In Garritano's case, his passion was an earmark for a high-speed rail from Northern California to Alaska. Never mind that the route passed through a sovereign country or that the business logistics of it were unsustainable. He believed that connecting the country together was of paramount importance and fulfilled manifest destiny, Canada's objection be damned.

"Of course not, Senator," she smiled.

Garritano sat back and scratched his cheeks in a way only geriatrics were comfortable doing in public. "Wilks and I have never seen eye to eye, him being a heretic of American exceptionalism. Why would he support me now?"

"I'll take care of Wilks." Jill gave him a reassuring pat on his wrinkled arm. Inside, Jill cringed. Wilks was going to wring her neck when he heard about this, but Garritano's vote was cheap.

"Well, little lady," Garritano winked. "You bought yourself a vote." He squeezed her hand in a way that made Jill want to dig out her sanitizer. Excusing herself as politely as possible, she left the senator's office and hurried to her next appointment.

That is five. One more and we have the filibuster.

Jill ticked off names in her head. She couldn't believe it, but things were falling into place. The past few days had come down to the wire. She had worked the phones frantically, wheeling and dealing, and calling in favors from her entire Rolodex.

At this rate, she owed a quarter of the Senate favors in one form or another to be cashed in at some future time. But in doing so, she had assembled a package of earmarks, bills, and amendments that were not only favorable to Wilks, but to the Prophus as well. The big losers in all this were the Genjix. She just needed a few more pieces to push them over the edge.

Jill left the Hart Senate building and walked across the street to a small Mexican restaurant nestled between an ice cream shop and a shoe shine store. Sitting in the far back, she met the last sweetener that should seal the deal.

"Jill," Senator Karn beckoned to her. He was in a tight primary race trending in the wrong direction. A true independent, none of his constituents liked him very much, but then that was what usually happened when you walked on the line instead of to the side of it. New polls showed him losing badly. His funding was pathetic, and pundits projected that he might not even have enough cash on hand to make it to primary day. This was where Jill came in. While Karn was a weathervane when it came to issues, he was still just one of a hundred votes that controlled legislation in the Senate. And now, she was going to buy him out.

Jill sat down opposite of him and spoke quickly. "Your approval rating is thirty-six percent. Your campaign war chest won't last another two months. You're down six points to an admiral, an American hero no less. You're dropping like a rock. How clear is this picture I'm painting?"

"You said I'd want to meet with you," he grumbled. "If I wanted a recap of how I'm getting my ass kicked, I'd just watch the news."

Jill leaned back and smiled. "Do you still want to win?"

"Do I want to go back to selling tractors in Wisconsin?" he spat.

"Good." She took a piece of paper and slid it across the table. "Here's a list of bills coming up for a vote in the next four weeks. We value your support on every matter. In return, Senator Wilks will campaign on your behalf during the upcoming holiday weekend. His political action committee will also make a sizable donation to your campaign."

Karn palmed the paper and slid it off the table. His eyes narrowed as he scanned the list. Then he tore the paper into pieces. "That's a long list. How large a contribution?"

"Mid five figures. Half up front, half after the holidays."

He shook his head. "Not for that many votes. Low six. Up front."

Squeeze him.

"The nerve!"

He was always a greedy one.

Jill leaned forward. He smelled like tobacco and road kill with a dash of Old Spice.

"Sir," she said in a low voice, "You know Wilks used to live in Wisconsin, don't you? He was the CEO who pulled that pipeline in from the badlands and created what, fifty thousand jobs? He's a hero there."

Karn snorted. "That was twenty years ago. My constituents have the memory of puppies. If you have to dig that far back, maybe Wilks' support isn't worth that much after all."

She stood up to leave. "Think it over. The offer is good until I walk out of the door." She turned and paused. "By the way, Admiral Back went to Annapolis, graduated '82? Interesting, so did Wilks. Perhaps the good admiral would like his old friend to make an appearance and regale the good people of cheese country with some of their old adventures together at the Academy. But then, the last thing Wilks did for them was twenty years ago. I'm sure it wouldn't mean much anymore." She began walking toward the door.

She was halfway across the room when she heard the "wait". She kept looking forward, a small smile escaping her lips. There was a pause, and then Karn said, "I think Wilks makes a convincing argument. I will consider supporting his positions." Jill continued walking out the door as calmly as she could. She had him!

I thought Wilks went to MIT.

"Annapolis, MIT, what's the difference?"

Think he will play?

"We'll find out. The first bill on the list is the energy renewal bill. If Karn votes for it, we're golden then."

Jill headed back to the Hart building and met with four other appointments. By evening, she believed she had built the political firewall she needed for Wilks not to have to meet with Hogan. The deals were rough, and details still had to be hammered out, but she was now in the driver's seat.

She went back to her office to prepare her notes to present to Wilks. When she finished, she gave herself a virtual pat on the back. It had taken an enormous amount of work but she had pulled it off.

Now to sell it to Wilks, which is far from assured.

"After all the work I did, I'll kill him if he says no."

No need to get your hands dirty. We can send a cleaning team in.

"I'm just kidding."

I am not.

A few minutes later, after weeks of cobbling support from every corner of Congress, she put all her cards down on the table and laid out the entire plan to Wilks. Some of her concessions made her feel downright dirty, and others would infuriate him, but her plate of offerings more than compensated for them. At least she hoped it would.

As expected, Wilks threw a fit at some of the deals made. He ranted about putting his name on the F-112 military plane allocation, slammed his fist on his desk when told he was taking the prescription pill plan amendment off Medicare, and literally screamed when told he had to increase corn subsidies for corporate farms in Iowa. And when he heard about campaigning for Karn, she swore he almost took a swing at her. Three very draining hours later, Jill thought the game was lost when he threw her out of his office and slammed the door in her face.

"That went more or less as expected."

I thought it went quite well, actually. Did you see the look on his face when he heard what Gastigone wanted with the military base in Turkey?

"I'm not going to lie, I almost slugged him when he called me a backstabbing turd playing for the other side."

You would have been justifiably excused if you had.

She turned to see Tammy, wide-eyed and pale, standing by the door. "Can I get you something, Jill?" she asked, voice trembling. "Coffee? A cup of water?"

"Tequila," Jill slapped her table. "You'll find a half bottle in the second drawer of my cabinet. And maybe an aspirin. Make that two."

She sat down at her desk and began to drink away her headache. She maintained a calm demeanor but inside, she was a wreck. If Wilks said no, all her hard work was wasted and she would lose all credibility in Congress. Her only remaining option would be resignation, which to be fair, didn't sound like such a bad thing right about now.

An hour later, Wilks came out of his office and sat down opposite her. His face was less red than before and he seemed to have regained some of his composure. Noticing the bottle of tequila, he helped himself to a generous pour.

"Let me ask you something," he said in a precise manner. She could tell he was choosing his words very carefully. "I looked everything over with a fine-toothed comb. And then I compared it with what Hogan offered me. None of it correlates. Yeah you sweetened my deal, but you're asking me to pay a higher price too. The only similarity between your deal and his is the sanctions he is so desperate to lift. Your entire agenda is to keep them. Why?"

"Like I said, the security and economic provisions–" she began.

"You see," he cut her off. "I don't care two shits about these sanctions. None of them affect my home state, and frankly I couldn't care less about trade with a region of the world where everyone is an ally, except for the egghead-shaped kid with the bad hair and nuclear ambitions. And looking at that crazy web of crap you just wove, I know you must have blown your wad on the Hill. So what are you fighting so hard for?"

Jill gave him a blank stare. She didn't have a good answer. She couldn't tell him that there was an alien species that wanted to move some really bad things to China to help their supply chain. She didn't even know what it was. Sitting in uncomfortable silence, she did the only thing she could think of. She poured herself another shot of tequila and tossed it back.

"Who do you really work for?" he asked suddenly.

Oh dear.

Jill spit the precious alcohol all over her desk. She pulled out a tissue and wiped down the mess. She handed Wilks one as well since half the tequila ended up on him.

"I work for you, Senator," she finally said.

He dabbed his probably ruined expensive shirt and tie and shook his head. "I thought you did. I'm not sure anymore."

Watch your words carefully.

"You see," he continued, "I've been in Congress for a long time now, and I'm privy to a lot of classified information. For over fifty years, the CIA has been aware of some sort of secret war going on that spans almost every government on this planet. It's hard to pinpoint, since we can't seem to nail down specific allegiances or central operations. The only things we have to work off are agendas. Now, I can't tell you any more without getting indicted for treason, but what you're doing here fits that description to a T." He leaned back and waited for her response. "Choose your next words very carefully, Jill, because I'm one finger away from calling Langley."

We have seen those reports. The government has a file on both the Prophus and Genjix, but little else. They believe we are secret societies.

"James, I have no idea what you're talking about," Jill stammered. Her pulse raced. She felt like a cornered animal.

"Here's what I do know," he said. "Stop me if this sounds familiar. This sanction is primarily an economic embargo on other first world countries that we are in technological competition with. Let's cut to the chase: it's for China. I've reviewed the embargo list. It's all crap that's only used for scientific, complex manufacturing and a bit of military tech here and there. It's either rare compounds like dysprosium or osmium, or military application compounds like holmium or promethium, or some other ism. Now, there's something on that list that you don't want China to get access to. What is it?"

"Baji, I'm going to tell him."

That is too risky. Tell him nothing!

"He is about to turn down the agreement and hand me over to the CIA."

Jill took a deep breath and chose her words very carefully. "James, there is a project in China that requires a weaponized mineral mixture being refined in the States. We need these sanctions to prevent them from succeeding. I'm trying to make sure it's not sent to China for its intended purpose."

"And where did you receive this intel from," he asked.

"I can't tell you."

Wilks scowled. "My finger's on the speed dial to Langley. You better talk."

"I can't, sir." Jill shook her head. "All I can say is that it's imperative for the country and the world that we keep these sanctions going."

"I see," he said, standing up. "You leave me little choice. Please don't leave your seat." He walked back toward his office.

"I need to do something!"

Kill him then.

"No!"

"Have you ever come across the word Prophus?" she blurted out.

Wilks stopped and turned around very slowly, the color drained from his face. "That's classified."

"And the Genjix?"

"That's classified as well."

"Let me guess. Scattered in intelligence reports over the years?"

"They're the real reason why the CIA was created," he said. "We thought the government was being infiltrated by secret societies. Seems they've been around for over a hundred years."

"Five thousand actually," she said. "And they're not like the Elks or the Stonecutters. It goes much deeper than that."

Wilks looked around the room and then approached her cautiously. "Jill, I have two questions right now. One, if I don't call the CIA, will you tell me everything? And two, am I in danger from you?"

Divulge as little as possible. The Sanctions must stand though.

"I'll see what I can do."

"You're in no danger from me, Senator," Jill said. "And I'll tell you as much as I can."

He nodded and sat back down in front of her. She pushed the coffee mug toward him. "I think you should pour yourself another drink."

CHAPTER THIRTY
UPDATE

It was a small consolation that my host, Yamsha-Adad, was beaten by a Quasing named Camr's host, Hammurabi. Thousands of years later, Hammurabi would be written into the annals of history as one of the greatest kings in history. But at that time, my pride was injured. Yes, even Quasing feel pride.

It was through that defeat that I realized how unique each human was. Most creatures on this planet, be they dinosaur or mammal, had instincts ingrained into their very being. I could inhabit most and reasonably deduce what their reaction would be to nearly all situations as long as I had experience in that creature before. This was not the case with humans.

Tao

"Are you fucking serious?" Roen pulled the knife out of his right boot and threw it the wall. It embedded hilt deep into the wall with a loud thunk. Then he pulled out the knife in his other boot and to chucked it even harder. This time, it bounced off the hilt and nearly skewered a cowering Stan. "I'm going to kill that asshole!"

Dylan, sitting sprawled on the couch with a beer in his

hand, shrugged. "There's a commandment somewhere about not being able to kill the man that officiated your wedding."

Roen looked for any other knives on his person, and when he realized he didn't have any more, made sure the wall was really dead by punching a hole through it.

Easy. This is a rental.

"Well, there goes the safety deposit."

Roen collapsed on the sofa, knuckles white as he glared off into space. "So let me get this straight. All this time, Wuehler's team was just decoys? And I was redundant in case you died?"

Dylan nodded. "The boys here were extra muscle if needed. Otherwise, their job was to keep the heat off my back. You were initially my replacement because Stephen didn't know if I was alive or not. Hell, even I'm impressed I survived my escape pod blowing up. I'm a tough son of a bitch. When I got in touch with the Keeper, she felt it was better for you to stay with the team until activated."

Makes sense. High availability in case one agent goes down. That and the Keeper just wants to screw with us any way she could.

Dylan continued, "If I didn't make it, you would have gotten activated and continued where I left off. Your original intel was very on-point, by the way. We'll make a secret agent out of you yet. Things were working well for a while. Hadn't heard a peep from anyone until last week. Then my job got harder and now I know why." He wagged a finger at Roen. "Make no mistake. The Genjix know you're in this area."

"Sorry," Roen spat. "Maybe if someone had told our team we were just a bunch of piñatas, we'd have stayed away. Why didn't the old man say something?"

Assigning Wuehler's team should have been a clue.

"He probably figured there was no need to know, and he's right," Dylan said. "What if the Genjix got their hands on one of you and beat the truth out?"

Stephen's always erred toward caution.

Dylan downed his beer and did a free throw at the garbage can across the living room. The can bounced off the wall half a meter from the ground. "He sent me the orders while we were being chased by the entire damn Chinese fleet. Initially told me he'd send me a team. I told him to not bother and to just light a fire on the other side of town. He knows I like to work alone."

Roen rounded on Faust. "Why didn't Ramez tell us?"

Faust looked just as angry. "He just told me just now. Said it was need-to-know and that no one needed to know unless Dylan was confirmed dead or failed to report in to the Keeper."

"I hate your Quasing," Roen spat.

"Yeah," Faust grimaced. "Join the club. So much for the circle of trust between host and alien."

When you are done pouting, we still have work to do.

Roen plopped down on the sofa and scowled. "So what's our situation now?"

"Kaohsiung is the trade front for the Genjix supply chain. With Taiwan's preferred trade status with most western countries, the Genjix are working around the most stringent trade restrictions. Anything that goes to China, Myanmar, North Korea, or Russia routes through this port. I've been attaching trackers for weeks to shipments and following the flow of cargo. It's starting to draw a pretty clear map of their operations in this hemisphere. That's how we pinpointed the prison camp in Tibet, the nuke base in Yukaghir, and the research program in Qingdao." Dylan leaned in close.

"I haven't been able to infiltrate the southern part of the harbor. It's heavily guarded, but I've got a plan cooked up." Dylan picked up a beer and tossed it to Roen.

Roen deftly caught it and cracked it open, sucking in the suds. He smacked his lips and then clinked cans with Dylan. "Is there anything my boys can do to help? I promised the lying bastard I'd get you home in one ugly piece, and I meant it."

"Got a meeting with the Keeper tonight. We'll clarify orders. I have eighty percent of the harbor already mapped and tagged. Another two weeks and I bet I'll crack that last twenty percent." He finished his beer and tried another free throw. The beer can flew straight into the trash can. He looked at the table and grimaced at the now empty six-pack of beer. "Maybe we can meet up with Stephen in Tibet after we do the deed here," he said, patting his belly.

"When's the meeting?" Roen asked.

Dylan checked his watch. "In about five hours. Middle of the night while we sleep."

Roen scowled. "Oh, one of those meetings."

Dylan nodded. "Yep, it's their world now. We're only living in it, mate."

There was a click and a soft beep, and then an electronic female voice chirped over the speaker phone in a bored tone. "Meeting place 41223 open for thirty minutes."

Tao looked over at Yen curiously who, controlling the sleeping Dylan, shrugged. "Cost cutting measure. Free for the first half hour."

"Quite a security risk using a public line." Tao didn't like stating the obvious, but in this case, felt someone had to do it.

"One we have to take," the Keeper's voice came across the line irritably. "Physical data centers can no longer be secured and with the Genjix influence everywhere, contracting a private third party is an acceptable risk."

"If the Genjix wish to troll the entire Internet to find us then by all means they are free to try," Yen added.

"But a free public channel?" Tao demanded. "That is just reckless."

"Tao, I do not know what that host of yours has done to you but ever since–"

"Can you all save singing Roen's praises for when I'm not here? He is still my husband after all," Jill's voice piped up. "Paula's here as well."

"Cheers, everyone!" Paula chirped. "I see we're all one big happy family again. Yen, it's bloody good to hear from you. The stories of your demise have been greatly exaggerated."

"I do not suppose we can have the ladies take a nap, so we can speak with Baji and Yol," Tao said.

"Sorry, love," Paula replied. "Jill and I have a dinner date. We're going out for sushi."

"How's Roen?" Jill asked.

"Irritable," Tao admitted, "and not sleeping well. Lin taught him a little lesson. You are to thank for that."

"Serves him right," Jill said.

"Down to business," the Keeper cut in. "We have a lot to cover."

For the next twenty minutes, the Keeper updated them on the bad news happening all over the world. The debt woes in Europe were affecting global operations on both sides. The concrete shortage in Asia was stymieing the otherwise fantastic growth of China, which was now suffering from its own housing bubble. Prophus analysts predicted that the corn plague spreading through the Midwest would devastate the plastics, gasoline, and beef industries. The Genjix also solidified total control over OPEC and two of the five largest oil companies in the world.

On the war front, a Genjix cell was just discovered operating within MI6. While its exposure was welcome news, it was disturbing that the enemy had somehow infiltrated a Prophus stronghold. The FBI, on the other hand, was now fully Genjix-controlled, while the NSA and CIA were still up for grabs. The only solid positive news was that the Prophus had tricked the Russian government into nationalizing Krakiev, a Genjix munitions company accounting for fifteen percent of their weapons inventory and three percent of their bottom line finances.

The few bright spots in her report didn't hold a candle to the avalanche of negative events. It was as if the entire world had turned against them, and no matter how hard they all fought and bled, the casualties continued to mount.

"There's one more thing," the Keeper added. "We received a report that ProGenesis is near completion."

There was a long silence.

"New Quasing for the first time on the planet," Yen grunted. "Never thought I would see that."

"No longer a slowly dying species," Tao added.

"There's more," the Keeper said. "We intercepted a supply manifest from Genjix test sites in India regarding Quasiform. They're developing a Quasiform catalyst prototype utilizing large quantities of osmium derivatives. We need samples of this catalyst to know its effects."

"First they figure out how to keep our species alive, and now they want to build a new home," Tao mused. "Maybe we *are* on the wrong side."

"Only if you don't care about the consequences," Jill said.

"Dylan spent four weeks infiltrating companies at Kaohsiung harbor," Yen said. "The only one we could not break into is Punai Corp. It has military-grade surveillance. We were devising a plan when Roen and his band of merry bulls crashed the party."

"Punai's lobbying arm is a confirmed Genjix front," Jill said. "They've been at the forefront of this legislative push." There was a rustling of paper. "They do refine a specialized Osmium Quintoxide that is only available from a military plant in North Carolina. I think this could be what we're after."

"That is one of the primary compounds in Quasar's atmosphere," Paula added. "Yen, can you and Tao get eyes on the material and retrieve a sample? It could go a long way to cracking this secretive Phase III."

"It is a lot of ground to cover," Yen replied. "And will take time."

"Have Wuehler's team assist you," the Keeper said. "That should expedite your search."

Yen looked over at Tao and grinned. "I guess I am stuck with you louses a bit longer."

Tao returned the smile. "It will be like the Bolsheviks all over again, except this time, neither of us gets executed."

"We hope," Yen laughed.

The bored female robotic voice popped into their conversation, reminding them that they had five minutes left in the meeting, and that if they wished to extend it, all it would require was a Visa or MasterCard.

"I am adjourning the meeting. I want an update in four days," the Keeper said. There was a pause and she added. "And just in case you are curious, the new Genjix councilman, Devin's replacement, has gone to meet Stephen on the field of battle. Stephen is winning, but has confirmed at least thirty Prophus sent to the Eternal Sea, and nearly ten times that number in humans. Our stakes are high. Remember that." And then their time was up. The line clicked and went dead.

CHAPTER THIRTY-ONE
TIDE TURNING

Even now, the Prophus fight against their own ultimate good. We forgive their ignorance, though their standing will never be that of a true Quasing. That is their penance.

The sacrificing of the Prophus toward ProGenesis is an unfortunate necessity. It is punishment for disobeying the Council and the will of the Genjix. We honor them still, for they are still Quasing, and their sacrifice moves us toward our ultimate goal.

Zoras

Enzo scanned the map as his scouts reported in one by one. It had been four days since the large-scale attack on the camp. Since then, the situation had stabilized, and Enzo's position was no longer as touch-and-go as it had been when he first assumed command. He had ordered another fifty meters of forest of the no man's land burned, and after a few more failed probes, the Prophus had all but abandoned their efforts to penetrate the perimeter. Enzo attributed this major turn of events to his superior tactics and leadership.

Two thousand new reinforcements and outnumbering the enemy nearly three to one might have something to do with it.

Zoras might have a small point. Dramatically outnumbering the enemy did give Enzo a slight tactical advantage as well. With plenty of manpower now, Enzo could afford to go on the offensive. For the past few days, his scouts had pushed deeper and deeper into the forest to establish a larger zone of control. With the proper manpower and constant surveillance of a five kilometer radius, there was no longer a threat of surprise attacks.

There had been one raid since, which had ended in disaster for the Prophus. The Genjix were prepared and flanked the attack from the forest. Enzo even came out of that last melee with prisoners, including two vessels. With additional breathing room, he ordered construction of the airfield to begin. Until then, heavily escorted convoys delivering small numbers to the Langtang Airport in Nepal ensured the uninterrupted progress of the ProGenesis project.

Right now, an hour before dawn, Enzo, with a contingent of nearly five hundred men, was pressing northeast through a mountainous forested area a day's journey from the camp. When the Genjix expanded their zone of control, they discovered several Prophus camps numbering anywhere from twenty to a hundred. These camps were loosely spread out, allowing them to cover large tracts of land. It was an effective tactic for intercepting Enzo's convoys. His men were now systematically hunting and destroying these camps, taking prisoners when they could and killing the rest.

Yesterday, one of his scouts reported what they believed was the enemy's main base camp, and Enzo had personally led a sortie. His forces were less than fifteen minutes from the coordinates and had already killed two lookouts. They still had twenty minutes until dawn, which meant that if he timed it correctly, the Genjix could sneak in under the cover of darkness and attack at first light. He ordered his men to spread out into attack formations, and then signaled for Palos and one of the scouts to accompany him to reconnoiter the camp.

After a brief protest about how he exposed himself too much to risk, Zoras acquiesced to Enzo. It was how their relationship had developed. It took time but his guardian eventually realized that Enzo was not like most other fervent vessels who obeyed their blessed ones like automatons. His guardian had come to understand that Adonis Vessels were vastly superior to mere humans. And it was for this reason that Zoras consented that, especially at his young age, Enzo needed to experience what his training could not provide. They were now more like partners, working toward the same goal, if not always seeing eye to eye.

The three crept along the thickets up a hill. Already, the forest was coming to life, and the cover of darkness was beginning to lift. The scout signaled for a stop and pointed at a shadowy figure standing on top of the reach. Enzo nodded and motioned for Palos to stay at his position. This lookout he wanted to take care of by himself.

Again, your youthful foolishness can ruin your great potential.

"Most vessels earn their guardian. I was groomed to be one. I still intend to earn my place."

A breeze from the mountains swept in, rustling the leaves to mask his movement. Enzo crept behind the lookout and came to a stop six meters away. There, he waited. And just as the lookout let go of his rifle with one hand to pull his jacket tighter to his body, Enzo went in for the kill.

With a lightning first step, he launched himself at the lookout, smothering his mouth with one hand and jamming a knife into the back of his neck with the other. He held the man still for a second and then slowly laid him down on the ground. Enzo focused on the lookout's eyes as the life left them and then signaled to the others.

They continued up the steep terrain until they reached the crest of the hill. Peering down at the valley below, Enzo saw a sprawling camp, neatly organized and situated under the forest canopy to avoid aerial surveillance. He counted sixty small tents and a larger central tent hung from an old tree. Less than a dozen figures wandered outside.

Large camp. Estimated numbers at four hundred.

"I need some men on the northeastern side. Our flank won't reach there in time. Need to cut off their escape."

No time. The sun is rising.

Enzo looked up and cursed. His men barely had time to get to the crest for the attack. He peered over the edge. Sixty meters at a twenty degree angle. The only way to prevent the Prophus from fleeing east would be to get the drop on them and attack at close range. They had the numbers to easily win a sustained battle. His losses would be higher, but he had the men to spare. It was worth the gamble.

Enzo muttered into his comm and ordered his men up. He had originally anticipated a larger enemy camp than this and had brought more than necessary. Still, it was better to assure victory through sheer numbers than have to win an equal battle through finesse.

"No incendiaries until the vanguard reach the camp. Then only onto the far edge," he ordered as the first line of men crept over the top and began to make the descent. Enzo waited with the sniper teams as everyone got into position. Still, with several hundred people, it was nearly impossible to avoid detection. At about thirty meters from the edge of the camp, the closest Prophus guard opened fire. Several guns must have been trained on him since he was instantly cut down by a barrage.

We are not as deep as we should be. Order the right flank to disengage and circle to the rear.

Enzo did so and proceeded to move with the second wave of men. With the outcome still in contention, the first few seconds of this battle would be key. During the medieval days, Zoras would never voluntarily engage in a fight unless he had more than half the number of the opposing army. With technology becoming so deadly, the number needed to guarantee victory had increased.

The first row of tents was shredded by machine gun fire. Enzo was halfway down the hill when he saw several groups of Prophus flee eastward toward the forest line. Some were caught by his men, but more got away.

Where is the right flank?

"Tomlinson, where are your men? They're escaping," Enzo yelled into his comm. There was no response. "Tomlinson, report!" Still no response.

Something is wrong. Prophus numbers are too low.

Enzo stopped near the base of the hill and took a quick count. His men were a quarter into the camp by now. He had seen less than sixty Prophus total. Then he looked up at the ridge line as his men continued to pour into this basin.

"Teams on the ridge, hold position," he ordered. "Teams on the ground–."

The forest came to life as machine gun fire ripped from the thick trees. Panic ensued with Enzo's ridge teams reporting an attack from the rear. Two of the tents exploded into plumes of fire and debris. The Genjix were suddenly being attacked from all sides.

It is a trap!

Enzo looked around wildly. How could he get his men out of this situation? Coming back the way they came in was out of the question. Pushing forward would force them deeper into the camp, which was laden with explosives. North was an even steeper climb than west. That left only south.

Leave them. Have the men lay suppression fire. Get all the vessels to safety.

"I'll lose the battle then."

The fight is already lost. Suppression fire to cover the south. Now!

Reluctantly, Enzo gave the orders, and six other vessels, with Palos and his personal guard at his side, began to make their way south as his troops were realigned to punch a hole through the enemy trap. They barely made it a hundred meters when the Prophus responded. Within the thick forest, the fight became up close and ugly. Soon, Enzo lost his guards among the foliage and found himself alone.

Suddenly, two Prophus agents attacked, the bursts of their rifles blinking like yellow stars. Enzo returned fire, strafing as he slid behind a tree for cover. Tree bark exploded into hundreds of small fragments. Enzo listened to the rhythm of guns. One was using an M model rifle with the loud hollow metal sound of the casing ejection. The other was using a G3 variant. He timed his attack perfectly, first pinpointing their positions, then attacking when the magazine expired.

The M reloaded first. Enzo stuck his arm to the right and then turned left, shooting with precision and taking the M gunman out with two hits. Then an image flashed in his head of where the G3 gunman was kneeling. Enzo fired blindly on faith and was rewarded with a kill shot to the chest.

He continued south alone, abandoning his men. Zoras' life was more important than all of theirs anyway. It stung to have walked into this trap, though. This Prophus commander had a lot to answer for when Enzo got his hands on him. He continued through the thick forest and ran into Palos and two of the vessels pinned down by enemy fire.

He spoke into his comm. "Palos, I have eyes on you at your nine. You're caught in the crossfire at eleven and three. Take out the three. I'll take care of the eleven. Out."

Before Palos could respond, Enzo charged behind the firing nest and took out three of the enemy before they could respond. He saw a shimmer in the air as a Quasing left one of the dead soldiers and floated away into the air. This vessel must be a person of rank. Enzo searched the body and found the vessel's comm. It came alive.

"Jackson, this is Stephen, you got more incoming your way. Fall back. Jackson, report!"

Enzo picked up the comm. "Hello, Stephen."

The only Stephen we have on file with Prophus Command is their Field Marshal. His standing is just below the Keeper's.

"Who is this?" Stephen said.

"I'm the mouse that got away," Enzo replied. "Your trap failed."

Stephen laughed. "It's messy, but I'd hardly call it a failure. Who am I speaking with?"

"The only person worth trapping," Enzo snarled.

"Let me guess," Stephen said. "You sound young. And pretty high on yourself. And you're a little pissed off." There was a pause. "Did Zoras' new boy toy leave the hidey hole for our little party?"

"The name is Enzo," he replied haughtily. "And Stephen, I thank you for letting me know who my enemy is. You have been a worthy opponent so far."

"I've been kicking your ass is what I've been doing."

"Maybe today, but not as of late. I've swept over a dozen of your camps the past few days."

"Well, hell, let me outnumber you five to one, boy, and let's see how you fare."

Enzo bit his lip. "We'll see, Stephen. You have failed to rescue your fellow betrayers. Rest assured they will all die well for the Holy Ones."

"We'll see about that. Oh, by the way, I just captured a whole bunch of your guys, including several hosts. I don't have a nice camp to hold them in and can't really follow the Geneva Convention right now. You wouldn't be up for a trade, would you?"

Enzo threw the comm against a tree, shattering it into pieces.

CHAPTER THIRTY-TWO
ADVANCE TRAINING

The history of the war is well documented. Both the Prophus and the Genjix suffered and gained equally in it, having lost much of our European networks and influence. There was a lull in our war after the Second World War. Both sides were weakened and we worked to reposition ourselves in the world.

The Genjix moved their influence to Russia while we stayed to rebuild Europe. Both fought for control of the vast lands in China and for the unblemished industrial might of the United States. The Genjix came out victorious in with their support of the Communists and fought us to a standstill in the United States.

Baji

Jill frowned at the row houses in the affluent part of the Georgetown neighborhood. She checked her watch and then took out the small piece of paper he had left in her mailbox. It was two in the morning and this was the right place. She looked down the block at all the attached homes, then back at the note.

"Says third floor. They're all two stories."

Marco is just being cute.

The transition to city training was not all Jill had hoped. Now that they no longer had to commute outside the city, they held two practice sessions a day. The new early-morning workouts were kicking her ass. And to make matters worse, Marco was always so chipper in the mornings. She just wanted to break those perfect white teeth of his. It should be illegal to smile that much before dawn.

She was also acquiring an impressive collection of bruises. When she wasn't diving on the concrete or practicing changing directions like a stripper spinning on a pole, he made her hang off ledges and scamper up walls. She had a sneaking suspicion that he was making her jump through hoops for his amusement. And then when her arm muscles failed, he had her sprint intervals. Jill could jog practically forever, but interval training was pure torture.

"I think being in labor was less painful," she had said.

Oh really? You should tell Roen that. Remember when he said he knew what being in labor was like when he had to hold his...

"He said that to my parents!"

Jill scanned the roofs. That guy had to be up there somewhere, waiting to spring one on her. Well, hated to disappoint him. It was too risky to scale the walls from the front. She walked around the back and trespassed through the backyards, easily scaling wooden fences. Training was starting to pay off. She still couldn't melee worth a damn, but her agility had improved, literally, by leaps and bounds.

It is the house with the blue trim.

She reached the backyard of the address on the paper and looked up. Marco, leaning against a chimney, gave her a lazy wave and beckoned her to join him. Jill scanned the wall and noticed the neighbor's gutter pipe. A moment later, she scampered up the two-story building and sat down next to him.

He was sipping a cup of steaming coffee in an open Styrofoam cup. "Nice of you to join me. Ready?"

Jill wondered how he had gotten that up here. She smirked at his cat burglar outfit, half-cap and all. Somehow, he still made it look stylish.

"Give me your best shot," she said.

He stood up, dumped the contents of the cup and wiped his hands. "Right then, let's give it a go," he grinned. He touched her shoulder. "Tag, you're it."

He took off, sprinting south haphazardly across the tops of the row houses. A second later, Jill was nine steps behind, trying to keep pace without stumbling on the uneven surfaces, assorted pipes, satellite dishes, and vents littering the roofs. She was surprised that he was running at full speed. It would be a minor miracle if one of them didn't sprain an ankle or break their neck falling off the sides. Regardless, she wouldn't let him get the better of her. Besides, they were six houses down from the end of the block. Where exactly did he think he'd go next? She found out the hard way.

Just as they neared the edge, he turned on a dime and launched himself at her. Her training and instincts kicked in as she ducked to the side, feeling the whoosh of his fist brush her hair. She tumbled onto the roof and skidded along the descending slant but was able to stop from falling over the edge. She put her hands down to maintain her balance and palmed a small piece of roof tile. Watching her closely, Marco feinted to the right and cut her off from getting away from the ledge.

"You're trapped," he grinned. "What are you going to do now, little girl?"

Little girl? That smirk again. While Marco had a beautiful smile, he used it far too often. And not only that, those oh-so-confident words grated on her. He obviously considered her harmless. Well, she'll show him.

"Here's what I'm going to do," she said, hurling the tile at Marco. He stumbled as it smacked him in the face. She then grabbed his arm and yanked. She watched with satisfaction as he yelped and toppled over the edge, landing on a row of shrubs below.

"I hope he isn't dead."

His legs moved.

"Good. I'd have a hard time explaining to Paula how I killed James Bond."

A minute later, she climbed down and found him sitting on the grass at the side of the house rubbing his forehead. There was a two inch gash from the center of his temple down to his cheek. It was turning a nice plum red. He shot her the same look that Cameron did every time she gave him a bath.

"Not a bad arm," he forced a smile, albeit not so wide this time around. "Could have picked a less beautiful place to mar."

"Good lord," Jill rolled her eyes and pulled him to his feet. She looked at the time. "So, how did I do?"

"Oh, we're not done yet," he said, drawing a very high-tech looking pistol. He pointed just to the left of her head and squeezed the trigger. The gun popped softly and a small puff of smoke exploded from the wall behind her, leaving a red circular imprint the size of a marble.

"Training gun. Fires projectiles that hurt," he warned, aiming it at her chest. "Can break bones at close range."

"You wouldn't!" Jill gasped.

Duck left!

Jill dove just as Marco pulled the trigger and another puff of smoke splattered the wall.

"Thirty seconds," he yawned, pretending to dig dirt from his fingernails.

Jill looked for cover. They were in a suburban block filled with houses! Where would she hide?

Quick, around back and up.

"How long do I have to escape for?" she asked.

He shrugged. "I got two clips worth, so until I run out of pellets."

She took off, hopping over the fence and sprinting through the back yard. She found another drain pipe three houses down and scurried up. She heard a soft poof and a puff of smoke exploded at her feet just as she pulled her leg over the side. Those thirty seconds went by really fast. Jill felt another zing past her ear and saw Marco scaling the wall. He couldn't be more than fifteen seconds behind.

Topple the piping.

Jill suddenly saw an image of a medieval siege. Baji's host at the time, a foot soldier by the looks of it, was on the parapet defending against a horde of armed soldiers with large red crosses emblazoned on their chests. Then her host used his pike and pushed against a ladder leaning against the castle wall. The ladder tipped over and crashed back to the ground, taking the nine men climbing with it.

Jill looked down at Marco, who was now halfway up the house. It felt almost cruel to do that to him again. Marco looked up and tried to shoot her in the face. She pulled back at the last second and narrowly avoided eating a dust pellet. The feelings of guilt disappeared.

Jill gave the gutter pipe a solid kick, snapping off the links holding it in place and sending it careening onto the lawn. She watched with satisfaction as Marco, flailing, fell into the pool.

"At least he fell into the water."

He will have a more difficult time chasing while wet.

Apparently, his gun still worked underwater because a second later, his head broke the surface of the pool, and he shot three more times at her. By now, the ruckus had woken up a bunch of dogs in the neighborhood.

Time to go.

Jill took off, speeding north along the houses. She reached the end of the block and looked over the edge. Across the street, there was a small open field and then the Potomac River. Very little cover in either case. To her left was another block of connected buildings, taller than the ones she was on. A small alley separated them.

Two meters across. Jump it.

Two meters might as well be two miles to Jill.

"Uh... I can break my neck here."

She turned and saw Marco halfway down the block. He would catch up to her in seconds. She looked back at the chasm between the two houses.

Jump or surrender.

The thought of surrendering to Marco made her queasy. Jill scrunched her face, took a deep breath, and sprinted toward the alley. Just as she was about to hurdle the chasm, she balked and almost tripped over the edge.

"Should have made the jump," he singsonged from behind her.

Voice coming from your back left. Duck right to the skylight. Grab the satellite dish. Fight!

Well, if she was going to get shot anyway, she might as well go down swinging. Jill dove behind the skylight, rolled to her feet, and yanked the satellite out of its base. She turned just in time to hear two patters strike the round dish.

Lean left and find cover behind the chimney. Get to open space to retreat back the way you came.

"It's not fair. I should have a gun as well."

Disarm him and take it, then.

Jill reached the chimney just as Marco fired another half dozen rounds.

"I can't believe your aim is that bad," she called out.

"It isn't," he replied cheerfully.

Then she heard the click of an empty chamber. This was her chance, else she'd just be target practice when he reloaded. She charged, wielding the satellite dish as a weapon and crashed into him. The exchange was short and brutal. She knocked the gun out of his hand and gave him a sharp rap on the knee with the dish. In doing so, however, he caught her in a choke hold from behind and squeezed tight. They spun in circles as she squirmed.

"You smell nice," he said.

That cheerfulness again. Well, she'd show him! Right as they spun next to the chimney, Jill pushed off it. Marco lost his balance and fell backward. They both fell on top of the skylight and crashed through into the house below. Thankfully, Marco's body cushioned her fall as they both lay gasping among the wreckage of broken glass.

Empty room. Door to your three. Get out!

Jill rolled off of him and checked for injuries. "Are you alright?" she asked.

"Now you care," he groaned. "Well, that escalated quickly."

They were in a guest bedroom by the looks of it. Thankfully, they had landed on the bed. The two stood up and brushed the glass off of each other.

Then the lights turned on and a terrified elderly man brandished a golf club at them. "Get out of here you thieves! I've called the police!"

There is our exit cue.

Marco reached into his pocket and pulled out a wad of money. "Sorry about your window, mate. I hope this covers it." He tossed it to the old man who bungled the catch. And in that moment of lost concentration, Marco grabbed Jill by the hand and pulled her past the old man. They scampered down the stairs and out the front door, laughing like teenagers.

"Well, that was a jolly good time," Marco said, slowing to a walk only after they were five blocks away from the scene of the crime.

"Did you give him enough money?" Jill asked, feeling a bit guilty. "We did break into his house after all."

Marco sniffed. "With the amount of money I gave him, he could build a new roof. Come on, let's get a drink. We deserve it."

"So who won?" she asked.

Marco flashed her a smile, a sincere one this time. "We'll call it a draw."

CHAPTER THIRTY-THREE
THE TRANSPORT

*For the next thousand years, I, along with the rest of my kind,
followed the Conflict Doctrine and expanded wherever the humans
could thrive. Like a swarm of locusts, we occupied every crevice of
this earth, sowing dissension and innovation everywhere we went.*

*In our defense, and I will argue that we did not feel we needed
any defense, we pushed humanity to greater heights. Krys had a
hand in the development of the chariot. The wheel was the work of
Galen. Chiyva's genius in warfare created the tactics of the Roman
Legions. Haewon, being one of the few like me who explored the
lands to the east, later trumped us all with the creation and advent
of the black substance now known as gunpowder.*

Tao

Two days after Roen found Dylan, the team was ready
to infiltrate the Punai grounds of Kaohsiung harbor and
wrap things up in Taiwan. Dylan already had a plan in the
works, so it just needed to be retooled for the eight member
team. The plan was surprisingly elegant, one that even Tao
admired.

Much like the Trojan horse.

"Head out to sea, hide in a container, and get shipped right in. That man is smarter than he looks."

Probably Yen's idea.

They had originally planned to leave at dawn, but after deciding to have one last breakfast, they ended up departing closer to nine. Hutch had convinced Roen to leave the entire security deposit for their landlord, much to his disappointment. The way he saw it, whatever of Lin's money was left after this mission was his to keep. But after doing a final walk through of the apartment, he realized it was the right thing to do. After all, eight guys sleeping in a tiny place for any length of time tended to leave the place somewhat of a disaster, especially if it was eight live-by-the-seat-of-your-pants killers with lax hygiene. All except for Hutch, though. He was the motherly and cleanly type everyone else took advantage of.

They traveled by subway back down to Kaohsiung International Airport, stopping by FedEx to ship any personal items back to wherever each person was from. They dumped anything unnecessary, expendable, or incriminating into a local landfill, and then chartered a private helicopter southwest.

"So is this captain is reliable?" Roen asked. "The entire plan hinges on buying passage on the ship."

Dylan grinned. "Of course. Manny and I used to run arms for the Philippine civil war. Now he runs routes up and down the coast. Stops by Taiwan every two or so weeks. I've used him dozens of times to sneak around. If you operate a trade ship in this region, you can't help but work for the Genjix one way or another."

"Doesn't sound trustworthy," Roen frowned.

"Money rules Manny's world," Dylan chuckled. "I wouldn't trust him otherwise."

A few hours later, Dylan pointed at a massive freighter, designation RPS *Imelda's Song*, with the P and the S half flaked off by the rust covering the hull. It was easily one of the largest ships Roen had ever seen, and he had watched *Titanic* four times. Though not possessing a nautical eye, he had enough experience aboard ships to know they were about to hitch a ride aboard an antique.

"This rusty behemoth is older than some Ming vases I've broken," he grumbled.

The sad part is, I think that statement is true.

"Really? When?"

Remember that French socialist? The arms dealer?

"The one with the gaudy wing of tacky furniture I shot up?

Gaudy yes, tacky no. You have poor taste. When you ran through there, I recognized some of the pieces.

"I was being chased by half a dozen guys at the time. Didn't have time to stop and admire the craftsmanship. There was a Ming vase there?"

I believe so. You smashed it over someone's head, picked up a shard, and stabbed another in the chest with it.

"Ah, good times."

The helicopter landed in front of a group of not-so-friendly-looking sailors. Dylan jumped off and made a grand gesture at their welcome party. Roen watched as the helicopter took off a minute later, stranding them on the ship.

"Talk about painting ourselves into a corner."

At least we outnumber them.

Ten more sailors appeared on the deck.

I stand corrected.

Roen leaned in to Dylan. "Are you sure about this? Our ride just left."

Dylan shrugged off his concerns. "Captain Manny is an old pal of mine. I'm sure he wouldn't mind us hitching a ride."

The eight of them walked across the fore deck toward the dilapidated bridge. When Dylan had first told them about the plan, Roen had imagined a tugboat flying into the harbor by night. This monstrosity was ridiculous. There must have been a hundred cargo containers here.

The price of passage will be steep.

"There goes my retirement."

Roen counted at least a dozen more not-so-friendly pairs of eyes staring as they walked on deck. A ship this size must carry a good size crew. Roen didn't exactly hate those odds, but who was going to steer the ship if it came to that? Still, he kept his hand near his pistol and hatched a quick plan to take over if things got rough. He moved a little closer to Faust and signaled for him to be alert, though he doubted Faust needed much warning.

"I don't see guns. I think I can take half of these guys on my own. Dylan can take the other half. Faust and the rest of the guys can man the ship and cook."

Roen must have grossly underestimated their numbers because shortly after, the count swelled to at least forty, with more showing up by the minute. To top it off, he saw at least four rifles and at least two spear guns. For some reason, being shot by a spear sounded much more unpleasant than being shot by a bullet.

Dylan acted as if he didn't notice any of the animosity, grinning and calling out to people he recognized. None seemed to return his greetings as they bunched closer and closer together. Finally, he leaned in to Roen and whispered. "Funny, they were so nice last time. I wonder what I did to piss them off. Maybe I shouldn't have slept with Manny's sister."

Roen's face turned white, and his hand reflexively reached for his pistol.

Dylan chuckled and pulled Roen's hand away. "Just kidding. But seriously, don't reach for your gun. They might be small, but it's a rough life out on the seas. These critters can fight like Tasmanian devils. Oh, wait, there's Manny now. Just you watch." Dylan broke out into the widest smile his burnt face would allow and waved at a crusty old sailor. "Ho, Manny, it's good to see you, mate! How's old *Imelda* treating you? She looks as fresh and clean as the day you took her out of the sack."

Roen studied Manny's facial expression, and if this man was what stood between them and a lynching, they were in trouble. Manny was shorter than most of his crew, which frankly was a feat in itself. He was a scrawny but wiry dark Filipino with a face so weathered that he looked like he was carved from tree bark. If Roen hadn't known better, he'd guess Manny was the grumpy cook or the old bilge cleaner. Only a torn-up captain's hat gave away his rank.

Manny held up two fingers and spoke in surprisingly clear English, though with a Singaporean accent. Roen knew immediately then that there was more to Manny than it seemed. Not intimidated by Dylan's size, the tiny Manny walked up to him and poked Dylan twice very hard in the chest. "That's four times now I offered you my services as a friend, and four times you bring trouble with you. You cost me and my men money. And every time you promise to pay what's owed, you scurry away just beyond trouble's reach, leaving us with trouble and no money."

"Well, Manny," Dylan's chuckle had a little hint of desperation in it. "Come now, you know it's just circumstances, mate."

"Don't 'mate' me!" Manny spat. "You owe my men a lot of money. So pay up now, or I have my boys throw you off!"

As if on cue, the sailors of *Imelda's Song* crowded toward Dylan, growling with outstretched hands as if a tide of zombies reaching to rend his flesh.

Dylan backpedaled and leaned into Roen. "I actually think he's serious. And I thought we were friends, that bastard."

"How much do you owe him?" Roen whispered.

Dylan shrugged. "I dunno. There was never any set amount. Just one of those bags-of-doubloons-at-the-end-of-the-rainbow sort of gentlemen deals. If I had to guess, maybe ten, fifteen thousand?"

Roen buried his head in both hands as the wave of sailors began to corral his men back toward the walkway. "Please tell me it's in Philippine pesos," he moaned.

Dylan laughed. "Not even the Filipinos trade in their own currency."

These sailors meant business, and no amount of talking would get them out of this mess short of flashing some money.

"Tao, you know how far out we are at sea? Maybe we can swim to shore."

You have the money. Stop being cheap and spend it.

"I hate you, Tao."

Roen raised both hands and yelled out. "Captain, if I were to take care of Dylan's debts, could we work something out?"

The wave of angry zombie sailors momentarily stopped. The ones who understood English began to chatter excitedly. They told the rest of the crew who didn't and another wave of chatter and jeers erupted. Manny looked him up and down, studying him as if he were estimating how much money Roen actually had to his name.

"Dylan's debt is no small matter," he began. "Last I recall, adding the troubles and fees I've incurred from him, the amount lies at thirty thousand Australian dollars."

Correction. You may have enough money. It depends on what Manny's going exchange rate is for the Taiwanese dollar.

Roen didn't bother masking his gasp and jerking his hand back as if he just saw a poisonous snake. He shot Dylan a look of death.

"Come now, Manny," Roen used his be-reasonable sounding voice. "I want to do you right, but you have to level with me. Look, how about we square up a fair number for Dylan, and we move on to taking my men where we need to go."

Captain Manny's eyes narrowed. "Maybe we should discuss this in private." He gestured at the closest door, and the sea of Filipino sailors parted ways.

That was an error. You just told him you have at least thirty thousand Australian and can offer more if needed.

"Well, what the hell else am I supposed to do?"

Now he will not even let you leave the ship until the amount that Dylan owes is paid, regardless whether you book passage or not.

"Watch them," Manny said as he followed Roen through the doors.

An hour and mostly broke later, Roen emerged from negotiations with Captain Manny to find the team lounging around a burning oil drum. Dylan was already drinking with a dozen of the sailors. He had made it a point to stop by the market on the way to the ship and purchase several cases of beer, which he was now using to buy the crew's affection.

"Ho, Roen, how did it go?" Dylan asked, tossing him a can.

"I thought you said you were friends!" Roen snarled. "He took the shirt off my back! Hell, I'm negative. I have to pay him more when I get home."

Master negotiator you are not.

"But we're square, right?" Dylan said.

"Square and broke," Roen grumbled. "First we're heading to Manila then to Macau before we detour back to Kaohsiung Harbor. Our good Captain Manny said it would appear suspicious to venture off the ship's manifest."

"Alright then," Dylan grinned. "We got a few days of R&R, let's take advantage of it."

CHAPTER THIRTY-FOUR
DEFEAT

The end game has begun for the Prophus. But like any dying and cornered animal, they are still dangerous. The Genjix's purity of purpose is what continues to drive us forward.

With the success of ProGenesis so close, we aim to play gods once more, but this time, to our own kind. After millions of years of slow extinction, it is the Genjix who will save all Quasing. And as it has always been, we will choose who is worthy to procreate. After all, we are the future and this will be our world.

Zoras

It took Enzo two days after the disastrous ambush to get back into their camp. He and Palos carried a barely alive bodyguard with them. All three of them were half dead on their feet. Abhinav, the bodyguard, had lost a lot of blood from a leg wound and had to be carried the entire trip back. Enzo had initially had wanted to leave the man for dead, but Palos wouldn't have it. He had lost enough men as it was, he said. Enzo reluctantly agreed. It would reflect well on him back at camp once news spread of his magnanimous nature.

Enzo helped Palos carry the semi-conscious man all the way back to the camp through the treacherous and unforgiving landscape. The first glimmer of light from the camp was such a welcome sight that his knees nearly buckled. If it wasn't for his pride, he would have fallen mere steps away from the front gate. Support personnel ran out and took the three of them to the infirmary, where for the next hour, Enzo was poked and prodded like a specimen on a table.

Inside, Enzo seethed with anger and felt such intense shame that he could barely keep himself from attacking the doctors. This was his first defeat as commander, and he was not taking it well. Before, with the *Scimitar*, he did what had to be done. With the first few weeks in the camp, defending and surviving was itself a victory. And now, with the upper hand, better supplies, and superior numbers, he was soundly defeated and mocked by this Prophus Field Marshal.

There is no shame in losing a battle. All the great leaders in history had to lose before they became great.

"I had the numbers! The higher ground! The advantage! What could I have possibly done different?"

You were outmaneuvered. By the leader of the entire Prophus military, no less. Stephen has a brilliant tactical mind. His Quasing, Camr, was one of the first to bring us together. He is one the Genjix still respect, even if he is a betrayer.

An unclear and washed-out image of a cave popped into Enzo's mind. There were strange and primitive trees just outside the cave entrance. Trees that Enzo had never seen before and knew no longer existed. Then, slowly, a shadow appeared to block out the sun, and in stepped the largest primate he had ever seen. It was three meters tall and seemed to take up the entire entrance. Enzo reared back, but the primate grabbed his foot. And then he felt a shock of recognition. Enzo snapped back to reality and found himself in the infirmary again with a slight headache. That had been a long memory. He touched the bottom of his nose and felt blood.

Camr was the will that built the Umayyad Caliphate and kept it together for centuries. His tactics with the Rashidun Cavalry changed the way war was waged during that time period. He later revolutionized desert warfare in a way that was relevant until the twentieth century.

Enzo flinched as the doctor closed a small wound with stitches. He bit back the urge to strike the doctor for his carelessness. "Zoras, telling me Camr's greatness is not making me feel that my failure is any less than it is."

The intent is not to spare your emotions. You were bested by the better human today. Tomorrow, you will not make that same mistake.

A messenger ran into the infirmary and bowed. "Father, there is an urgent communique from the States."

Growling and grunting in pain at the same time, Enzo swatted the doctor aside and limped toward the war room. It was the longest forty-meter walk of his life. Still, Enzo knew that everyone he passed was watching him, their failed leader barely able to put one foot in front of the other. He seethed even more. It didn't matter that Stephen was their Field Marshal or that Camr was one of the greatest Quasing. When Enzo got his hands around his neck, he would squeeze the life out of him. He reached the war room not a moment too soon and collapsed onto the chair.

"What is it?" he demanded.

"Message from operations in DC," the communications officer said. He pushed a button on the comm.

THE DEATHS OF TAO

"Father," Simon's voice came over the speaker. "I have grave news. The Prophus have successfully upheld the sanctions. I'm working on an alternative. The political process here is encumbered and once legislation is approved, it will take time to unravel it."

"That is unacceptable." Enzo slammed his fist so hard onto the table that he cracked it. "What are your options to speed up the process?"

"None, Father," Simon apologized. "The Prophus opposing this has been skillful. Please be patient. I can defeat–"

"I am out of patience," Enzo snapped. "ProGenesis is near completion. I will not allow delays to Phase III. Execute Operation Eagle Purity. Call in additional support to the eastern seaboard and take out all the Prophus at the capital!"

Enzo! You are being rash! The Council has not approved this.

"I am being a decisive leader. Victory is worth the risk, Zoras. The price of America and the Phase III are worth the risk."

Hear me now. If the battle here at this camp falters and we lose our test subjects before ProGenesis is completed, your standing on the Council will be lost. However, if Operation Eagle Purity fails, I will have no choice but to order a forceful transition and your life is forfeit. It will be the only way to appease the Council for your failure. Do I make myself clear?

It took a few seconds for Zoras' words to sink in. Finally, Enzo's lips curled into a smile and he chuckled. "Your will, Zoras. So be it. I accept the risk."

"Simon," he said aloud. "Proceed with Operation Eagle Purity. How long will it take to completely resuscitate the operation?"

"A day, maybe two, but Father," Simon stammered. "The fallout–"

"Deal with the fallout later. That's what our PR teams are for." Enzo snapped. "No more games with these damn Prophus. We are the ones in power. We do not need to play by their rules. We play by ours! Handle it, Simon. Don't fail me again. If you do, Simon, Biall's standing will fall and your life will be sacrificed for a worthier vessel."

Enzo cut Simon off before he could respond. The entire room was quiet. What Enzo had commanded was the most brazen attack in the history of their war. If it was successful, America would be theirs and it would be Enzo who would have handed one of the superpowers to the Council on a silver platter. They would have no choice then but to elevate him to the Council. If it failed, well, he was well aware of what lay in store for him.

The choice is made. Now live with the consequences.

"Gladly, Holy One, The die has been cast. Greatness cannot be achieved without risk. I have been studying this war all my life. The time has long been ripe to land the killing blow, but the Council is too full of tired old men. I will show them what true leadership means and will either take the Genjix to new heights or die. This I accept."

CHAPTER THIRTY-FIVE
LOSING OPTIONS

After the Second World War, I moved from host to host until I inhabited a young Prophus agent named Dania Hunter. She operated in the central and eastern portions of the United States, which were hotly contested regions of our war. During those years, the Prophus were hard-pressed. We suffered grave defeats and lost many friends.

She met an agent named Jordan Lyte while working on the General Dozier kidnapping task force and the two fell in love. They married the next year, and a few years later, had a daughter named Sonya. Then, during the crisis known as the Iran-Contra Affair, Jordan was killed trying to extract six Prophus agents from newly Genjix-controlled Iran.

Baji

It had taken her all night to convince Wilks not to have her arrested, but she finally got her point across to him about the Quasing without naming them. As far as he was concerned, she was part of the Templars or some secret foreign government agency. With Baji's help and a mountain of historical data, she was able to draw the bigger picture for him. Wilks wasn't completely sold, but for now, he was content to let her put all her cards on the table and see what happened. Then he'd decide if he needed to haul her in for treason.

You would definitely have to kill him then.

"I prefer to not kill United States senators if I don't have to."

Wilks had thrown his weight behind the sanctions, and they flew straight through committee. Tomorrow was the day all of Jill's wheeling and dealing would go on the Senate floor, and she had been working non-stop to keep her complex plan in place. While Tammy and the other aides had long since called it a day, she had no intention of sleeping until all the votes were counted. She rubbed her eyes and tried to focus on the forty-page briefing she was compiling for him.

Now she just had to wait until the morning session to see if the Genjix political arm could respond. Who knew how the landscape might change tomorrow. The Genjix had the money and influence to override the Prophus if they had time to unravel her secret deals, but Jill had cleverly set up this vote to be right before the holiday break, giving the Genjix too little time to get all their ducks in a row.

And even if they did somehow scrounge up the votes to bring the sanction down, she now knew enough about their operations to single out Punai Corporation and what they were refining and exporting. In every scenario, the Prophus had won, or so she hoped. Simon had left her a particularly vile voicemail threatening everything from her bodily person to the grandchildren she didn't have.

Jill had been up for nearly twenty hours, and she was fighting a losing battle against her drooping eyelids. She stood up and stretched, poured two cups of coffee, and walked into Wilks' office. There were a lot to work out still. Simon could come at them from several angles, so they had to be ready to fend him off.

"Cite the limited refinement tonnage and their recent import of heavy water," she stressed.

Wilks furrowed his brow. "You're not implying there's any nuclear refining going on, are you?"

"Please don't say that on the floor, Senator. We want to inject doubt, but we can't make that sort of accusation without proof."

"That's because we have none," he snapped. Jill checked the time. Wilks was getting more and more irritable the later it got. He wasn't a young buck anymore.

"Maybe we should continue this in the morning," she sighed. "There's just a few main–"

There was a knock on his office door. Jill froze. Looking puzzled, Wilks was going to call out to whoever it was when she signaled him to be quiet. She distinctly remembered hearing Tammy locking the front door when she left. Motioning for him to remain quiet, Jill picked up one of Wilks' heavy lifetime achievement awards and crept to the side of the door. Then she gave Wilks a nod.

Looking more confused than worried, Wilks said in a loud voice, "Come in."

Simon, wearing a trench coat and a very unfashionable set of sunglasses, walked in. "Senator Wilks."

"Simon?" Wilks began. "Why are you wearing sunglasses at night?"

Night vision goggles! An attack!

Before Jill could act, Simon drew a pistol and shot Wilks, knocking him off his chair. She leaped from the corner and blindsided Simon, slamming the large metal award against his face, followed by a knee to the groin.

Get Wilks out of here!

Simon groaned as she walked over him to check on Wilks. She eyed his smug face and brought her fist down on it, feeling a satisfying crunch as the bridge of his nose suddenly made a sharp detour on the way up to his forehead. He passed out.

"That's for threatening my kid." She kicked him in the gut for good measure and ran behind the desk. She found Wilks lying on the ground, clutching his left shoulder. He had ducked just enough for the bullet to miss his heart.

This was a bold attack. Simon must have backup.

"Can you stand?" she asked. He grimaced as she helped him up. "We need to get out of here," she said.

Wilks picked up the phone and punched a few buttons. A second later, he dropped the receiver. "Phone's dead," he said, gritting his teeth. "Is this the other team you've been telling me about?"

She nodded.

There is bound to be a secondary unit.

"Baji, what are they doing here? We're in the Senate building for God's sakes."

Attempting to assassinate a sitting senator basically implies they couldn't care less about that. The front door and back will be watched. Exit through the side of the building.

"There aren't any doors at the side."

Her bangle beeped and Marco's voice came on. "Jill, is everything alright?"

She raised it to her mouth. "We just had an assassination attempt on the senator. He's alive but injured. We need to get out of here."

"It's worse than you think," Marco replied. "I just received reports of this occurring all over the capital. All our agents are under attack. We've lost forty so far."

She gasped. Forty operatives in the government. Dead in an instant. How could this be?

It is a cleansing. The last occurred during the Spanish Inquisition. The Genjix have decided that removing us from power is worth the fallout.

"I'm coming for you, but it's chaos on the streets. There are Penetra vans everywhere." Marco said. "For now, get out of the beltway or get underground. I'll find you."

She turned to the fallen senator. "Listen carefully, James," she whispered. "There's a coup going on. The enemy is trying to wipe us out in order to control the government. We need to get you to safety. Keep quiet and follow closely."

He nodded and grimaced as they left his office. She picked up Simon's pistol and checked the clip. Wilks' eyes widened in surprise when he saw her handling the pistol like a trained expert.

"This is crazy," he whispered.

"You don't know the half of it," she muttered.

Get the night vision goggles.

Jill picked up the pair of night vision goggles and turned them over in her hand. From afar, a person wouldn't be able to tell them apart from regular sunglasses, but that seemed kind of silly. Wouldn't a person attract more attention for wearing sunglasses at night? Someone didn't think this through very well.

Worry about fashion later. Move!

Jill put the goggles on and led Wilks out the door. Together, they left his office and sped down the hallway, passed the elevator banks on their way toward the center of the building. She risked a glance through the atrium window and saw half a dozen dark figures on the ground level wearing the same goggles.

She grabbed Wilks by his good shoulder and dragged him around the corner to the stairwell leading to the lower levels. She motioned for him to hide in a cubicle while she scouted the stairs. She found two Genjix guarding the exit on the ground floor.

Kevlar. One with a combat shotgun. The other with an assault rifle.

"Take them out?"

Too risky. Taking out two fully armed agents in armor will be difficult. It will also draw attention. Not to mention you are wearing a pencil skirt.

Jill swore under her breath. "Second floor plunge it is. Sometimes, I hate this job."

I thought you hated being an attorney.

"I hate that too."

The problem is not the job. You just need a better attitude.

"Shut up."

See.

Jill went back to the second floor and led Wilks toward the southwest end of the building where it joined with the Dickson Senate Building. They moved slowly, hiding behind cover and in cubicles wherever possible. There was a small garden with several large trees on Constitution Avenue nestled between the two buildings where Wilks liked to smoke when he didn't want anyone to see. With luck, they could climb down a tree or at the very least jump onto a nice bed of flowers to soften the fall. As luck would have it, there was another guard near the entrance to that section of the building. Wilks was about to call out to the guard when she covered his mouth with her hand.

"We're not sure if he's compromised," she whispered. Then she motioned for him to stay still. She stayed low to the ground and crept forward toward the guard.

"He's wearing a federal uniform. Maybe he's a good guy."

I am sure the Genjix have several federal uniforms for Halloween. You cannot risk it.

"I don't see a rifle or Kevlar. I think he's a regular."

Do not risk it. If he is a regular guard, the best thing you can do is put him down non-lethally. He would not stand a chance against Genjix squads.

Jill cursed under her breath as she inched closer. The closer she got, the more she was sure he wasn't the enemy. For one thing, he looked relaxed and was completely oblivious to his surroundings. If he were a Genjix agent masquerading as a bored guard, he should be nominated for an Emmy.

She crept up to the cubicle adjacent him and waited. And waited. And waited some more. The guy was so lazy he kept staring straight ahead, at one point yawning and leaning against the wall. Finally, feeling a sense of urgency, she picked up a stapler on the desk, stood up, and chucked it at him. It clipped him on the ear. Jill leaped out of the cubicle, swept his legs, and choked him out.

Well, that was not elegant.

"No style points there, but it did the trick."

Jill went back to retrieve Wilks, and they continued to the next room. By now, his shoulder was pouring blood, leaving a trail for anyone to find. They had to get out of there fast. They reached the corner of the building with the small garden. She looked out the window. It was a decent drop, but not more than what she had trained for with Marco. She took aim and put three slugs into the window, shattering the

WESLEY CHU353

glass. She dragged Wilks to the ledge, apologized quickly, and pushed him out. Then she leaped out of the second floor window and landed on a bed of tulips, rolling as she was trained into a kneeling position with pistol drawn.

I see the training is paying off.

"Didn't stick the landing, but I give that a six."

Hearing the clatter of footsteps approaching from the east, she grabbed Wilks by the collar and dragged him westward between the building and a row of bushes. He was in sorry shape by this time. The fall might have broken his leg. She wrapped his arm around her shoulder and dragged him down Constitution Avenue. There was a flash and the pop of gunfire. Jill threw herself to the ground and returned fire. A squad of Genjix appeared across the street and closed in. There must be a Penetra van nearby. She was a sitting duck. Then she saw one of the Genjix agents approach with a small round object in his hand.

Flash incendiary. Hold until range. Open fire during throwing motion.

She opened fire right when he was about to toss it at her, taking him out at the leg. A moment later, there was a blinding flash and then another hail of bullets ripped through the air right above them.

"You alright, James?" she whispered.

"Ain't the first time I've been shot at," he replied.

The Genjix closed in. By her count, there must have been seven or so. Far too many to deal with. At best, she could take out two before they pinpointed her location. Still, two was better than none. Jill tensed and waited for them to get in range. Thirty meters. Twenty-five. Just as they were within twenty meters, two of the Genjix suddenly dropped. The squad turned to engage the new threat. Jill got up and fired as well. The five remaining Genjix agents didn't stand a chance in the crossfire. A new figure sprinted toward her from her left. She dropped to one knee and aimed.

Marco held out his hands. "Whoa, whoa, it's me. We have to move. Bogies converging on our position. The entire beltway is under Penetra surveillance." He looked down at Wilks. "Hello, James, need a hand?"

Wilks' entire body was shaking. A veteran of both Vietnam and Korea, he didn't scare easily, so he had to be in a lot of pain. "You're part of these shenanigans?" he demanded. "I should have figured."

Marco picked the large man up by the waist and started to half-carry and half-drag him as if he were a piece of luggage. "We're still on for golf, right?"

"I'll pay for the beer if we survive," Wilks grinned.

Jill rolled her eyes. They got off the main streets and navigated through the smaller ones leading out of the city. The night was eerily loud for the capital at two in the morning. The center of the city, where the government buildings were located, had very little night life surrounding it. Usually, everything inside 495 shut down early, leaving the Hill a semi-ghost town. Tonight, though, felt more like the Fourth of July. She could hear continuous pops in the distance, followed by low rumbles that couldn't be mistaken for anything other than low-grade incendiaries. The capital was a battle zone tonight.

"We need to find a place to hole up outside of Capital Beltway," Marco was saying, snapping her back to reality.

"What's going on?" she asked. "Have you spoken with Paula?"

"She's out trying to bring people in," he replied. "We're stretched thin enough as it is and getting massacred out here. Last count was seventy confirmed casualties. The rest we aren't sure about."

Seventy. That is twenty percent of our influence in the government. That means we just lost the United States.

Jill stopped dead in her tracks. The States were lost. How could this happen? She stared in stunned silence at the lone flag waving in the night sky next to a government building. The Genjix controlled the United States now.

Marco turned around and snapped his fingers in front of her face. "We have to move. There are more Genjix teams filtering in by the second. Paula is working on establishing a rendezvous point. Until then, we need to stay low and out of danger."

"What about Command operations?" she asked.

He shook his head. "The first place attacked."

Jill gasped. "The Keeper?"

Marco exhaled, the usual twinkle in his eye gone. "She left for European Command last week. Paula was able to take the helm and fight off the first Genjix wave, and then they escaped through the manufacturing district. I'm waiting for confirmation on a rally point. The existing safe houses here are all considered compromised."

"We have nowhere to hide?" Jill said. "Wilks can't stay on his feet much longer."

Marco shook his head. "We're in a bad state. Without a place to regroup to and Penetra scanners everywhere, we're sitting ducks. We need to avoid all major cities for a few days until Paula figures things out. Unfortunately, that's where all our safe houses are."

"Wait," Jill said quickly. "I know a place. Can you get a word out to Paula and the rest of our people?" He nodded. "Good," she picked up her pace. "I guess my good for nothing husband is good for something after all."

CHAPTER THIRTY-SIX
THE FALL

There were others like me who wandered the land, searching for greatness. While most were unsuccessful – finding the special humans who have the power to change history was as difficult as finding Quasing during the Gathering – a few were successful, though sometimes with unexpected results. Huchel and Camr succeeded with King Solomon and Hammurabi. With Alexander the Great, Cualm showed us what could happened if we lost control of a host with unbridled ambition. Both Zoras' hosts, Nero and Caesar, were cases where the Quasing lost control as well.

Tao

The trip around the South China Sea at the freighter's snail-paced twenty knots became a mini-vacation of sorts. Though Roen had paid enough to get them all housed at the Ritz Carlton for a year, they were given cargo containers down in the hold as apartments. It seemed that in the distant past, Dylan had indeed dated Manny's niece, and the two men had once been close and dabbled in cockfighting together. Now, Manny's niece was a nun and Dylan was on Manny's permanent shit-list. However, Dylan had saved Manny's life more than once from bad wagers in the arena, so the old captain put up with him.

Roen and his men spent much of their days practicing their golf swings on the makeshift driving range at the aft starboard side. This was the first real downtime the team had had since they arrived in Taiwan, and the men's individual talents were coming out of the woodwork. Jim had been an opera major and a pretty decent baritone, Ray had once been a semi-pro figure skater, Grant had graduated from culinary school, Faust had made it to day four of one of the World Series of Poker tournaments, Hutch was a Golden Gloves amateur champion, and one would never guess, but skinny Stan could drive the golf ball nearly three hundred meters. Roen had no idea why Stan bothered being a Prophus agent. If Roen had that kind of skill, he'd ditch Tao and join the PGA in a heartbeat.

Thank you for the loyalty and support.

"I've seen the chicks pro golfers nab. You still owe me a Brazilian lingerie model."

When not working on their golf swings and swilling lambanog, a liquor brewed in the engine room, the team passed the time sparring. Their friendly fights became so popular that it soon became the ship's main attraction. Grant had to make a fight schedule to accommodate the crew and even set up a relatively complicated system for them to bet on. Within two days, the team was able to amass a tidy enough sum to pay for all the lambanog they could drink.

What also impressed Roen during these sparring sessions was the skill his men had in hand-to-hand combat. These weren't the green grunts that he had encountered guarding doors at Command. These were the best shock troops the

Prophus had to offer. Roen wasn't about to admit that any of these guys were better than him, and all the betting odds backed his confidence, but all of them had at one point given him a run for his money. There were quite a few upsets during the fights, from Ray with his flashy dance-like moves to Stan's old-school Chinese Hong Fist to Grant's "I'm impervious to pain" Neanderthal beat-down. It wasn't pretty, and he ate punches by the bunch, but once Grant got his paws on him, it was pretty much over. Now Roen knew why the rest of the guys called him Zangief. Hutch, on the other hand, gave him the most problems with his boxing. His odds against Roen were nearly one-to-one.

Their Pacific cruise finished its leg in Manila on the second day and reached Macau on the fourth. They spent two days in port, loading new cargo before chugging back toward Taiwan leisurely. The sun was out, and there was a gentle breeze coming in from the west making the weather perfect for just lounging and drinking copious amounts of alcohol. All in all, this was the best and only vacation Roen had had in years.

And you needed it, Negative Nancy.

"All work and no play..."

And as karma would have it, just as the going got good, bad news had to rain down on their parade. They were a day out from Taiwan when disturbing information from the States came across the Prophus sub-channel. Roen and Hutch were playing tetherball with a punctured soccer ball when Stan came sprinting out onto the deck.

"We're all needed in the communication room," he gasped, breathing so hard he barely got the words out.

Roen looked down at his watch. "I'm not on radio duty for another thirty minutes."

"We've just lost the government!" Stan said.

Roen looked puzzled. "What happened to the Keeper?"

"No, the United States!"

This cannot be true!

Roen only thought of Jill as he rushed to the tower, followed closely by the rest of his team. According to bits and pieces from scattered Prophus reports, Washington DC had fallen to the Genjix. The team huddled around the communication array, hitting every back channel they could find. Nine hours later, the Keeper had verified their worst fears. The capital of the United States had fallen to a brazen military coup, and the Genjix were now in firm control of the country.

Roen spent those hours huddled in a ball next to the radio. Some of the information was conflicting, and he didn't know what to believe. It trickled in slowly and in bits, and it only got worse. Senator Thompson was missing. Secretary of Defense Jayloh, Director Sun of the FBI, and Representative Forbeck, a respected nine-term congressman, were all confirmed dead alongside their Quasing. Federal appellate Judge Cole, Secretary Kowal of the Department of Education, and Vice Admiral Andrews were only a few of the growing list of important Prophus figures missing. The number of dead Prophus operatives climbed higher and higher. Initial estimates were fourteen, then forty, and then over a hundred. One bit of data stood out to him though. Senator Wilks had been shot and presumed dead. Scenes of Jill facing a hit squad of Genjix assassins played over and over in his head. His face drained of all color as he clutched his knees, listening for any piece of news that would prove his worst fears false.

I cannot believe they can be so brazen as to risk such an attack.

This was a coordinated attack, one inconceivable a few short years ago. For the Genjix to risk this sort of exposure and cause this kind of public upheaval was beyond any Quasing's understanding. This went against strict Quasing doctrine both sides had followed for thousands of years.

What the hell are those assholes doing?

Tao kept muttering that phrase over and over. It worried Roen to hear him say that. Tao was incensed to the point of being incoherent. Usually nothing rattled him. This was the alien who had conquered half the world several times.

Are they insane?

During those hours, Tao had retreated into a shell, staying silent for the most part save for a few random angry outbursts. Finally, during the tenth hour into their vigil around the radio, Tao made a disturbing proclamation.

We have lost.

Roen, dozing against the table, snapped his head up, suddenly alert and attentive. He glared at the others huddled in the room in various states of consciousness and snapped. "Who said that?" He climbed to his feet, nostrils flaring. "Which one of you said we've lost?" The other guys looked up at him with dull, blank stares.

"No one, Roen," Ray said. "It must be Tao."

"Tao would never..." Roen snarled and then stopped. "Tao, did you say we lost?"

The war is over. Without the United States, the Prophus have lost.

"Come on, that's bullshit. We're not giving up."

There is no longer a path to victory. Without support from a superpower in this world, we have no choice but to capitulate to the Genjix. It will save lives in the long run. We should advise the Keeper to consider the inevitable. Had we kept at least one superpower neutral, we might have been able to hold off the Genjix until we found a long-term solution, but with both China and the United States actively working against us, the war is lost.

Roen suddenly couldn't breathe. He stormed out of the communication room and barreled past several startled crewman. He sprinted up the stairs and burst out onto the deck. He inhaled the cool night ocean air, taking in the salt and water as he stalked toward the bow of the ship. Between Tao's shocking concession and his fear that Jill was dead, he couldn't take it anymore.

Roen leaned over the railing and screamed as loud and as long as he could. All he could think about was how he was half a world away from Jill. He should have been by her side. He should have been there to protect her! He rounded on the nearest inanimate victim, which happened to be a rusty ventilation shaft jutting up from the deck, and punched it as hard as he could. He followed up with another punch and then a kick that rang the round tube like a dull church bell.

"Ow."

Careful. You might need that foot still. We could be on the run for a long time.

Roen was pretty sure his hand wasn't broken, but he couldn't say the same of his foot. If he had hurt the ventilation shaft, it didn't show it. That shaft was a lot sturdier than it looked. Instead, Roen turned his back to it and sat down, leaning on it for support. He rubbed his injured hands and foot as his mind raced. Was Jill lying dead in her office? Maybe in a ditch? Had she been executed by the Genjix? Every thought tore out a little piece of him. Lin's words echoed again in his head. His wife was probably dead, and he could be soon as well. His son would be an orphan. He should have been there! Roen slammed his fist into the deck.

Get ahold of yourself.

"This is your fault, Tao! I should have been by her side!"

There was a long pause.

You are right. I am sorry, Roen. When this is over, we will find Jill. I promise you. You have done enough for the Prophus. It is time we put your loved ones first.

Roen leaned against the railing. "You mean it?"

I do. Finish this mission, and we will catch the next plane out.

Then Roen saw a smattering of lights in the distance. The lights multiplied and grew larger and larger. A minute later, the outline of the city came into view.

We have reached the southern port of Kaohsiung. Get the men inside the container.

Roen didn't move. His eyes followed the blinking lights as they got closer and closer. "What's the point if it's all over?"

Until told otherwise, we still have a mission to carry out. And even if the war is lost, it is not like we can back out now. Prepare for infiltration.

CHAPTER THIRTY-SEVEN
EX-EXTINCTION

The eve of humanity's evolution is coming to a close. Like the early primates that we sacrificed when we deemed their evolutionary worth was at usefulness' end, so too are humans.

With that, the vessels who serve will continue on in another form. Those who do not will cease. Once Quasiform completes, it will only be the Quasing who will remain. And thus, the destiny of Earth will be fulfilled.

Zoras

Enzo scanned the black and green specks of the forest interior, searching for signs of movement. Somewhere in there, the enemy lay in wait. Last night's razed eastern tree lines still glowed angry red, drifting thick black smoke into the otherwise pure blue air. After the disaster at the Prophus camp, the lines had once again been redrawn.

The Genjix had taken heavy losses and were no longer able to maintain the heavy escorts, base defenses, and widened perimeters. One of his tactical advantages had to go, so Enzo was now blind again in the forests and unable to go on the offensive. The Prophus had again pushed all the way to the edge of the forest. Yesterday, while his construction crews were working on the runway, the Prophus had attacked, massacring thirty.

The news coming in from America was much better. The United States government was now theirs, free of Prophus influence. The results of the cleansing had thrown the government into disarray. It would take months for their public relations arm to cover up the incident and calm the government. For now, the Genjix pushed the conspiracy of Middle Eastern terrorist attacks. Others thought it a military coup. Even more thought it was a religious fundamentalist rebellion.

Those fools could think what they wanted. As long as their attention was elsewhere, Enzo did not care. The situation would blow over in a few months, and by then the Genjix would have free rein over the country without the meddling Prophus getting in their way. It was a good trade off.

The Genjix Council had also finally come around. With the Genjix's control of the United States assured, the ProGenesis project nearing completion, and his continuing successful defense of the camp, they had no choice but to offer him full status on the Council. When it was brought up during the last meeting, only Vinnick opposed his standing.

Well, Enzo planned to take care of the Russian billionaire soon after his business at the camp was complete. In fact, he considered neutralizing the old man's power an important matter. The primary facilities for Phase III were based within Vinnick's sphere of influence. With the ProGenesis near completion, all Genjix initiatives would shift toward Quasiform. Whoever controlled Quasiform controlled the Council. If Enzo was not careful, Vinnick could steal the project from underneath him.

Your ambitions are admirable. However, do not forget your goal or who you serve.

"I serve you and the Genjix, Zoras."

As long as you serve our purpose. Power struggles are encouraged among the Genjix. It keeps the vessels strong and hungry, but do not overstep. You walked when you should be crawling. And now you want to run.

Palos walked up and bowed. "Chow is reporting in, Father."

Enzo nodded without tearing his eyes away from the trees. This wasn't their scheduled meeting. He must have good news, for there was little reason to report his continuing failure. Enzo trotted to the main building with Palos in tow.

He spared his first a regretful look. After their time in Tibet was over, he would have to release Palos from his duty as his personal guard and assign him to another role. Being a bodyguard was beneath a vessel. Of course Enzo would keep him under his command, but it would not be the same. He had become accustomed to Palos; it would be difficult to replace him.

He walked into the war room and saw Chow's face already on the screen. He was sweating like a pig on a spit. He was excited though, moving about animatedly and shouting at his assistants off-screen. Enzo sat down and coughed. Chow gave a start and then began talking so fast Enzo couldn't understand what he was saying. The only words he could make out were "three days" and "still alive". As far as he was concerned, those were all the words he needed to hear.

He put up a hand to shut Chow up. "Are you saying ProGenesis is a success?"

Chow nodded so fast that he thought the man's neck might snap. "Yes, Father. Three days. Tested among all six of our prisoners. All still alive."

Has one of ours survived?

Enzo kept his rising excitement inside. There would be no celebration until everything was confirmed. "Have you done final verification?"

"I have not." Chow replied. "That is what I'm calling you for. I need permission to do that."

"Proceed. Quickly, and today. Do we have a volunteer?"

Chow nodded again. "Heisenberg, a lowly regarded vessel, and his Holy One Danli have volunteered to be the sacrifice. We are prepared to translate Quasing light signals."

Enzo allowed a smile to break out on his face. "Very well then. Have Danli enter the vat immediately. You better pray you are successful, Chow. If so, your standing has been raised. Your place among all the Holy Ones is secured, and you will be honored for your accomplishments from this point on until the Eternal Sea. If this is another false positive though, I will have your hide."

Then Enzo sat in front of the screen and waited, watching as the scientists scurried around, preparing the first Genjix volunteer to enter the vats. Then he watched Heisenberg jump into the vat. Interestingly, this current formula dissolved human flesh. Within minutes, Heisenberg was nothing more than a pile of bones floating in the container. Then he noticed Danli floating within the red liquid, blinking. A few minutes later, Chow reported in again with a simple message from Danli:

CONDITIONS ARE IDEAL INDISCERNIBLE FROM QUASAR PROCREATION POSSIBLE

"Get four other volunteers in quickly!" Enzo ordered. "I want results on an attempt immediately."

The next six hours were the longest in Enzo's life. He spent the entire time watching the screen, not leaving the war room unless he absolutely had to. Enzo cursed for not being back at Qingdao to witness this triumph in person. Still, he sat and waited and watched patiently as four other volunteer vessels sacrificed their lives in the vat alongside Danli. For those hours, he stayed glued to the screen while the five Quasing mingled. Even when the Prophus launched an attack, Enzo sent Palos to take care of the defense. He would not leave until this latest experiment was concluded. Finally, a message from Chow came through loud and clear. The five Quasing had successfully created life.

A new god had been born.

Unbelievable. It has happened.

Unbelievable was right. Enzo stared at the screen for a good five minutes as Chow relayed the news. Inside, he could feel Zoras churning with excitement. To Enzo personally, this was just a passing milestone, a step on his climb to leading all of the Genjix. He had only been involved in the project for a few months and while proud, he could not even begin to feel the jubilation his Holy One felt. He was simply the right vessel at the right time.

For Zoras, this was a milestone after millennia of maneuvering, the culmination of a century of planning from when the Genjix first realized that the Quasing might become extinct before they accomplished their original goal of returning to Quasar. With ProGenesis, Zoras had just ensured that the Quasing would continue on even if their numbers dwindled. This victory also sealed the Prophus' fate. It wouldn't be a surprise if the Prophus unconditionally capitulated once they learn that the Genjix had successfully birthed new Quasing.

"Your will, mighty Zoras. Your victory."

A victory for the Genjix. For all Quasing.

Today was a great day. Enzo stood up, rubbed his tired eyes, and looked outside. It was dark except for the tower lights scanning the perimeter. He had been so focused on what was occurring in the labs that he had forgotten everything else. Not that anything else mattered. His mission was a success, and now the Genjix could move to the final phase: Catalyst.

The necessity of this camp was also now in question, as were the prisoners. These were just loose ends that needed to be cleaned up. He considered his options. He could just do it quietly and with little trouble, but it seemed a waste. Why not force the Prophus' hand? Make them grind their forces toward certain death through no-man's-land toward entrenched Genjix forces. It seemed to Enzo a fitting end to this conflict. He still owed Stephen a debt, after all.

Enzo turned to Palos leaning against the door. "Build a platform, gather all the prisoners, and then shoot them; publicly for all the Prophus to see."

CHAPTER THIRTY-EIGHT
HIDEOUT

His death broke Dania, who immediately retired from active duty.
She lived out the rest of her life in peace, raising young Sonya.
During those years, I was kept out of the war. However, I did not
mind. Dania had experienced great loss and deserved her peace. She
developed cancer and died with Sonya by her side, and I enjoyed a
rare peaceful transition.

I began to train Sonya. She benefitted from having known of
us since she was a child. Even at a young age, Sonya proved gifted
in all ways that a Prophus finds valuable. Beautiful, physically
talented, intelligent, and forceful, she was extraordinary and
showed potential for greatness.

Baji

Jill leaned into the microphone hidden within the recess of
the stone wall and paused. Then she looked back at the sixty
survivors, the remnants of the Prophus political operation
in the United States. Out of nine senators, twenty-eight
representatives, one cabinet member, twenty-four federal
judges, and nearly three hundred aides and officials, only these
scared and exhausted souls had made it out of the city alive.

The Genjix had brazenly swept into the city with overwhelming numbers. Some of the pitched firefights had numbered fifty combatants, turning the streets of the capital into a veritable war zone. Command estimated that two thousand Genjix had encircled the beltway and squeezed in. Paula's team of two hundred had stood no chance of mounting a defense. The only thing they could do was delay the enemy long enough for survivors to escape. It was to Paula's credit that even this many had made it.

Marco was currently out with the scouts herding stragglers to this rendezvous point. Time was of the essence. There were still pockets of Prophus hiding, having eluded the Penetra vans. The longer the remaining operatives stayed out there, the greater their risk of discovery.

Initial reports of casualties were catastrophic. Both Senators Brant and Lim were dead. Eleven Representatives were confirmed dead alongside their Quasing. Judges Rhiew and Hellen were captured and presumed dead. Of those in Congress, only Senators Thompson and Wilks, and Representatives James and Howard had made it here. The rest of their people were unaccounted for.

Jill put her hand on Paula's arm. "You saved a lot of people." The woman looked like she was about to fall over.

"Just open the bloody rock," Paula muttered.

Jill coughed and spoke in a hushed voice. "Baby bear versus the big city." The panel dinged like a bell signaling tea time, and a green light lit up. There was a hiss from the side while the door swung open. Jill turned and waved everyone through.

"Baby bear, huh?" A small smile escaped Paula's face as she walked by.

"Long story," Jill shrugged. "He's quirky like that."

The survivors dragged themselves into their new temporary home and made themselves comfortable. Already, Paula's team was setting up a command post in the kitchen while the non-military personnel erected an infirmary and living quarters in Roen's bedroom and living room. Within a few minutes, Roen's hole in the mountain transformed into the new base of operations.

Too exhausted to sleep, she decided to explore her husband's home. The first time she was here, she had been too drunk and tired to get a clear feel for the place. Now that she was sober, she had to admit Roen's hideout was impressive. Walking through one of the side corridors, she discovered that this old missile base went a lot deeper underground than she realized.

She found Roen's treasured ammo dump in the second silo, which was circular in shape, similar to the living room. However, in place of couches and a coffee table, this one was stocked to the brim with crates of what she presumed were weapons and ammunition. He wasn't exaggerating when he said he had stockpiled enough for a nuclear winter. There were enough arms here to equip Ecuador. She cracked open a few crates. Tucked in beds of straw were caches of weapons from grenades to Browning M2 heavy machine guns to crossbows. In one crate, there were several hand-propelled rocket launchers and in another, a flamethrower. She even found a jousting lance on the floor.

"At least he'll be ready if Normandy invades. I couldn't shoot all this stuff in two lifetimes."

Some of it looks older than the Cold War.

"Ammo is ammo."

Old ammunition is dangerous. I would rather use bows and arrows. At least they will not explode in your face.

Jill was about to leave the room when something off to the side caught her eye. At first, it looked like a tall mini fridge. She frowned and upon closer inspection, whistled in disbelief.

"Is that what I think it is?"

A miniaturized Penetra scanner without a power source. One of the newer models the Genjix have been testing. I do not know how Roen acquired this. Command has been trying to get their hands on one of these for months now. Soon, the Genjix will have miniaturized it into a hand held. Then we will be in real trouble.

"He can be resourceful when he puts his mind to it," she murmured, wiping the dust off the scanner and checking the interface. It was the first time she'd seen one of these scanners. The Genjix guarded them very closely.

Leave it. We have more pressing things to worry about.

Jill exited the ammo room and continued down the corridor to the next silo. This one was Roen's doom-prepping storage. There must have been more than five thousand canned goods in here. She counted several hundred gallons of water, mounds of assorted dried fruit, and six lifetimes of ramen. In the corner were a dozen cases of scotch. To the right of that, she stumbled onto a pile of toilet paper twice as tall as she was.

Booze and toilet paper. At least he has his priorities straight.

"He's nothing if not consistent. How much do you want to bet I find a couple crates of chocolate bars?"

It would be a bad bet to take.

The last silo was Roen's office. A metal desk sat in the center, enclosed by a ring of shelves filled with computers. On the desk were a state-of-the-art computer and several pictures of Cameron. Jill picked up a picture of Cameron's first birthday. She wiped off the dust, her fingers brushing his chubby face and that look of joyful bewilderment at the lone candle on a cake. Moments after that picture was taken, Cameron had grabbed the candle and burned his fingers. She chuckled. He was so much like his father, even at this young age.

Jill sat down at the desk and tried to log into his computer. First she tried the baby bear password and then several others that they shared, combining hers and Cameron's information. She tried a few more passwords, such as her favorite phrase, Cameron's first toy, and his old cat Meow Meow. When none worked, she leaned back and pondered. Roen wasn't exactly a creative genius with passwords. He was sentimental and a creature of habit. He tended to rotate the same three over and over again with slight variations.

We should not waste time on this. Though if his birthday had worked, Command would have to reconsider allowing him into our network.

A second later, Jill's face cracked a grin after she typed in "pretzels&beer" and got in. Jill checked her watch; six minutes to hack in. She beamed and mentally patted herself on the back.

He often mentioned that phrase. I never understood what it meant.

"It's what we had for dinner on our first date. Pretzels and beer at the Cubs game."

It is sweet but pathetic, like his entire life revolves around that day.

"It's momentous event for him, right up there with the first day of football season. What can I say? He loves me."

Jill paused. Roen did love her. He was an idiot and was terrible at showing it, but it dawned on her right there that his life really did revolve around her.

Yet not enough to stay when you begged him to.

"I blame his alien and his messed up view of how best to protect his family."

Jill rummaged through his files. Being a computer nerd in his previous life, Roen was meticulous with his systems. While a slob in reality, his virtual cleanliness was unsurpassed. She was able to find important documents on his hard drive within seconds and soon had schematics of a dozen Genjix bases laid out before her. She was surprised at how thorough Roen was with his surveillance. His specialty rarely ventured toward the softer side of covert operations. The photos he had nabbed were first rate, though.

"My man is growing," she murmured.

Better late than never.

"He's still one of the best agents."

That I concede and take a fair amount of credit for. When Sonya first trained him, he was two left feet and no brains. Now, he is a no-brained killer on par with Sonya.

"Could you get any more backhanded with your compliments?"

The day you forgive him, I might too.

"You're sweet, Baji. You have a funny way of showing it, but you are."

She pulled up his mission itinerary and was surprised to discover that he had been very busy. Within the past eighteen months, he had ventured to forty-two places all over the world. And by the looks of them – Kurdistan, Siberia, Mongolia, Libya, among others – none were vacation hotspots. For the next hour, Jill delved into what he had been up to for the past two years.

It began with Roen chasing clues to an obscure Genjix reference known as Phase III. There were some unexplainable trips that she found curious that had no notes attached. There was one trip where he flew from Istanbul, back to Virginia for two days, and then back out again to Istanbul. Jill furrowed her brow. It seemed he was funding his frequent flier miles with a savings account that she didn't know about.

"That damn guy," she growled. She shook her fist in the air. "Roen! You're in so much trouble when I get my hands on you."

You hide one from him too.

"That's different. I use mine to buy shoes and pretty sundresses. A woman needs her own little spending account. He uses his to jet set around the world."

It says here he bribed a courier to stow away on an Air India transport. Hardly jet setting.

"You're supposed to be on my side."

Damn you, Roen!

"Much better."

On page nine of his expenditures, his account ran dry, and he subsidized his lifestyle by running guns on the black market.

Jill shook her head. "My husband is a felon."

Quite ingenious. I did not think he had it in him.

"Look, he broke out of a Pakistani prison last December."

That explains why he did not call Cameron on Christmas.

"Now I feel kind of bad for yelling at him about being a bad parent."

The data began to paint a picture of several large industries purposely releasing large amounts of toxins, carbon, and different variants of methyl into the air. It was a conspiracy that he estimated had been occurring for the over fifty years. Jill could see the case he was building. The last entry was three months ago when he discovered the name of Phase III: Quasiform.

"What a busy bee," Jill exclaimed, closing the documents and opening the next folder. She was startled to find dozens of photographs of her. Most of them were surveillance shots from afar on the Hill. Shockingly, some of them were her on assignment, including at the United Nations, at the London G8 conference, and at the assault on the Genjix naval yard in Newfoundland. Somehow, he always found time to shadow her missions. Then it dawned on her the lengths that he had gone to be there for her. Her eyes began to water.

I give him credit for who he is. He is many things, but he does love you and shows it in his own way.

The last folder was pictures of Cameron. Hundreds of them. As far as Jill could tell, Roen practically had Cameron's life chronicled daily in pictures. That wasn't unexpected. He had developed an interest in photography when his son was born. What was interesting, though, was that he had somehow snapped pictures of Cameron even after he had left. There were pictures of Cameron at preschool, playing at the park, even playing in their condo.

Sadly, those pictures stopped the day she sent Cameron to Louis and Lee Ann's. Working for the senator and the Prophus had just gotten to be too much for a single mother with a toddler. She had received a harsh phone call from him about sending Cameron away without his permission. He had received an even harsher retort from her. And then they hadn't spoken for three months.

Later that night, Jill stood outside the missile silo entrance and stared at the stars. There were a lot more of them popping out here in the boonies than there were in the city. She missed stars. There was something magical about them as they filled the blackness of the universe. Quasar was somewhere up there, filled with billions of her people, waiting for Baji to come home.

Technically, you cannot see Quasar right now.

"You're ruining my moment of serenity with facts. Stop it. You think Roen and Cameron can see these same stars?"

Cameron maybe. It is daytime where Roen is.

Jill looked to the west at the furthest star on the horizon. Then, with a tear falling down her face, she took out her phone and called Lee Ann.

Her mother's voice was a welcome sound after tonight's horror. "Hey, Jill, how's my favorite daughter?"

"Still hanging in there," she said, forcing a smile onto her face. Lee Ann had this crazy ability to always know how she felt even if they were halfway around the world. She couldn't let her mother catch on. She didn't want what could be their last conversation to be sad.

"Is everything alright in DC?" Lee Ann asked. "There was something in the news about gang violence on the streets tonight. You're staying home, right?"

"Yes," Jill said. Of course the Genjix would have the news blanketed with alibis before their assault tonight. The less her mother knew, the better. "How's my little guy?" she asked.

"He eats as much as Louis and is already growing out of his old clothes. Louis and I are arguing about enrolling him in public or private school. There's this wonderful magnet school here that teaches French Immersion. Of course, your father thinks it's a waste..."

Jill didn't hear the rest. These were decisions that she was supposed to make. She should be the one grousing about his growth spurts or worrying what schools he should attend. She stayed silent for most of the conversation, just listening to Lee Ann go on about Cameron. Finally, she asked for her son.

"Mommy?" Cam's beautiful voice came on the line.

"Hey, buddy," she sniffed. "How's it going?"

As usual, Cameron began to blab about his day. Jill stayed quiet and just enjoyed the sound of him as well. His conversation with himself moved from Eva to his first soccer practice to scraping his hands on the slide and then back to Eva. Eventually, he exhausted his vocabulary.

"Mommy," he said. "I miss you and Daddy."

"I miss you too, Cam Cam." She felt her strength ebb away and another tear escape the corner of her eye.

"All my friends have mommies and daddies."

That broke the dam. Jill buried her head in her hands. "I'm sorry, Cam, we'll all be together soon."

"I had a bad dream last night. I went to find you when I couldn't sleep again."

"If you ever need to find me, just look up at the stars," she tried to say. The words came out a blubbery mess. Finally, after several more minutes of trying to say she loved him and hearing him say he loved her back, Jill hung up.

She leaned against a boulder in the ravine and broke down, burying her face in her hands, her entire body shuddering as she sobbed. After what seemed an eternity, long after her tear ducts had dried out, she just sat there looking up.

"I don't know how much longer I can keep it together."

This war is for Cameron as well. If we lose, his future will be lost.

Jill palmed her face and wiped away the tears. "I already lost a husband. And I lost two years with my baby. I'll never get those back."

I promise you. After this is over, you will reunite with Cameron, even if you need to walk away from the Prophus. I owe you this much. But for now, you need to hold it together just a little bit longer.

Jill closed her eyes and sucked in through her nose. She held it for a few seconds and slowly exhaled. "I don't want just my son, Baji. I want my husband too. They're everything to me. Promise me both, and I'll fight the Genjix until the end of the Earth."

When this is all over...

Several headlights suddenly appeared in the distance, rumbling down the ravine at high speed. Jill frowned. Were they discovered?

Get inside.

"No time. If it's the Genjix, they'll be right on my heels. I can't open the vault door for them."

It was suicide, but she scrambled up the ravine and hoisted herself onto a small cliff jutting out of the side. Lying flat against the cool stone, she watched as six cars screeched to a stop. She did a quick head count on the bodies getting out and prepared to run.

"You can come down, Jill," Marco called up to her.

With a sigh of relief, she peered over the edge and slid down to greet him in a rough embrace. "I was that invisible, huh?" she asked. "Some ninja I turned out to be."

He squeezed her tightly. "Nah, the ninja detecting bangle gave you away." He let her go. "Listen, we need to get inside. There are Genjix on our trail. They'll be here soon."

Jill gasped. "You led them there? You idiot! Why?"

Marco motioned his men inside and pushed her in as well. "Not us. They intercepted Paula's recall signal. We came to get you out." He stopped just as they entered the tunnel and looked outside as several new headlights appeared in the distance. "Too late," he said grimly. "Get inside. Guess we'll make a final stand here."

CHAPTER THIRTY-NINE
THE PORT

*The Roman Empire became our philosophical paradox. We became
so adept at manipulating humanity that we were able to dominate
them by creating the largest empire the world had ever seen.
However, in doing so, we also created a stability that directly stifled
our Conflict Doctrine.*

*Therefore, in order to maintain both the empire and the
doctrine, the Quasing pushed the empire further and further out.
This led to the eventual corruption and rotting of the empire. It was
at that time that I decided to venture eastward to Asia and try my
hand at unspoiled lands.*

Tao

It was a rough couple of hours for Roen and his band of very un-
merry men as they were tossed around like dice in a cup in one
of the shipping containers marked to be unloaded at the Punai
warehouse. Between the cranes, trucks, hooks, and conveyor
belts used to move these containers about, they were jostled
around constantly and violently until they finally reached their
resting place. They presumed it was somewhere on the Punai
grounds since the container was virtually pitch black inside.

Otherwise the men passed the time in silence though, the recent news weighing heavily on their minds. Most had been with the Prophus for years if not decades, and all of them believed fervently in the cause. They knew what was at stake if the war was lost, not only for the world but for them personally as well. If the Prophus fell, they were all dead men walking. Roen spent his time worrying and napping. There wasn't much else to do other than have his imagination run out of control. At midnight, Tao woke him up. He always said having a built in alarm clock qualified as his one super power.

Game time.

Roen checked his watch out of habit and then shined his flashlight around the room. He saw his men's long faces and decided to give everyone a pep talk. After all, they could all use a morale boost, even though Roen felt like he needed cheering up the most.

You should say something. Be the leader.

"Technically, Faust is. Or Dylan since the Keeper assigned him to run this."

Dylan is the tactical lead, but he is still a stranger to the men. Faust is still not right in the head. The job falls on you.

Roen stood up and paced the container, watching each man tending to his own little part of the world. Grant had a son who was in Tibet fighting with Stephen. Hutch's wife worked on the Hill with Jill. Ray's brother was in Greenland with the Keeper. Being part of the Prophus was more than a job; it was a family affair. And now everything they stood for was on the verge of falling apart. Hell, it was all Roen could do to not bust out of this metal coffin and swim across the ocean to search for Jill.

"Tao, I don't know what to say."

Everyone feels defeated. Just be honest.

Roen cleared his throat. "Alright, huddle up. I know the situation sucks, and we're probably screwed."

I was hoping for a better opener.

"We have loved ones and friends all over the world who are in danger," he continued. "We don't know if anyone is still alive, and all we want to do right now is ditch this mission and go look for them. At least that's what I want to do. My wife's out there somewhere in the thick of it. Right now, I could give two shits..." he gestured at the container "...about this shit."

You are making things worse. Stop talking while you are ahead, or better yet, repeat after me.

"No, Tao, I got this."

Roen scanned each face. At least he had their attention. Well, most of them. Hutch was still sleeping. Roen raised his voice. "And I'm so frustrated right now that I just want to hit something!" He emphasized his anger by punching the wall. The ringing woke Hutch, who reached for his rifle.

Easy, Tyson. Last thing we need is to be discovered.

"But I'm in the same boat as you," Roen continued. He pointed at the wall. "We still got a job to do. And at least we know that some of the people responsible for endangering our loved ones are right outside. Our mission is still important. We can still hurt the enemy."

Roen's speech was met with silence. And though he didn't quite expect an enthusiastic huzzah after his speech, he had hoped for some sort of positive reinforcement. Grant looked stone faced, Hutch tired, and Stan resigned to their fate. Only Dylan wore a smile, but then, when didn't he?

"You know," Ray said. "I've always been told that if the Genjix win, humanity's doomed. Is that still correct?"

"Even more so than ever," Dylan said.

"So what does it matter if the Prophus lose the States? I mean, we haven't lost the planet yet."

"I'm not dead yet," Hutch added. "We keep fighting until we win or die."

"I don't know about you boys, but I'm in it for the fame and fortune," Faust added.

That brought about a round of laughter and seemed to have broken the ice. The men became their normal selves again as they bantered and ribbed each other. Roen sat back down and smiled. These were a bunch of good guys, every single one of them. Wuehler might have been a prick, but he knew how to assemble a team with quality men.

"What does that say about me, Tao?"

That Wuehler does not get it right all the time.

Suddenly, Roen's watch beeped. The chattered died immediately and the group began to gear up, from armor to ammunition to night vision goggles to rifles. They were a veteran crew and knew when to get serious. Within four minutes, the team was ready to go.

Roen grabbed the door latch and slowly turned it, making the entire container creak as he moved the lever ninety degrees. Then he opened the door a smidgen and looked outside. They were in a massive storage yard. They were two stories above the ground, stacked on top of another container. A cool blast of air flowed through into the stuffy container. The midnight sky was as black as he could have hoped for.

Roen turned to the men behind him. "Alright, do your job, stay safe, and hit them where it hurts." He grabbed Dylan on the shoulder as he was about to jump out. "Manny's dependable?"

Dylan nodded. "Yeah, old *Imelda* will be ready."

Roen conveyed last-minute instructions and encouragement to each person as each left the container. Within seconds, he was the only one left inside. He peered out the opening and watched as his team headed toward their assigned sections of the Punai grounds. He dove out head first and rolled gently to a kneeling position, rifle aimed forward.

A large barbed fence separated the storage yard from the warehouses, Roen's assigned section. Intelligence bought from the Bamboo Union indicated half a dozen guards manned the night shift at the warehouses while three manned the refineries. Roen had put himself on the more difficult assignments and had sent the lumbering beasts to the refineries. Tao had objected strenuously.

You are heading tactical. You should not be prowling at all.

"Limited resources, buddy. Gotta make do with what you got. Besides, six guards is a lot for anyone to juggle, let alone these lumbering hulks. There is a grand simplicity to being a shock trooper after all. Just point the way and let the carnage begin."

If it were that simple, I would have steered you toward that role a long time ago.

"I'm much more sophisticated than that. More a scalpel than a butcher knife in my execution."

You are as much a surgeon as Leopold a humanitarian.

"Which one is that?"

The one that liked to explore and meet new people in foreign lands, and then kill them.

Roen spent the next few minutes scouting the perimeter of the fence separating the container yard and the warehouses. Once he was ready, he followed the fence north until he came up to a small hill. There, he settled in and studied the pattern of the four floodlights. Within minutes, he had timed all four. Then he watched the guards making their rounds until he was comfortable predicting their routes.

The rest of the team should have arrived at their designations around the complex by now: Jim at the northwest warehouses; Ray, Grant, and Hutch searching the refineries; Dylan at the administration building. Hopefully, with all of them spread out, they could find this catalyst and be out within the hour. Then it depended on Faust and Stan at the docks to direct their exit strategy.

"How we looking, fellas?" he whispered into his mic.

"In place," Dylan whispered back. Jim echoed the sentiment. Grant grunted his affirmative like he always did.

"Going in now." Roen stretched, feeling the ligaments in his body pop. The past five years had done wonders and horrors to his body. From losing fifty kilos and training to run an ultra-marathon to being shot half a dozen times and rupturing organs, his body had run the entire gamut. He wondered how much longer he could keep this up.

Already thinking about going out to pasture?

"Only if there's a hot filly involved. Wait, don't tell my wife that. But really, guys like me don't retire. We just do one mission too many."

Can I tell you how much you sound like Edward right now?

"I'll take that as a compliment."

Roen's eyes trailed the moving floodlights as they floated across the concrete field between the fence and the first building. He'd have forty seconds to scale the fence, run across the forty-meter clearing, and get behind cover. He took off at a sprint.

Watch the barbed wire on top of the fence.

In three bounds, Roen launched up the four-meter fence, using his feet and hands to effortlessly scamper to the top. Using his upward momentum, he log-rolled onto his back just as he reached the crest of the fence, keeping his chin tucked against his chest and letting the Kevlar take the brunt of the sharp barbed wire. A second later, he landed softly on the ground and flattened into a crouch. Then he was off again, sprinting at full speed while still hunched over.

You are better at running low.

"Can't believe it took me six months to get this down, not to mention the number of times people snickered while I trained to run like Igor."

Small price to pay for ninja mastery.

"I'd pay double to disappear in a puff of smoke and glide among tree tops."

Roen reached the wall of the first building in exactly thirty-three seconds. He checked his watch and then slid toward the first window, peering into the darkness. Once he was satisfied that no one was inside, he moved on to the end of the building and checked around the corner. A patrolling guard had just exited the building and was moving away from Roen's position.

Once he disappeared around the corner, it would take him nine minutes to make it back around. This should be plenty of time for Roen to get into the building, check it out, and then move on to the next. As long as he stayed just behind the guard's route, he would be fine. He looked up at the floodlight again.

"Time before it hits that door?"

Forty-six seconds.

"That's cutting it tight. I'm not good at lock picking."

That is because you usually lock pick with a gun.

When the floodlight passed, Roen took off, sprinting along the side of the building to the wall. He took out a set of bump keys and picks. One glance at the lock and Roen knew he was destined to fail. It was an industrial-grade keypad lock and that part of his breaking-and-entering game was weak. He fiddled with the lock for exactly thirty-nine seconds before abandoning the door and going back around the corner.

Do you even know what you are doing?

"Yes. Well, no."

He retreated around the corner with just over two seconds to spare before the high beam swept the building. Roen's game of cat and mouse with this white light continued for several rounds. Each time it passed the building, he would run back to the door and spend the next thirty-eight seconds trying to work his locksmith magic. Then when he failed, he would flee back to the safety of the corner as the light came back around the building. By his seventh attempt, he was so irritated that he was ready to shoot the lock. Unfortunately, a silencer was not one of the tools his team had deemed necessary to rescue from the original safe house. Roen clenched his fist, knuckles white as he racked his brain for a solution. This delay was proving costly.

Maybe...

"Shut up, Tao. Just shut up. I don't want to hear it."

"I'm in the first warehouse," Jim's voice cackled over the comm.

"How did you crack the door?" Roen whispered.

"Spotted the guard on patrol. Sniped the code as he went in. How else do you do it with a level-six industrial grade

lock?" The way Jim said it so nonchalantly made Roen
cringe. He felt his ears burn.

Well, that was an obvious and simple solution.

"Why didn't you think of it? You're the smart one."

You were so eager to try. I did not want to shatter your confidence.

Roen moved off the wall and sprinted across the field
to the side of the adjacent building and hid behind a stack
of crates. There, with his scope trained on the lock pad, he
waited until the security guard came a minute later. Roen
watched as the guard punched a few buttons on the key
pad, went inside, and then left a minute later.

Did you get that?

"3385. Well, that was easy. You have failed me, brain."

You have your own brain. You just choose not to use it.

Roen waited sixty seconds until the guard was out of
sight, continuing on his rotations, before he moved in.
A few seconds later, he was inside the large cavernous
building with a massive door on the north end. On the
near sides, two cranes built into the walls like giant arms
hovered over the crates. A variety of colored metal crates
were stacked in the center of the room, reminding Roen
of a giant Rubik's Cube. Roen did a quick run through the
building, opening crates and containers, and checking drum
barrels. Most of the stuff here was missile parts: guidance
systems, seeker heads, fuel pumps. Nothing you couldn't
find in any second-rate army. He checked the window for
the guard and headed out to the next warehouse.

It was a short run to the next building. There he found
several pallets of neatly categorized boxes filled with assorted
electronics, ranging from high-tech research instruments
to parts Tao identified as Penetra scanner modules to what
looked suspiciously like the proton packs used by the

Ghostbusters. Each of these containers was marked for delivery to exotic locations throughout the region, from Myanmar to Siberia to Russia. There were even some marked for delivery to North Korea via Liaoning in China.

"Somalia, huh? Don't tell me the Genjix have a facility there."

It is the perfect place to have a research facility.

The next warehouse at the corner of the Punai grounds was the most disturbing. Inside, Roen found rows upon rows of reactive metals, molded into long tubes and conical ends. They stacked on top of each other by the dozens and were marked with orange triangular danger signs and the Taiwanese flag. The design of these particular types was unmistakable though.

"Long-range ballistic by the size of them. Proprietary US military grade. What's equipment slated for the Taiwanese Defense Force doing here? And there's enough in this warehouse to blow the planet up. What the hell is going on?"

If this is for Quasiform, now we know their delivery system.

"I thought Taiwan and China didn't get along. How do they even get this across the South Sea?"

The Genjix do not care about human political tensions. And if enough people are bribed, no one sees anything. Their influence over this region is as strong now as it was over Europe at the turn of the twentieth century.

Roen found his breakthrough in the last building. There, he found several rows of metal crates that were more fortified than the ones in the other warehouses. Roen pulled out a Geiger counter and checked its readings. Even the most secure container would show traces. Fortunately, it all came back negative. His team was ill-equipped for that kind of stuff. The last time Roen had dealt with radioactive material, he ended up bedridden for two months. It was a great way to diet though. Checking his watch, Roen made his way to the first crate, and with a little muscle and a metal rod he found on the floor, pried it open.

"Think it's the catalyst?"

The side of the canister says Catalyst Mark II. Take a sample and get a sit rep from the others. It has been over an hour now. Time to head out and go home. Good job.

Inside, he found nine silver transport tubes not unlike the ones used to for radioactive materials. Again, feeling the apprehension of dealing with radioactive material, he checked the meter again. Still nothing.

"I feel like Han Solo approaching the Death Star for the first time." He reached down and gently lifted a tube out of its protective covering.

That is not a moon. It is a space station.

Roen stopped, a grin growing on his face. "I don't say this enough, but I love you, Tao."

You should say that to your wife more.

"Now I don't love you anymore. Keep my wife out of it."

Undoing the metal latch and unscrewing the lid of the metal cylinder took an excruciating thirty seconds. He half-expected to discover a green glowing rod that would melt his face off and grow another head out of his belly, but instead, found a cool black metal rod sitting in a bath of clear liquid. He reached down to pluck it out.

I would not do that.

Roen retracted his hands. That was probably a good idea. He screwed the lid back on the canister and tucked it into his backpack. Whatever this thing was, it needed to go to a lab to be analyzed. Best-case scenario, it was a new material for glass figurines, though they had better be precious collectibles to justify that packaging. Worst-case scenario was a weaponized material for a bomb or something equally bad.

"God, I hope it's not biological."

Doubtful. The Quasing understand the dangers of biological warfare better than humans.

"How you guys doing?" Roen asked over the comm as he checked the area outside the door.

"In and out of the processing facility," Ray's voice crackled back. "Heavy water generator and micro assembly plant here. Not sure how this all fits together."

"Ghost town here," Dylan replied. "Grabbed some interesting plans."

"And Faust?" Roen asked. No answer. "Faust, you read?" Roen cursed and counted down from fourteen as his spider sense went nuts. The night leading up to now had been so quiet, but it could still go to hell if Faust's part fell apart.

"Faust here," the whisper came hurried and breathy. "Extraction ready. Heavy guard presence though. Eyes on six. Avoiding if possible."

It has been almost an hour. Time to not press your luck.

Roen switched over to the team channel as he made his way to the door. "Grant, get your team's ass back. We're bugging out. Faust, where you at?"

"Drydock Two. Second from the–" Roen heard a grunt and a squeak of a throat constricting, then the sound of automatic fire, a pause, and then more popping. In the distance, an alarm began to howl.

"Get to extraction. Move, move!" Roen ordered, bursting through the warehouse door and sprinting toward Faust's last known location. "Jim, you're closest. Rendezvous on the dock security building. Grant, double time."

He continued barking orders as he zigzagged around the floodlights and guards, haphazardly staying in shadows only when it was convenient. It was a wonder he wasn't discovered. He had just about reached the dock entrance when Jim, hiding behind a row of forklifts, beckoned him over. Roen dove into a dark corner with him just as a beam passed near his position.

"You're making more noise than a stampeding rhino," Jim muttered.

Roen ignored him. "How's it look in there?"

Jim pointed at the door of a large building with a massive "2" painted on the walls across from their hiding spot. "Dark."

"Let's go," Roen said. The two moved quickly to Drydock Two. Once inside, Roen gestured to Jim and pointed left, then gestured to himself and pointed right. The two split off and continued down the length of the long rectangular building, always keeping in contact with each other. Halfway down the length of the room, they found Stan's body sprawled against a drum barrel with two taps, one in his neck and one in his head. Faust appeared out of the shadows.

"Make that seven guards," he shook his head. We took out five, but the last two got a few shots off. Stan..." He grimaced.

"Get his body to the boat," Roen ordered.

A moment later, the rest of the team straggled in. Four minutes later, they were on a small tugboat heading out of the harbor. They were a klick out to sea when the entire dock lit up like Vegas during AVN Awards week. It was too late, though. Roen and his team had escaped. Exactly fifteen minutes later, they were standing on *Imelda's Song*'s aft deck.

Well done. Could not have gone much smoother.

Roen stared at the dwindling lights in the horizon. "Hardly smooth. We lost Stan. You know, he could have been a pro golfer, but he felt he had a higher calling. And now he's gone."

Stop.

"All this death and destruction is starting to mess with my head. With everything that's happening in the States... I can't stop thinking about Jill. Damn it, Tao, if I could get on a plane right now..."

Stop it now.

"I'm on this goddamn rusty boat in the middle of the goddamn..."

I mean it. Shut up. Listen.

"You know, all these years, she's the love of my life, and I took her for granted..."

LISTEN! That sound. Do you hear it?

Roen paused mid-rant and stayed very still. The waves were rolling all around, breaking against the hull of the ship. Below him, he could just make out the low hum and the clicking of the engine. If he listened carefully, he could just make out someone playing Filipino pop music down on the second level of the port deck. Other than that... Then he heard it. It was faint, easily missed, a soft *whup whup whup* sound. Roen closed his eyes and concentrated. It was coming from behind the ship, somewhere out in the ocean. He turned and scanned the horizon, watching for anything out of the ordinary. On his second pass through the darkness, he saw it, a large black shadow skimming just above the ocean waves, looming larger and larger.

Large. Transport size. Chinooks or Z-8s. Estimated intercept at rate of incoming is less than two minutes. Carrier capacity anywhere up to fifty. Rally the men. We are about to be boarded!

CHAPTER FORTY
DESPERATE MOVE

To this day, Sonya's fate fills me with regret. It was a needless death, caused by a series of events that were completely avoidable. I cannot simply let go for not only was she my host, she was also my daughter.

My anger is misplaced, I understand and apologize, but in this sense, I have reacted as any human. Quasing are not perfect, nor do our millions of years of existence protect us from emotions. I still blame Tao to this day, and will do so until the Eternal Sea.

Baji

The silo was a hive of activity when Jill and Marco came running in. Paula, standing on the coffee table, was directing troops and lighting fires under asses. An hour ago, the room looked like a refugee camp. Now it reminded Baji, who in turn reminded Jill, of the makeshift barricades erected by citizens in Paris during the French Revolution.

Past the barricade, the rest of the room had changed into the furniture version of trench warfare. The agents had moved every piece of furniture and turned the main room into a bizarre maze of lamps, desks, shelves, and couches that the Genjix would have to wade through. Several men pushed by Jill. She watched as they tossed anything from kettles to books to a pinball machine on top of piles comprising the maze, as if growing some monstrous Ikea barrier reef.

"Stack 'em up, boys," Paula shouted. "No more than waist level. Make them work for every inch. We need every able body. Anyone who knows how to use a gun is fighting."

"How many Genjix are out there?" someone called out.

She shrugged. "A dozen? A hundred? Does it matter?"

Two men brought out weapon crates from the ammo locker and handed out rifles. Jill took an old Kalashnikov and examined it. The thing looked older than she was.

"Stack those weapon crates when they're empty. Not so straight, idiot!" Paula hollered, jumping off the coffee table. "You want to make it easy for them? There's only one way in and out of this place, so we need to capitalize on the real estate in here."

Something about that statement didn't ring true. Then it hit her.

"Baji, there's a back door to this place!"

Be discreet. Do not cause a panic.

Jill pushed her way through the living room to the back hallway. There, in rear of the third silo, she found a rusty metal door hidden behind a shelf. Scanning the room, she saw a sad-looking ant farm. Add ant genocide to Roen's list of sins. She reminded herself to not let Cameron bring Eva back to their home if they ever reconciled. She found the key under the ant farm and tested it on the door. It clicked open.

Jill rushed back to the dining room and pulled Paula aside. "We can all sneak out the back with the Genjix being none the wiser," she told her.

Paula furrowed her eyebrows. "The enemy's at our doorstep. If we all leave at once, they'll find us and catch us out in the open. We need to engage the Genjix, lock them into the fight, and then have our people trickle out in twos and threes to avoid detection." She put a hand on Jill's shoulder. "I need to manage the fight at the front. I'll leave the evacuation to you."

"I'm sending Thompson and Wilks first," Jill said.

"Wilks isn't a host. I'd rather Quasing escape."

"They're two sitting senators!"

Paula sighed. "It doesn't matter if they're in Congress anymore. America's lost. And with her goes any hope of victory. It's over."

Paula's words stopped Jill dead in her tracks. She knew the situation was grim, and this recent attack on the capital was a serious setback, but she didn't think it was the Prophus' death knell. Only now did she realize how critical her role was in the war. Except it was too late. What minor successes she had achieved in the past few weeks were worthless. She had won the battle while the Prophus lost the war. Nothing could prevent the Genjix from assuming control of the United States government.

Suddenly, a dangerous and radical idea occurred to her. "You're still getting reports in from the outside? How? Through Roen's system?"

Paula nodded.

"Can we patch through to the Keeper?"

"I already had a call with her about reinforcements. Unfortunately, the bulk of our forces are in Tibet. The rest here are too occupied with the evacuation of the country."

"I need to speak with her. Meet me in the computer room," Jill said quickly, running out the door.

"What are you trying to do?"

"Just get me the damn Keeper now!" Jill roared. "And find Senator Thompson!" She high-stepped it to the infirmary and found Wilks lying in bed.

"Jill," he exclaimed. "What's that racket outside? You mind if I turn into a grumpy old man and tell them to shut the hell up?"

"No time, Senator. The enemy's trying to break in."

She gave him a moment to let those words sink in. He took it surprisingly well. Actually, he took it so well that it shocked her. He looked thoughtful for a second and then tried to sit up. "Well, get me a gun. A rifle, mind you. Can't hit a chicken in a hen house with a pistol."

"This isn't your fight, Senator," she said. "Listen, you need to come with me."

"You're not leaving me on the sidelines, counselor," he argued. "I've fought through more wars than you can count."

"I can count to two, James." Jill wasn't in the mood for any of this. "Come on, you need to meet someone."

She dragged him to his feet and felt a little guilty for how rough she was being when he grimaced in pain. Then she dragged him to the computer room, where Paula and Thompson were already waiting. The Keeper's face was on the large computer screen.

"What is he doing here?" the Keeper demanded.

Wilks squinted. "Meredith Frances?" he said, his surprise clear.

Paula looked at him curiously. "You two are acquainted?"

"She's one of my largest campaign contributors," he said. "Meredith, don't tell me you're involved in all this brouhaha."

"I run this brouhaha, James," the Keeper said dryly. She turned to Paula. "The National Guard has been called. The Navy is blockading Chesapeake Bay, and the Air Force is on high alert. The Genjix claim it's a terrorist attack. By morning, the entire eastern seaboard will be under martial law. The good news is the Genjix have until dawn to take your fortified position before they need to disperse. The bad news for you is you have to hold out until dawn."

"How do we retake control of the government?" Thompson asked.

The Keeper looked at Thompson with a deadpan expression. "We don't. The Americas are lost."

Thompson gasped. "If the Americas are lost and China is already gone..."

"The war is over," the Keeper said. "We cannot sustain our fight with the Genjix with the two superpowers of this planet siding against us."

Wilks held up his hand out. "Can someone explain to me how the United States is lost? We're still here, governed by the people. The President..."

"You don't understand the situation. The people you speak of haven't been in control of your government since 1850."

Wilks furrowed his brow and did a little mental president-counting in his head. "Zachary Taylor?"

"What do you think the Civil War was really about? Now please shut up."

"I always knew you were a bitch, Meredith," he shot back. "I was just nice to you because of your money. No one controls the freest country in the world!"

"You're not campaigning right now, James." The Keeper turned to Paula. "Get him out of here."

"Wait!" Jill yelled over Wilks' protests. "There's another way."

All eyes turned to her.

This is a dangerous proposition.

"Does it matter if we've lost the war anyway?"

Agreed. If that is so, might as well slash and burn our defeat.

"There's a way," Jill repeated. She looked the Keeper in the eye. "Tell the world. Tell them everything." She pointed at Wilks and Thompson. "They're senators. Give them our data. Roen has a portable Penetra scanner in his ammo locker. Have Wilks expose us."

The room became silent. Even the Keeper's famously stoic face betrayed her.

"You mean to end all Quasing," the Keeper said at last. "I will not partake in our extermination."

"Our extermination is already a forgone conclusion if the Genjix control the United States," Jill said. "At least there's a sliver of hope if the people fight back."

"This could stop the Genjix from taking the country," Paula said slowly. "Perhaps even loosen their hold on the other countries. The people won't stand for it."

"We'll be hunted," Thompson said.

"So we send the two senators with a Penetra scanner, our historical records, and let the inhabitants of this world decide," Jill said. "Let them judge us for our actions. If what we have been doing all this time is really for the good of the planet, they will come to our side."

"Or exterminate us," the Keeper added.

Jill shrugged. "We're walking dead right now anyway."

"So, Wilks and I just walk up to the Hill and lay it all out?" Thompson said.

"Not you," the Keeper said. "You're a host. You will be the first one exposed. They will arrest you immediately."

Wilks turned to Jill. "What does she mean by Thompson being a host?"

"Baji, should I tell him?"

Might as well.

Jill took a deep breath. "Senator, there've been aliens living on Earth since before humans walked the planet. They survive by living in us and have guided humanity since the dawn of time. These secret societies that I told you about, well, it's an alien civil war. And our side is losing."

Wilks' face turned sheet white. He stammered for a second, looking from face to face in the room, and then at the Keeper, who only nodded.

"Get outta here!" he said.

Thompson stepped up to the screen. "Keeper, Haewon and I insist on going. We are volunteering to be exposed. Wilks will need to prove to naysayers that he is telling the truth, and I doubt that any Genjix will volunteer to be scanned, so might as well make it one of us. I am a senior Prophus. I have the authority and knowledge to negotiate with the humans. Besides, if I volunteer to be exposed, the Prophus might garner sympathy. It might give us a chance to tell our side of the story."

"Sympathy is the last thing humanity will offer us." The Keeper had a pained look on her face. "Very well, then. It seems we have few options here. Good luck, Haewon. We have been friends since before our time on this planet. I hope to see you again in our true form or in the Eternal Sea."

"The honor has always been mine, Keeper." Thompson bowed. "But let us not kid ourselves. The only way the people will believe us, Penetra scanner or not, is if they see Haewon's true form. I am willing to make that sacrifice."

Jill had not realized that Thompson's Quasing was Haewon. If there was ever an important Quasing, she was it. And now, Haewon had just volunteered to sacrifice herself to the mercy of humanity. And Senator Thompson had just volunteered to die in order to expose them. This was madness!

One of Paula's men ran into the room. "The Genjix are moving a demolition team through the tunnel," he said.

"Get out of here!" the Keeper said. "And may you all finally rest in the Eternal Sea."

Paula sped out of the room, barking more orders. Jill typed furiously on the computer and then pulled out the hard drive. She led Thompson and Wilks to the ammo locker and pointed at the Penetra scanner.

"Take that with you," she said.

Wilks scratched his brow and looked puzzled. "I thought you said it was portable."

"That *is* a portable one," Jill replied. "Trust me, Senator, they don't come much smaller."

Thompson shook her head. "It's portable but still too big to carry around."

Wilks walked up to the scanner and picked it up. "Not too bad," he huffed. "Lighter than it looks. I can carry it a ways, I think. Worse comes to worst, we can hide it off the side of the road and pick it up later once we find a ride."

Jill nodded, stuffed a pile of documents and the hard drive into a backpack, and then led them to the hidden exit. "Guard this bag with your life. It will have everything you need to expose us."

She turned to Thompson. "If our network is still active, make sure Wilks has access to the historical database. We need irrefutable evidence."

Thompson nodded and gripped Jill's arm. "Baji..."

The sound of heavy gunfire ricocheted across the metal walls.

"Go!" Jill screamed, pushing them through the dark tunnels. She rushed to the dining room to organize the evacuation from the silo. All the able-bodied people were fighting in the living room while the injured had been moved to the infirmary. Jill began to mix the groups, sending the healthy and injured out together at ten-minute intervals so as not to attract attention. To her surprise, many refused to leave. Representative Valkner, a host who had to be pushing eighty, with rifle in hand, actually shoved her out of the way and went back to the front line.

When he was young, Valkner was a one-man sniping army. There is a rumor, mostly perpetuated by him, that he once kept an entire Vietcong division pinned down for six hours until the reinforcing army got into position.

"How did he do that?"

He said he shot anyone who got within five meters of the river they were trying to cross.

"So the river stopped them."

According to him, he did. The river just helped a little.

The sound of fighting was deafening. Gunfire, explosions, and screams filled the air. She glanced over at the barricade and saw the Prophus desperately trying to keep the Genjix from climbing over it. It was like the trench warfare of the Great War condensed into a room the size of a tennis court. The fighting ebbed and flowed and eventually bogged down into a stalemate. The Genjix were unable to utilize their superior numbers in cramped quarters, and the remaining Prophus didn't have the numbers to push the Genjix out. What was particularly eerie was the number of Quasing that suddenly appeared in the air, having been expunged from their hosts during the chaos of battle. Jill had little doubt that the majority were Prophus. Slowly, the tide moved in the Genjix's favor. The Prophus began to give way step by step as the casualties mounted.

Over the din of the chaos, someone screamed "RPG!" and then the entire room shook. There was a deafening screech and explosion as the barricade vanished. A column of pressurized fire blew Jill backward like a rag doll. She blacked out.

When she came to, the world felt strange. For one thing, everything was fuzzy, and she was having a hard time breathing. People were running and shouting, but there were no sounds. It was like watching a silent film. Now that she thought about it, she couldn't hear anything at all except for a slightly unpleasant humming near the back of her head. Suddenly, she heard a pop like a balloon bursting, and then a sound like water draining in the bathtub. Then an avalanche of sound punched her in the gut.

Strange hands dragged her to one of the back rooms. She looked up, eyes glazed, as Paula sized her up, reared her hand back, and brought it down toward her cheeks.

Jill's blocked the slap at the very last second. "That's not necessary," she shouted. "Really not necessary."

"I thought you were in battle shock," Paula yelled over the din of battle.

"I'm going through a rocket-blew-up-near-my-face shock, not battle shock," Jill screamed back.

Paula shrugged. "I did it for Roen once. I thought it was like husband, like wife." She offered her hand.

Jill took Paula's hand and stood up. "Roen froze in battle?"

"Just once when he was green," Paula said. "You're taking it much better than he did. Now, if you'll excuse me?" Paula was gone again, running toward the remnants of the barricade.

Jill got back to work as well. She sent more noncombatants out in groups of twos and threes, making sure the injured or old were accompanied by at least one able-bodied person. She knew that many of them would not make it to a Prophus evacuation site, but at least they had a chance now. The ones fighting wouldn't make it. They knew this silo was going to be their graveyard.

It is not over yet. We are still alive.

"For how long?"

You are starting to sound like your husband.

"If only I had listened to him then."

You would have probably ended up here as well.

Jill paused and considered the possibilities. "That is true. Now I'm depressed."

By 4am, Jill could barely stay on her feet. The Prophus had lost the main silo and all the rooms adjacent to it. All they had left was the last two silos on the far end. The Genjix had tried to blitzkrieg through the tunnels and had nearly succeeded in taking the ammo dump. If that had happened, the fight would have been over. Luckily, Marco had led a charge that pushed them back. The casualties were heavy on both sides.

Could they hold out? Jill's left arm was bandaged pretty tightly with a wrap of her own making, and she limped from a ricocheting bullet that had grazed her leg. Still, she was better off than most of the others. Standing next to her in the tunnel leading to the ammo locker, Marco kept watch over her. Blood dripped down the left side of his face as they continued to hold their position. If they lost access to ammunition, the fight would be over very quickly.

Paula suddenly scampered to their hiding spot. Throughout the entire night, she had somehow kept the defenders from panicking, seeming to appear everywhere at once.

When Marco had overextended his counterattack, it was Paula who had covered his retreat, most likely saving his life. When there was a lull in the fight, it was Paula who had led them into the fray. When one of her men lost his leg to a close-quarter shotgun blast, it was she who had dived into the melee and pulled him back.

If we had a few more of her fighting alongside us, the war could be a different story.

"It's too bad we're stuck with me, huh?"

I have no idea what you are talking about. The work you do is just as important. Sonya would have been proud.

"Yeah?"

Yes. I am proud of you.

"I'm sorry. What did you just say?"

Well, Sonya would have cleaned house and probably had breakfast cooked by now.

"What's our situation?" Marco said to Paula.

Paula leaned heavily against the filing cabinet they were hiding behind, a look of exhaustion briefly clouding her otherwise stoic face. "Twenty-two left, none at full fighting strength. Seventy percent of my team is dead. Six injured and still alive in silo four. Estimated enemy strength is at sixty percent with approximately a hundred casualties."

"We got thirty-three out," Jill added. "Including all the hosts except for us and Valkner. He won't leave."

"At least we bloodied their nose," Marco grumbled.

Jill did a quick calculation in her head and then checked her watch again, and then she sat there stunned, her brain telling her something she just couldn't accept. She looked up. "We're not going to be able to hold out until dawn. It's time to get the rest of our people out."

Marco had the audacity to smirk. "Jill, ever the optimist. But then I forget that this is your first time in one of these stickies."

"No, I'm serious–" she began.

He exchanged a smile with Paula who put a hand on Jill's shoulder. "Not all of us are leaving. We knew that, love, when they first breached the door. Someone has to stay and keep the dance going. The only one left to leave is you."

"You're staying?" Jill gasped. "You'll die!"

Paula shrugged in the way only a professional soldier facing death could. "We bloodied their nose. Now let's break it."

Jill, I have an idea. Ask Paula how many she needs to hold this position for fifteen minutes. I want you to take a few men through the back tunnel.

"Baji, I won't leave all these people just to save myself."

I am not asking you to.

Baji quickly told Jill the plan, and in turn she relayed the instructions to Paula. Paula ordered her two healthiest men to accompany Jill.

"You should be the one going," Jill said.

Paula shook her head. "Miss, I can barely stand. Besides, I'm the captain of this ship. I'm not abandoning her. We can hold out for twenty, maybe thirty minutes tops. If we hear your signal, we'll blow ours. Understood?"

Jill nodded.

Then Paula leaned in close. "Listen, if it looks like the plan's going to fail, your job is to run with Marco. My boys will cover your escape. Is that understood?" Jill was about to tell Paula to kiss her ass when Paula grabbed both shoulders and shook her. "That's an order. Go back to your baby, and for God's sake, make up with Roen. That daft boy loves you more than life itself."

Jill suddenly reached out and hugged Paula, squeezing her as tightly as she could. "It'll work," she whispered. "You just make sure you're on the right side."

The sound of a man screaming tore them away from their moment. Valkner's aide carried him into the back room. He had been shot in the chest, and blood was gushing out of his mouth. The aide gently laid him down and hovered over him.

"Get your arse back to the front," Paula ordered, pushing him away. She then leaned in close. "George, can you hear me? George!"

Eighty-two year-old George Valkner, representative of the great state of the Idaho Third District, decorated soldier and grandfather of seventeen, reached up and grabbed Paula's Kevlar vest. "Do it! Save Eymi," he said in a hoarse voice. "Give him a chance."

Paula nodded solemnly, gestured toward Emerson, one of the two handpicked men she had assigned to Jill, and then pulled out her pistol. Emerson knelt down next to Valkner and whispered something to his ear.

Valkner nodded and looked up at Paula. "Thank you."

"To the Eternal Sea, my friend," Paula nodded grimly, holding the barrel over Valkner's heart and pulling the trigger. There were a few moments of silence as everyone watched Eymi, glittering and beautiful, hover above Valkner's body before sinking into Emerson. While Emerson writhed on the floor, Paula left the room and came back moments later carrying a duffel bag filled with a Cold War era RPG launcher, three grenades, and Roen's smelly workout clothes. She dragged Emerson unceremoniously to his feet and handed the bag to Jill.

"Get going," she ordered. "I'll see you on the other side or in the Eternal Sea, whatever comes first."

CHAPTER FORTY-ONE
FINAL FIGHT

Now, Quasiform begins and soon, once the catalyst is deployed, Earth will begin its final cycle toward an Eternal Sea. Once the transformation to a new Quasing home world is finished, the human prophecy of their heaven on Earth will have come true.

Zoras

"Sir," Kowal, staring through a pair of binoculars, called out. "You'd better see this."

Stephen looked up from reviewing their supply lines at the makeshift command tent. He walked up to Kowal and took the binoculars. The elevated platform the Genjix had been building for the past few hours was now complete. It reminded Stephen of a medieval gallows used for hangings. The camp was a mess of activity as the Genjix soldiers moved to defensive positions. Then he saw several guards push a crowd of prisoners to the center of the camp. He recognized Stein, Bedford, Singh, Howlzer, and Fromme, among others.

"Joe is still alive?" he muttered. He thought Director Joseph Fromme of the German *Bundesnachrichtendienst* intelligence agency had died in Tunisia two years ago. During his younger days, when Stephen had been stationed in France, he and old Joe used to bike up to the Pyrenees every year to spectate the Tour De France. They had lost touch over the past fifteen years when Stephen transferred to the States and began to climb the Prophus ranks, but those were some of his fondest memories.

"What's that little psycho doing now?" Kowal asked.

Then Stephen's worst fears were realized. The Enzo boy walked in front of the group of prisoners and gestured for a prisoner to be brought to the platform. She was a communications lieutenant by the name of Ginny. Stephen had met her once or twice on the *Atlantis*. Pretty face, tiny body, and a blow horn voice that would have made Charlemagne take notice. The guards forced her to her knees in front of the boy.

"No," Stephen whispered.

In one smooth motion, Enzo pulled out his pistol and shot her in the head. As her body crumpled to the ground, her Quasing, Bizoo, rose into the air. Then another guard stepped forward and a jet of flame engulfed Bizoo.

"Damn him!" Stephen swore.

Enzo motioned for another prisoner to be brought forward. The horror show repeated itself. They were executing all the prisoners one by one. There could only mean one thing. The prisoners were no longer needed, which meant ProGenesis had succeeded. The Prophus had run out of time.

Stephen scanned the guards around the perimeter, goading him to attack. There was another loud bang of a pistol followed by the whooshing sound of the flamethrower and another Prophus died. Stephen handed the binoculars back to Kowal, his mind racing for a solution. Sending his people through no-man's-land toward the teeth of their defense during the daytime would be suicide, but he had to do something.

"Form up. All sides!" he instructed. The command post came to life as his lieutenants coordinated all their forces. The sound of the pistol and flamethrower continued. Five deaths already, but how many more if he sent them in? It would be a massacre. Still, this horrifying transgression couldn't be overlooked. A few minutes later, Kowal signaled that all units were a go. Another bang and whoosh punctured the air.

Then, suddenly, incredible courage saved Stephen from deploying his men into a suicide mission. The prisoners, knowing their fate, turned on the guards. With nothing more than their bare hands, they chose to die fighting than be slaughtered one by one. The camp fell into chaos as the guards surrounding the prisoners were taken by surprise and temporarily overwhelmed.

Stephen saw a surge of them attack Enzo, forcing his bodyguards to pull him back. The soldiers at the camp perimeter had to turn their attention inward. There was the sound of automatic fire and the sparking lights of Quasing leaving their hosts' bodies. Then Stephen saw Joe, as if clairvoyant, jump on top of a bunker and looked straight at him, waving both hands desperately. There was another loud crack in the air and then Stephen saw his old friend's body go limp and fall forward. Meina rose from Fromme's body into the air and flitted toward the forest. Stephen hoped Meina could reach one of the friendlies in time. It was now or never!

"Artillery on the perimeter!" he yelled. "This is the day, men! We win this, get our boys out, and we go home. All units, charge!"

The entire Prophus force, one thousand five hundred soldiers plus the six hundred freed prisoners, charged in unison. The last day of their battle in Tibet had begun. Normally, Stephen ridiculed Starfleet's landing party command structure with the captain going on every off-ship mission. Out of all the fantastic suspension of realities he had had to endure with that show, that one was the worst. Sending the senior staff to the front line was the equivalent of Roosevelt and Churchill parachuting with the 101st Airborne during Normandy. It was completely asinine.

Now he took it all back. Normally, he stayed well behind friendly lines and planned his tactics in a safe zone. Not this time. The only tactic now was a full-on charge, and Stephen intended to be right there at the front. He owed it to old Joe Fromme.

To their credit, Stephen's surprised staff was alongside him without hesitation. McDaniels, his quartermaster, hadn't seen live combat in two decades. Yet, the sixty-five year old was keeping pace, wielding a pistol that probably hadn't been fired since Reagan was in office. Stephen couldn't be more proud of his people than he was right then as they rushed across no-man's-land. The carefully placed artillery he had ordered began to fire down the perimeter, blowing apart the makeshift fences. It also provided a little cover as the defending forces covered up.

By now, the riot inside the camp had spread. Only a few of the machine guns were spitting out death to Stephen's men. Most of the guards were locked in close combat with the prisoners. The prisoners wouldn't last much longer without backup, though. Already, Stephen counted at least ten Quasing floating in the air.

To his left, Smitty, his second division commander, fell to a spray of bullets. Stephen veered to the right as a stream of small eruptions on the ground zinged at him. He dove to the side and huddled behind an upturned patch of earth. He peered over the top, shot two Genjix, and continued on. Before he knew it, he had reached the splintered fence and was climbing over the mound into the camp.

Stephen was nearly impaled by a destroyed section of fencing as he jumped down into the makeshift trench and killed an enemy with a point-blank shot to the face. Then he dove to the side as a line of bullets sprayed just over his head. He pressed on, the image of Fromme's face etched into his head. He was going to save all his people today or die trying. The melee continued as small groups of Prophus and Genjix collided.

Stephen and his staff took on a larger group of Genjix from behind, eliminating half of them in their initial charge. He took out a Genjix's kneecap and finished him with a crushing blow to the face. He grappled a guard from behind and snapped his neck as the guard beat on one of the prisoners. And then the prisoners joined his gang, swelling their numbers.

The fighting raged on, with the Prophus slowly pushing the Genjix toward the center complex. Enemy snipers from the upper windows in the building became an issue, and the offensive stalled. As long as his men were outside, they were sitting ducks. The enemy had fortified themselves inside. They had to press on. Stephen roared and led the charge, knowing his men and women would follow. And they did.

The battle intensified as the fighting became concentrated at the three narrow entrances of the building. Leading the charge on the northern entrance, Stephen saw the young psychopath in the thick of the melee. Enzo, wielding a machine gun and a machete, was a whirlwind of death, taking out anyone who got within reach. In a span of five seconds, he took out six Prophus soldiers, including one host. Even more impressive was that Enzo was speaking through a mic, giving orders without missing a beat. Somehow, the boy was effectively managing the battle while wading through the thick of it. Stephen had to admit he was breathtaking.

Stephen, withdraw. You have control of the exits and the majority of the prisoners. You cannot match an Adonis Vessel.

"I'm not that old yet, Camr."

The boy is not worth it.

He saw Fromme's face again, and Ginny's, and his friends who had died in the laboratories. That boy needed to be put down. If this boy wasn't worth it, he didn't know what was. Zoras being on the Council was just a bonus.

Stephen charged straight in.

Enzo was having the time of his life. This was the glory he'd always envisioned. No more hiding behind fences or plowing through thick forests into ambushes. He reveled in the honest combat where two sides locked themselves together until one fell, where a warrior could see the will drain out of his beaten foe's eyes. Guns and technology had made boys out of men. Now, in this chaos, the fight reverted back to how man was meant to kill: with his bare hands. Still, even though Enzo reveled in this melee, he was not an unthinking beast. There was a plan in this defense, and it was working to perfection.

Do not push out, but do not retreat too quickly. Draw them in. Give them a reason to press on.

Their tactic was working and would prove to be the linchpin to winning the day. Enzo admitted that while he thought he was versed in matters of war, he was like a babe next to Zoras. He may have been knowledgeable in strategy and command and was quick to identify and forecast tactics, but Zoras really understood the timing and flow of a battle. That came from the experience of centuries of warfare. Enzo would be wise to learn.

Meyers is reporting that they've broken through the Prophus line. Order him back.

The frenzied battle had raged for thirty minutes, and the initial disruption caused by the prisoners had proved costly for the Genjix. They had lost the advantage of being a defending force. Whatever sport claimed the best offense was a great defense, it was doubly so for war. The mark of a great general was the control he had over his troops amidst the chaotic battle. By fighting in the interior and keeping the Prophus in a holding pattern, the Genjix could inflict heavy casualties while replenishing some of their tired and injured ranks. It also left the Prophus wildly exposed. All it required was Enzo's exacting control over his men. His lips curled into a sneer as his men baited and repelled the Prophus at the steps leading up to the doorway. Meanwhile, snipers on the upper level decimated Prophus ranks.

Suddenly, a body charged forward and slammed into him, pushing him into his men. The Prophus surged at just the right time, and the northern exit point crumbled. Enzo twisted around and grappled with his assailant.

It is Camr!

When he realized it was Stephen, he smirked. Things had just gone from good to better. Still being pushed back by Stephen's momentum, Enzo locked onto the other man's arm and twisted, throwing him through a window, shattering the glass, into the corner room.

Stephen's specialty is Aikido and boxing. Utilizes little footwork but has power in both hands. Do not count on him to tire.

He put his hand on the nearest officer. "Maintain choke points. Under no circumstances do you push forward. And make sure I am not disturbed."

He turned back to climb over the window only to take a punch to the jaw that snapped his head back. Now, a lot can be learned about a person by how they react to being sucker punched. It's one thing when a person knows a punch is coming. It's another when his mind isn't prepared to get the brain rattled. Well-trained fighters instinctively cover up and protect their heads. Almost all take a step back to try to access the situation. The unlucky ones freeze like deer watching the headlights of a fast approaching semi-truck.

Enzo was none of these. He was an apex predator, and when an apex predator is attacked, he attacks back. Even as the bone of Stephen's knuckle cracked against his chin, momentarily causing his vision to blur, his hands reacted the only way they knew how. Three quick blind jabs, two of them connecting with Stephen's face, were his body's response. Both men fell backward, but it was Enzo who recovered first and leapt through the window into the room.

"You and I are about to have a long, painful talk, old man," Enzo said.

Stephen, who was still picking himself off the floor, had the audacity to grin. "So you're that smart ass chosen one who's pissed everyone off." He made a face. "Thought you'd be taller."

Enzo launched a vicious attack, swinging a nine-strike combination with his legs, fists, and elbows, tossing in a head butt for good measure. He thought the best the old man could do was duck the first few hits before the withering barrage overwhelmed him. Instead, Stephen took the first punch, sidestepped, and using Enzo's forward momentum, shoved and tripped him from the side. Enzo crashed into the wooden door and knocked it off its hinges. He found himself back in the crowded hallway.

You are taking him too lightly. He is a master of counterattacks. Watch his left hand.

Enzo's earpiece crackled. "Father, we have a situation on the eastern flank. Requesting reinforcements."

"Not now!" Enzo snapped. He grabbed the two men who positioned themselves between him and Stephen. "This one is mine. I do not wish to be disturbed. Keep the rabble out."

Then a brazen Prophus fool tried to charge past the line to reach Stephen. He pushed past the initial Genjix line and almost made it into the room. Enzo caught him by the neck, threw him down on the ground, and killed him with a punch to his throat. He looked up at the nearest officer. "I said, keep the line intact! Do not disturb me!"

He stepped back into the room and paid Stephen a bit more respect as they sized each other up. Stephen stayed just out of range of the taller man's reach and seemed in no particular hurry to engage.

After nearly a minute of the two just circling each other, Stephen spoke. "Well, this is fun."

"Come at me, old man," Enzo sneered.

"You know, I'm only in my fifties. Early fifties that is. I consider myself middle-aged, thank you."

"The body is the first..." Enzo stopped as a loud yell from his comm popped into his ear.

"Enemy occupying southeastern corner room. They're coming in through the windows!"

You need to finish this quickly. Your forces have no leader.

"Send the auxiliary–" Those were the only words Enzo got out before Stephen charged.

The old man's first step was quicker than Enzo realized. He parried the initial strike, but fell victim to an arm lock as Stephen cranked his elbow, nearly dislocating it. He gritted his teeth and pushed back. On a lesser man, Stephen's move would have snapped the limb, but Enzo was the product of the Hatchery. He tightened his arm and muscled his way out of danger. He followed with an uppercut cross combination that Stephen just barely ducked.

He clicked on his earpiece. "Auxiliary on eastern stairwell, relocate to the southern–"

Again, Stephen attacked before he could finish his sentence. This time, there was a hint of desperation and wildness to his charge. Enzo easily countered it, picked him up, and slammed him against the wall. Stephen bounced off with a thump, but was on his feet once more, though a bit unsteady.

"Already weakening," Enzo smiled. "I haven't even broken a sweat yet."

Stephen pressed the attack, this time a lengthy exchange that felt half-hearted. Enzo fought him off easily, wondering what this tactic would buy the old man. Surely he must know that he would tire before Enzo. He was just wasting his time and energy. Then he noticed the band around Stephen's throat, and for the first time, realized that he was using a throat mic. The man had been giving orders the entire time, and Enzo had been oblivious to what was going on.

"It's not going to be that easy, old man!" he yelled, launching a vicious attack.

"It already has been," Stephen smirked.

Enzo's fury was too much for Stephen to handle. Gradually, the superior strength and speed of the Adonis Vessel began to overwhelm the tiring older man. Enzo knocked him down and pounced. He began to rain blows down on Stephen. Whenever Stephen tried to cover up, Enzo knocked his arms aside and continued to pummel him until his fists were red with blood. He took immense satisfaction in each blow, bringing his fists down harder and harder. Eventually, he did tire, but by that time, Stephen's face was unrecognizable.

Sucking in large gulps of air, Enzo stood up and spit on Stephen's face. "My will. My strength. Know your betters, betrayer."

To his surprise, Stephen summoned the last of his energy to pull himself into a sitting position and chuckled. Enzo watched in perplexed amazement as the broken body of his opponent struggled to stand. It was almost comical. Finally, Stephen got on his feet and leaned against the wall for support. His bloody hands palmed the window, leaving a red handprint on the glass.

"Win the fight, lose the battle," Stephen coughed, blood dripping down the corner of his mouth. "My teams have broken into your central holding room and have freed all the prisoners. The rest of your men are pigeonholed in this wing making sure your fun is undisturbed. It's all just about over. You lost!"

Enzo suddenly realized he had no idea what was going on with the battle. He had lost his earpiece beating Stephen. He picked it up off the ground and put it back on. "Report!" he screamed.

The news was just as Stephen had predicted. The chain of command had broken and his men were paralyzed without his leadership. Once the Prophus took the entrances and pushed Enzo's forces to one half of the building, they were able to lay suppression fire on the windows long enough to release all the prisoners. Now, they were fleeing into the forest. They had all escaped. Every single one.

"I still have you, old man," he snarled, tossing the earpiece onto the floor. "You and your betrayer!"

"You got me, alright," Stephen grinned, showing bloodstained teeth, "but I'll be damned if I let a two-bit punk like you get a hold of Camr. Always a step ahead of you." Stephen swung his hand into the window, shattering the glass. He grabbed one of the shards and jammed it into his neck. Blood gurgled out of his mouth as he slid down to the ground in a heap.

"Goodbye, Camr," he whispered. Then he looked up at Enzo and stuck out his middle finger as his body went limp. Enzo could only watch in dismay as Camr rose from Stephen's body, circled over it as if paying final respects, and then flitted out of the window into the Tibetan sky.

CHAPTER FORTY-TWO
COMING OF AGE

I do not blame you, Jill. I hope you understand that. I tell you this because you are my host and because you are my daughter as well. You have come far, and will go much further. The future is uncertain, and the road ahead will be dangerous. Know that I will be with you every step of the way, for the end times of this war are near.

With the recent revelations you and I have caused, we will either save all of humanity, or cause the destruction of the Quasing, or both. I fear that for the first time, I might have earned the title of Prophus, of betrayer, for I might be the first to doom my kind.

Baji

Jill, Marco, Emerson with newly acquired Eymi, and a spry dark-skinned agent named Felipe, left through the hidden tunnel and made their way toward the light on the far end. The tunnel was built similarly to the entrance at the first silo, except it had collapsed long ago. Now, there was barely enough room to squeeze single-file through the fifty-meter passage. It had taken Jill longer than she would have liked to get through to the open air. Every minute counted, and she exhaled in relief when she felt the cool breeze entering her lungs. It wasn't dawn yet, but she could just make out the faint amber of sun in the distance.

That took five minutes. You do not have much time.

They were on the other side of the hill in one of the tertiary ravines connecting the paths cut from the dry riverbed. They could hear the faint patter of gunfire echoing in the distance. Marco got his bearings and immediately took off running. The rest followed him around the bend and down to the side path. It was another five-minute sprint over rough terrain before they reached the entrance. The sky was getting lighter by the second. If they did not hurry, they would soon lose the cover of darkness.

The group stopped short of the entrance and took cover behind a row of thick bushes. There were two dozen cars and vans parked in the ravine and roughly fifteen people milling around the outside gate. Five of them hovered over the hood of a Range Rover that was being used as a makeshift command table. Jill recognized Simon among the group. Her eyes narrowed.

Put him out of your mind. You have lives to save. Killing him is a bonus, but we have other priorities.

Marco gathered them around as he doodled in the dirt. He and Jill would draw the Genjix away. Emerson would carry the launcher while Felipe brought the RPGs. Hopefully, these old relics still worked. Once the heat was on them – mostly Marco; she was supposed to hide and snipe – it was their job to cave the entrance.

"Should someone else be carrying these?" She tried to hand the grenades off. "They make me nervous."

Marco shook his head in resignation and chuckled. Jill wanted to smack him right there. He turned to Emerson

and Felipe. "You've got one chance. See you chaps in five."
And then the two men were gone.

*A grenade is not like a DVR. You just pull the pin and throw it.
There are no other buttons to press.*

"I'm not comfortable handling them. Besides, I suck at
softball."

You throw knives just fine.

"It's different. Knives don't explode."

Emerson and Felipe disappeared behind the fleet of cars
and made their way from directly opposite the entrance
while Marco and Jill went in from the side. They crept
closer, hiding between cars until they were within a stone's
throw of the Genjix agents.

Marco pointed to her and then to his left. Then he lobbed
a grenade toward the group of Genjix and ducked back
behind the car. Jill heard the bonk of the grenade bouncing
off the hood of the car and the cries of alarm from the Genjix
diving to the ground. The explosion never came.

"Oh bloody hell," Marco growled. "Toss yours. I'll lead
them away." He stood up and opened fired, running away
from her location.

With badly shaking hands, Jill pulled the pin of her
grenade and then nearly dropped it.

Steady. Just throw it!

An image of the Genjix around the Range Rover flashed
in her head. She noted the three cars in between their
positions. Hefting the weighty explosive in her hand,
she stood up and lobbed it as far as she could toward the
makeshift table. Unfortunately, throwing the damn thing
felt like tossing a shot put. The grenade fell ten meters short
of the target. Fortunately, there was a reason for the saying
about horseshoes and hand grenades. The grenade bounced

off the hood of one of the Range Rovers and rolled forward directly into the path of half a dozen Genjix agents were rushing after Marco. The resulting explosion knocked her off her feet. She saw at least two bodies fly through the air, slamming into car windows and landing on hoods. Jill picked herself up and ran in the opposite direction to Marco.

Remember your training. Roll to your left now!

By instinct, she followed Baji's every command. Weeks of constant training kicked in and her body moved reflexively. She saw a quick mental image of a Genjix agent kneeling against the side of a car. She dove left just as he opened fire.

Over and on the hood. Shoot at your one.

She rolled out of the somersault gracefully and jumped on top of the car hood. Mid-jump, she turned toward the Genjix, flattened her body, and fell on her side. She aimed at her one o'clock, took a split second to adjust her shot, and fired. It took three shots to find her mark, but the Genjix fell, clutching his leg.

One from your two and three at your ten converging on Felipe and Emerson. Distract them.

Jill rolled off the hood and landed flat on her stomach. Peering under the car through the weeds and rocks, she saw a pair of boots sprinting toward her. She unloaded her clip and heard a satisfying cry of pain as whomever the boots were attached to fell. Then she began to trail the three engaging Felipe and Emerson. The two Prophus agents were pinned down by those three and another two near the door. Time was running out. In a few seconds, someone from the inside would notice the fight outside and then their opportunity would be lost. Then, she saw Felipe fall from a bullet to the chest.

Get them off Emerson

"Where's Marco?"

Busy with six Genjix.

Jill ducked back behind the car and moved to a better vantage point. A pattering of bullets striking metal sparked all around her. Sensing a figure out of the corner of her eye, she spun to the side, changed levels, and fired twice. She was rewarded with a high-pitched cry of pain. Jill rolled to her feet and looked at her would-be killer. It was Simon.

Jill approached him cautiously. He was writhing on the ground in pain, having taken two shots to the abdomen. His pistol was several meters off to the side. He pushed himself into a sitting position as he stared at her warily. Then he smirked. "Hello, counselor."

"Simon," she replied, approaching with pistol held up.

Finish him quickly.

"I guess it's your move," he said with labored breath. "What are you going to do?"

"I'm going to kill you, Simon," she said, voice deadpan.

"I don't blame you," he spit out blood. "It doesn't matter to me. Biall will still live. And as long as my Holy One does, I will live forever."

"You care a little."

"Go to hell, bitch," he spat. "Get it over with. Shoot me!"

We need to get back to the others.

"I'm not going to shoot you, Simon," Jill said, holstering her gun. She took out the last grenade, pulled the pin, and dropped it a few feet away from Simon. "I don't think Biall is going to get very far either." Then she sprinted for cover.

"Noooooo..." was all she heard before the explosion sent her tumbling to the ground.

Well done. Biall will not survive that.

Jill moved back toward Emerson's last known location. Moving around the back of a gray Range Rover, she caught sight of the two Genjix near the door. Two targets at thirty meters behind cover. Jill wasn't confident about the shot.

Relax. Clear your mind. Exhale and make the shot.

Instead of clearing her mind, an image of her friends popped into her head. Paula, battered but still fighting, giving away ground in that silo inch by inch, buying time with their blood. Valkner, older than her parents, fighting with his last breath. Even dying, his last concern was for the safety of Eymi. Wilks, a man who yesterday wasn't even involved, now trying to pull the Prophus away from total defeat. Then she thought back again to an injured Paula, waiting for that explosion so she could pull her people out. There was no way in hell Jill was going to let them down after all that they had sacrificed. She bit her lip, went down to a kneeling position, moved her sights back and forth between the two targets, and then took them both out with two shots.

Great shots.

"Time for pats on the back later."

She made her way toward the last Genjix and found him lying face down on the ground with Emerson kneeling over him. He was still carrying the launcher on his back, but looked like he was about to fall over. His chest and shoulder was crimson red all the way down to his arms. "What happened to you?"

Emerson looked at the torn flesh exposed just below his collarbone and then shrugged with his good shoulder. "I got nicked by a bullet or three." He grimaced as he tried to unstrap the launcher. "I don't think I'm going to be able to shoot this puppy. You're going to have to."

Jill blanched. Shooting a RPG was not part of her training.

It is easy. Point and pull the trigger, like operating a vacuum cleaner.

"I don't know what sorts of house cleaning you're used to, but the ones I have–"

We do not have time. Just do it.

Jill stared at the dull long metal tube for a second, and then knelt down and propped it on her right shoulder. It was heavier than she thought.

"I'll help steady it," Emerson said, "but you're going to have to aim. Go for the top of the entrance."

Move a bit closer but no more than thirty meters. At this distance, expect heavy blow back. I would rather you hit the target though.

They knelt down next to the Range Rover in front of the entrance. Jill saw a dozen or so Genjix in the tunnel. They noticed her just as Emerson rapped the launcher with his fist and told her he was ready. Two of them tried to charge out of the tunnel as she squeezed the trigger. The resulting explosion knocked her onto her butt. She didn't see the trajectory of the RPG but the shock wave was so massive she momentarily blacked out. When she came to, Emerson was dragging her away from the wreckage with his good arm.

"Did we hit it?" she gasped.

He smiled and helped her to her feet. "You were about half a meter off the mark, but let's face it, precision work wasn't necessary here. You did it. We blocked the passage. Let's hook up with Marco and get back to the tunnel."

Marco! Jill hoped he was alright. He had dealt with the most of the Genjix. They backtracked the way they came and found him leaning against a boulder having a cigarette. There were six dead Genjix lying about.

He saw them coming and waved. "I would have gone to check up on you, but I seem to have walked into a shotgun blast, and now this bloody leg is being a bad dog."

Jill ran up to him. "Oh my God, you took a full shotgun to the hip?"

"Well, it was a bird shot," he inhaled and puffed out a cloud of smoke. "So I'm sure it's probably in parts of my chest and arms as well."

As she got close, she noticed that he was bleeding all over and gasped at the amount of blood pouring out of his body. How he was still conscious was beyond her. Suddenly, there was another explosion and the mountainside shook. The three of them looked up as debris came tumbling down the sides.

"That must be Paula. You two stay here," she ordered. "I'm going to go check up on her. And then we'll get you to a doctor."

Marco waved her away. "No rush, take your time." He turned to Emerson and offered him a cigarette. "By your accent, dear fellow, Northern Ireland? First time in the States?"

Emerson accepted it and sat down next to him. "Aye, came across the pond with Paula. Much chillier here than I thought it'd be."

Jill shook her head and left the two boys to their own devices. She still had to round up all the survivors and move them to the evacuation site. Then they could lick their wounds and plan the next step. She walked around the ravine back to the hidden entrance. It was exhaling a small cloud of dust that reminded her of puffs of a cigar. Rather than waiting outside, Jill went in to help the survivors. Twenty meters into the tunnel, she found the cave in. She stopped and looked frantically for another way through.

Oh no! Paula must have had to cause the cave in before they could escape. They are all trapped with the Genjix.

Jill collapsed to the ground and stared at tons of earth and rock for God knows how long until Marco and Emerson eventually found her. Refusing to give up, she picked up a rock and banged on the rubble, making loud tapping noises that echoed through the tunnel, hoping for a sign of life from inside, but none ever came.

CHAPTER FORTY-THREE
SHIP FIGHTING

The rest of the story you know. My triumph and fall with Temujin, my time with Zhu as emperor, and everything else since is an old shared story between us. So why did I start at the beginning? Because you, Roen, needed to know. Now we are whole, you and I. I am laid bare before you as all Quasing are before humanity.

The rules have changed. Humans can now throw off the yokes of our influence. I am not absolved of the Quasing's crimes. I admit to my role in humanity's enslavement. I am as guilty as most. My only solace is that I, along with the rest of the Prophus, saw the error in our ways and tried our best to atone for our crimes.

Tao

We cannot hold this line. Sound the retreat!

"Already? That didn't last long."

Roen ducked behind a shipping container and yelled as loud as he could. "Everyone get the fuck out of here! Pull back!"

You could have said it in a less panicked way.

Truthfully though, the fight was going exactly as Roen had sounded. He abandoned his position and scurried toward the tower, occasionally diving behind cover and taking a few pot shots at the Genjix troops overwhelming their position. Everywhere he looked, the defenders of *Imelda's Song* fell back with as much dignity as anyone who just had their asses handed to them could. In other words, it was an all-out rout three minutes into the fighting.

Roen's team and the crew had never stood a chance. Though the crew was determined to defend the ship, no amount of untrained men armed with spear guns, pistols, and enthusiasm could overcome twenty heavily-armed shock troops. He gave the crew credit for standing their ground even that long.

"Get below deck. Regroup at the mess hall," he yelled over the sounds of automatic gunfire.

Duck!

Roen dove to the side just as a hail of bullets plastered the wall where he was just standing moments earlier. He rolled onto his knees and opened fire, felling one of the Genjix. Then he realized he had just put himself badly out of position and was now exposed.

Genjix top left and ground level right. Two more approaching.

An image of four Genjix flashed into his mind: one standing on top of a container, one trying to flank him from the side of the ship, and two charging forward from the far back.

Roen looked for cover, already knowing that he wasn't going to make it unless these Genjix were really bad shots. He tried to scramble for cover, but bullets kicked up dust around him, and he flattened against the floor. Just then, Hutch appeared next to him and began to empty clip after clip.

"Get on your feet, sir," he growled. "Let's go!"

Together, they retreated, still shooting as they fled toward the stairs leading down to the lower levels on the starboard side of the ship. They were almost to safety when Hutch gasped and fell. Roen grabbed him by the collar and dragged him to the stairs and down a few steps.

"Argh, can't feel my legs," Hutch growled. "Leave me."

"Save your breath," Roen said, wrapping his arms around his waist. Hutch pushed him away and waved him off.

"I got you covered, sir," he said. "They won't take these stairs without paying for it."

He is right. Get going.

"God damn it!" Roen slammed his fist on the steps. "I'm not leaving–"

"Shut the hell up, Roen," Hutch spat out blood. "You're a good guy but you talk too much. I'm done for. Now get out of here before it's too late!"

Roen hesitated, and then ran down the stairs. Behind him, Hutch roared and rained wrath down on whichever Genjix was unfortunate enough to try to approach those stairs. He made it down two more levels and halfway to the mess hall when Hutch's yelling died. Roen stopped for a beat and paid homage to Hutch's courage. There was going to be hell to pay for this. When he got to the mess hall, Dylan and half a dozen of the crew were waiting for him.

"Is this it?" Roen asked, looking around. If this was everyone who had made it, they were in really bad shape.

Dylan shook his head. "This is everyone from the tower. Manny should be along shortly. He and two of the guys stayed at the bridge to disable the engine. I was able to get a distress call out to Prophus sub-channels, then we rounded up everyone we could find and brought them down here."

A minute later, Faust and Jim appeared with another five of the crew in tow. Then Grant and two more joined in after them.

"Where are Jim and Ray?" Roen asked, already fearing the worst.

"Jim covered the port flank while everyone ran," Grant said. "A grenade blew him out to sea. I haven't seen Ray." He looked around the room. "Hutch?"

Roen gritted his teeth and shook his head.

"How many confirmed kills do we have?" Dylan asked.

A couple of guys raised their hands. Even more said they'd struck one but doubted it was a killing shot. These Genjix shock troops were pretty heavily armored after all. He estimated their remaining strength to be at approximately twelve. Eight Genjix killed compared to over twenty team and crew.

"We need to get deeper in," Faust said. "Fight a guerrilla war. The crew knows the lay of the land. We can hide in the ship for days and hit them when they're not expecting it."

Dylan disagreed. "They'll have control of the bridge by now. If they take over the entire ship, they'll steer it toward China. Then we're as good as dead anyway."

That much was true. Next to North Korea, China was the worst place in the world for a Prophus. The last Prophus agent in North Korea disappeared in 1948, shortly after Kim Il Sung, host of a Quasing, coincidently named Sung, assumed control of the country. Since then, it had been a black hole, and the Prophus, like the rest of the world, avoided it at all costs. It was rumored that Sung was a family heirloom handed down from father to son as a symbol of their power.

The sounds of men yelling "clear" could suddenly be made out in the distance. Roen put his finger to his mouth and pointed at the door. Everyone in the room got up and followed Dylan toward the front of the ship. Along the way, they ran into Pedro, Manny's first mate.

THE DEATHS OF TAO

"We busted the engine controls," Pedro said, "but then one of those gringos came to the bridge. The captain gutted him with a machete." He was in tears. "I told the captain we have to go, but he didn't want to leave the bridge."

"It's alright," Roen said, patting Pedro on the shoulder. "You did what you could. Let's go."

Together, the ragtag group moved across the entire length of the ship and down several floors, finally coming to a stop in one of the shipping containers holding pallets of bananas and oranges alongside several crates of opium and cocaine.

"Get some rest," Faust said. "This place is as good as any."

Roen looked around. The team looked no worse for wear but the crew looked like they'd been dragged through the ringer. Getting some rest here was as good as anywhere else. There were enough nooks and crannies on this ship that it would take a stroke of luck for the Genjix to find them. He closed his eyes, and just as he was about to doze off, the PA system squealed and emitted static.

A grainy but familiar voice began to speak over it. "To whoever is still alive, we have control of the ship and captured several of your people. We do not care about the crew, just the passengers on board. Hand them over and the rest of you go free. Else, once we reach a Chinese military port, all your lives are forfeit. The choice is yours."

It is Jacob.

Roen swore under his breath. That damn punk kid. "I should have killed him when I had the chance."

Really. When was that?

"Good luck getting anywhere with the engines disabled, asshole," Dylan chuckled.

Suddenly, the unmistakable sound of the engine sputtered and began to rumble.

"Aww, crap," he added.

"And as a bonus," Jacob continued. "Until you comply, we will interview your friends over the PA system, starting with this Prophus agent. What's your name?" Then they all heard the sickening smack of a fist to flesh and the grunt of someone trying desperately to not cry out.

"Ray..." Faust whispered. The beating continued for several more seconds in an almost rhythmic pattern.

Jacob continued. "We'll be at the tower chatting with your man here. He'll be beaten until he dies. And then we'll move on to the next prisoner until you give yourselves up. If you like, you can listen in."

Over the next few minutes, Ray's groans echoed across the entire ship. The weary people in the container exchanged glances. Roen was pretty sure he knew what everyone was thinking. The team probably worried about their captured friend while the crew probably considered turning them in. Yet no one moved a muscle as they sat in silence, trying to push out the sounds of torture playing in the background.

Do not do it, Roen. He is as good as dead. Do not throw your life away.

The guilt ate at him. He saw Hutch's face, then Wuehler's, and then Sonya's. And then he thought back to his friends who had died fighting the Genjix while he had stood on the sidelines chasing conspiracy theories. It didn't pain him any less that those theories had turned out to be true. He still wasn't there when they needed him. And now, he was hiding in a container while that punk Jacob beat his friend to death.

"I can't just sit here." He stood up and headed out the door.

"Where are you going, Roen?" Dylan asked.

Roen turned to him slowly. "I'm going to check up on Ray and see what I can do."

"I'll come with you." Dylan replied, picking himself off the ground and joining him.

A few minutes later, Roen watched horrified through a pair of binoculars at the scene on the outside deck of the bridge on the fourth floor of the tower. Two Genjix held Ray up while a third beat him. He was such a bloody mess that Roen couldn't even recognize him. There were five more crew lying face down on the deck with their hands behind their heads.

Next to them, that little psychopath Jacob lounged in a chair drinking a jug of the crew's lambanog. It seemed all four of them were taking turns using Ray as a punching bag. Roen wasn't sure how long Ray was going to last but it couldn't be that much longer.

"I'm going to get him out."

That is suicide.

"We're basically dead anyway. Might as well die trying to rescue my friend."

Roen, I count nine on the bridge and outer deck. You would not get within... Wait.

"What, Tao?"

There are nine Genjix on the top of the tower. If they are all there...

"Then there is barely anyone guarding the engine room," Roen murmured aloud.

"What did you say?" Dylan asked.

Roen pointed to the tower. "There's nine Genjix up in the tower. That means there's less than five Genjix in the rest of the ship."

"We should hit the engine room," Dylan mused. "Blow it up to smithereens."

You should be able to blow the engine and disappear back into the hull if you strike fast enough.

"And while you're hitting the engine room, I'll rescue Ray and the rest of the crew. Once the Genjix find out the engine room is being attacked, they'll send most of their men down. It'll give me the chance to sneak up and get Ray out."

No!

"That's a dangerous and kind of stupid," Dylan said.

Roen shrugged.

"What the hell." Dylan shrugged as well. "Let's do it. I'll go get the guys. You hang tight. When you start hearing fireworks and the Genjix clear out, you make your grab."

Roen nodded, extending a hand. "This might be it. I'll see you, one way or another. What do you say? Grab a drink later, either on the deck or up at the Elysium Fields?"

"Hey, son," Dylan said, clasping his forearm. "Just wanted you to know I appreciated you coming for me in Taiwan, even if you did do too good a job. I know it must have taken a lot to bring you back into the fold after what happened with Command."

"What are brothers for?" Roen said as they clasped hands.

"I want you to do something for me." Dylan's usually jolly expression turned solemn. "If there is an instance where you can live to see your family, do it. I'm an old man with no one waiting for me back at home. Hell, I don't even have a home. This place is as good as any. Go see your wife and kid, got it?"

"Bite me," Roen held back the tears. Dylan would never let him live it down if he cried. "We're not dead yet."

"Hoorah," Dylan nodded, and left to rouse the others.

Roen crept closer to a container near the base of the tower and waited, slowly counting the seconds and carefully listening for sounds of battle. His stomach growled. He hadn't eaten since before they infiltrated the port and it was now reminding him of the neglect. He patted his pockets for a snack and found none.

"Tao, we're screwed, aren't we?"

We will get out of this. We have survived worse.

"Can't think of a worse time, sorry. I'm so hungry I could eat someone, but I won't because I'm a gentleman after all."

A gentleman is something I will never mistake you for. But I agree. Cannibalism is never the solution.

"At least when I die and go to hell, I can tell the devil that I've done a lot of bad things, but at least I was a decent enough fellow to never eat another human being. This could be the last time you get to bestow your Tao wisdom on me. Any last words? Maybe tell me one last story. A happy one, please."

Did I ever tell you about the time around 6,000BC... I do not know the exact date. We did not keep accurate numbers back then due to Christ not being born yet. My host had fallen off his fishing boat and was eaten alive by a shark.

"That's the happy tale? Your host must have been a dick if that's the good part."

No. I joined with the shark. Then for a hundred years, I survived in the Persian Gulf, moving from one shark to another, until I was in a whale that got beached. I admit it was not a bad life.

Roen looked perplexed. "I don't get it. What's the point of this story?"

I am trying to tell you, that if all else fails, jump into the ocean. I should be able to survive. Now, do you feel better?

Roen stifled a laugh.

"You know, Tao, it does make me feel better. You're the only thing I ever did right in this world."

What about Jill?

"Nah, she deserves better than me. That's the only thing you ever steered me wrong on."

Getting her to marry you?

"No, that was a good thing. You steered me wrong in convincing me to leave her and Cameron. I should never have done that."

There was a pause.

You should not have. I was wrong. I forgot the words that Kathy had told you. I did a disservice to Edward in leading you away from your family. I am sorry, my friend.

"Meh, it is what it is. I bet if we never met, I'd still be that fat miserable fuck eating pizza every day. Would probably outlive me where I am now though."

I doubt it. I know you well enough to know you would have come to somehow. I just prodded you along. Besides...

In the distance, the now familiar sounds of gunfire broke the night's silence like popcorn in a kettle. Roen watched the top of the tower as several shadows merged into one blob and then broke off and disappear from view. He counted only three remaining.

"Alright, show time."

A few minutes later, he went through the aft entrance of the tower. It was pitch black, which suited him fine. The noise of the ocean and the slow groaning of the ship made this infiltration almost too easy. Roen pulled out his knife and crept up the flight of stairs, careful to stay in the shadows and make as little noise as possible. He found a Genjix at the top of the third-floor stairs with a pistol in hand.

"Not exactly the best sentry position."

These guys suffer from the same problem Wuehler's team did. Being elite shock troops does not make them good security. The stairs are too steep and loud to cover the distance. Use the knife, sixty degree slant, catch the body. You will need to step into their sights to get the angle.

With one fluid motion, Roen stepped into sight of the guard and flicked his wrist upward. The knife whistled through the air and stuck into the man's jaw. The sentry made one soft gurgling nose and pitched forward. Roen raced up the stairs as quietly as he could and caught the body just as it fell down the stairs. He laid the body gently down on the stairs, pulled his knife out, and wiped it on the dead man's shirt.

Nice throw.

"I was aiming for his neck actually."

I know.

He reached the third level and crept toward the far end of the passageway, which opened to a set of stairs outside the tower that led to where the prisoners were. With luck, maybe the Genjix would think no one was dumb enough to assault the tower and leave it deserted except for maybe one or two Genjix to guard the prisoners. It was a good thing Roen was dumb enough to do just that.

He stayed low and inched down the hallway, tilting his head through the opening on the first door on the left. Inside, he found one of the Genjix sorting through a stash of guns. Roen slid his knife out again and in a single bound leaped forward and jammed it into the guy's neck with one hand and covered his mouth with the other.

Two down.

Roen exited the door leading to the outside and crept up the deck. There was one Genjix guarding the prisoners, and he was busy scanning the deck below. A few seconds later, Roen had crept up behind him and snapped his neck.

Three. Well done. You really are becoming a master at this.

Roen rushed to the unconscious Ray lying on the floor.

Leave him. Untie the crew first and have them carry him. Escort them to safety and then help Dylan.

Roen grudgingly complied with Tao's orders. Luckily, the crew seemed to understand what he said and picked up the unconscious Ray by his hands and feet. Suddenly, the bridge door opened, and Jacob and the three other Genjix walked out onto the deck. Roen open fired point blank and struck one in the chest, but he was too close to get a good shot at the others.

"Get Ray out of here!" he screamed, barreling into the remaining three Genjix and pushing them inside the bridge. A blow to the side of the head knocked him off balance. Roen pivoted toward the attacked and pulled the trigger, just missing Jacob.

"It's Roen! I want him alive," Jacob snarled.

Another blow struck Roen in the eye and someone else swept his legs. He crashed to the floor, losing his rifle and tried to cover up as blows rained down on him. Then everything went dark.

CHAPTER FORTY-FOUR
IN THE NAME OF THE GRANDSON

We are no longer the puppet masters hiding behind the curtain. We are now on display for all to judge. I fear that the sentence handed down by our former wards will not be kind. Were we your guides or your slave masters? That is for you to decide. I find small solace in the belief that revealing our existence was the right moral decision. In the end, that means very little.

For the first time since we crashed onto this planet, the future is dark. I do not know what lies ahead and that is foreboding. The balance between human and Quasing has been disrupted, and now, humanity is in control of our destiny. All that we have built, we have put into humanity. And it will be you, our children, who can cut us down. And I cannot blame you if you do.

Tao

Roen, wake up!

"Five more minutes. It's too cold to go jogging this morning."

You have to stay with me, my friend.

A hard slap across his face shook his entire body. Roen blinked and woke to a blurry picture, as if he were watching a Van Gogh television show. Suddenly, the nerves just below his skin began to pound on their pain receptors to let his brain know they weren't feeling great at the moment. He groaned. Another blow snapped his face to the side.

"What happened?"

Stay quiet. You were beaten. Your eyes have been closed, but by the voices, at least three individuals. Jacob Diamont is here.

"Well, that sucks."

Indeed.

"I'll just pretend to still be unconscious."

That plan went out the window a second later when he felt what could only be a cigarette burn on his arm. Roen's nerves screamed and shot pain up his arm and through his entire body. He opened his eyes and gasped, gritting his teeth as he tried to pull his arm away. The jerk burning him clamped a hand down on his forearm and grinned. Finally, Roen couldn't tolerate the pain anymore, and a moan escaped his lips. His vision blurred and tears welled up in his eyes. Then jerk let go of his arm and Roen collapsed onto the ground.

"Pick him back up," a voice he recognized as Jacob's said.

When Roen had regained his composure, he lifted his head and saw Jacob sitting on a chair, studying him intently. On his left, a Genjix soldier was patting a steel rod in his hand. On his right, the man with the cigarette was taking a drag.

Looking around, he saw that he was slumped over on a chair in the bridge. The entire room was at a slight incline. The sky was still dark, so he couldn't have been out that long. Outside the window, a large fire burned at the rear of the ship. Dylan and the guys must have done it. The engine was destroyed and now *Imelda's Song* was adrift. A lone gunshot pierced the air. At least that meant his guys were still fighting.

"Hello, Mr Tan, welcome back to the world of the living. Rest assured, it'll be a short visit," Jacob said.

"You know..." Roen tried to enunciate the words but with all the blood pooling inside his mouth, it came out a bit mushy. He spat to his right, shooting the blood onto the pant leg of the guy with the cigarette. "Smoking can lead to emphysema, which could cause death, or at the very least make you bad at soccer." His smart-ass comment was rewarded with a punch to the jaw from the guy with the smoking habit.

He was about to receive another when Jacob held the guy's arm. "That's enough. Mr Tan and I have unfinished business. You two, go help mop the rabble downstairs."

"Are you sure, sir?" Cigarette Man asked, shaking the hand that had so carelessly rammed into Roen's head a moment ago. "He's dangerous. He killed most of squad four."

Jacob brushed him off. "Leave him to me. He's half dead, anyway. Now!"

If Jacob felt the need to send these guys to deal with Dylan, then maybe the fight was going better than he thought. The two soldiers bowed and left the room, leaving Roen alone with Jacob Diamont. The boy was so confident, Roen wasn't even tied up. Not like he was in any shape to do much anyway. They had really worked him over. Roen moved his fingers and toes to make sure nothing was broken. He took a deep breath and felt a stabbing pain in his chest.

"Ooh, that's a cracked rib."

Probably two.

"Quick Tao, tell me what I need to do to beat him. Analyze our last fight."

There is nothing to analyze. He beat you too quickly last time to gauge his abilities.

"Well, that's a tad disheartening."

Here is what I do know. He is faster and stronger than you. And as much as I hate to say it, from what I could tell, he has better technique as well.

"Remind me to never have you in my corner during a fight."

However, Jacob is young, prideful, and easy to anger. Push him into doing something stupid.

Joseph leaned forward in the chair. "You left far too quickly last time, Mr Tan."

"Look Jacob," Roen said. "I think the ship is sinking. Maybe you have something better to do right now than beat on me. Like get off the ship maybe? You have the rest of your life ahead of you. Go date. Find a girlfriend."

Jacob leaped forward in a blur and slapped Roen in the face with a crushing backhand.

"And stop slapping me, you sissy!" Roen snarled. "God, what's with all you Genjix and slapping people?"

Jacob grabbed Roen by the collar and lifted him with ease. "Do not make light of this situation. I have been dreaming of you ever since I learned that Grandfather was killed by an insignificant Prophus named Roen Tan. I have dedicated myself to honoring Grandfather and seeing you dead." He pushed Roen back in the chair so hard that he tipped over and fell onto his back.

It took a second for Roen to get all his limbs moving the way his brain told them to. Trying to appear calm, he picked himself up from the ground, turned the chair right side up, and sat back down. He went as far to brush some of the dirt off his shirt.

You are overdoing it.

"You really didn't know your grandfather well, did you, kid?" Roen said in a forced patient tone, one that he remembered his father using on him when he was young. "I don't know where all this hero worship is coming from, but Sean was a really bad man. To be honest, he was also kind of a prick."

Roen noticed Jacob flinch at those words. To him, Grandpa Sean stood on a pedestal.

"He wasn't even that great of a fighter. I mean, you even said I suck, and we both know I kicked his ass."

That last comment did it. Jacob roared and tried to knock Roen's head off. Roen managed to duck, just barely. If it had connected, he had no doubt that the blow would have shattered a bone in his face. But luckily for him, Jacob was predictable. Just as the swing flew over his head, Roen popped Jacob right in the solar plexus, following it up with an uppercut that snapped his head back. He then cleared his mind and fell into his combat mindset, letting his body dictate his movements, continuously changing angles to confuse the boy. There would be no brute forcing this kid. Roen had to rely on his training and his skill to beat him.

His cleared mind lasted a whole twenty seconds. Roen successfully battered and confused the boy through several feints and counters before Jacob did the combat equivalent of "to hell with this nonsense" and grabbed the first thing he could get his claws on – which in this case was Roen's shirt and forearm – and tossed him across the room like a rag doll. Roen's back smashed against a window pane, cracking the glass, and he fell into a heap on the floor.

"God, he's strong. What the hell are they feeding them at the Hatchery? Steroid burgers?"

Comes from years of doing nothing but training. He also has a severe reach advantage.

Roen picked himself up off the ground and managed to give Jacob a bloody grin. It seemed Roen's surprise flurry had done some damage at least. Well, a bloody lip and a cut eye wasn't exactly debilitating, but at least he had scored some points on the young Ivan Drago. Except now, Jacob wasn't messing around anymore. Roen recognized the classic shotokan stance again as they circled each other.

"I wish I had my knife still."

Or a gun.

"Or a grenade."

That would kill you both.

"Would be worth it."

What happened to seeing Jill and Cameron?

"In my current situation? Those odds are depressingly low. Best I can hope for is taking both of us out in a blaze of glory."

The two began their deadly dance. Now that they were fighting from neutral positions in tight quarters in which Roen couldn't maneuver as easily, Jacob's superior range became a serious issue, and the boy knew how to maintain his advantage. Coupled with his speed, Roen was getting pot-shotted to death, though he was getting his fair share of hits in as well.

By the end of the first minute, Jacob's face was turning a beautiful shade of puffy red. Unfortunately, Roen's was such a hot bloody mess that he probably wouldn't recognize himself in the mirror. The kid must have sharp knuckles because his punches kept cutting gashes open on Roen's face. And to top things off, Jacob liked to trash talk.

"You're an old has-been, old timer," he smirked as Roen ate another punch to the nose that rearranged his face.

"And you're... redundant," Roen growled as he threw a hard right that only hit air.

He is using his speaking to distract you, and as a form of kiai. Study his breathing.

Roen realized then that Tao was right. Jacob didn't blab unless he was pushing the pace. Unfortunately, he pushed the pace and blabbed quite a bit. Roen was slowly getting beaten to a pulp.

"I'm down on points, Tao, going into the championship rounds. What do I do?"

He is as good with his legs as with his hands. Crowd him and put him on his back.

Jacob shuffled forward and attacked, throwing three straight blinding punches and following up with a chambered side kick. Roen was able to dodge and block the trio of punches but took the side kick full in his mid-section, right where his ribs were cracked. He blacked out from the pain while flying backwards from the impact. The saving grace was that he was already unconscious when his body broke through the window and flew out onto the bridge deck. Roen slid across the deck until he slammed into the railing, which briefly brought him back to consciousness. He looked down at the drop into the ocean below. Then everything darkened once more. He woke to more slaps on the face.

Stay with me, Roen!

"Can't have you unconscious when you die, Mr Tan," Jacob sneered.

"First of all," Roen mumbled, "stop slapping me. It's not manly. Second of all, you can call me Roen, you little psychopath."

Jacob grabbed him by the side of the face and slammed his head against the metal railing. "As you wish, Roen." He pulled Roen in close. "This is for Grandfather, you evil Prophus bastard." And then he threw Roen over the side down toward the deck, four stories below.

Just as Roen went over, he reached out and grabbed at the railing. Grabbed at anything, really. An image of Jacob's face and collar popped into his mind and instead of grabbing the bar, Roen got his hand on Jacob's shirt at the collar right at the base of the neck. The kid fell forward and nearly decapitated himself on the metal railing. He saved himself by pushing his hands against the bar at the last moment. And there Roen dangled, with only his tenuous hold on Jacob's shirt keeping him alive. He reached up with his other hand. Jacob's face was turning purple as he tried to hold up Roen's weight with his arms and neck.

See, I told you I would figure something out.

"Your dumb luck strategy has succeeded, great Napoleon."

No need to antagonize me at a time like this.

Roen looked down at the deck as several cargo containers made a slow slide into the water, sinking into the black depths. Then he saw Dylan and two other figures he couldn't make out run onto the deck. At least some of his guys were still alive.

Another explosion in the back of the ship shot a plume of fire up into the air. *Imelda's Song* was singing her swan song, pun intended. Roen tried to will his arms to pull himself up, but it was all they could do to hang onto Jacob's collar.

"Hey Tao, at least you got one of your wishes. We'll fall into the ocean. You can find a new host then."

Roen, listen carefully, if you swing to your right, you can try to land on the lower platform.

"Fat chance, Tao. My tank is on empty."

"Mr Tan," Jacob growled, obviously choking. He pulled Roen's up enough to grab Roen's wrist and tear his grip away from the shirt. "It seems your friends are down there, which mean I no longer have the luxury of killing you slowly. Why don't you do them a favor and join them below?"

Jacob let go and all Roen could feel was the sensation of weightlessness before everything went black.

CHAPTER FORTY-FIVE
EPILOGUE

Roen, my friend, I have told you all of our history so that you can know and understand. The real reason I tell you this, though, is so that maybe you can hear me. I do not know if you are still here, but I pray that I am not alone in your body. You are my friend and always will be. In case you do not survive, you will live forever through me.

Tao

Enzo was in a hurry. He had been gone for nearly a month, but with the recent birth of new Quasing and the beginning of Quasiform, this was not the time to keep his eyes from the prize. With Phase III officially under way, his true life's work was about to begin. The sideshow in Tibet was just that, a minor distraction that had to be taken care of. Some on the Council might call the encounter a loss, with the Prophus freeing the majority of the prisoners, but Enzo saw it differently. The delivery of test subjects was uninterrupted. That was the important thing. Add the fact that their overall strength had been diminished by that encounter was just an added bonus. In a game where pawns were exchanged, the side with superior numbers always came out ahead. With the death of their Field Marshal, his victory in Tibet was near-total. Stephen was just under the Keeper on the priority list, and it was Enzo who killed him. He had cut off the head of the snake, and now the body of the enemy was writhing aimlessly.

A momentary victory is not to be savored. Only the conclusion is worth noting.

Enzo jumped out of the helicopter before it touched down on the ground. He sped directly toward the research wing. While the reports from Chow had been glowing, Enzo knew better than to believe everything at face value without seeing it with his own eyes first. Immediately, the entourage that had been waiting on the platform organized around him as if an honor guard. Within moments, he had received a data dump of the events of the twenty-four hours since his last briefing.

"The Council is requesting a meeting at your convenience."

Requesting.

"At my convenience? Interesting," Enzo said, amused.

"The earliest possible, Father."

Be wary of their reaction. Your victory in Tibet was not absolute. They might seize the advantage.

"The rest of the Council might still try to take Quasiform from me?"

Possibly.

"Still, their tone has changed."

"Arrange it," Enzo said. It would be interesting to see how they treated him now. They must feel threatened by his success. After all, he had accomplished more in a few short months than what most of them had in decades. Regardless of how they would try to spin it, they could not take away his accomplishments.

"General Marec, head of port operations, has reported an incident."

"With the catalyst prototypes?"

"Among others." Amanda clicked on her tablet. "Port security has concerns about the trade hub in Taiwan. There was a security breach and he believes it is a vulnerable single point of failure in this hemisphere's operations. The Americas are still in turmoil."

"Once our legislators assume full control of the States, that port will no longer be important," Enzo said. He was at the cusp of a new era on this planet and all Amanda could do was ply him with silly logistics.

Supply lines must be maintained until that change takes place.

"Of course, Holy One."

Enzo reached the research building, walking at a pace his aides found difficult to keep up with. He could feel Zoras' anticipation as they reached the lab. This was an exciting time. Under Zoras' direction, the future of humanity and this planet would bend to his will. He was truly blessed by the Holy Ones.

He bounded into the main lab with his entourage close behind. Chow was giving orders to the two dozen or so scientists in the lab. Everyone in the room stopped what they were doing and bowed. Enzo ignored them. He ignored everything but the glass vat and the swirling liquid inside. Except now, the red liquid was filled with thousands of small bursts of white light, as if there was a bubble universe right within the confines of the container.

"Praise to the Holy Ones. What is that?"

It is beautiful. Five Quasing are incubating two right now. We have birthed the first of our kind on this planet!

Enzo's eyes traced the swirls circling around a large membrane that pulsed with a white light so bright that it was difficult to look straight into it. Yet, if he focused, he could make out the shapes of five separated individual blobs attached to each other. And in the very center of the combined form, two smaller membranes orbited each other. It was a celestial sight, and to Enzo, further proof of the Quasing's divinity. He ordered the lights dimmed and for half an hour, just stood there and watched the kaleidoscope of Quasing incubation. Suddenly, one of his aides rushed to this side and grabbed him by the arm so forcefully it took Enzo by surprise.

"How dare you!" Enzo hissed.

"Apologies, Father," the aide said, panicked. Then he pointed at one of the television screens on the side wall where a press conference was taking place. Then, one by one, every screen in the lab changed to that channel. Enzo's face turned white.

On the screen, two United States senators stood behind a podium and addressed dozens of reporters on live television.

"My name is Senator James Wilks," the man said. "As you know, there was an attack on our nation's capital a few days ago and I was presumed dead. As you can see, I am very much alive. I bring ill tidings to the American people. There is a conspiracy in this world that affects all of us. It is foreign, and when I say that, I mean extraterrestrial." The bank of reporters began to mutter. He held up hands. "I have evidence."

The other individual, a good-looking older woman, spoke. "I am Senator Mary Thompson, and I too was a victim of the reckless brutality. Make no mistake, it was a coup d'état by this same group that my colleague Senator Wilks speaks of. Except the attacks and the conspiracy go far deeper. There have been aliens in our midst since the dawn of humanity. You see, I have one of them in me, and we have the technology here to prove it."

What have those fools done?!

Enzo could only stare at the screen, frozen in shock. The world as the Quasing knew it had just collapsed.

The air ambulance transporting the survivors of *Imelda's Song* landed on the helipad of the Queen's Hospital in Honolulu, Hawaii at three in the afternoon. None of them had slept much since the fight at the ship nearly two days ago. Well, none except for Roen and Ray. Both were in medically-induced comas.

The survivors of the freighter were picked up by the remnants of Stephen's air support, which had been redirected to search for them when Dylan had sent the distress signal out. The search and rescue teams had looked for the better part of a day and were about to call off the search because of the increased presence of the Chinese Air Force canvasing the same area. Luckily, a large explosion on the freighter in the middle of the night had pinpointed their location. The Prophus were able to get their people out minutes before the Chinese teams got there.

From there, it was a race to an airspace that the Chinese would not yet dare violate, regardless of their Genjix allegiance. Jill was waiting for them on the helipad as the medics unloaded everyone and rushed them to the emergency room.

The prognosis from the doctors weren't good. They gave Roen less than a twenty-five percent chance of pulling through his injuries. He had spent a day clinging onto debris in the ocean with half a dozen broken bones and severe internal bleeding. Several of his injuries had festered and he was severely dehydrated. If Roen wasn't going to survive this, Jill was determined that her son would see him one last time.

Jill swallowed the lump in her throat as the doctors lifted him onto the gurney and rushed him down the hallway. She ran alongside him, holding his hand as they weaved in and out of traffic. Dylan had taken over security and an entire squad of Prophus operatives were clearing the path for them to the operating room. Once the doctors and the nurses were there prepping for surgery, she was barred from going inside and ended up waiting just outside in the lobby.

Two hours later, Louis and Lee Ann arrived with Cameron. She rushed to her son and held him tight, tears flowing down both their faces as she told him how much she missed him. He didn't know what was going on, and part of her thought it might be cruel to bring him to his father's death, but she also knew that was what Roen would have wanted. It hurt her to know that Cameron was not at his father's side until the last moment. They both deserved to have this and it was a lesson Cameron needed to learn.

"Jill," Lee Ann said, giving her a hug. "What happened? Is he going to pull through?"

She dug face into her mother's shoulders and wept. "I don't know. It's too early to tell. They just went in a while ago."

Louis joined in on the hug and squeezed her tight. Then he pulled back and stared at her. "Why are you carrying a pistol?" he asked, looking wide-eyed at the holster half-hidden beneath her vest. Then he looked around at the half dozen Prophus agents standing watch. His eyes narrowed. "What's going on?"

It is time.

Jill wiped the tears from her eyes and exhaled. "We better sit down."

Then she told them everything, from the moment she met Roen to the incident at Monaco to the time she went to basic training to when she was positioned with Senator Wilks. She kept the Quasing out of it. That would require a lot more explaining to do. For now, her parents wanted to know about her and Roen. She was about to tell them about her work on the Hill with the Senator when something to the side caught her eye. Wilks was on the television. Her face drained of some of its color as she pointed at the screen.

"Isn't that your boss?" Louis asked.

She nodded in silence. Everyone in the room watched Wilks and Thompson detail not only the conspiracy of the Prophus and Genjix, but the technology of the Penetra scanners. The conference went on for another hour as Thompson laid everything out in the open, from the crash landing to how the Quasing had influenced humanity for thousands of years to their civil war to how they had infiltrated every aspect of human government. The conference would have gone on much longer had the FBI not interrupted it and taken them both away.

Jill knew this was coming, but she was still unprepared for it when the full brunt of reality smacked her in the face. After years of hiding the Quasing from the world, it was now all out in the open and she felt starkly naked.

"Shit just got real."

No shit.

"I think that's the first time I've ever heard you swear."

If this is not the most appropriate time, I do not know what is. Also, that is also because you do not understand Russian.

Lee Ann turned to Louis. "Were they just talking about what I think they're talking about?"

Louis only nodded with a dumbfounded look on his face. "This is a prank right?" He turned to Jill. "That's your boss. What's this..." his voice trailed off as he looked again at the guards standing about.

Jill nodded. "I'm one of them, Dad."

And then she told them about Baji and about the Quasing. There was too much to tell in one sitting, so she chose the important and less frightening aspects of her life as a Prophus. She was halfway through when a young operative walked up to her and bowed.

"Mrs Tan," he said. "Lieutenant Jackson Riley, naval intelligence. I've been sent from Command."

"For what," Jill said sharply.

"In the event that Mr Tan does not pull through. I have been assigned to Tao. I just wanted to introduce myself in case the worst happens. I'm sorry for your loss."

"He's still alive!" she snapped. At that instant, Jill wanted to claw his eyes out and punch that old hag Keeper in the face. Her husband wasn't dead yet and those vultures were already circling his spoils. But after taking several moments to compose herself, she knew it had to be done. It wasn't this young man's fault. He was just following orders. She thanked him and watched as he took a seat at the other end of the room. Then they all sat down and waited.

Six hours later, Dylan limped out of the emergency room and signaled for Jackson to follow him back in. Jill felt a lump crawl up her throat. That could only mean one thing. She picked up Cameron and ran after them, pushing past the two guards into the emergency room where the doctors were working frantically on Roen. The ECG was going off the charts, bleeping several times a second and the nurses were prepping a crash cart.

WESLEY CHU   459

A minute later, Roen flatlined.

Jill held on to Cameron tightly as she watched in horror, being nothing more than an observer of her husband's death.

"No," she moaned.

I am sorry.

After a minute of attempts with no change to the ECG, the doctor pulled off his mask and read the time of death. Jill collapsed to the ground in sobs. Dylan knelt next to her and held her tightly as her body shook.

A sparkle of light left Roen's body and circled the room. Tao flitted around the ceiling of the room and then moved down to where she and Cameron lay. Then he brushed by her face as if trying to reassure her, blinking softly.

Tao says he is so sorry and that he loved Roen more than anything.

Then Tao swirled around Cameron, as if caressing him, as if trying to tell him something as well.

Jackson walked up at attention to Tao and bowed. "Tao, by the request of the Keeper, I would be honored to be your host. Please, sir, when you are ready."

Tao rose up to eye level with Jackson and paused, his membrane pulsating with light as he studied his new assigned host, and then he moved past Jackson's head and circled around the room. Then finally, instead of settling into Jackson Riley, he moved back down to Jill and Cameron.

A second later, Cameron began to scream with pain. His voice echoed through the room like a piercing siren. Jill clutched her little guy as tightly as she could as he writhed in pain.

What is Tao thinking?

"What Roen would have wanted I think."

Then, joining Cameron's scream, the ECG suddenly blipped. Once. Twice. Three times.

A lone figure, haggard and dirty, limped up to the MP at the gate of Caserma Ederle in Vicenza, Italy. He shuffled forward as if a zombie, half dead, weaving left and right, barely able to stand on his feet. The man was nearly bald with odd tufts of white hair sticking out of his head. All the other parts of his head were red with blood, as if he had been tearing hair out by the fistful. He stank of alcohol and stale clothing. His odor reached the two MPs before they even saw him. His eyes were vacuous and he moaned as he crept toward them.

As he got closer, the two MPs exchanged glances and lifted their rifles. "This is a United States Command Post. Step back immediately. This is your only warning."

The half-dead man stopped and stared at them for several seconds. Then he opened his mouth and spoke in broken English, the words misshapen as if foreign to the tongue speaking them. "Code: The greatness of man is secondary to his use." He paused, as if still formulating the thoughts in his head, before speaking again. "I am Shiva the Destroyer, and I must see Zoras. You will take me to him right away."

ACKNOWLEDGMENTS

I never expected to write another acknowledgement so soon after the release of *The Lives of Tao*. After all, it's only been a short six short months since my debut novel was introduced to the world and now *The Deaths of Tao* is following hot on its heels.

For that, I have to first thank all the readers and fans that made Lives such a smashing success. You guys rock! The first book in the Tao series was received so well the overlords at Angry Robot Books decided to bump the release date for Deaths up from Summer 2014 to Fall 2013. You guys get all the credit for that.

To the folks at Angry Robot, Thank you for your continuing support and keeping my crazy at bay. You guys – Marc, Lee, Amanda, Caroline, and Mike – are awesome. Special thanks to Bruce Hogarth, Stew and the rest of the crew at Argh! Oxford for the jump-off-the-shelves covers.

To my kick-ass agent, Russell Galen, this is only the beginning. Special thanks to Sasha, who moved a mountain when I needed one moved.

To my crack beta reading posse, you will always have an open bar when you're with me.

461

To my family, Mike, Yukie, Stephen, and Amy, your support means the world to me. Special thanks to my nephews Roen and Cameron, I hope you're enjoying the ride.

To Paula, my source of inspiration against self-doubt, hopelessness, and pessimism, you are my cure-all and phoenix down all wrapped up into one.

Special thanks to my Airedale terrier, Eva, for being the only reason I work out these days.

Lastly, to Tao and Roen. Hey, I know I put you two through some rough shit in this book. I'm sorry. Actually, no I'm not. Suck it up. It's going to get worse.

Wesley Chu, Chicago, October 2013